Fathe...
L...

Psst!
Don't tell Father,
but he's in for a surprise…

Love and marriage don't necessarily go together.
When that happens,
Mother
might just have a little secret
that

Father Knows
Last!

Two complete novels by your favourite authors!

Emma Darcy nearly became an actress until her fiancé declared he preferred to attend the theatre *with* her. She became a wife and mother. Later, she took up oil painting—unsuccessfully, she remarks. Then she tried architecture, designing the family home in New South Wales. Next came romance writing—'the hardest and most challenging of all the activities,' she confesses. Emma Darcy has now written over fifty romance novels and is an author of great international acclaim.

Jacqueline Baird began writing as a hobby when her family objected to the smell of her oil painting, and immediately became hooked on the romantic genre. She loves travelling and worked her way around the world from Europe to the Americas and Australia, returning to marry her teenage sweetheart. She lives in Ponteland, Northumbria, the county of her birth, and has two teenage sons. She enjoys playing badminton, and spends most weekends with husband Jim, sailing their Gp14 around Derwent Reservoir. Jacqueline has had ten romance novels published and her titles are loved by romance readers around the world.

Father Knows Last!

HIGH RISK
by
Emma Darcy

GUILTY PASSION
by
Jacqueline Baird

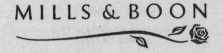

MILLS & BOON

*All the characters in this book have no existence outside the imagination
of the author, and have no relation whatsoever to anyone bearing the
same name or names. They are not even distantly inspired by any
individual known or unknown to the author, and all the incidents are
pure invention.*

*MILLS & BOON, the Rose Device and By Request
are trademarks of the publisher.
Harlequin Mills & Boon Limited,
Eton House, 18-24 Paradise Road, Richmond, Surrey, TW9 1SR*

High Risk was first published by Mills & Boon Limited in
a single volume in 1993.
Guilty Passion was first published by Mills & Boon Limited in
a single volume in 1992.

High Risk © Emma Darcy 1993
Guilty Passion © Jacqueline Baird 1992

ISBN 0 263 79623 X

*Set in Times Roman 10 on 12 pt
05-9604-109714 C*

*Printed in Great Britain by
BPC Paperbacks Ltd*

HIGH RISK

Emma Darcy

CHAPTER ONE

SHE HAD TO GO TO HIM.

The idea had been nagging at Carrie's mind for days, and she had kept pushing it away. The last thing she wanted to do was go to Dominic Savage for help. But she had already tried everything else. There was no other option left. Or none that Carrie could see.

Dominic would be able to get Danny out of the clutches of those officious welfare people. All it would probably take was a telephone call to the right person. From him. The rules and regulations, which were so cast-iron for unimportant people like herself, were always bent to accommodate those with power and wealth and influence. Carrie had seen that happen too many times to have any doubt about it.

Bitter times forced bitter decisions, she reflected. The wealth and power in Dominic's world had once evoked awe in her, until she learnt that they also excluded her from ever being a permanent fixture in his life. Since it had cost her dear in the past, Carrie felt she had a right to use it now. For Danny's sake, more than her own. And only just this once.

She would be running a risk—a high risk—inviting even this slight involvement with Dominic Savage. Any association with him had to be strictly contained to today's meeting. Carrie didn't want old wounds reopened. All she wanted was a quick efficient solution to her problem. With no follow-up. She had quite enough to cope with without any more disastrous repercussions from her move back to Australia.

She wished she had stayed in Fiji where at least she had friends. It was so lonely in Sydney with her mother gone and Danny taken away and no one she knew well enough to even pass the time of day with. Yet there was no way in the world she could have foreseen what had happened since her return. However, *if only* thoughts were a total waste of time, Carrie told herself sternly.

The question to be faced was, considering the nature of their brief relationship, would Dominic Savage help her?

Because she remembered him, it didn't follow that he remembered her. Eight years was a long time, and for him it had only been a holiday fling. After she had found out what was really happening, she had ended it there and then. Even left the country to get farther away from him.

Had he married the other girl?

She didn't even know anything as basic as that about him.

A bleak shadow passed over Carrie's soul. She shook it off. What Dominic Savage had done with his personal life was not her problem. Her problem was getting her child back. There was no point in worrying whether Dominic would remember her or not. If she had to, she would tell him who she was and make him remember. He was the only person she knew that she could turn to, and when she considered what was happening to her, surely to heaven it wasn't much to ask of him.

She would have to go to his office, Carrie decided. Calling him would be useless. It was all too easy to refuse a telephone call when the name given might not mean anything to him any more. Even in person, he might not recognise her, but she would not be turned away without seeing him first.

She pushed herself up from the bed, moving slowly so as not to bring on the awful dizziness quick action invariably triggered. This lingering weakness was a source of intense frustration.

She had never had a serious illness in her whole life, never had a day off work through sickness—until now. To be struck down by viral pneumonia just when she needed everything to go right was the cruellest trick Fate could have played on her. And this convalescence period was dragging on far too long. She had to get well again, and quickly. So the sooner she forced herself to move, the better off everyone would be.

She searched through her wardrobe for the most suitable thing to wear. Pride insisted that she look her best for the meeting with Dominic. In her present state it was clearly impossible to look her *absolute* best, but she had to do her utmost to look her *relative* best.

She had lost so much weight that all her clothes hung loosely on her. Carrie finally chose a green and white dotted cotton shirtwaister. It had a belt she could pull in and long sleeves to cover the thinness of her arms. Having to bend over to put on tights made her head whirl, but she managed to get them on eventually. The white low-heeled sandals were not exactly dressy, but she didn't feel safe in high heels, not with the balance problem she had at the moment.

She grimaced at the reflection that looked back at her from the bathroom mirror. Her face looked older than its twenty-seven years, tired and drained of any healthy youthful bloom. Her dark blonde hair was no longer lightly streaked from the sun. It hung lifelessly to her shoulders and badly needed a good cut. She brushed it hard but couldn't get any shine into it. It felt like straw.

Carrie had never been in the habit of wearing much make-up. Never needed it. She only had a couple of lipsticks, so there was nothing she could do about adding some artificial lustre to her green eyes, or even putting some healthier-looking colour onto her pallid skin. She tried rubbing a smear of lipstick over her cheekbones, but it gave her a garish appearance, which looked even worse. She cleaned it off.

It was one o'clock when she left the dingy little apartment in Ashfield. She was glad to be out in the sunshine for a while. It had appalled her that such a dark, depressing place was all she could afford in the high-rental climate.

Of course, she hadn't anticipated remaining there beyond the three-month probation period of the job she had secured before coming back to Sydney. Assistant chef at a well-reputed restaurant paid well enough for her to find better accommodation, but Carrie's natural caution insisted that she be frugal until she was sure of permanent status on the staff. Which was just as well, since she had only been working for a week before going off sick. She couldn't blame the management for not holding the position for her, but if she didn't get well enough to hold a job soon, she would have to move to cheaper and worse accommodation.

It was bitterly ironic that when she had been in Fiji, she had been homesick for Australia. Now she yearned for what she had left behind. Fiji was a fine place. The sun was almost always shining. The cost of living was low. The Fijians were the friendliest people in the world. But living there for six years had not prepared her for the high cost of housing in Sydney, forced to astronomical heights by the huge Japanese investments in property. Still, Carrie refused to give in to pessimism. Today was the day. She was going to get Danny back, no matter what it cost her to do it.

It took her an hour to reach the huge APIC building in Bridge Street. One bus went straight past her. The next was so crowded she had to stand in the aisle for part of the way. Then she alighted at the wrong stop and had to walk three blocks. It was slow going with all the halts she had to make as she fought off waves of dizziness. When she finally reached her destination, Carrie was exhausted.

In times gone past the APIC building had dominated the Circular Quay area. Now it was just one of the many skyscrapers that comprised the inner-city business district. Nevertheless, it was still imposing. There was certainly nothing derelict about the polished marble exterior, nor the rich gleaming Jarrah woodwork and marble in the foyer.

She read the directory on the wall beside the bank of lifts, then rode up to the first floor, which was designated Reception and Enquiries. She stepped out into a spacious area that spelled prosperity in capital letters, took a deep breath to steady herself, then approached the long enquiry desk behind which several smartly dressed young women were working.

"How can I help you?" one of them asked, greeting Carrie with a polite smile.

"I'm here to see Mr. Savage," Carrie said, adopting a brisk, confident manner. "Could you please direct me to his office?"

"Take the elevator to the twenty-seventh floor. The receptionist there will direct you to the managing director's suite," the woman supplied helpfully.

"I meant Mr. Dominic Savage, not his father."

The woman gave her an odd questioning look. "Mr. Dominic Savage is now the managing director. He took over two years ago when Mr. James Savage died," she added pointedly.

Carrie stared blankly at her, slowly absorbing this new item of knowledge. She had thought of Dominic Savage frequently enough in the intervening years, but never of specific events happening to him. At least, nothing like the death of his father.

Of course Dominic's life had moved on, just as hers had. Eight years was a long time. She had lost her mother. He had lost his father. And now he was in an even more exalted position than she had imagined him to be. Nevertheless, that didn't change anything. In fact, the more important the position he held, the more influence he could wield. If he would. He had the power now, as well as the name.

"Thank you," she murmured, and headed to the lifts, conscious of the woman's eyes boring into her back. Carrie wondered if a call would precede her to the twenty-seventh floor, giving a warning that someone very strange was on the way up.

When she arrived, however, that anxiety was quickly erased. The receptionist apparently had no compunction whatsoever about directing her along a wide corridor towards the managing director's suite. "You'll find Mrs. Coombe's office down there," she said, passing Carrie up the line of authority with the words, "Mrs. Coombe handles all Mr. Savage's appointments."

Carrie thanked her and moved down the corridor. This led to a large open waiting room, which was presided over by a middle-aged woman at a massive semicircular desk.

Mrs. Coombe was not a welcoming figure. She looked every inch the guardian of the citadel of power. Her iron-grey hair was cut short in a trim mannish style. Horn-rimmed spectacles added emphasis to steely grey eyes. Her stout body was encased in a professional black suit, and the cameo brooch that was pinned to her pristine white blouse was the only touch of femininity she apparently allowed. Her stern face did not crack the slightest smile. Carrie was subjected to sharp scrutiny as she approached the woman. She had the feeling that she was judged and found wanting. The woman's face assumed a superior condescending expression, which boded ill for Carrie's purpose.

"Good afternoon," Mrs. Coombe said crisply. Eyebrows rose fractionally as she added, "How can I help you?"

"I wish to see Mr. Dominic Savage," Carrie stated flatly. She was feeling ill again. It was all the movement, she supposed. Soon she would have to sit down and rest.

"You want to make an appointment?"

Carrie concentrated fiercely, willing her body to behave as it should. "No. I want to see him this afternoon," she said firmly. "As soon as possible, really."

"I'm afraid that's impossible, Miss . . . ?"

"Miller. Caroline Miller."

"Miss Miller." The steel-grey eyes had swept over Carrie's fingers. The voice continued with a huff of exasperation. "Mr. Savage is a very busy man. His afternoon is already filled with appointments. If you'll state your business and give me a contact number, I'll confer with Mr. Savage when he's available and let you know when an appointment would be convenient."

Another evasive runaround. Just like at the welfare department. Carrie wondered why no one seemed to realise when something was very important. It goaded her into digging her toes in. She was not going to be stopped by red tape here. Dominic might turn her away, but she wouldn't be turned away by this woman or anyone else.

"I've come on a personal matter, Mrs. Coombe. An urgent personal matter," Carrie said emphatically. "Mr. Savage and I are old acquaintances. I appreciate the fact he is a busy man, but I'm prepared to wait until he can see me. I'll wait all afternoon, if necessary."

The grey eyes glittered with suspicion. "I'm acquainted with all Mr. Savage's friends, Miss Miller. Your name is *not* on my list."

No doubt she didn't measure up as an acquaintance, let alone a friend, Carrie thought with grim irony. It was all too obvious that she didn't have the wealth or the style or the presence of someone from the right stratum of society. That had been the problem eight years ago. She had run away from it then. But she was no longer a naive, inexperienced nineteen-year-old. She was not going to run away from it now. This woman's opinion did not matter to her. Not one whit. Only Danny mattered.

Her head swam. She could feel her forehead going clammy and perspiration breaking out over her body. She had to concentrate very hard to produce a rebuttal to Mrs. Coombe's argument. "I've been out of the country for many years," she explained. "Mr. Savage would have no reason to give you my name, Mrs. Coombe. But if you'd be kind enough to tell him I'm here, I'm sure he won't turn me away."

She was not at all sure of that, but if she didn't exude confidence, her case was lost. And what alternatives did that leave her? None that Carrie could think of. Perhaps tomorrow she would get another idea.

"Mr. Savage is in conference," the woman said officiously. "I expect he will be there for another hour, Miss Miller, and I have the strictest instructions not to interrupt a conference. Except in the direst of emergencies."

That was precisely the situation as Carrie saw it, but she was not in a position either to explain it or to be demanding. "Then I'll wait until you can speak to him," she stated as matter-of-factly as she could.

"As you wish." Mrs. Coombe gave a cold little nod of dismissal towards a group of armchairs, then ignored Carrie's presence, dropping her gaze to whatever paperwork she was doing.

Carrie was glad to sit down at last. The strain of getting here was fast catching up with her. She needed a rest before coming face to face with Dominic Savage. Time to regather her meagre resources of energy. An hour was nothing when so much hung in the balance.

For a long while Carrie mentally rehearsed what she would say to him if she got to see him. If he still remembered her and was kind enough to see her. She exhausted all the possible opening gambits at her disposal, and eventually her surroundings impinged on her consciousness. The pale blue-grey and white decor was very modern. Understated class. The paintings on the walls were watercolours—undoubtedly originals—and subtly suggestive of many things without being truly representational of anything.

The telephone on Mrs. Coombe's desk rang from time to time. Carrie tensed as the woman answered its summons, not knowing if they were incoming calls or in-house communications. She eavesdropped unashamedly. The secretary didn't once mention Dominic's name, handling each call with an air of assurance and competent efficiency.

There were two sets of double doors leading off the office waiting room, one to the right of where Carrie sat, the other to the left of Mrs. Coombe's desk. She suspected that the doors closest to the secretary would lead to Dominic's office. She watched them, waiting for them to open and emit the members of the conference.

But it was the other set of doors that were eventually thrust open, the silence abruptly broken by an accompanying burst of male voices. A phalanx of men spilled into the room, spreading out near the doorway like a guard of honour for the man who emerged last.

Carrie's heart squeezed tight at first sight of him. If anything, Dominic Savage was more handsome in maturity than when she had met him. Then she had thought him the most handsome boy she had ever seen, so compellingly attractive that she could hardly stop looking at him; eyes so blue, face just the right mixture of perfect features and strong masculinity,

and the intriguing dimple at the base of his chin to
break the rather uncompromising power of his square
jawline.

Now he was very much the man. Although he could
not be taller than she remembered him, he looked
bigger and broader, the lean athletic physique of his
youth obviously having filled out over the years,
lending him a formidable aura of authority. Even his
thick black hair had been tamed into a short, stylish
cut, which added to the impressive executive air that
a formal business suit gave him.

He paused to speak to one of the men. Carrie
pushed herself out of the armchair, her pulse leaping
erratically at her temerity—or perhaps it was at seeing him again in the flesh. Whatever, if she brought
herself to his notice, forced a meeting so that her
presence could not be ignored... It was a chance to
bypass the dragon of a woman who guarded his lair.

He finished speaking. His listener nodded. A satisfied smile curved his mouth as he moved forward
again.

The blue eyes gave Carrie a swift cursory glance.

There was not the slightest flicker of recognition.

She was dismissed from his notice almost in the
same moment he saw her, and the shock of that dismissal rendered Carrie speechless. He passed on by,
heading for the doors on the other side of Mrs.
Coombe's desk.

Carrie gazed helplessly after him, too stunned by his
failure to acknowledge her to make any move. Somehow, in her heart of hearts, she had wanted Dominic
to know her instantly. Despite the brevity of their relationship, despite the change in her appearance, de-

spite the years. It hurt that he didn't. It hurt so much that she even forgot why she had come.

Suddenly he checked in mid-stride. His back stiffened. He half turned, subjecting Carrie to a sharp, searching look. It lasted only a second or two, but it was enough for Carrie's frozen heart to leap alive again, enough to make every inch of her skin prickle with an electric awareness, enough to unlock thoughts and emotions that she had no right to have.

His head jerked forward again, and so did his legs. "Mrs. Coombe. In my office please," he rapped out as he passed his secretary. He didn't pause or wait for her. He went straight into his office, leaving the door open for Mrs. Coombe to follow.

As she stood up from the desk, the dragon shot a quelling frown at Carrie, clearly warning her to stay precisely where she was and not make any trouble. Mr. Dominic Savage had not acknowledged her as an old acquaintance. A second glance meant nothing, particularly as it had been followed by a second dismissal. As far as Mrs. Coombe was concerned, Miss Caroline Miller was here under false pretences, and she would certainly get her come-uppance later for having disturbed Mrs. Coombe's peaceful existence with her intrusive behaviour.

The wild rush of adrenalin that had been stirred by Dominic's second look at her drained quickly away, leaving Carrie shaking. The cold sweat broke out again on her forehead. She flopped into the seat rather than sat down. She might have fallen down, and again she cursed the debilitating weakness that swept over her.

She tried to push away the feelings Dominic had evoked. She couldn't still love him. Not after all these years. That was impossible. She had so carefully controlled all those awful wilful feelings. It was crazy to want what they had once had together. And what was obviously impossible for them to share. It had only ever been on her side, anyway. To him she had been available, willing, a bit of fun to be enjoyed until his friends arrived. That was how he had used her. Now she was only a vague memory, jogged for a moment, then dismissed as not worth pursuing.

So much for that episode in her life!

For a few intensely bleak moments Carrie wished she could die right here and now. Then she remembered Danny and slowly gathered her purpose for living. What she had shared with Dominic Savage was dead long ago. She had always known that. It was stupid and self-defeating to let such feelings influence her.

Even though he hadn't recognised her, she had expected that, hadn't she? It didn't mean she should give up on Danny. There had to be another way. She would think of it. Tomorrow. In the meantime it was useless to stay here. It was another good idea gone wrong. And it had always had the potential to make trouble that she would rather avoid. She had been weak minded to even consider such a high-risk venture. Better to avoid it now.

She pushed herself out of the chair. Despite the ringing in her ears she pushed her feet one after the other down the corridor to the bank of lifts in the reception area. She stabbed a down button, then pressed her forehead against the cold marble wall. It seemed to help. The cloud of dots that jagged across the front of her brain seemed to slow down. She would be better soon.

"Miss Miller."

Carrie jerked her head up. Mrs. Coombe was
breathing hard, as if she had run down the corridor
after her. But that couldn't be right. Carrie had to be
mistaken. Mrs. Coombe carried herself like a senti-
nel, with irreproachable dignity. She would never run
anywhere.

"Mr. Savage will see you now," she announced, as
though bestowing a great and undeserved privilege.

For a second or two Carrie couldn't take it in. Then
a great tremor ran through her. It wasn't relief. Now
the moment was upon her, she was gripped by an
overwhelming fear that she wouldn't be able to handle the interview in the manner she had planned. Before she had seen Dominic. If she said the wrong thing
now... but she mustn't. Too much was at stake.

"Miss Miller?" The secretary was frowning at her.

Carrie steadied herself as best she could. "Thank
you," she pushed out through dry lips. Her legs were
weak and shaky but she willed them to move down the
corridor again. For Danny, she recited fiercely with
each fateful step she took. Mrs. Coombe led the way
to Dominic's office, opened the door for her, then
stood aside to usher Carrie into his presence.

It was a large office—spacious and luxurious, as
befitted the chief executive officer of APIC—but
Carrie didn't take in any details. She only had eyes for
the man whose help she needed. He was standing at a
large window, which undoubtedly gave a panoramic
view of Sydney, since they were on the twenty-seventh
floor. His back was turned to her. Carrie noticed one
hand clenching and unclenching at his side.

The door was closed quietly and discreetly behind
her. Dominic turned at the sound, slowly, as though
he didn't want to face her but was forcing himself to.

They stared at each other across the room, across the distance of eight long years.

She could feel his tension as he studied her, knew he was contrasting the Carrie now with the Carrie he remembered and finding quite a lot gone wrong. The intense scrutiny gave him no pleasure. The grim expression on his face attested to that.

"It's been a long time," he said quietly, the blue eyes probing hers like twin lasers, intent on boring through to her soul.

"Yes," she agreed, her voice barely a whisper. "Thank you for seeing me, Dominic."

"I couldn't believe it was you out there, Carrie. Not until Mrs. Coombe confirmed it."

"I thought you hadn't recognised me."

"I didn't. Not at first," he said with a touch of dry irony. "It takes a bit of getting used to."

Carrie worked some moisture into her mouth. She couldn't let the memories crowding in on her divert her from her purpose. She had to get on with it. "I won't take up much of your time," she blurted out. "I'm sorry for barging in on you like this. When you're so busy."

"Take all the time you need, Carrie," he invited softly. "Tell me . . . what you need."

She flushed at his kindness. "A few minutes, perhaps a little more . . ."

He frowned, obviously not caring for her dismissal of his generosity. "Is that sufficient to catch up on eight years?" he asked, projecting a light tone that was not reflected in his eyes. "Eight years and two months, if my memory serves me correctly."

Why Dominic should want to "catch up" Carrie couldn't imagine. Probably it was only a polite remark. Dominic's manners had always been more than gracious. Class and style, she reminded herself. They were qualities that had once fooled her into believing more than she should have.

In any event, she didn't want to talk about her life. Not what had happened to her in all that time. She didn't want to know what had happened to him, either. In fact, the less she knew, the better. All these years she had shut him out of her mind and heart, not always successfully, and she didn't want a prolonged meeting with him now. It was too disturbing, unsettling, and fraught with too many pitfalls. She had to achieve her purpose and get out of here as soon as possible.

"Dominic, this isn't a...a social reunion," she said with an edge of desperation, her green eyes begging his indulgence. "I've come because I need your help. I didn't know anyone else who could do what needs to be done. You're my only chance. Otherwise I would never have intruded into your life."

"Of course. What else?" he murmured. The blue eyes gathered a cynical self-mockery. "I never thought your visit was connected to doing something for me, Carrie."

The rush of blood that had scorched her cheeks receded with devastating swiftness. Carrie knew that what had to be said and what had to be done had to be said and done quickly. She was feeling less and less in control of herself with each second that passed. She managed one step towards him, lifted her hand imploringly.

"I'm so sorry to be a nuisance—"

"You aren't." The quick retort was clipped. "What can I do for you?" The manner of his words was not harsh, but he looked so remote and controlled. He moved towards his desk, seeming to retreat from her.

"It's my baby..."

Close enough to the truth, Carrie thought. Danny was her baby. Always would be. However, the effect of her words on Dominic Savage was both instantaneous and incomprehensible. A bleak frozen stillness washed over him, enveloped him, making him appear rigid and stern.

I've lost this encounter, Carrie thought wildly. He's not going to help me at all. Was he judging her harshly for having a baby?

The floor tilted crazily. The black dots came swarming back. Not now, she told them.

"What about your baby?" The words were shot at her on a flat trajectory, totally devoid of emotion.

Carrie harnessed all her willpower to deliver the final message, and she managed to get the words out. "I want you to find Danny for me. I *need* you to get him back for me."

Then she was falling towards the thick grey cloud of carpet, and it came up to meet her halfway. She felt no pain at the contact. It felt warm and soft and comfortable and secure, like being wrapped in cotton wool. Just where I want to be, Carrie thought.

It was the last conscious thought Carrie had for quite some time.

CHAPTER TWO

SOMETHING COLD AND HARD was moving over her chest. It felt terrible, and Carrie wished it would go away. She didn't have the strength to push it away. She willed it to stop. It seemed to work. The cold hard object was abruptly removed.

She wondered about opening her eyes but decided against it. The effort required was too great. It was much, much easier to leave everything the way it was. She felt exactly right here. Warm. Comfortable. Heavenly, really. The best she had felt for quite some time.

Then she became aware of one intrusion. There were voices murmuring in the background. Carrie strained her ears to catch what was being said.

"What's the problem with her, Doctor?"

That was Dominic Savage's voice. It carried a note of anxiety. Memory rushed into Carrie's consciousness. He probably thought I was going to die on him, she wildly surmised. And a death in his office would hardly be good for business. No wonder he's anxious!

But if doctors were involved, Carrie had to stir herself fast. It was the last thing she needed. She had already had far too much to do with doctors. She had to get up, get out of here, leave Dominic Savage behind and think of some other method for attacking this problem. She tried to move, then reflected that another minute or two of resting wouldn't do any harm.

"Hard to be certain, really."

That had to be the doctor's voice. Low and disembodied, and like all the doctors she had ever met, disinclined to be certain of anything. They just made her feel angry and frustrated. Carrie listened to his *uncertain* diagnosis.

"There is fluid on the lungs. The heart may be overstrained . . . diaphoresis . . ."

So it was a stethoscope that had been moving over her chest and causing her distress! She had learnt to hate stethoscopes in hospital. They were so coldly intrusive and impersonal. And she could never tell what the doctors learnt from them. They always hummed and hahed as though they were pontificating over something important, but they never said anything definite.

"Without more tests it's impossible to be sure—" the doctor's faraway voice intoned.

Not more tests, Carrie promised him, with a violence of feeling that set adrenalin running through her veins.

"But my provisional diagnosis is that the basic problem is malnutrition."

What rot, Carrie thought.

"You must be joking!" Dominic's voice was filled with anger and disbelief.

Carrie silently approved.

"Take one look at her!" the doctor said pointedly.

So I'm too thin, Carrie conceded reluctantly, but it's not my fault I can't find much appetite these days. All the same, I must try and eat more, she told herself.

There was a disquieting silence.

"That's my opinion until tests confirm it or disprove it," the doctor went on.

"What are you going to do about it?" Dominic asked with a tight thread of concern.

"I'll call an ambulance and get her admitted to Royal Prince Alfred Hospital. Then . . ."

Movement was instantly triggered by the well of protest that surged through Carrie. Her eyes flew open. She forced her limbs into action and managed to sit up. Her head swam. But she could see why she had been so comfortable. Not only was she on a soft leather sofa, but her head had been on a pillow and she had been swathed in blankets. Two male heads swivelled towards her.

"Not going!" Her voice was just a croak, but as far as she was concerned the tone was both incisive and decisive. From the very beginning, hospitals and doctors had created the problem she was having now. A repetition of that was too much to endure. In fact the more distance she put between them and her, the better chance she had of getting Danny back.

"Carrie, you heard what the doctor just said." There was a harsh edge of disbelief in Dominic's voice. "You have to do what he advises. In fact, you'll follow his advice to the letter!"

Carrie focused on Dominic Savage. She had never seen him look like this before, dominating and imperious. She remembered him as always being easy and relaxed, full of camaraderie, gaiety and laughter. She shook her head. He didn't appreciate what was at stake here. But he did look very handsome and compelling with that authoritative look on his face.

"Not going," she repeated dully. She didn't really like going against his wishes. She just had to.

"Oh, yes, you are!" His square jaw looked very determined. Even the dimple seemed to flatten out.

But Carrie was even more determined. She knew better. "Over my dead body!" she told him.

He looked even more grim at that. "It will be if you don't do as you're told."

Carrie decided he wasn't going to understand anything. "Sorry," she said, with a terribly leaden feeling in her heart. Somehow she dredged up the strength to stand up without falling over again. "Going home," she stated decisively.

Dominic seemed to lunge at her. Then his hands and arms were wrapped around her shoulders, steadying her, as if to protect her from falling again. Which could happen, she admitted to herself. She did feel weak and shaky.

"No ambulance," he conceded. "I'll take you to hospital myself."

"No. Going home," Carrie insisted. "Sorry for nuisance. Goodbye, Dominic."

For a moment she let herself lean against the warm breadth of his chest. It felt so good. She was just regaining her strength and balance. That was all. He had changed his after-shave lotion from what he used to use. She liked it, though. It was very...manly. She wondered if his hair still felt soft and springy. Like the curls on his chest. She could feel the hard muscular power of his thighs. Somehow that made her own even more quivery. Very weak.

"Carrie, you don't have any choice."

His voice had a raw, gravelly sound to it. Exasperation, she thought. She was being a lot of trouble to him. She had to make a stand and get it over with. She couldn't really fool herself that the weakness coursing through her was entirely due to her sickness. Dominic had always had a sort of melting effect on her.

But that had to stop. She was indulging herself when she should be thinking of Danny. Only Danny. And that meant no more doctors saying she was too sick to have her child back. And definitely no hospital. She forced some stiffening into her spine and lifted her head, meeting Dominic's eyes with defiant and unshakeable purpose.

"If you so much as try to force me..." She concentrated her mind as best she could. "I'll charge you with kidnapping, invasion of privacy, abduction and—" she searched desperately for some other threat "—deduction."

That last word wasn't quite right but somehow it fitted together into the general pattern. Perhaps she was getting light-headed. It was so important to get the right words.

The blue eyes seemed to sharpen in intensity. "Please, Carrie! For my sake!"

"Sorry!" She was definitely repeating herself. "Not for your sake, Dominic," she added for good measure.

"God damn it!" That raw, gravelly tone *was* exasperation. "You're being stupidly wilful! And impossible!"

"Yes," she agreed, not wanting to annoy him any further. "That's exactly right."

He kept one arm clamped around her shoulders as he swung to face the doctor. "Isn't there something we can do?" He seemed to be imploring for some authority from the medical profession.

Carrie wasn't going to take that. Not after her re-
cent experiences!

"If the young lady is adamant...it is her right to
refuse treatment. She cannot be forced," came the
considered reply.

And about time someone recognised my rights,
Carrie thought belligerently. If only she could get the
welfare people to do the same thing, there wouldn't be
a problem.

Dominic's chest heaved and fell. "Thank you for
your time and trouble, Dr. Burridge," he said on a
strained note of resignation. "I'll let you know when
something can be done."

The doctor gave a rueful grimace. "I wish you
luck."

Carrie was glad to see the back of him. It wasn't that
she had anything against him personally. He was
probably a very nice man. But she had been messed
around in hospital for far too long. And certainly the
treatment hadn't seemed to help all that much. In fact,
she had begun to feel like a guinea pig, and she wasn't
going to get caught up in that again. She could get
better by herself. Viruses didn't live forever. At least,
she didn't think they did. She would get well in her
own good time. And a lot faster if her worry about
Danny could only be lifted.

As soon as the door closed behind the doctor,
Dominic put both his arms around her again, holding
her more firmly against him and giving her very secure support. She nestled her head against his shoulder, wondering if his strength could flow into her.
Certainly she was beginning to feel better with him
holding her so close. She would make an effort to get
going soon. But just for a moment or two...she could

dream a little, couldn't she? Dream that he loved her, had always loved her, and she had come home.

"Tell me about your baby, Carrie. Tell me what the problem is. Ask me whatever it is you want me to do."

The words were spoken in a curiously flat manner, totally neutral as far as any feeling was concerned, but Carrie could feel the warmth and the kindness behind the intent. She was a silly little fool for dreaming of more from him. One could never really go back. And the past had all been a lie, anyway, on his side. She had come for Dominic's help. He was offering it. So she would gratefully accept it. Then go.

Carrie took a deep steadying breath and began her story at the beginning of the problem. She had been sick. Someone had rung for an ambulance. She omitted to tell Dominic that it was Danny who was so concerned for her that he had rung for help. That was irrelevant to the problem. Everything had worked fine until they got to the hospital. The authorities there had found out Danny didn't have anyone to look after him.

She was too newly back in the country to have any friends or acquaintances she could trust. Her parents were both dead, and any family relationships that still existed had all been estranged when her mother and stepfather had married. She didn't even know where they were. So the welfare people had been called in to look after Danny.

At first she had been intensely grateful. The problem had developed later. She had signed herself out of hospital when it was obvious that they weren't doing anything more for her. Then she wanted Danny back. The welfare people refused point-blank. They said she wasn't well enough to look after a child. Which was, in her opinion, totally unjustified. They had no right to keep a child from his own mother.

"You don't think they might have a point?" Dominic's voice was filled with dry sarcasm.

"I would have coped," Carrie replied defensively "I always do. After all, I got to you, didn't I?"

"Only just."

"But I did it."

"Yes," he said heavily. "You did it."

"And looking after Danny wouldn't be nearly as much effort. He's never any trouble. He's the best child in the world. And I want him back. He'll be fretting for me, not knowing what's going on. He probably feels unloved. Strangers won't give him the kind of attention I do, and nothing will be familiar to him like in Fiji. . . ."

"Fiji?"

"That's where we came from. What he's used to. He could be psychologically scarred in an institution over here with everything unfamiliar to him. He needs me. It's wrong to separate a child from his mother. I have to have him back, Dominic."

She lifted her head, wanting to make her appeal straight to his face. Her eyes pleaded her case as eloquently as they could. "All I'm asking is that you make one or two little phone calls. To the right people. To cut through the red tape. The small-minded rules and regulations. To get Danny back with me where he belongs." She searched his eyes anxiously, pleadingly. "Will you do that for me, Dominic?"

He slowly nodded his assent. "Yes, I'll do that for you, Carrie."

A feeling of wild triumph overtook Carrie. She had succeeded. Against all the odds. Her head dizzied with

delight. She leaned it on Dominic's shoulder, just for
a few moments. He couldn't know what it meant to
her. She would be gone soon. Out of his life again. But
Danny would be coming back into hers. It was
enough. She felt a new burst of purpose surging
through her body. I'll get better quickly now, she
promised herself.

"Thank you," she murmured in heartfelt relief, and
nearly added, "that makes up for all the pain you've
ever caused me," but that would be a mistake. She
must never confess the agony of mind and heart that
Dominic Savage had given her. That was too long ago.
Instead she said, "I'll always remember you for doing this." She would anyway. There was no lie in that.

"But first, I'm taking you home, Carrie."

The grateful glow was instantly dispelled by a wave
of horror. Oh, no, she thought, not that! She couldn't
allow Dominic back into her life. That would be a
road to disaster. Maybe worse than what she already
had. He would reopen wounds and make more. And
he would see where she lived, and that alone would be
too dreadful. And . . . and . . . somehow she had to put
a stop to this idea immediately.

"You can't do that!" she cried in alarm, lifting her
head to assert herself again. His face had an even more
determined look than before, and the blue eyes blazed
with immutable resolution. But Carrie would not be
shaken from the course she had to take. "All I want
from you is a little telephone call," she insisted.
"Nothing more."

"If you want that telephone call to be successful,
Carrie, I need the facts. All of them," he stated grimly.

Then, while she was still frantically trying to see a
way around that argument, he scooped her legs off the

floor and she found herself cradled firmly against his chest.

"No! No!" she protested, panicking at having control taken out of her hands. "Put me down, Dominic!" An idea came. Any evasive tactic was justified. "You can't take me home. Not today."

There was a chilled pause. His eyes gathered suspicion. "Why not, Carrie?"

"Your whole afternoon is booked with appointments. You're a busy man. You can't let those people down."

She had him there, Carrie thought triumphantly. Apparently she knew the facts about him better than he did himself. It was lucky she could remind him. He had to let her go. So near and yet so far, she thought with painful regret. But she couldn't accept his help if he meant to pursue her problem beyond what she'd asked of him.

"I'll look after that," he said grimly, and began striding to the door, holding her tightly clamped to him. She couldn't even struggle against the grip he had on her.

"You can't carry me like this," she cried in desperation.

"Yes, I can."

"I'm too heavy," she pleaded.

His eyes raked hers in challenging disbelief. "You're lighter than an armful of fairy floss. And something has to be done about that whether you like it or not! You want that telephone call to be successful, don't you?"

"Yes."

"Then we have to give ourselves every chance."

"But..."

"No buts! Every chance! Remember that!"

Her head whirled with frightening uncertainties. This wasn't what she had planned at all. She couldn't let Dominic go so far. The risk of terrible trouble was too high. Far too high! But how to stop him?

CHAPTER THREE

DOMINIC OPENED THE OFFICE door while Carrie was still churning over how to change his mind. He walked out of the office, then paused as his secretary's desk. Mrs. Coombe's eyebrows flew to the top of her head.

"Cancel all my appointments for this afternoon, please, Mrs. Coombe."

"Yes, Mr. Savage." It was amazing Mrs. Coombe got the words out, her jaw had dropped so far.

Carrie's last glimpse of the dragon was her look of suspended disbelief. Her whole face was frozen like a cartoon, her eyebrows near her hairline, her chin sagging down near her bosom. She was obviously shocked right out of her orderly officious mind.

Although Dominic's action was not what she wanted, Carrie had to admit to a little stab of satisfaction that it was the formidable secretary who had got her come-uppance, and not her. Next time, although, of course, there wouldn't be a next time for her, Carrie suspected that a visitor such as herself would not be subjected to red tape and officious delays. The dragon had better believe it when someone said it was urgent.

Dominic was hurtling down the corridor to the reception area. Carrie got her mind into gear. She could not allow this to go any farther. In fact, it was paramount that it be stopped forthwith.

That was easier decided than done. Dominic was a difficult force to be reckoned with now that he had the bit between his teeth. It really wasn't fair that he was so strong and she was so weak. She only had her wits to fight him with, and for some reason her wits seemed to be slowing down. Before she had managed to gather them into an offensive weapon Dominic had her at the lifts.

"Call down to the car park," he said to the receptionist. "Tell them to have my car ready for me. Immediately. I don't want to be kept waiting."

"Yes, Mr. Savage," the woman answered, her eyes goggling at the vision of her boss carrying off a woman like a latter-day pirate.

"Dominic, you must let me go," Carrie hissed at him. "What will people think?"

"I couldn't care less."

Carrie could hardly credit such an irresponsible attitude. As it was, gossip about this extraordinary incident would be rife among his employees. If he persisted in taking her home, it would make it ten times worse. She had to be more insistent, not only for her own sake, but for his, as well.

"Think of your wife!" she whispered urgently.

His face underwent an almost violent change. Hostility, anger, a rage of intense frustration blazed down at her. "That's precisely whom I am thinking of," he rasped, the blue eyes as bitter as a winter storm and total disapproval spiking through every word.

Carrie instantly shrank inside herself. If he was using her as a weapon to hurt or get back at his wife in some way, she wanted no part in his schemes. She wished she hadn't brought the subject up. Of course, he had married that girl—Alyson Hawthorn, the Super-Sophisticate and Bitch Extraordinaire. It was always going to happen. Alyson had not only told her so, but had left Carrie in no doubt about the nature of their proposed marriage.

It was obviously a marriage that wasn't wearing too well with Dominic at the moment. Carrie had never understood the kind of relationship that accepted flings on the side, but she had been forced to believe it. She remembered Alyson's derisive laughter at the idea of being offended that Dominic had slept with Carrie. "We all do it," she had said, as if it was nothing at all, and her eyes had mocked Carrie's naïveté.

She looked at Dominic, unable to conceal the pain in her eyes. "I'm sorry," she whispered. "I shouldn't have said that."

"Best to get it out in the open," he muttered irritably.

Carrie sank into deeper misery. I was right never to go back, she thought, never to see him again, never to make any contact at all. That's one decision I can be proud of. But today's decision had been a bad error of judgement, despite her own and Danny's need. The high-risk factor was getting riskier by the moment. Somehow she had to stop this right now, before everything got out of hand.

"Please ... I'd rather you call me a taxi," she begged.

"The facts, Carrie. I need the facts," he reminded her.

The lift doors opened, and Dominic had her closed into the small compartment with him and whizzing downwards before her frantic mind could produce a solid protest.

"This isn't what I planned," Carrie protested vehemently.

"Will you stop making objections?"

"I didn't mean for you to go to all this trouble."

"I can see that."

He bestowed a stern look on her that gave Carrie an odd quivery feeling in her heart. She had the distinct suspicion that when Dominic Savage made up his mind about something, not even a full-scale battle would deter him from seeing it through. It must come from being in charge of APIC, she thought. He hadn't been at all imperious when she had known him before. But she wasn't one of his employees he could order around at will.

"You can't do what you like with me, Dominic," she warned him. "I'm a free agent, you know."

"You've obviously become doggedly and impossibly independent, Carrie. But you did ask for my help. That's what you came for, and that's what you're getting."

"Only to get past the bureaucrats."

"I have to know the relevant facts in order to achieve that," he said with grim patience.

The lift doors opened. Dominic started moving again. There were people eagerly offering assistance, a Daimler waiting with its front doors open and its engine humming at a low thrum. Carrie was lowered onto a cold leather seat, and Dominic's arms slid away from her.

"All right?" he asked softly.

Reluctantly, wearily, she lifted her eyes, feeling raw and very vulnerable as she met the sharp concern in his. "I made a mistake, Dominic," she said flatly.

"Please . . . just forget I ever came. Forget everything I said. I'll manage without your help."

His mouth thinned. He pulled the seat belt across her and pressed the buckle into its slot. Then his eyes met hers again, and somehow her own feelings seemed to be reflected in their dark blue depths. "It's too late for that, Carrie," he said quietly.

Then he shut the door on her and quickly rounded the car to the driver's side. Someone was holding his door open, then closed it after him as Dominic settled on the seat beside her and fastened his own safety belt. One hand gripped the steering wheel, the other curled around the gearshift. He didn't look at her again. He simply said, "Tell me where you live, Carrie."

A trip home, she silently resolved, and that's all. She would definitely dismiss him then. It was bad enough having to put up with him taking her home this one day. She would have nothing more to do with him. Ever! Her anxiety over Danny, and her sickness, had obviously dulled her brain this morning. But this was where solid common sense took over.

"Ashfield," she answered tersely. "Eleven Bond Street."

The Daimler purred forward. All the luxury fittings of the car screamed money. But then everything about Dominic had always screamed money. She had been so flattered, so excited, so awed, almost, when he seemed to return her own mad attraction to him on that holiday so long ago. A brief summer madness it was, not grounded in reality at all. It had come to a brutal end when reality had caught up with her in the form of Alyson Hawthorn. And Dominic's other high-living friends.

It all came down to money, Carrie thought bitterly.
Like this car. Like Alyson Hawthorn, who was another symbol of status and class, with her high con-
nections in the gentocracy, or whatever it was called.
The people with old money. They inevitably inter-
married. That was the way the world was made to
move. Carrie had recognised that even then. The same
reality was just as brutal now.

The drive to Ashfield seemed to take forever, although it could only have been twenty minutes or so.
The feeling of strain and tension in the car made light
conversation impossible. Besides, they really had
nothing to say to each other. They came from different worlds, occupied different worlds, and Carrie
spent the time wretchedly castigating herself for being such a fool as to invite even the briefest connec-
tion between them.

They turned into Bond Street. The tenements had
been built late in the last century—dingy, squalid
semidetached houses planned for manual workers who
did not need light or sunshine or hope in their lives,
only a hand-to-mouth existence with a roof over their
heads. Carrie saw Dominic Savage's mouth grimace in
distaste. In his life, he rarely had to face such grim
relics of the labouring class, Carrie thought. It was so
different to what he was used to. She had known he
would disapprove of the kind of home she could afford.

He parked in front of the entrance. Carrie managed to get out of the car before Dominic could get to
her to help. It was most important that she assert her
independence as quickly as possibly and get on with
her life without him.

"Which flat is it?" he asked.

Number eleven was a three-storey tenement, and Dominic had his head tilted, looking at the top storey.

"It's the basement flat," Carrie answered. "Down these steps."

She hurried ahead, quickly grasping the thin railing of the rusty cast-iron fence that lined the stairway to keep herself steady.

"Let me help you."

"No, Dominic. I'm all right now."

He caught up with her and took her arm anyway as she bolted down the steps. She didn't bother protesting. She kept her gaze averted from him, not wanting to see his face. No dreaming now. Stupid to have indulged herself even for a few moments. She knew only too well what his expression would reflect.

The tiny porch in front of the door seemed hopelessly crowded with him standing next to her. Carrie snatched the key out of her handbag, jammed it into the lock and opened the door. She stepped into the hallway and switched on the light. Even in the daytime that was necessary.

She didn't try to stop Dominic from coming in. Give him his way now, Carrie thought fiercely, then refuse anything he suggests. Refuse point-blank. That would get rid of him.

He followed her to the kitchen at the back, pausing momentarily to look into the single bedroom and cast his eyes around the cluttered living room. He muttered something under his breath that sounded distinctly like an appalled oath, but Carrie determinedly ignored it.

"Well, this is home!" she said with forced cheer. "And now that you've got me here, you've discharged any sense of duty you were feeling. Thank you for your kindness and consideration, and—''

''Carrie, this is dreadful!'' he cut in, his brow furrowed with concern, his eyes stabbing her with their total rejection of her definition of ''home,'' his face set in an even grimmer mould of disapproval.

''You shouldn't say things like that,'' she reprimanded with stiff pride. ''Even if you do mean them.''

''This is no place to bring up a baby,'' he said in a softer tone.

''We cope,'' she said defensively. ''We always have and always will.''

His expression slowly changed into a more disturbing one. Carrie told herself she had to be mistaken, but he seemed to be looking at her with an intensely hungry yearning, as though she had something he wanted very much. Her spine prickled with danger warnings. She eyed him warily, afraid that he was going to spring something on her that she wouldn't like at all.

''In your condition,'' he continued softly, ''and in this place, I can understand what the welfare people think. They believe they're doing the child a favour—''

''They're not!''

''Don't interrupt, Carrie. Open your mind to the problems they see. That I see. It's quite obvious to me what is needed if you want your baby back. If you want the best chance of getting him and keeping him. What we have to do is present them with a different situation. One where no doubts about your welfare can arise—''

''What are you suggesting?'' Carrie leapt in, the worst suspicions forming in her mind.

"I have a large home with live-in staff. Plenty of space for you and Danny. I want you to come home with me now, Carrie. We'll get things organized for Danny, and then I'll have the strongest possible case to present to the welfare people. You'll have your baby back tomorrow. I promise you that."

Carrie stared at him blank-eyed as her mind whirled in horror at his scheme. She had suspected something, but not this! What did he think he was doing? Setting up a ménage à trois with her and his wife? Was he trying to get at Alyson, teach her a lesson? Was Alyson playing around too much and not giving Dominic what he wanted? Carrie recalled his reaction when she had first spoken of her baby. Was Alyson refusing to give him children?

But bringing a former lover into his home! No way could Carrie be a party to that! The very thought curled her toes with revulsion. She sat down on the wooden stool in the kitchen, suddenly feeling quite ill again. She shook her head in an attempt to clear it.

"No, Dominic," she said very firmly. "Thank you, but no. I won't do it."

"Carrie, you're not thinking straight," he argued. "If you refuse, it might mean more delay in getting Danny back."

"I won't do it," she said, her eyes fiercely defying and denying the persuasive appeal.

It wasn't even a dilemma. For her and Danny to be placed in the situation that Dominic proposed would be even worse than the situation they were in now. And if he got even a hint of how matters really lay, it could lead to the dislocation of so many people's lives. She had no choice. No choice at all. No matter how much hurt and anguish it caused her, she had to refuse the treacherous option that Dominic was holding out to her.

"Carrie, you're not being reasonable," Dominic pressed. "It must be because you've been so sick..."

Funny how people could distort their lives and twist things up. She had never understood the values by which he and Alyson lived, but this was truly warped.

"I'll never change my mind. Not about that," she repeated for emphasis.

There was a nerve-tearing pause, then very quietly he put the question, "What did I do that was so wrong, Carrie?"

It trapped her into looking up, and she was momentarily caught in that black empty place in the past—the time when she had turned her back on his kind of life and walked away with desolation in her heart. Her own pain seemed to be reflected in his eyes, yet he couldn't be thinking of that. Her walking away couldn't have hurt him. Not really. Only perhaps his male ego. For a little while. And, of course, he always had Alyson to help him forget.

Besides, he couldn't be talking about that. He was referring to today's encounter. She was messing up his plan. "It's just wrong for me, Dominic," she said flatly.

"Do you hate me so much?" he asked, each word slowly enunciated like the clap of doom.

Dominic really did have everything distorted, Carrie thought sadly. He had so many good points, and her feelings towards him were the very opposite to hate. If only... but she wasn't going to start on if onlys again. Reality had to be faced, however brutal it was. She managed a wry little smile.

"I don't hate anybody, Dominic. Particularly not you."

"I see," he muttered, but he didn't seem to see anything at all. His eyes had a glazed look as though they were focused inward.

"I'll find another way around the problem," she said dully. Perhaps she would leave Sydney and find a place in the country. Taree, Dubbo...any large country town might offer some form of work that was in her line of training. Perhaps a pastry cook at a bakery. Or in a homemade pie shop. She didn't have to be a chef. And living would be cheaper out of the city. If she could get a job...

"I'll find another way, too," Dominic said in a tone of strong resolution.

She frowned at him. "Please let it go. All I wanted was a telephone call—"

"I'll do that."

"—nothing else."

"Leave it to me."

Carrie didn't know whether he meant it or not, but she couldn't take any more from him. "Goodbye, Dominic," she said flatly.

His eyes locked on hers for a long tense moment, then slowly he nodded. "I'll let myself out."

"Thank you," Carrie whispered, her voice choked by a huge lump of suppressed emotion in her throat.

"Goodbye, Carrie."

The way he said it was almost a caress. Tears pricked at her eyes. He was going...out of her life forever this time. She heard his footsteps receding down the hallway, heard the front door open and shut quietly behind him. For a long while Carrie sat totally immobile, her face white, her body lifeless. Then, for the first time in many years, she buried her head in her arms on the kitchen counter and sobbed bitterly into her loneliness.

CHAPTER FOUR

YESTERDAY HAD BEEN more weakening than Carrie had expected. She felt limp, drained, without purpose, will or energy. She berated herself for letting this happen to her. She could not rely on Dominic Savage for anything. She had to pull herself together. And the first thing she had to do was start eating more, even if she had to force food down her throat. Then maybe she would have the energy to get herself better organized instead of trying to think of some easy way out of her problem.

She cooked herself some scrambled eggs and managed to consume a piece of toast with them. Then she made coffee with milk. It was a bit rich for her taste but she drank it, determined to put weight on any way she could. She had been existing on soup lately, not wanting anything more than that. But obviously it was not enough.

In fact, if she had remembered to have some lunch yesterday before setting out to see Dominic, she might have fared a lot better instead of succumbing to that awful weakness. Today she would set herself a proper diet and follow it rigidly, no matter whether she felt like it or not. If those welfare people thought she was suffering from malnutrition she would soon set them straight.

The thought came to her that she could ring or write to her member of parliament. It was a pity she hadn't registered herself on the electoral role as soon as she had come back from Fiji, but it was the kind of official duty that everyone let slip until a looming election served as a reminder. She would see to it today. Then she could proceed along that line, even though it meant more red tape.

She washed up the few things she'd used, fired with new purpose to get going and achieve something. She did feel better for having made herself eat a more substantial meal than she had become accustomed to. As she went to her bedroom to dress, she couldn't help looking at the flat through Dominic's eyes.

He was right in one respect. This was no place to bring up a child. It compared so badly to the sun-filled *bure* that she and Danny had occupied in Fiji. This was nothing but a dingy little hole in the ground. When she had first occupied it, it had been filthy with old grime. She had scrubbed and cleaned, even fumigated the place. However, the only difference now was that it was a clean dingy hole instead of a dirty one. Even the bright curtains she had put up did not make up for the lack of sunlight.

She had to move. Her ambition to be a chef in a top restaurant was not as important as having the right kind of place for bringing up her son. She knew Danny hated the flat as much as she did, although he had never grumbled or complained about it. He had accepted her insistence that it was just a temporary place until she had a permanent position. But that kind of position was not easy to get in Sydney, Carrie had found, despite her excellent references and years of experience. A country town was better anyway,

Carrie decided. It would get her right away from Dominic Savage.

Having made up her mind on a new course of action, Carrie got herself moving. She put on a brightly flowered skirt to cheer herself up. It had an elasticised waist so she didn't have to worry about it falling off. The matching T-shirt with the hibiscus-flower motif looked very baggy on her but she tucked it in, then bloused out the looseness so that it didn't look too bad. At least she could wear her flat comfortable Roman sandals today, so walking shouldn't be too much of a problem.

She made her way to the electoral office at Ashfield and registered herself as a voter. Next she bought a writing pad and envelopes. She also purchased a newspaper to read advertisements for jobs up the country. At the very last moment she remembered food. The tomatoes looked good at the fruit shop. She bought some salad things. That was healthy. She also stopped at a bakery shop and bought a custard tart. It would help put weight on.

Despite her good breakfast, Carrie's burst of energy was fading fast. On her way home she rested in the park for an hour or two. She felt a bit too dizzy to read the newspaper. Focusing on little print seemed to make things worse. She could do that later, Carrie decided, when she felt better. She watched the birds as they wheeled and soared, free and unhindered by any welfare people or red tape. They twittered happily between themselves. Life was good. And so it would be for her and Danny again, once they were back together.

After a while, Carrie remembered the custard tart and ate it. Birds swooped down to pick up the crumbs.

She smiled at their antics, pleased to be passing the time so pleasantly. She wondered if Danny was pleased with anything, wherever he was living. She hoped so. She hoped he wasn't too miserable. Soon, she silently promised him. I'll get you back soon, my little love.

It was mid-afternoon by the time she returned to Bond Street. The first thing she saw was a Daimler parked outside number eleven. She halted dead in her tracks, her heart palpitating at an alarming rate. "Oh, hell!" she thought. "What is Dominic up to now?"

Then she remembered the telephone call he had said he would make, and the thought that he might have brought news of Danny had her feet instantly scurrying forward.

He didn't hear her coming. He was sitting on the basement steps, irritably throwing small pebbles at some invisible mark on the wall. His brow was furrowed. Despite his maturity and the superbly tailored business suit he wore, he looked like a petulant little boy who had lost his favourite lolly. Carrie's heart did a funny little flip. But it was no good thinking of him like . . . like she might think of Danny. No good feeling anything for Dominic Savage. That was forbidden territory.

"Hello, there!" she called out brightly. "I hope I haven't kept you waiting too long."

The frown instantly disappeared. He rose eagerly to his feet, but when he turned to her his face had assumed a guarded look, the blue eyes wary and watchful. "No," he said. "I've had a fair bit to do. The appointments from yesterday afternoon."

"Of course." She flushed. "But that wasn't really my fault. I did—"

"I appreciate that, Carrie," he cut in quickly.

Her eyes searched his anxiously, hopefully. "Have you found out anything from the welfare people?"

"Yes."

She looked at him in expectant appeal.

He gestured towards the door. "May we go inside?"

"Oh! All right." She hurried forward, ready to agree to almost anything just to hear about Danny. Any news was better than no news at all.

"Let me carry your parcels."

She handed them over reluctantly, but they were getting heavy and she needed her hands free to get out her key anyway.

"Have you been overdoing it again?" Dominic asked sternly.

"Don't fuss. I'm fine," she insisted, although his presence did make her feel a bit shaky and feverish. She probably needed to sit down. Not so close to him. When she was close to him the memories were all too sharp, and she couldn't afford them. Not if she was to remain sane and sensible.

She quickly unlocked the door and led him to the kitchen. He placed the plastic bags on the counter and sat down on Danny's stool, on the living room side of the kitchen counter. He looked as if he meant to stay for some time, and Carrie couldn't exactly dismiss him. At least, not straight away.

"Would you like a cup of tea? Or coffee?" she asked, driven to be polite in her need to know about Danny.

His serious face cracked into a slight smile. "Thank you. I would."

"Which one?"

"Whatever you're having."

"Tea."

"Fine."

Carrie put the kettle on to boil, then sat down on her stool, facing him across the counter. "Well?" she pleaded, unable to wait any longer.

A wave of resolution passed over his face. "Danny will be coming back tomorrow."

Carrie had not been aware of how tensely wound up she was until that firm pronouncement hit her and she let out all the tightness in a shuddering sigh. A well of jubilation flooded her mind. A spring of happiness bubbled through her body. She wanted to leap off her stool, to hug Dominic Savage, to kiss him, to thank him, to show her gratitude. All of which was impossible.

"I'll never be able to repay you," she said feelingly. "To say thank you simply does not express—"

"There is one proviso."

Carrie stopped in full flight. Her stomach turned over. He couldn't be returning to his proposal of yesterday. He just couldn't! She had been so definite in her rejection of it. If he was trying to blackmail her... Surely Dominic could not stoop so low, no matter how pressed he felt to achieve his purpose. Whatever that was.

She stood up, too agitated to remain seated. The blood rushed from her face, but the light of bitter battle was in her green eyes. "What proviso is that?" she demanded icily.

Dominic rose from his stool, his expression clearly indicating that he was prepared to do battle. "Don't look at me like that, Carrie," he shot at her. "It's not what you think. I'm not double-crossing you. This is genuine concern for you and your baby," he insisted vehemently, then tempered his tone to a more reasoning note as he added, "Please hear me out. For your own sake. And the child's."

"I'm not going to your home, Dominic," she fired at him. "I don't care what you say or how you twist it. I'm not going!"

His face tightened. "You made that abundantly clear yesterday."

"Then what is this proviso?" Carrie demanded tersely, every atom of her being poised to explode in fiery rebellion.

Dominic's chest rose and fell as he administered a deep breath to his lungs. He made a visible effort to relax, to speak calmly so as not to upset her. "Your accommodation here. It is a stumbling block, Carrie. Truly it is."

"Then what are you suggesting?" Her eyes flared a hot warning.

Dominic did not flinch. He held her gaze steadily, projecting calm reassurance. "My company owns an apartment. We use it for interstate executives, business associates, overseas clients...people we want to accommodate who prefer not to stay in a hotel. And with the way property values are moving, it's a good investment. It's more appropriate housing for you than here, Carrie. You and Danny could use it until such time as—"

"And put myself further in your debt?" she flashed at him, a fierce pride putting a sharp edge on every word.

"Not at all. There's no reason you shouldn't use it. Until you're better."

"While your company is inconvenienced by not having ready accommodation for your executives, associates and clients," she sliced back sarcastically.

Dominic grimaced, shook his head as though in some pain, then tried again, slowly and patiently. "At the present moment, the apartment is being redecorated. It's already been cleared of most of its furniture, leaving only the barest basics. If you can put up with the nuisance of an interior decorator coming and going, and doing things around you, at least you will be in better living quarters than this place can offer. It's spacious, with well-appointed bathrooms and kitchen. And lots of windows to let in the light."

Carrie was tempted, despite her suspicions. "This is a genuine offer, Dominic?" she asked. "I won't accept charity. I can always pay—"

"Carrie, I've explained it all to you. Our company doesn't really need your money. The apartment is not expected to earn an income. That's not its purpose. What more can I say?" he replied with every appearance of earnest sincerity. "The main point is, the welfare people approve of the plan. They'll release Danny tomorrow. If you agree."

She was plunged into a quandary. It was an opportunity too good to miss, yet if it meant a continued association with Dominic... If he had some problem with his marriage, she didn't want to get involved in it. In fact, she couldn't really afford any involvement with him at all. There was always Danny to consider, apart from her own disturbing feelings.

Some of her agony of mind shadowed her eyes. "I don't want you... coming to see me, Dominic."

The relief on his face seemed to make nonsense of all her thoughts on the matter. Apparently he didn't want to see her. Had she got everything wrong? Or had he changed his mind since yesterday, realising that it was totally unfair to use her need as a means to settle his own?

"Only if it's necessary," he said, obviously anxious to reassure her.

Maybe he felt guilty for what he had formerly proposed. And she had always thought Dominic kind and generous by nature, even though some of his morals didn't bear too much inspection. She hesitated for a while, tossing alternatives around in her mind. Her need to be reunited with Danny won out.

"All right. I accept."

"Thank God!" Dominic breathed, his relief becoming even more pronounced. "You're being reasonable for once. I'll go and bring the suitcases in."

He had turned away when Carrie was struck by a hornet's nest of uncertainty. "You expected me to accept, Dominic?"

He swung back, ready to appease again. "It was the only sensible decision to make, Carrie." He gave her a wry little smile. "But I must confess I wasn't at all certain you'd make it. I brought suitcases just in case, so to speak."

"I see," she said, trying to quell the nervous flutters in her stomach. She had the feeling that she had just crossed a line that wasn't as straight as she would have liked it to be. But Danny was on the other side of it, and her yearning for him could not be denied. "Thank you, Dominic," she said, not very firmly.

"It will be all right, Carrie," he assured her. "I promise you."

She trailed after him as far as the bedroom door. At least she hadn't been here long enough to gather much stuff, she thought, so the packing wouldn't take long. She had given away all unnecessary belongings before leaving Fiji.

She sat down on the bed, feeling weak from the stress of being with Dominic. But after tomorrow she wouldn't see him again, unless it was necessary. Which it wouldn't be. She could cope with everything. If this company apartment didn't work out, she could always leave. Once she had Danny back. And once she was well, she would get a job in the country. This was only a temporary measure, and it would stay a temporary measure.

Dominic came in with two large suitcases and set them open on Danny's bed. He opened the top drawer of the chest near the bed and began scooping clothes out.

Carrie gaped at him. "What are you doing?" she asked, shocked that he would take such a liberty. "They're my underclothes!"

"I thought I'd help you pack," he said matter-of-factly.

Blood had rushed to Carrie's face. "No, you won't!"

"Why not? You look as if you need a rest, Carrie. I've done this plenty of times for my wife—"

Mention of his wife tipped Carrie into a maelstrom of violent emotion. "I don't want you touching my underclothes!" she cried vehemently.

He gave her a look that told her he remembered touching far more intimate things than her underclothes. Carrie burned. Her heart pounded a frantic protest. She told herself it was the humiliation of it all, but she knew it was more than that. She was just too frightened to examine what she was really feeling. It was far too dangerous to her sense of rightness.

"That was eight years and two months ago," she stated tightly, trying her utmost to get in control of herself. "Before you married!"

"Yes. I remember," he answered softly, and there was something infinitely disquieting in the vivid blue eyes. Again that look of haunted, raw, naked pain crossed his face.

"Things have changed," Carrie said, flustered. "I've changed. You've changed. And I don't want... I don't want..." She lifted her hands helplessly, unable to hold the gaze that remembered too many things that had to be forgotten. And stay forgotten!

"May I pack food from the kitchen?" he asked quietly.

Carrie could feel the tension flooding from him in waves. She nodded, too choked to speak.

"Then I'll go and get boxes out of the car."

Carrie got up to pack. She was trembling so much she had to sit down again. But when she heard Dominic returning with the boxes, she forced her legs to hold her and moved to the chest of drawers, determined to start the packing. And finish it. At least in the bedroom.

Dominic brought her a cup of tea. She had completely forgotten that she had put the kettle on to boil. She thanked him abruptly, and he did not linger with her. She instantly regretted the abruptness. It had been kind of him. But she couldn't allow herself to go soft. If she gave him an inch, she had a dreadful suspicion that he might take the inevitable mile.

He took boxes out to the car while she slowly filled the suitcases. She had almost finished when he stopped in the bedroom doorway.

"What about the furniture, Carrie? Is it yours?"

"No. Only the curtains."

"I'll take them down for you and put them in a box, too," he said. "I've cleared the kitchen and the laundry at the back. Is it all right if I do the bathroom?" he asked tactfully, aware that it could be personal to her.

"I'll do that," she said.

"Okay," he agreed, and briskly collected her cup and saucer before disappearing again.

When Carrie finally went to inspect what he'd done, she found he had been amazingly efficient. Everything had been tidied as he had packed, and he had left nothing behind except what belonged in the flat. The whole place was as spick-and-span as she would have left it. She looked at him in questioning amazement.

"I am house trained," he said dryly. "I even cook when called upon."

Heaven above, she thought, he has changed! The old Dominic she had known would have had no more idea about cooking than the man in the moon!

"Thank you again for all your help, Dominic," she said stiffly, doing her best to let him know she would not be calling upon him for anything more.

He made a dismissive gesture. "Are you ready to go now?"

"Yes."

She locked the flat and they drove to the real estate agent that handled the rental. Dominic insisted that Carrie remain in the car and rest while he handed over the key and finalised matters. She did not argue. She felt exhausted, mentally, emotionally and physically.

She realised after a while that she hadn't asked Dominic where the company's apartment was, but then decided it didn't really matter. So long as the welfare people accepted it as suitable for Danny. That was all that counted.

CHAPTER FIVE

WHEN THEY GOT GOING AGAIN, Dominic headed the Daimler into the city. Carrie closed her eyes. It was easier to shut out Dominic's presence if she couldn't see him. Besides, she was very tired. It had been a more active day than she'd had for some time. An extremely wearing day.

"Carrie?"

She didn't really want to respond to the soft call of her name. Her body did, completely without her volition. The tone he used, the caring it implied . . . Little quivers fluttered through her stomach. She should never have gone to him. It was all coming back. Not just a memory any more. Raw reality. But it would be over soon, she told herself. Meanwhile, politeness demanded a reply. "Yes?" she asked wearily.

"There wasn't any baby food stocked in the kitchen cupboards." There was a puzzled note in his voice. "And what about a bassinet or a cot? If you're sleeping with the baby, you won't get your proper rest," he added in anxious concern.

Carrie heaved a deep sigh to relieve the tension that instantly tore at her nerves. He had to know the truth now. At least, as much of the truth as he needed to know. After all, he would be meeting Danny tomorrow. Carrie concentrated on injecting a matter-of-fact tone into her voice.

"I'm sorry, Dominic. I may have misled you just a little bit. I think of Danny as my baby. He is. But he's not exactly a tiny cuddly thing any more. He's a real little boy. He eats what I eat. And that was his bed you put the suitcases on."

"Oh!" It was the sound of relief. "That's all right, then. A bed," he added, as though to himself, and as if it was a matter of some importance.

To Carrie's relief, that ended the conversation. Of course, it was bound to be resumed tomorrow, after Dominic met Danny, and she had to get herself mentally prepared for it. But there was time enough to think about that. Once over that hurdle she was home free. If everything went right.

Once they were in the inner city, Carrie snapped alert again. She wondered if Dominic was returning to his office for some reason, but they passed Bridge Street and went right down to Circular Quay, turning into the basement car park of an ultra-modern skyscraper that stood on the waterfront of the harbour.

It made sense when Carrie stopped to think about it. APIC would naturally want their important clients or associates placed at the hub of things and in a prestigious area. Harbour frontage was always prestigious. The welfare people couldn't possibly look down their noses at this address!

Dominic wouldn't let Carrie lift anything from the car. He hefted the two large suitcases over to the lifts. He used a slot key to open the doors of one lift and quickly ushered Carrie inside, following her with the packed bags.

"I hope you're not nervous of heights, Carrie," he said anxiously, as the lift started upwards.

"Not at all," she assured him.

Again he looked relieved. "All the glass in the apartment is laminated and break-proof, and the whole place is air-conditioned. So it's completely safe. I'm sorry it isn't comfortably furnished as yet, but it will be, bit by bit."

"It'll be fine, Dominic. Anything will be fine as long as it means..."

"You get Danny back," he finished for her, giving her a smile of intimate understanding that took Carrie's breath away.

For several rocky moments, it was as if there had been no eight years and two months. They were sharing together, just as they did before his friends had come and Alyson had put a different face on their relationship. Then Carrie wrenched her gaze from his and stared at the doors, willing the lift to stop, willing the doors to open, urgently needing to escape the intimacy Dominic had evoked. Endless seconds ticked over. She felt her nerves stretch to snapping point before the lift co-operated with her frantic willing and came to a halt.

The doors opened and she stepped out, concentrating fiercely on her new surroundings, doing her utmost to shut Dominic out of her mind. Her body was a weak mess, but at least she could control her mind. She had to, or she would never get through this ordeal.

The private lobby that led into the apartment was tiled to an old Etruscan pattern. Reluctantly but determinedly, she followed Dominic into an enormous living room, carpeted in off white, which would be a nightmare to keep clean, Carrie thought. In fact, it must have been recently cleaned, because it looked as good as new. The only furniture was two blue-grey leather armchairs and a Travertine coffee table, all of which looked vaguely familiar to Carrie. Were they duplicates of the ones in Dominic's office?

She dismissed the thought as her attention was pleasantly distracted by the magnificent view of Sydney Harbour from the floor-to-ceiling windows. "How high up are we?" she asked.

"Um ... nineteenth floor, I think. The elevator is private, so you'll have no trouble coming and going, Carrie. It's only a short distance from the Botanical Gardens, so you'll be able to take Danny for walks. There are shops along the quay...."

"You business people really do yourself proud. The best of everything!" Carrie remarked drily, then realising she might have given offence, she offered an apologetic smile. "This is—" she gestured towards the view "—fantastic!"

He grinned with deep pleasure. "Good! Have a look around while I bring all your things up."

Carrie steadfastly battled the effect of his grin, turning to the view as he retreated to the lift. Her heart gradually steadied. Dominic probably grinned at everyone like that. It meant nothing personal. Not really personal. She had been difficult about coming here. Now he had won his point. That was all.

This must be what they call a penthouse apartment, Carrie thought, and could not help wondering what it cost. Probably close to a million dollars, with this view and position. Perhaps more. It was going to be an awful comedown when she had to move out, but in the meantime, she might as well enjoy the high life. It was an experience she never expected to have again.

The dining room had a large laminated table and four rather ordinary chairs that didn't suit the place at

all. Perhaps it was a workplace for the interior decorator, Carrie thought, and would be replaced by an
appropriate suite when the time came.

There were three bedrooms, each with its own luxurious bathroom and beautifully crafted built-in
wardrobes. The master bedroom was the only one with
furniture—a king-size bed, already made up, and a
bedside table on which sat a portable television set.

The kitchen seemed huge and was the last word in
modernity. It had a computerised microwave oven as
well as double fan-forced ovens, a barbecue grill beside the burners, a dishwasher, even a garbage disposal unit. Carrie dreamed of the meals she could
cook with such excellent facilities.

The laundry was spacious, with a top-brand automatic washer and matching dryer, as well as a tub and
ironing facilities. Of course, living up here, there
would be no pegging the washing on a clothesline,
Carrie thought, bemused by another new experience
for her.

She returned to the kitchen for a further exploration. There was a huge two-doored refrigerator, and
when she opened the freezer side, she found it stocked
with ice cream and cakes and pies and all sorts of frozen meals and snacks. Dominic came into the kitchen
with a box of food from the flat. She hid the instant
rise of inner tension as best she could and turned to
him enquiringly.

"There's a whole lot of food in here, Dominic."

He shrugged. "Someone comes and does that. You
might as well use it up, Carrie. Otherwise it will get
thrown out before we install anyone else in here.
Whatever is usable, use it."

She frowned. "You'd better tell whoever does it to stop doing it," she said. "Until I'm gone."

Telling herself to keep acting naturally, she opened the other door of the refrigerator. It revealed a huge stock of soft drinks and fruit juices, butter and margarine, a wide variety of cheeses and even some oranges and apples. Carrie shook her head. "I think you should take these things home with you, Dominic."

He slid her an ironic smile. "I assure you, I don't need it. In fact, if I took it home my housekeeper would think I'd gone insane and hand in her notice. Do me a favour and just use it as you please. It'd be a pity to waste it."

Amazing how rich people could just throw things away, Carrie thought with a dash of her own irony...bitter irony. She imagined they didn't think twice about it, while she had always had to think twice about everything. Except for that month with Dominic.

Carrie instantly clamped down on that treacherous memory and opened the doors to a built-in pantry. There were tins of food galore, packets of biscuits, bottles of sauces, all the basic ingredients for all sorts of cooking, spices and condiments—almost a real chef's pantry.

"Use what you like of that, as well," Dominic said carelessly. "Before it goes stale. We'll make a clean sweep of everything when the decorating's done."

It was sinful extravagance to throw it away, Carrie thought critically. "You're sure?" she asked, not wanting to take any advantage that she shouldn't, but unable to countenance such waste.

"Positive," Dominic insisted.

She sighed in relief. "I won't have to shop for weeks," she remarked, her eyes feasting on all the provisions.

"You'll need meat and fruit and vegetables," Dominic said with a disapproving frown.

"Yes. You're right," Carrie quickly agreed.

"I've brought everything up. Do you want to unpack yourself, Carrie?"

"Yes, I do. And thanks! I'm terribly grateful for all you've done, Dominic."

Either he sensed her anxiety for him to leave or he wanted to leave anyway, because he didn't press her except to say, "Promise me you'll take it in easy stages and not wear yourself out."

"I promise." She found herself giving him a smile before she could stop it, and he smiled back, unsettling her all over again.

"OK. Come and I'll show you how the intercom works. The interior decorator will be coming in the morning and you'll have to let her in."

She steeled herself to go with him and listen to his instructions. They were easy to remember. He gave her the key then stepped into the lift.

"I don't know what time I'll get here with Danny tomorrow afternoon, Carrie. You just take care of yourself so you'll be fine when we come. OK?"

"I want to come with you, Dominic," Carrie pleaded, wanting to see Danny as soon as possible and also afraid of Dominic's possible reaction to her son. There were so many uncertainties about how Danny would react to Dominic, as well.

Dominic reached out and took her hands before she could stop him, his warm fingers curling around hers, sending her pulse haywire. He pressed them ear-

nestly, as earnestly as his eyes begged her coopera-
tion.

"Believe me, Carrie, this will all work out much
more smoothly if you leave it to me. I know how to
handle these people and I can do it better alone.
You're sure to get emotional, Carrie, and that's not
the way. Let me get your son for you. Trust me."

She couldn't doubt his sincerity. He did mean well.
And maybe she had been her own worst enemy in her
futile dealings with the welfare people. Dumbly she
nodded her head in compliance with his plan. Trust-
ing him, though, was a different matter. She had
drunk at that well once before. The aftertaste had been
bitter, and the effects had lasted a long time.

He squeezed her hands in a final reassurance.
"Everything will be all right," he promised.

Carrie hoped so. She nodded, too choked by another surge of emotion to say anything. He released
her hands and smiled again. The doors finally closed
on his smile, releasing her from the need to keep her
composure.

Only one more meeting with him, she assured herself. It would probably be the most difficult and the
most testing, but she would get through it somehow.
The problem was that every atom of common sense
she possessed dictated that she never see him again
after tomorrow, but she wanted to.

She wanted to drown in his smile, to feel his eyes
caress her with soft caring, to hear his beautiful voice
say anything, anything at all. Or sing to her as he used
to. She wanted him to hold her again, close, lovingly...

Dominic couldn't be happy with Alyson Hawthorn.

The uncharitable thought slid into her mind, and even as Carrie tried to crush it, it gave her satisfaction in a way. The truth was, she didn't want Alyson and Dominic to be happy.

But they were married!

And it would be utter madness for her to invite any further involvement with him. No matter how unfair it was, no matter what she felt for him or what he felt with her, it had to end tomorrow! The parting of the ways had to come.

CHAPTER SIX

THE SOUND OF MOVEMENT in the kitchen woke Carrie with a start. Who could it be? An intruder? Certainly not the interior decorator, because she didn't have a key. Had Dominic come back for some reason?

Carrie looked at the clock she had placed on the bedside table. Nine-thirty. She had overslept dreadfully. Not at all like the sleeping pattern she was used to recently, where she hardly seemed to close her eyes before she was awake again. But this king-size bed was so roomy and comfortable after that sagging single bed in the flat, and the pillows had been just right. Even better than that, though, was the knowledge that Danny would be with her again today. It had removed so much stress and given her peace of mind.

Meanwhile, she had better find out who was doing what in her kitchen. Carrie slipped out of bed, donned her wraparound housecoat, tied the belt securely, then moved uneasily to the doorway.

"Is anyone out there?" she called, wanting some warning of whom she had to confront.

"Yes. I'm here."

Carrie had heard that voice before, as recently as two days ago. The dragon!

"It's me. Mrs. Coombe, dear."

Wonders will never cease, Carrie thought. I'm now "dear." I've obviously been added to Dominic Savage's list of friends and acquaintances and even granted special honours! Seeing me carried out in Dominic's arms must have really impressed the dragon.

Carrie headed for the kitchen, figuring she had better check what Dominic's secretary was up to. He hadn't given any warning about a visit from her.

Mrs. Coombe was standing over a shopping trolley, transferring parcel after parcel to the refrigerator. She glanced up as Carrie walked in. "I didn't want to wake you," she explained. "You were sleeping so peacefully."

Ah, Carrie thought, so she had been tiptoeing around, seeing what was going on. "You shouldn't have worried about it," she said. "I needed to get up. I was going shopping..."

"I've already done that for you, dear."

"What?" Carrie gaped at her, even more so when Mrs. Coombe gave her an indulgent smile.

"Yes, this is your meat here. A nice tender fillet of beef, a few sausages, a leg of lamb, some hamburger..."

Carrie was slow to recover. "Mrs. Coombe, you can't possibly...this isn't necessary."

The dragon rearranged her face into the more familiar stern look. "Mr. Savage doesn't want you wasting your strength on mundane chores."

Carrie had the mad impulse to stand at attention, salute and say, "Yes, sergeant-major." But she controlled herself and said, "This is so kind."

"Not at all. You've got to get well. I've brought a notepad and I'll put it by your bed. Anything you want, just write it down and you'll have it the same day. And, of course, you must telephone the office for anything urgent. I've put down the number you can call for a direct line to me. Any time at all. Don't hesitate."

Carrie stared in astonishment. The dragon certainly had a new appreciation of "urgent matters." Where Carrie was concerned anyway. And I'm really being pampered, she thought. It made her feel a trifle uncomfortable. Useless, really. She was so used to being self-sufficient.

"I can look after myself," she said defensively.

"I see that," Mrs. Coombe answered with a very dry look that threw Carrie into confusion. "I've brought fresh milk, and here are your vegetables and fruit," she continued with her air of competent efficiency. "If you like, I'll put them away for you. The grapes are seedless and..."

"That's enough to feed any army," Carrie protested.

"Convalescents need a lot of little delicious delicacies to tempt the appetite," Mrs. Coombe said in her no-nonsense manner. "I should know," she added in her best don't-argue-with-me voice.

Carrie felt her hand coming up to her forehead and only resisted the salute at the last moment.

The intercom rang.

"That will be the interior decorator," Carrie said distractedly. "I've got to let her in."

"Go on, then," the dragon urged. "You'll have your hands full, helping with that today. I'll finish here and quietly slip away so as not to disturb you."

Carrie didn't understand how she was supposed to help, except by keeping out of the interior decorator's way, but the intercom rang again, so she didn't stop to argue. "Thank you, Mrs. Coombe."

It was a pleasant surprise to find that the interior decorator was a young woman, about the same age as Carrie, with an outgoing, friendly manner. She introduced herself as Georgina Winslow—"But please call me Gina. Everyone does"—and handed Carrie her business card. Carrie knew she had to be good at her job, despite her age. No one got to do a prestige job like this unless they were good. She suspected Dominic Savage would automatically hire the best.

And of course, the woman looked very professional, her auburn hair cut in a short chic style that suited her rather round face, which was attractive without being conventionally pretty. Her nicest feature was her bright hazel eyes. Her clothes were very smart. A cream dress printed with a geometric design in amber and brown, and a fancy leather belt that screamed designer wear.

Carrie suddenly felt extremely conscious of her unkempt appearance. "Sorry I'm not dressed...or anything. I overslept."

"That's fine. I want to look around and take some notes and measurements. Do you mind?"

"Of course not. I'll get dressed. Do you want me out of here today? Will I be in the way?"

"Oh, no!" came the quick assurance. "I'd much prefer it if you were here. People can have such different tastes. It's a lot easier if we can talk."

The strange remark left Carrie somewhat bemused. Her opinion didn't count at all. But if Gina wanted to sound out her ideas on her, Carrie didn't mind. It would be interesting to see how an interior decorator went about furnishing a place like this. And at least she didn't have to go out and perhaps miss Danny when he arrived. So this arrangement suited her admirably.

By the time she had showered, dressed and tidied herself, as well as the bedroom, Carrie found that Mrs. Coombe had gone and Gina was spreading sample books out on the dining-room table. "Would you like a cup of tea or coffee?" Carrie asked.

"Coffee, please," came the smiling response.

In the kitchen, she found that Mrs. Coombe had set out a glass of orange juice, a bowl of freshly cut fruit salad, a jug of cream and a plate of muffins that smelled as though they had been baked this morning. Tempting my convalescent appetite, Carrie thought drily. And no doubt I'll get lectured tomorrow if I don't eat everything.

She would have to stop Mrs. Coombe's visits. However kindly meant they were, Mrs. Coombe was too closely connected to Dominic Savage. Carrie made a mental note to pay him for the extra food supplies this afternoon. She would not accept charity from him. She owed him too much as it was.

Since she couldn't bear good food to be wasted, and the fruit salad was tempting, Carrie poured some cream over it and ate it while she made the coffee. Then she loaded a tray with the coffee mugs and the plate of muffins and carried it into the dining room.

"Oh, lovely!" Gina beamed at her and quickly cleared a space for the tray. "I skipped breakfast this morning and I'm starving."

"Eat as much as you like," Carrie invited.

"You must have some, too," came the quick retort. "I'll feel like a pig otherwise."

Carrie already felt full from the fruit salad but she forced down a muffin just to be companionable. Out of curiosity, she asked Gina how she set out to tackle a project such as this.

"Well, first you must know the theme the client wants. In this instance my instructions are to produce the homey touch rather than a showpiece. A place where people can really relax and feel comfortable."

That made sense, Carrie thought. If Dominic's clients preferred not to stay in hotels, they wouldn't want an impersonal atmosphere here.

"And that's where you can help me most," Gina said, looking at Carrie expectantly. "Tell me what colours you feel happy with. We don't want anything too neutral. We need warmth as well as restfulness."

"Well, I like most colours," Carrie answered, not feeling comfortable about influencing the decorating. Besides, what she said about colours was true enough. She did like most of them.

"Mr. Savage mentioned you had a little boy. What about him?"

Carrie laughed, happy at the thought that Danny would be with her in a few more hours. "Oh, he loves red and orange and yellow. He's spent most of his life in Fiji, and people in the islands seem to naturally gravitate to bright colours. It's what he's used to. But Danny is only seven years old, so what he likes won't matter."

"Sounds good to me," Gina said consideringly. "I can work with that. A lot of people like bright, cheerful colours. And red and orange and yellow are warm."

Carrie grinned. "More like hot."

Gina grinned back. "So we'll have one very hot bedroom. Let's look at fabrics and see what choice we have."

It was fun looking through the sample books and talking to Gina. The young woman seemed eager to have Carrie's opinion, so Carrie gave her preferences, but always waited until Gina had pointed out the possibilities she favoured. After all, a professional interior decorator obviously knew her job far better than Carrie did.

They were interrupted by the intercom buzzing a summons. It was a delivery man, wanting to bring up a bed. Carrie gave him entry and Gina took over, showing the man where to put it in the second bedroom. Then she asked Carrie if she could make some telephone calls.

"Now that we've chosen fabrics for this room, I'll get coordinating linen delivered for the bed so it will be ready for Danny," she explained.

Carrie felt some protest was in order. "You shouldn't really be taking any notice of what we prefer, Gina. You know, we're not permanent guests here."

Gina looked perplexed for a moment or two, and then her face brightened. "That doesn't matter. This is working out well. Let's go for broke!"

Carrie shrugged. In the end, whatever the result was, it would be Gina's responsibility. "Whatever you like," she said, secretly delighted at the thought of Danny having a nice room of his own. A bright, cheerful room. At least for a while.

She felt so happy that she went out to the kitchen to prepare a really nice lunch, hoping that Gina would share it with her. The time was passing quite easily with the young woman's company. Gina was only too pleased to accept the meal Carrie offered her.

"This is sumptuous! Really lovely! But you mustn't make a practice of feeding me." She laughed. "I don't want to end up overweight. And I don't want to be any trouble to you."

"It's no trouble," Carrie assured her. "I like doing it."

Besides, it made her feel better about using the food that had been left here. If she saved Gina some time, then she was saving Dominic time and money.

She put her individual touches to the salmon salad, and Gina enthused over the tasty dressing. "What is it? I'll have to buy some."

"It's my own special recipe." Then with a sense of pride and a rueful little smile, she explained, "I don't give away my secrets."

"I knew it!" Gina rolled her eyes in appreciation. "You're a professional at this, aren't you? The way you arranged the salad—the dressing, the taste! Come on, Carrie, admit it!"

Carrie laughed in pleasure, thinking how lucky she was that Gina was so appreciative. "I have had a bit of experience," she acknowledged, but wouldn't elaborate. It sounded too much like bragging to tell her about Ports o' Call, the premier restaurant at the Sheraton in Fiji, and arguably one of the finest restaurants in the world. She felt in such good spirits that it wasn't hard to eat a reasonable helping of salad herself.

The linen for Danny's bedroom arrived after lunch. The sheets and pillow slips were cream with thin lines of orange forming a geometric pattern. A vibrant orange blanket accompanied them, and there was a set of bathroom towels in exactly the same colour. Carrie made up the bed and hung the towels in the bathroom. The orange looked super there against the white and beige tiles. At least, in Carrie's opinion.

Gina seemed pleased with the effect, too. She didn't stay much longer after this, excusing herself to go hunting for the rest of the furniture for Danny's bedroom.

Her departure left Carrie at a loose end. She suddenly felt tired and decided to have a rest. It had been an eventful day, and the best event was yet to come. It wouldn't do to be feeling weak and worn out when Danny arrived.

Gina had kept her mind distracted from worrying over what was happening with Dominic and Danny, but now that Carrie was alone, with nothing to do, all sorts of possibilities presented themselves, and none of them allowed Carrie to rest easy. She kept telling herself not to cross bridges until she came to them. But there were definitely a few dangerous chasms ahead of her.

First and foremost were the feelings that Dominic aroused in her. They had to be kept under rigid control. Then there were the questions he would inevitably raise over Danny. She had been sidestepping that issue, but it couldn't be sidestepped any longer.

Last but not least, she had to be very firm about Dominic staying out of both their lives. She couldn't afford to start being dependent on him for anything. It was going to be hard enough to leave this place when the time came. It would be a thousand times harder if she didn't remain self-sufficient.

It was a few minutes past four when the intercom buzzed again. She raced out to the lobby, then answered the call in as steady a voice as possible.

"We're on our way up," Dominic announced.

Carrie's heart fluttered between excitement and apprehension. But the most important thing was that Dominic had Danny. He had done what he'd said he would do. He had brought her son home to her. And whatever the cost for her to pay in that, Carrie wasn't counting it at this particular moment. It was almost two months since Danny had been taken away from her, and just the thought of seeing him again was pure bliss.

She positioned herself in the centre of the lobby, directly in front of where the lift doors opened. She was trembling from the sheer force of her emotion when the doors finally slid apart. For a moment, Danny looked stunned, as though he hadn't expected to see her. Then he hurled himself forward, and Carrie dropped to her knees to wrap him in her arms and hug him tight.

"Mum, Mum," he cried in relief and longing and love, almost strangling her as he wound his arms tightly around her neck.

"Oh, Danny! I've missed you so," Carrie half-sobbed, rubbing her cheek against his soft dark hair in her own silent ecstasy of love for this precious child of hers. She was vaguely aware of Dominic Savage stepping out of the lift, then moving aside, stepping towards the living area, leaving her and Danny alone together. But the focus of her attention was entirely on the little boy who meant so much to her.

"I told them I could look after you, Mum," Danny said fiercely. "But they wouldn't listen. They said you were too sick. And I was so scared you would die and I'd never see you again."

"I know, I know," she soothed. "They said I was too sick to take care of you, Danny. But I'm all right. Truly I am. I'm getting better all the time."

He eased away from her enough to take a good look at her, his blue eyes moist and heartbreaking in their concern for her. "You feel awful thin, Mum."

"I just couldn't eat much, Danny," she explained. "But I can now. I'll soon put weight on. You'll see."

He took a deep breath. "I tried to get back to you, Mum. I was at some place near the Hawkesbury River and I asked the other boys how to get to Ashfield. I would have made it, but I was caught getting onto the train." He pulled a disgusted grimace. "After that they kept a good watch on me and I couldn't get away."

She smiled, her heart so full of love it was almost bursting. "It doesn't matter now, Danny. We're back together again."

He took another deep breath, then grinned his cheeky boy grin. "They sure won't get me another time. I'm staying with you."

"You sure are!" she affirmed vehemently and hugged him again, rocking him in a fierce embrace.

"I was scared coming with Mr. Savage and Mrs. Coombe," he confessed. "I figured you would have come with them if everything was all right. I thought it was a trick to take me somewhere else."

She rubbed his back comfortingly. "I'm sorry, Danny. I wasn't much good at convincing the welfare people that they should give you back to me. And I wanted you so badly, I would have tried anything."

"That's okay, Mum. I was only worried about you." He pushed back to give her his assurance. "Now that I'm here, I'm going to look after you real good."

"I know you will."

He gave her a happy grin, then his head swivelled around. "Where's Mr. Savage?"

Carrie's heart performed a double loop. She knew there was no escaping this final confrontation, but that didn't make it any easier. "I think he went into the living room."

"I'd better speak to him, Mum," Danny said anxiously. "I didn't believe all those things he said to me, so I wouldn't answer him back. He must think I'm awful."

"I think it would be a good idea to thank him. He's gone to a lot of trouble for us. Even lending us this nice place to live in until I'm strong enough to get a job. So we've got a lot to thank him for."

She stood up and took his hand, drawing strength from the strong little fingers that curled around hers.

Dominic was over by the windows in the living room, apparently studying the view of the harbour, but Carrie was not deceived by his seemingly relaxed pose. The taut set of his shoulders betrayed his inner tension.

"Mr. Savage?" Danny called eagerly.

He turned slowly, his eyes sweeping hers with probing intensity before dropping to her boy. She knew it was only natural that he should wonder. She had known that from the moment it became inevitable he would meet Danny. Not that the boy looked like him. He didn't. Unless you counted the blue eyes. But lots of people had blue eyes. It was Danny's age that fed Dominic's speculation.

He made a visible effort to soften his expression. "Happy now?" he asked.

"Yes," Danny replied with feeling. "Thanks a lot, Mr. Savage. I'm sorry for not answering you before. I thought you were tricking me, and until I saw my mum..."

"That's okay, Danny," he said quietly. "But I do need some answers from you now. To enrol you at a school I have to know your age, for a start."

It was done so smoothly, without the slightest hint that anything was amiss. Carrie let the matter of enrolling Danny at school pass for the moment, aware that it was best for everything to be out in the open now.

"I'm seven," came the prompt reply.

Dominic nodded as though it was precisely what he had expected. He posed the critical question without missing a beat. "And when is your birthday, Danny?"

"The tenth of September."

Carrie could see him doing the calculation—a bare eight months from the time they first met. And she could see the disappointment in his eyes. He could not be the father. And then, of course, there were other conclusions he could come to, as well.

Carrie didn't want Dominic's mind dwelling on the sensitive subject of who Danny's father was. Nor did she want any discussion of that painful time in her past. She had taken full responsibility for Danny from the beginning, and it was going to remain that way.

"I'll see about enrolling Danny in a school myself, Dominic," she said briskly. "You've already gone out of your way so much on our behalf, and I'm terribly grateful for all you've done, but there's no need for you to be concerned any further. I can handle everything from now on."

There was a weary mockery in the eyes he raised to hers. "Do you have a particular school in mind?"

She flushed. "There was a primary school at Ashfield. I guess there must be one around here somewhere."

He shook his head. "Some aren't as good as others. I've had practical experience with it. And you're not exactly well, Carrie. Don't you think, for Danny's sake, it's wiser to leave it with me?"

She frowned, feeling that she was being painted into a corner where she didn't want to be, yet she couldn't deny the sense of Dominic's argument. All the same, she wasn't that sick. She could get around the problem if she took it easily.

She lifted pained eyes. "I can cope, Dominic. I don't want to put you to any more trouble."

He gave her a little smile, then shifted his gaze to Danny. It was a severe jolt to Carrie's heart when she saw the question still lingering in Dominic's eyes. It was an even worse jolt when it was followed by a hungry look that said more plainly than words that he wanted this boy to be his own. She suddenly remembered the bleak, frozen stillness that had enveloped him when she had first spoken of her baby. Was that one of the problems in his marriage? Was it childless?

"I don't mind," he said quietly. "You trust me to pick a good school for you, don't you, Danny?"

"Sure!" Danny replied confidently, then shot a worried look at Carrie. "It doesn't matter if Mr. Savage picks my school, does it, Mum? I don't want you getting sick again."

Carrie silently fretted over the situation. Perhaps it was best for Dominic to make the most suitable choice for Danny. She did trust him to do that. Nevertheless, his involvement with her and Danny had to stop. If he kept wanting Danny to be his child . . . It was a terribly dangerous situation.

"It is necessary to get Danny enrolled quickly, Carrie," Dominic said pointedly.

She heaved a deep sigh and faced him with reluctant resignation. "All right."

The blue eyes were steady with purpose, wiped clear of whatever other thoughts were harboured in his mind. "I'll be in touch when I have it organized."

Carrie looked at him with her own determined purpose. "Just ring me, Dominic. There's no need to visit."

For a moment he challenged that statement, then seemed to accept it. "Very well. I'll get on my way now." He smiled at Danny. "Take good care of your mother. Don't let her overdo things."

"I'll look after Mum. And thanks for everything."

"You're welcome."

There was affection and pride in Dominic's eyes when he turned them back to Carrie.

"Goodbye, Dominic," she said firmly.

"I'll be seeing you, Carrie," he returned softly, and as she watched him leave, Carrie knew this wasn't the end. Dominic wasn't going to let it be the end. Not so long as he had any question about Danny's father in his mind. Sooner or later she was going to have to settle that. Somehow.

CHAPTER SEVEN

IN THE JOY of having Danny home and the worrying issue of Dominic's response to him, Carrie had forgotten all about Mrs. Coombe's visiting programme. When she rose the next morning, she certainly did not expect to find the dragon in the dining room setting out a jigsaw puzzle on the table, nor Danny on obviously friendly terms with her.

"Look what Mrs. Coombe brought me!" Danny cried with excitement. "And a whole lot of books and games."

"My sons have long outgrown them," the dragon explained, her stern face incredibly relaxing into benevolence. "I thought they might help keep Danny occupied when you're resting."

Carrie took a deep breath. She could hardly deprive Danny of the pleasure that was so clearly written on his face, yet acceptance of this charity went very much against her independent grain. "That's very kind of you, Mrs. Coombe. And very thoughtful," she forced out as graciously as she could. What else could she say?

"Not at all. I know what boys are like. I've had three of my own. All grown up now and leading their own lives." She heaved a rueful sigh. It made her disconcertingly human. And when she followed it up with an indulgent smile, there was no trace of the sergeant-major at all. "Is there anything you need, dear? I can get it for you before I go to the office."

"Thank you, but we're fine, Mrs. Coombe. Truly," Carrie assured her emphatically. "We won't need anything for a week at least, and then I'm sure I'll be strong enough to do my own shopping, so you mustn't worry about me any more."

The sergeant-major was instantly evoked. Mrs. Coombe rose from her chair in iron command. "You can't be too careful in cases like this. Relapse can be just around the corner. I know. I've given Danny my telephone number. In case he's worried about you over the weekend." She shot Danny some severely lowered eyebrows. "You won't lose it, now, will you?"

"No way, Mrs. Coombe! I'm going to look after Mum real good," he promised her. Carrie thought he should have saluted, but instead he only offered a big grin. "And thanks for everything!"

"My pleasure." The sergeant-major beamed approval at him, and Carrie caught some of the afterglow. "You have a fine boy."

"Yes," Carrie meekly agreed, beginning to feel that her independence was being systematically undermined.

Mrs. Coombe definitely departed the victor from this encounter. Having drafted Danny as an enthusiastic and well-rewarded ally, and established herself as an authority on Carrie's state of health, she had effectively squashed all possible protests. Not only that, she had already given Danny his breakfast and Carrie's was waiting for her in the kitchen. It was perfectly plain that when the dragon adopted a stance, it was going to take an awful lot of firepower to shift her.

The kind of firepower Dominic had, Carrie thought. Except she had more than a crawling suspicion that to shift Mrs. Coombe, she had first to shift Dominic. Or perhaps it was the other way around.

Gina arrived. And so did the furniture for Danny's bedroom. All day long! First came a number of segments of a wall unit, which, when all fitted together, formed a chest of drawers, a corner desk, a large set of bookshelves, a corkboard to pin papers on and another desk for a personal computer. It was all made of polished pine and looked first class.

"I decided this room could double as a private study," Gina informed them.

A comfortable and adjustable office chair arrived, upholstered in the same vivid orange as Danny's blanket. A marvellous painting of parrots among tropical foliage was hung on the wall. Another portable television was delivered and installed on the chest of drawers next to Danny's bed. A video recorder came with it. Finally, a massive orange beanbag chair made its appearance.

"The curtains and bedspreads and the decorative cushions for the bed will be a few days," Gina said regretfully, "but it's shaping up very well, don't you think?"

"It's fantastic!" was all Carrie could say.

Danny was in seventh heaven.

"We'll decide what to do with your bedroom on Monday, Carrie," Gina said, glowing with satisfaction. "So start thinking about what you'd fancy having around you. It's so helpful to have your ideas."

Gina had left and Danny was busy putting things away in his new chest of drawers when Dominic telephoned. As soon as Carrie heard his voice, her whole body tensed, fighting against the emotional weakness that threatened her peace of mind.

"How are you today, Carrie?" he asked softly.

"I'm fine," she replied, a little too curtly in reaction to the sudden galloping thump of her heart. She did her best to temper her tone. "Danny and I are both fine, thank you, Dominic."

"I've enrolled Danny in a fine school at Bellevue Hill. He'll be starting on Monday week. There's a good bus service to the school from Circular Quay, so there's no problem with transport. I'll take him myself on the first day and introduce him to the headmaster."

"I can do that, Dominic." She had to stop him from involving himself further with them. It had gone too far already. Just the sound of his voice was disturbing, making her want what she couldn't have.

"I'd like you to be there, Carrie."

The warm eagerness in his tone clouded the sense of what he was saying for a moment. Then Carrie realised he was suggesting that she accompany him, the two of them together, like parents.

"Strangely enough," he continued, "in an imperfect world, these things do matter."

"I meant that *you* don't need to go, Dominic," she said, squirming with embarrassment at the kind of false position that might be presented and feeling more and more desperate to evade any further encounter with him. "I can do it by myself," she added insistently.

Silence for several seconds. Then rather slowly, as though feeling his way with infinite care, he said, "Carrie, I thought ... I hope you don't mind. This is for such a relatively short time ... It seemed a good idea for Danny to have the best, at least this once. I know the headmaster of this school personally. In fact, he's a former teacher of mine. It would be a discourtesy if I didn't turn up with you."

It was clear that Dominic had used his personal influence to get Danny placed at a really good school. Apparently education rules and regulations could be bent like those at the welfare department for a man of consequence such as Dominic Savage.

"As I said, it's an imperfect world," he acknowledged, perhaps sensing her resentment of how easily this world worked for the big people. "First impressions make a difference, Carrie. I can help," Dominic added persuasively.

That was a reality Carrie couldn't brush aside. It was all too true that little people were ignored or given very little consideration. She had already had a heap of that frustrating experience, and the memory of it was still bitter.

Why should Danny suffer in any way just because she wasn't important like Dominic? Danny was just as good as any other boy and a lot better than most, in her opinion. If Dominic's presence could ensure Danny every advantage the system had to offer, and give him a good start at his new school, then she owed it to her son to accept this one last favour.

"All right, Dominic. Just this once," she conceded, telling herself it would be the very last favour she would accept from him.

"I'll call at the apartment for you. Eight o'clock, Monday week."

He rang off before she could discuss the matter any further. Carrie hadn't even thanked him for making the school arrangements. However, she resisted the

impulse to call him back. There were nine days before
Danny had to go to school, nine days for her to get a
lot stronger. When she saw Dominic on Monday week,
she had to make sure she didn't give in to him again,
no matter what issue he raised. She had to insist upon
complete independence. As it was, she had already
accepted too much from him. Although what would
she have done without him?

Carrie shook her head. Now she had to learn to live
without him all over again. But even that was worth it,
just to have Danny back with her.

They had a wonderful weekend. On Saturday they
had a leisurely walk through the Botanical Gardens.
On Sunday they took a ferry ride up the harbour to
Manly and back. They ate well, played some of the
games Mrs. Coombe had brought, completed the jigsaw, watched television and generally enjoyed being
with each other.

Mrs. Coombe turned up on Monday morning, saying that Mr. Savage had given her the day off to take
Danny shopping for his school uniform.

"There's no need!" Carrie protested.

The dragon laid down the law. "You are to rest.
Shopping is far too exhausting for you at this stage.
Particularly for school clothes, which aren't a simple
matter at all. There's sports clothes, proper black
shoes, gym shoes, different socks and goodness knows
what! It's a long and tedious business and not suitable for a convalescent."

"And Gina wants you here to do your bedroom,
Mum," Danny piped up, filling the role of trusty ally
to the hilt.

Carrie frowned. Gina had asked for her help. "Then
we can go shopping tomorrow, Danny," she insisted.

His face fell. "Why can't I go with Mrs. Coombe?" he demanded.

Which was a difficult question to answer.

"My dear, you must learn to trust me," the dragon said, eyeing Carrie severely.

"Oh, I do, Mrs. Coombe...."

"Then that's settled! Come, Danny!"

Damn, thought Carrie! I've been trapped.

The dragon bore Danny off, an all too eager and willing victim, before Carrie could figure a reasonable way out of the trap. The lift doors closed on two triumphant smiles. Totally outmanoeuvred, Carrie thought in disgust. The games and books now made perfect sense. Bribery and corruption to win Danny over to her side! But the dragon wasn't going to get away with it a second time, Carrie vowed.

She brooded over Danny's cheerfulness about going off with Mrs. Coombe until Gina arrived and distracted her from that unprofitable train of thought.

"What do you think about apricot as a main theme?" she asked. "Perhaps a floral with that colour so we can highlight it for impact interest."

Carrie was immediately attracted to the idea, and once again they pored over fabric samples. By the time Mrs. Coombe delivered Danny home, along with a formidable array of packages, all the furnishings for the main bedroom had been decided upon.

"Remember what I said about polishing those black shoes every morning, Danny," Mrs. Coombe commanded as she took her leave. "Don't be expecting your mother to do it."

"No, Mrs. Coombe. I mean, yes, I'll remember, Mrs. Coombe," said Danny—the ideal army recruit!

"What about the cost of everything?" Carrie called after her.

"Oh, you'll have to see Mr. Savage about that, dear," the sergeant-major said, passing the buck to a higher authority with sublime confidence in her own position. "I put it all on his credit card."

That night Carrie toted up all the price tags on Danny's new clothes. A good school, she found, cost a lot of money even before the first lesson began. The amount she finally arrived at for the whole school uniform was positively formidable. All of this . . . for just a short period of time!

Part of the problem was that Mrs. Coombe had bought the best of everything, whereas Carrie would have hunted for bargains. But she supposed she couldn't very well complain. After all, she wasn't paying any rent. Besides, pride whispered, she didn't want Danny to feel he was less well-dressed than the other boys. Although it would make a substantial hole in her wages for some time to come, the clothes wouldn't go to waste. Apart from which, her cost of living was virtually negligible at the present moment.

Thanks to Dominic.

Carrie felt uneasy with this thought. She felt uncomfortably like a kept woman, even though she knew that wasn't the case. She worried over how she could repay Dominic for all he had done for her, but found no satisfactory solution to the problem.

She couldn't ask him to dinner without his wife. The impropriety of such an invitation was all too clear to Carrie, and she instinctively shrank from inviting any meeting with Alyson Hawthorn. She could just imagine how odiously patronising Dominic's bitchy wife would be to her. Carrie knew the attraction had to be there for a marriage to keep going, but she would never understand it. How Dominic could have married that woman...

But he had married her! And that was that! It was none of her business, and she wasn't going to start making it her business. On this last meeting with Dominic at the school for Danny, she had to clear up all outstanding matters so that there would be no need for any further involvement.

The days flew by. Danny's bedroom was completed and looked absolutely marvellous. Carrie's bedroom began to take on a new look with additional pieces of furniture. Fabrics for the furnishings in the living areas were chosen. Gina came and went, milking Carrie for advice on ideas all the time, then delivering the most amazing and wonderful results.

Danny made a point of wearing his new shoes for longer and longer periods each day. Carrie suspected this was on Mrs. Coombe's instructions, but since it *was* sensible, she couldn't very well countermand the sergeant-major's orders. Mrs. Coombe did not reappear until Friday morning, when she came to check that all was how it should be and was told very firmly by Carrie that there was no shopping to be done.

Just for once, the dragon didn't argue or even try to override or outmanoeuvre Carrie. She actually said Carrie looked a lot better, but then spoilt it all by complimenting Danny on looking after his mother so well. It took the shine off Carrie's sense of triumph.

All the same, Carrie was satisfied that she did look better. Her cheekbones were definitely less prominent and her eyes were brighter. However, the state of her hair left a lot to be desired. She eyed Gina's shining cap of auburn hair with envy.

"Who does your hair, Gina?" she asked. "I desperately need something done to mine." It was probably stupid pride, but she felt compelled to look as good as she could when she took Danny to meet the headmaster of his new school. And, of course, it would also be her last meeting with Dominic.

"I'll make an appointment for you with my hairdresser, if you like," Gina instantly offered. "He's a whiz at cutting. Uses a great conditioner, too. I promise you'll look like a million dollars when he finishes with you," she added with an encouraging grin.

Carrie decided this was one time when she wouldn't count the cost. The appointment was made for the next morning, and Gina insisted on taking her and bringing her home, saying it was small enough return for the free lunches Carrie had given her. Danny went with them and was intrigued by all the activity in a hairdressing salon.

"Gosh, Mum! You sure look different now," he remarked when she finally emerged.

She laughed, delighted with the effect of a cleverly shaped bob that curved down to her jawline, and soft feathery fringe, which made her face look softer as well as highlighting her green eyes. Her hair was shining after a long massage with some special conditioner, and Carrie was almost ready to declare Gina's hairdresser a magician.

"Good different, or bad different?" she asked.

"Oh, good!" Danny assured her. "Real pretty like you used to be before you got sick."

Which was certainly telling her straight, Carrie thought ruefully. However she was secretly pleased that Dominic would be left with a nicer memory of the girl he had once known than the image she had re-

cently presented. Not that it was of any real consequence, she told herself. It was sheer vanity on her part
to be thinking like that, and pointless vanity, as well.
In fact, it was flirting with danger to remind Dominic
of those days in any way whatsoever.

On the other hand, it wasn't really for Dominic. Her
improved appearance would certainly make a better
impression at Danny's school, and she wanted Danny
to be proud of his mother. That thought settled any
uneasy twinge of conscience.

Over the weekend, Carrie coached Danny at walking from the apartment to the bus depot at Circular
Quay and back again, making sure he was familiar
with the whole area so that he couldn't possibly get
lost once he started school.

She felt as though her nerves were jumping out of
her skin as she got herself and Danny ready on Monday morning. She rigorously denied to herself that it
was caused by any excitement about seeing Dominic
again. It was simply that starting at a new school was
a big step for Danny. She wanted everything to go
right for him. It was for this reason alone that she
fussed over her appearance.

She wished she had bought a new dress, then chided
herself for craving a needless extravagance. But she
couldn't wear the green shirtwaister. It would remind
Dominic of her fainting fit. Besides, she wanted to
prove to him that she was quite well enough to stand
on her own two feet.

The only other outfit she had with long sleeves was
a lightweight suit in brown and white spotted linen.
She had to make two tucks at the back of the skirt with
safety pins to secure it around her waist, but the hip-
length jacket covered that little adjustment. In fact,

the jacket successfully hid the looseness of her white blouse, as well. She pushed the excess fabric around to the back so she presented a neat smoothness at the front. With some carefully applied apricot lipstick and her blonde hair looking bouncy and healthy, Carrie was reasonably satisfied with the result.

Danny looked very smart and suddenly quite heart-wrenchingly grown up in his school uniform. She could hardly call him her baby any more, Carrie acknowledged ruefully. And Mrs. Coombe would have soundly approved the high polish on his new black shoes. You could definitely see your face in them.

They were ready and waiting when Dominic arrived. He stepped out of the lift and into the apartment on the dot of eight o'clock and took Carrie's breath away with his smile. He looked so impressive in his dark grey business suit, both handsome and commanding, and the blue eyes were as warm and as brilliant as a summer sky.

"Carrie..."

Surprise, pleasure and something deeper and infinitely disturbing rolled through the soft caress of her name. Her heart turned over. The memory of their very first meeting eight years ago leapt into her mind and lingered. He had looked at her just like this...surprised, pleased, wanting to know more of her, wanting...

He wants me now!

And the hell of it is, I still want him!

"That hairstyle really suits you. Although I used to—"

Love it long, Carrie finished for him, remembering how he had stroked it and wound it round his fingers, saying it was like spun silk.

He made a visible effort to check himself, pull back, adopt a less revealing expression. "I do believe you've put on some weight," he said, his gaze roving over her in a far too intimate appraisal.

A flush swept over her skin wherever his gaze alighted, and there was nothing she could do about the erratic acceleration of her heartbeat. "I told you I could get better on my own," she said defensively.

A shadow dimmed the brilliance of his eyes, and he turned quickly to Danny, who was raring to go. "Looks like you've done a good job of looking after your mother, Danny," he said warmly.

"Mum doesn't get tired so fast now," Danny informed him, glowing with pleasure in Dominic's approval. "And we've been eating a real lot."

Dominic laughed and his hand reached out to stroke Danny's hair. Carrie was thrown into more emotional turmoil at the fondly paternal gesture. It was bad enough that Dominic stirred this dreadful yearning in her. Surely he wasn't still harbouring thoughts that Danny might be his. It would be totally unreasonable.

Frantic to get this meeting on a businesslike level, Carrie quickly held out the envelope that contained the cheque she had got from the bank.

"This isn't all I owe you, Dominic, but I'll pay you back the rest when I can," she explained with considerable embarrassment.

He frowned. "As far as I'm concerned, there's no debt between us, Carrie."

The caring in his eyes was almost her undoing. Once again she was drawn back to the time when she had believed that look of caring, believed it so utterly that she'd thought nothing could have shaken it. But she had read much more into it than there ever was. Besides, she couldn't risk following that treacherous path again. There was not only herself to consider this time. She forced away temptation and gathered her resolution.

"I can't let you pay for Danny's uniform, nor the food Mrs. Coombe bought for us that first morning," she insisted. "Please take it."

The blue eyes warred with the fierce independence in hers, then slowly retreated into a self-mocking resignation. He reached for the envelope and took it without any argument, much to Carrie's relief.

"I guess we'd better be leaving," he said with a rueful little smile. "Ready to go, Danny?"

"I've been ready for ages!" Danny replied with impatient excitement.

As they rode down in the lift Danny peppered Dominic with questions about the school. Dominic's answers were all reassuring and delivered in a kind indulgent tone, which aroused a deep sadness in Carrie. It suddenly seemed terribly wrong that Danny had always been deprived of a father to stand by his side and do the kind of thing that Dominic was doing for him now. Yet there was nothing she could do about it. And even if she could live the past over again, she would not have chosen differently. There had never been any other way.

A wave of deep depression rolled over her as they settled into the luxurious comfort of the Daimler. She told herself she should be grateful that Dominic had accepted her independent stance, that there was no longer any reason for them to see each other again, and that there could be no more crossing points in their lives. This car alone hammered home their different stations in life. It was part and parcel of the kind of marriage he had.

But she didn't feel grateful. She felt wretchedly miserable. And not even her love for Danny could fill that other aching emptiness in her life.

It was almost agony sitting beside Dominic, being aware of everything about him, remembering how it had once been between them, listening to him chat so charmingly with Danny and Danny's eager response to his interest. She wished she could touch him, look openly at him, meet his eyes with that special intimate togetherness she had once shared with him.

If only they could be taking Danny to school like real parents who were proud of their son. But she couldn't afford to indulge in that fantasy. It could never never happen. She had to accept that. And the intimate togetherness she thought she had once shared with Dominic was only an illusion. She had to keep remembering that, as well.

If she slipped up, if she let Dominic see how she felt about him, she suspected he would have no more conscience about taking what he wanted than he had in the past. If an engagement had not been any impediment to gratifying his desire for her, a marriage was not going to get in his way, either. Particularly the kind of open marriage he undoubtedly had with Alyson. However much she wanted him, Carrie would not accept being a fling on the side. The consequences of that were all too clear to her.

The Daimler slowed to a crawl. Carrie was too deep in thought to take any notice. They had been halted by traffic scores of times on their way to Bellevue Hill.

"Is this it?" Danny asked, a bright expectation in his voice.

It startled her into looking out the window, and Carrie instantly suffered another shock. Superb and immaculately kept playing fields seemed to stretch forever. Everything about the school—tennis courts, swimming pool, gardens, the grounds, the buildings themselves—trumpeted wealth. Old wealth! This was no ordinary public school. It had to be one of the most elite private schools in Sydney!

"This is it," Dominic confirmed, turning the car through a wrought-iron gateway.

Carrie barely had time to recover from her shock before they were parked in a special visitors' bay in front of what was obviously the administrative building. Then Danny was scrambling out of the car, almost jumping out of his skin in excitement, and Dominic made a swift exit as well, striding around to open Carrie's door for her. Her eyes stabbed a thousand tortured questions at him as he helped her out. He fended them off with a look of brick-wall determination.

I'm trapped again, Carrie thought despairingly, as Danny joined them, chattering nineteen to the dozen, obviously thrilled that this marvellously impressive place was *his* school. The arrangements had been made, his clothes had been bought, and they were here, on the brink of meeting the headmaster.

Somehow Carrie could not force out the words to declare the whole proceedings null and void. It was wrong. It was all terribly wrong. And there was a dreadful panic welling up inside her at the thought of what this might all mean. But when Dominic took her arm and steered her towards the path that led to the arched entrance ahead of them, she could not find the strength of resolution to make a sensible stand. With Danny looking on, listening, it just wasn't possible!

Once inside, they were immediately ushered to the headmaster's office. Dominic's old teacher welcomed them warmly and was most interested in the fact that Danny had spent most of his life in Fiji. Danny was asked a lot of questions, which he answered with an uninhibited confidence, stirring Carrie's maternal pride, despite all her underlying misgivings about the whole situation.

"I think young Danny might turn out to be as good a scholar as you were, Dominic," the headmaster declared, obviously pleased with the interview. "You can leave him with me now. I'll take him to meet his teachers personally."

This was certainly favoured treatment, and Carrie felt profoundly embarrassed as she recognised the speculation in the headmaster's eyes throughout their leave-taking. He was undoubtedly putting one and one together and getting more than two. Although nothing overt was said either by Dominic or the headmaster, Carrie sensed that some private understanding had been reached between them when the arrangements had been made.

Carrie hoped that she had performed creditably enough, for Danny's sake, but she was churning inside as Dominic escorted her to the Daimler. As soon as they were both enclosed within the intimate privacy of the car, she turned on him with all the vehemence of feeling that the meeting had aroused.

"You had no right to enrol Danny in this school, Dominic," she said to him.

His mouth set grimly as he switched on the engine, put the car into gear and drove it towards the gate.

"Why not?" he finally replied, a fine tension edging the calm, reasonable tone he employed.

"You know why not," she accused. "The fees must be astronomical. And you didn't consult me."

"You wanted a good school for Danny. You agreed to leave the choice to me. I know this is a good school."

"That's not the point!"

"I took responsibility for the fees. And they weren't so high, Carrie. It's the school I attended throughout my primary education, and old boys have certain privileges. Discounts..."

"I'm not stupid, Dominic!" Carrie retorted angrily. "That kind of thing only ever relates to families."

His face tightened, but he spoke very quietly and with slow, deliberate emphasis. "How do I know that Danny isn't part of me, Carrie?"

Her heart stopped dead, then catapulted into mad overtime. It was finally out in the open! And she had to answer it! But how?

"I'd like to reach a better understanding with you, Carrie," Dominic said softly. "And I'd rather try to do that when I'm not driving in peak-hour traffic. Would you mind if I come up to your apartment when we get back?"

There was a dreadful tightness in her throat. Her voice sounded half-strangled as she replied, "I think...I think that's a good idea."

Carrie was not sure it was a good idea at all, but Dominic's actions in regard to Danny left her little choice. She should have resolved the matter before, when she had seen the questions in his eyes. She had taken the coward's way out. Yet to go through all that hurt again, to go back through all that had happened . . . She closed her eyes and willed herself to be strong.

What had to be done, had to be done!

She could not allow herself and Danny to be drawn into Dominic's kind of life, no matter what considerations he offered her! She fiercely wished she had never gone to him, never let him back into her life for any reason. The risk she had taken, for Danny's sake, had been too high. It was now paramount to convince Dominic that he had no reason to pursue a relationship with either one of them.

CHAPTER EIGHT

THE JOURNEY TO Circular Quay was accomplished in far too fast a time for Carrie. Nevertheless, she did determine one thing. Some questions she would not answer. Those she did, however, would be entirely truthful. In that regard, she would not deceive Dominic.

He kept a grim silence, even in the lift up to the apartment. Carrie's stomach was in knots when she finally led the way into the living room. It was still empty apart from the blue-grey leather armchairs and the coffee table. Today was one of the days Gina was out scouting for the right furniture for it, so they were completely alone. There was no risk of interruption.

"Do you want to sit down?" she asked with stiff politeness, making an awkward gesture towards the armchairs.

"You sit, Carrie," he returned quietly.

But she knew she couldn't relax, couldn't even appear to relax. She dropped her handbag on one of the chairs and moved on, stepping over to the windows, pretending to take in the harbour view because she didn't want to meet Dominic's eyes.

"I applied for a copy of Danny's birth certificate."

It felt like an iron fist was squeezing her heart. "You had no right to do that, Dominic. It's an invasion of privacy."

"I thought I might have a right, Carrie," he suggested softly. "The father's name is not filled in."

"It usually isn't in the case of an illegitimate birth."

She heard the hard edge to her voice and winced. But she had to be hard. This was no time to be weak. She waited patiently, all her senses as alert as they had ever been in her whole life. This was the moment of truth. What she had gone out of her way to avoid all these years.

"Danny was born eight months after—" he was going to say our affair, but he changed to "—eight months after we were together."

Carrie kept her face impassive. This is how people play poker, she told herself. She committed herself to a clipped, "You already know that."

His next words were more tentative, but determinedly probing nevertheless. "Sometimes, even the most well-intended precautions aren't a hundred percent safe. Accidents happen." He paused, waiting for her to comment.

The iron fist squeezed even tighter. She said nothing.

"And some babies are born prematurely," he continued, relentlessly pressing the question.

She waited, waited for the inevitable.

"Carrie, is that what happened to you?"

Somehow she forced the necessary words out. "However hard it is for you to accept, Dominic, most pregnancies go full term."

There was a long nerve-tearing silence. Then slowly, painfully, Dominic dragged out his next question. "Are you telling me that you were already pregnant by some other man at the time we were together?"

Her mind and heart were awash with sheer agony. Carrie knew she had to take the initiative. Otherwise these statements and future questions would never stop. She summoned up all her willpower, commanded her body not to betray her in any way, fixed a mask of calm indifference on her face then slowly swung around.

Dominic was no more than a few paces away, and the pained look on his face triggered a surge of savage resentment. What did he know of pain? He had taken his pleasure, hadn't he? Then moved back to Alyson, having enjoyed his little fling on the side.

"Are you criticising my life-style, Dominic?" she demanded harshly.

His head jerked back as though she had hit him, and she could see his inner torment warring on his face, darkening his eyes. I've lost him, she thought, lost him forever. And all her fierce resentment dwindled into the deep inner chasm of emptiness she had carried for so long. But then she remembered she had never had him. This confrontation was not about her. It was about Danny. And she would not let Dominic or anyone else make an emotional battleground over the child she had borne and raised.

She saw acceptance gradually emerge from his torment, but Carrie felt no relief. The emptiness spread through her whole body, making her feel numb, beyond pain or any other feeling or emotion.

"I'll never criticise you, Carrie."

She heard the words, even registered that they were spoken in a gentle, forgiving tone. On a rather distant level her mind kept ticking over. She wondered if he regretted the way he had played musical beds. Probably not, she surmised. However liberated women were today, there were still different standards for men and women. And always would be. Particularly where children were concerned. The more things changed, the more they stayed the same. Because the pain was still there, just as always.

She turned to the window and stared at the water traffic in the harbour, vaguely noting the ever-widening wakes left by the boats as they carved their way through the water. Her time with Dominic had had a long wake, but it was over now. And whatever kind of possessiveness had been aroused in him by the thought of Danny being his child would quickly be laid to rest. She did not want to watch him go. She had to lay her own ghosts to rest. Forever.

Dominic did not go. He came up behind her, his fingers curling lightly over her shoulders. His head was near hers. She could feel his breath on the newly cropped nape of her neck. Her mind told her that he wanted something more from her. Some appeasement, perhaps, for all the trouble he had gone to.

"I'm sorry you're disappointed in me, Dominic," she pushed out huskily. Her throat was dry, like the lonely desert inside her.

"Not disappointed. Other things," he murmured vaguely.

Carrie didn't question what the other things were. She didn't want to know what they were. Things said could never be retracted, and they caused too much hurt. Best left unstated. Just let me go, Dominic, she thought, unable to summon the energy to voice the words. Let it all go.

His mouth grazed over her hair, down by her ear. His lips touched her cheek, a light tender pressure that stirred a tingle of life... of need. Carrie leant back against him, angled her face towards him, then belatedly realised what she was doing. The impulse to turn around in his arms, to accept his kisses until she was totally mindless, to beg him to make love to her, to lead him to her bed...that impulse rampaged through her body with almost irresistible force.

But he was married, the voice of sanity reminded her. He had a wife. Maybe even children. But she didn't want to know about that. And she had to stop this madness before it took hold of her. She turned her head away from the tempting contact.

"I don't think...you should touch me, Dominic. That's not fair." Somehow she couldn't put the proper amount of coldness into her voice. Rather, the words were said with all the aching love and tenderness in her heart.

She felt Dominic's body stiffen against her. Then abruptly he moved away. "I'm sorry," he rasped, and the gravelled anguish of loneliness in the brusque apology smote her brittle defences.

Alyson was no partner for him. Every intuition Carrie had was screaming out that he shared the same bleak emptiness she herself felt. The thought that she could have let Dominic make love to her came unbidden to her mind, and it took a lot of stern repression to make it go away. Such an act was no solution, but the beginning of the end. For her.

"You don't have to be sorry." Inadequate words she knew, and said so stiltedly that Dominic surely had to take them as the ultimate rejection of anything between them, even sympathy.

But still he did not go.

She heard him pacing the floor behind her, apparently struggling to come to terms with the situation.

Carrie remained where she was, staring blindly out the window, unseeing and forcing herself to be uncaring. Or as uncaring as she could be. Eventually he stopped moving. She heard him draw in a deep breath and slowly expel it. When he spoke his voice was quiet and carefully drained of any emotion.

"So you came to me on the rebound. From some other love affair that ended unhappily."

"Something like that," Carrie agreed dully.

"No wonder things worked out the way they did. That explains so much."

His voice sounded as dull and despairing as her own. Carrie remained silent. She had no more to say. If Dominic thought everything was explained, however he had worked it out, there would be no more questions.

He gave a mirthless little laugh. "The great irony," he said savagely, "is that all the precautions we took to stop you getting pregnant were unnecessary and useless."

Carrie felt a well of unjustified anger surging destructively over the control she was trying so hard to keep. "As it turned out," she said curtly, once again turning to face him, her green eyes blazing her condemnation of his unkind mockery, "and with the benefit of hindsight, yes! They were useless! That much is certainly true."

The sudden passion in her voice startled him, shocked him.

"But, Dominic," Carrie plunged on, uncaring what his reaction was, just desperate to get this over, "I do not wish to discuss *our affair*." She enunciated those two words with particular emphasis, needing to get the past stamped with its actual reality. "I certainly do not wish to have it recollected with a blow-by-blow description!''

He winced, his mouth twisting into a pained grimace. Then he shook his head in an anguished denial before finally bringing himself under control and facing her with bleak resignation. "I guess it's time for me to go," he said flatly.

"I think that's the best decision," she affirmed, and regretted how distant—how callous—she must sound. Yet there was nothing that could be retrieved from this situation.

"At least I'm grateful to you for putting our... *relationship*—" he stressed the word with bitter irony "—into its proper perspective. I had the wrong impression. I thought it was different from what it was."

He turned away.

Carrie was too stung by those words to hold her tongue. The impulse of anger and scorn proved too strong. Why was the woman always held to blame? "I don't know what you think," she said in frayed anguish. "It doesn't matter any more now than it did then." Bitterness crept into her voice. "But whatever else you may think of me, at least *I* never played musical beds."

He paused in mid-stride, turned swiftly, violent emotion working over his face. "Are you implying that I did?"

Carrie shrugged indifferently, but her green eyes flicked scorn at the supposed innocence he was projecting. "You are what you are. What you do is none of my business."

She knew she had made a bad mistake even before she saw his expression change. She should have kept her mouth shut and let him go, no matter how unfair a slur he cast on her for the break-up that his attitudes had caused. All she had done with her stupid pride was prolong the inevitable and make it even more tortured.

Dominic stood absolutely still. All conflict had been wiped from his face. He could have been a statue except for his eyes. They probed hers with intense directness, as though trying to bore through to her soul. Carrie met them with all the resistance she could muster, denying him entry to the churning cauldron of emotion this delay had provoked.

His brow furrowed in thought. There was a perceptible straightening of his shoulders. His chin angled with determination, his brow cleared of its furrows, and a look of resolution transformed his face.

"So, everything is resolved," he said enigmatically, "and yet nothing is resolved."

A devil-may-care look glittered into his eyes and curled his mouth into a provocative little smile. He covered the floor space between them with a casual stride that belied the tension Carrie felt sweeping from him and entangling her in his purpose. She didn't move. Somehow she couldn't. Her heart was slamming against her chest as he lifted a hand and gently cupped her cheek. His thumb tilted her chin with a persuasive little caress.

"There is one last thing I have to know, Carrie," Dominic said softly. "And I figure there's only one way I can find out."

He took her by surprise, his head bending swiftly to her own, his lips sealing hers with a seductive sensuality that sent shock waves through her entire body. She trembled, and a strong arm instantly scooped her against the warm security of his body. She felt her mouth softening pliantly to the persuasive movement of his and told herself to pull away, to stop him before... before his tongue started its tantalising temptation... before she succumbed to its erotic invitation to deepen this forbidden intimacy... before she gave in to the need that screamed to let him do as he liked because she liked it, too... wanted it... craved it.

And then it was too late.

He kissed her with all the passion of a starving man, and her eight-year hunger rose to meet his in overwhelming waves, drowning her conscience, drowning any thought of past or future, feasting on all that was offered and could be taken now, no matter what hell had to be paid later. Perhaps it was the despair lurking somewhere in her subconscious that inspired her mad wantonness, that made her wind her arms around Dominic's neck in feverish possessiveness, that made her press her body to his in blind seeking need, that made her ride this wild roller coaster of total insanity, and all because sanity was suddenly too hard to bear.

It was Dominic who withdrew first, lifting his mouth from hers and showering her face and hair with impassioned kisses. "I thought I'd lost you," he breathed in a whisper of yearning that found a deep echo inside Carrie. "Lost you forever." Then in a burst of relief, "But it's not so. Thank God it's not so."

His arms tightened around her. His lips trailed down to her ear. "You can't deny me now, Carrie," he pleaded softly. "Say you love me."

The words were there, embedded in her heart, quivering for the expression he demanded. Carrie wanted to say them. She had promised herself she would speak only the truth to Dominic. Had to speak the truth. And her body had already betrayed that truth, anyway. Yet the memory of what had happened last time came back to haunt her. It was all too one-sided. Where was his commitment to her? He asked too much. And he would leave her to go back to his wife, his marriage.

She opened her eyes and lifted her head back to challenge him. "Why don't you say those words to me, Dominic?"

The blue eyes caressed her with all the promises she could wish for. "I love you, Carrie. I always did love you. Only you."

He said the words slowly, simply. Carrie could almost believe they were true. Dominic Savage, the ultimate deceiver, a bitter voice whispered. And he hadn't changed. The only difference now was that the impediment to any serious relationship between them was out in the open. And being conveniently ignored by him.

"And that's why you married someone else, Dominic?" she asked scornfully.

"What does that matter now?" he pleaded. "Now that we've found each other again."

A bitter little laugh erupted from her throat. "It may seem odd to you in this day and age, but it does matter to me. It matters very deeply."

Anguish darkened his eyes and roughened his voice. "Carrie, you must know from your own experience that there are different kinds of relationships. We had something special between us. And it's still there. For me and for you, Carrie. I need you in my life. And I think you need me just as much."

It was a need she had learnt to stifle long ago, and she simply had to keep on stifling it. Her green eyes were hard and implacable as she delivered her reply. "Let's not fantasise, Dominic. You are as much a realist as I am. There's no going back." Not even to assuage his loneliness, or hers, she added silently. However unsatisfactory he was finding his marriage, she was not going to let him use her to make up for it.

He shook his head. "I don't understand you, Carrie. Your lips, your body, are so soft and pliant...telling me what I want to hear from you. Yet your mind is like steel."

Her mouth twisted with sad irony. "Put me down as an aberration in your life."

"And if I won't?"

She dragged her hands down to press lightly against his shoulders. Every jagged nerve in her body clamoured a vehement protest at the thought of breaking from his embrace, of severing the body contact that was still arousing so many pleasurable sensations. She hesitated, riven once more by temptation.

Could she live with being Dominic's woman on the side? Did it really matter that he was cheating on Alyson? After all, with her attitudes, she was undoubtedly cheating on him.

But where could it lead?

And what about the effect on Danny?

No. She couldn't be blindly selfish. Nor did she want to face the consequences of another fling with Dominic. She shook her head.

"There's no future for us, Dominic," she stated flatly.

It was he who released her from his embrace, lifting his hands to cradle her face with infinite tenderness. His eyes begged indulgence from hers. "Carrie, I don't believe you. I can't. And I won't. I don't think you know your own mind. You've been under so much strain lately—"

"It's not that."

A finger instantly slid to her lips in a soft, silencing caress. "Don't say no to me, Carrie. Think about it. Think about how you felt with me just now. Think of how it might be . . . for us . . . together. I'd be good for Danny. As if he were my own son. At least think about trying it, Carrie."

Dear heaven! He knew how to twist the knife!

He removed his finger and dropped a light and infinitely sweet kiss on her lips. "I won't pressure you, Carrie. Perhaps this has all been too much for you too quickly. Just think about it. And let me know."

He touched her mouth again with his fingertips, as though sealing his kiss there as a lingering memory. His eyes made their demand with more compelling intensity.

Then he turned and left her.

To think about it.

And let him know.

CHAPTER NINE

CARRIE DID THINK ABOUT IT—hard—because it was all too easy to let her emotions influence her thoughts. She wanted Dominic Savage. Had always wanted him. There had been no other man in her life since she had left him eight years ago. She *wanted* to believe she had made some dreadful mistake then, that he had really loved her and it wasn't just a fling to him. Even though it meant that all these years had been wasted, Carrie still wanted to believe Dominic had always loved her.

But it wasn't true.

She knew it couldn't be true.

It simply didn't add up that way.

From the very beginning she had felt it was too good to be true. Their meeting had been like a fantasy, and of course, that was precisely what it was...

The two weeks at Surfers' Paradise was to be her first real holiday away from home and away from her mother. She had saved all year for it. On her very first night there she had visited Jupiters Casino. Not to gamble. Just to look, because it seemed to be the most glamorous place to go. She had been intrigued by the people there and the games being played.

Dominic had been at one of the blackjack tables. As soon as Carrie saw him, the rest of the huge gambling hall faded into total insignificance. She watched him play. He looked up and caught her watching him. He had smiled at her, and Carrie had smiled back in automatic response. The compelling blue eyes began inviting her involvement, sending her twinkling signals—should he sit on the cards he had or buy in for another one? The silent flirtation was the most exciting thing that had ever happened to Carrie.

He didn't play for very long. He gave his seat to someone else and literally swept Carrie away, taking her to the disco, to supper, then inviting her home with him to the fabulous apartment on the beachfront. She knew he was out of her class even before then, but she had stars in her eyes and didn't want to see any reason she shouldn't be with Dominic. She might be Cinderella compared to him, but that didn't mean she couldn't enter his world, particularly when he had invited her and wanted her there with him.

They had two idyllic weeks together—every girl's dream. Dominic had pampered her. Cost was no object. He took her everywhere, showed her all the tourist highlights on the Gold Coast. Carrie could have whatever she wanted. Not that she wanted much. Just to be with Dominic. The time she enjoyed most was when he brought out his guitar and sang to her as they sat on the balcony at night, with the stars overhead and the ocean a soft background thrum to the seductive lilt of Dominic's fine tenor voice. When he had asked her to stay on with him for the entire month of her vacation leave, Carrie had been only too happy to do so.

The problem started when Dominic's crowd arrived, and it was immediately obvious that whoever had planned this group holiday had not planned for Carrie. There was one female too many. Her! And they very smartly let Carrie know it in subtle and not so subtle ways.

Carrie hadn't liked Alyson Hawthorn from the first. Alyson, Carrie recognised, was trouble with a capital *T*. Nor had she trusted her. Even when she was all sweetness and light towards Carrie in front of Dominic, the sweetness had a streak of acid and the light invariably had a shade of condescension.

Carrie didn't fit in with the crowd at all, and they were as quick to realise it as she was. They were more Dominic's age than hers, sophisticated in their attitudes, widely travelled and used to all the trappings that money could buy. They teased Carrie unmercifully—at least the women did—although never in front of Dominic.

At first Carrie had played it down. If she had Dominic, it didn't matter. She might be a square peg in a round hole, but she could grin and bear it. They were Dominic's friends, although she found it difficult to believe. They were so different from him. Yet this was the kind of social set to which he belonged.

She would have endured it, and perhaps in time come to learn how to be more sophisticated herself. She never got the opportunity. The climax came within a few days.

Dominic had gone with his friends to surf while the girls sunned on the beach. Carrie had excused herself to do a bit of necessary shopping, but eventually, reluctantly, she returned and forced herself to join the others on the beach.

Alyson instantly started baiting her. "What's it like to be in love, Carrie?"

The other five girls tittered their amusement at what was coming.

"I'm coping very well," Carrie had snapped back.

"Oh, honey! You are such an innocent," Alyson had patronised. "I bet you were a virgin. And Dominic fancied being your tutor. But you can't expect to keep him, you know. It's really only kind to warn you you're simply a temporary aberration, a little fling on the side."

"I don't believe you," Carrie had protested vehemently.

Alyson had shrugged. "More fool you, honey! But if you need some hard evidence to get things into perspective—" she held out her left hand and waggled a huge diamond solitaire ring in front of Carrie's eyes "—this is the ring Dominic gave me as a token of *serious* intentions."

If it had just been Alyson, Carrie wouldn't have believed it. Even when all the other girls agreed that Alyson and Dominic were indeed engaged to be married, she still clung to the belief that it was some cruel, sick joke. But they had an answer for everything.

To the question about Dominic's blatant infidelity, they had mocked her with knowing grins. "We all do it," Alyson explained condescendingly. "But when it comes to marriage, honey, that's really about property. Money marries money. It's the way the world turns."

"Why haven't you been wearing the engagement ring before?" Carrie had demanded hotly.

Alyson's smile was a belittling taunt. "Dominic fancied a bit more time with you."

"So why are you showing it to me now?"

Alyson heaved an impatient sigh. "I'm not the jealous type, but I am getting a bit sick of those gooey green eyes following Dominic around like a dog, and him petting you along. The problem with Dominic is that he's always been too kindhearted. Particularly with underdogs. It's time you woke up. I mean, you really are getting to be a drag on the whole holiday. You're not with it, and you're keeping Dominic out of it.''

The other girls were very vocal in seconding that opinion.

Alyson delivered the final punch with infinite weariness. ''Why not do us all a favour, Carrie, and get the hell out of here? You're so far out of your depth it's not even funny any more. Dominic's done you enough favours these last few weeks. He's given you a good time, hasn't he? So do something for him. Make a quick, easy break of it. Just hop on a bus and go back to wherever it is you belong and play with your own kind.''

So much of what Alyson said struck true, even past Carrie's blind love for Dominic. Too sick at heart to brave out a confrontation with him in front of Alyson, Carrie had gone to the apartment and packed her things. It was impossible for her to stay on, given the attitude of his friends towards her, and even more impossible if all they said was true. But she didn't want to go without speaking to Dominic first. However painful that might be, she still nursed a little hope that he truly shared what she felt for him.

When she had finished packing, she watched from the living room windows, waiting for him to finish surfing. When he finally walked up the beach, Alyson went to meet him. They talked. He gripped her upper arms as though thinking of drawing her into an embrace, then apparently dropped the idea to take the towel she had brought to him. He accompanied her to where the others were grouped together, then lay down on the beach with them.

His life.

His world.

And the woman he would marry.

The despair she had felt then was the same despair she felt now. Nothing had changed as far as she and Dominic were concerned. She was still a fling on the side in his mind, a *different* relationship from that which he maintained with his wife.

The most sensible course was to get right out of his life, as she had eight years ago. Not discuss it with him. Just do it! Except that that wasn't quite so simple in her present circumstances. And she wanted him, even more now than she had then. She wanted him for herself and also for Danny.

Carrie's mind kept going around in torturous circles, but no matter which way her thoughts leaned, there was still one inescapable fact. Dominic was married. He might be able to ignore that fact, but Carrie couldn't. To have a relationship with a married man, even though he was married to *that* woman, was not acceptable.

If Dominic really loved her and wanted her to share his life, to be together, to be a father to Danny, he had to divorce Alyson.

She could let him know that!

But quite obviously that was not what he wanted to hear. Or he would have said it himself!

It came as a shock to her when Danny arrived home from school. She hadn't noticed the time passing. She was still in the suit she had worn this morning and hadn't even thought of having lunch. Danny was ravenous after his exciting day, and Carrie immediately set about supplying them both with a sumptuous afternoon tea. She couldn't afford to let herself get weak again.

Her heart shrank as she listened to Danny extol the wonders of his new school—Dominic's old school—which was clearly beyond her means and status in life. Danny liked all his teachers. The sporting facilities were super, and there was even a computer room where the mysteries of computers were turned into easy-to-learn skills.

"And the teacher said we have a lesson on how to use them every Tuesday afternoon and Friday afternoon. I can't wait till tomorrow!" he enthused. "We never had computers in Fiji."

As she listened to his excited comments about this new kind of education, Carrie found some consolation in the thought that she had been right in her decision to leave Fiji. She wanted Danny to have every opportunity to pursue whatever ambitions he might nurse as time went by. Fiji was a fine place to live, but it provided only limited opportunities for the young.

Times had changed so much since she had been at school, Carrie reflected. The whole world was changing with the escalation of new technology. She wondered if the state schools were as well equipped with computers as the wealthy private school Dominic had chosen for Danny. Probably not, she decided.

If she agreed to what Dominic wanted, Danny could stay at that school and probably have the best education money could buy. Maybe that was worth bending her morals. Maybe Dominic would be good for Danny in lots of ways. He could give him so much that Carrie couldn't, and never would be able to by herself.

And Danny liked him. Of course, that was only natural, since Dominic had rescued him from the welfare institution and brought him back to her. And all the exciting things that had been happening since Dominic had entered their lives—this fabulous apartment, the new clothes, the school. It had to affect Danny's opinion of Dominic.

And all the good things would go on, if she agreed to what Dominic wanted.

But for how long?

And eventually Danny would start asking questions about their relationship. How would she answer those questions?

Carrie repressed her inner turmoil as much as she could and concentrated hard on responding naturally to Danny's excitement. But it was a relief when his bedtime finally came.

She lay awake for a long time that night, a host of wayward desires fighting hard common sense, which dictated that she had to cut her association with Dominic as soon as she could. The longer it went on, the harder the break would become, both for her and Danny. It would be easier for Danny to adjust to a new school if he wasn't given the time to settle too comfortably into this one.

The next day she started on job applications. Every morning she checked the listings for positions vacant in the *Sydney Morning Herald*. There weren't many, not in the locations she preferred, but whenever she found the odd one or two, she wrote to them.

The days slipped from one week into the next. Carrie kept on writing about jobs and waited anxiously for some response to come by mail. She wished people could make up their minds as fast as she had to. Although Dominic had said he would wait for a response from her without pressure, she suspected he would not wait indefinitely. Yet she shied away from contacting him in any way whatsoever, afraid she might weaken without the bolster of a decisive commitment to a job somewhere.

The furnishing of the apartment continued at a high rate of knots. Gina was totally indefatigable in determining what should be done and doing it. Carrie grew concerned that everything would be finished and she still wouldn't have anywhere definite to go. It was some secret relief to her when Gina declared there would be quite a long wait—two months at least—for the dining room furniture, which was being made to order. Surely by then, Carrie kept assuring herself, she would have succeeded in securing a job and knowing where she had to move for it.

The decorating served to fill Carrie's days with much-needed distraction while Danny was at school, and Gina was always stimulating and cheerful company. Carrie learnt quite a lot about the art of interior decorating, and Gina picked up a number of helpful hints about the preparation and presentation of various meals. It was a mutually satisfying and rewarding association.

Then, several weeks since she had last seen Dominic, Dr. Burridge called at the apartment. Carrie instantly realised that Dominic had sent him to check up on her. She felt a twinge of guilt. After all Dominic had done for her—for whatever reasons—she should have at least telephoned him to allay any further concern over her state of health. While she had no desire whatsoever to submit to another medical examination, Carrie felt it would be ungrateful and discourteous to turn the doctor away.

Besides which, she didn't have to take any notice of what Dr. Burridge said. She knew she was getting better almost every day now. Only occasionally did she get a slight attack of dizziness, and that was invariably when she had bent over for something and straightened up too fast. She could walk quite long distances without feeling exhausted, and her clothes were definitely not just hanging on her any more.

Indeed, when she admitted the doctor to the apartment, his surprise at her improved appearance told its own tale. Nevertheless, he still wanted to use the dreaded stethoscope on her, and Carrie resigned herself to the vagaries of medical science once again.

"Well, young lady, I have to concede you didn't need further hospitalisation after all," he finally declared with a satisfied smile. "You've managed very well all by yourself. In fact, one of my best cases."

Carrie couldn't resist a triumphant little snipe. "So, I did the right thing. I got better all by myself."

"I'll put it this way," the doctor pontificated. "This time it worked out all right." Then more thoughtfully, "Of course, if I hadn't thought it would work out for you, I'd have been back much sooner. With you, I had to use one of the most advanced techniques known to the medical profession."

Carrie looked at him dumbfounded. "You believe you had something to do with me getting better?"

"Of course."

Carrie felt a surge of righteous indignation. She just couldn't let him get away with such an outrageous statement. "What technique did you use?" she demanded.

"Masterly inactivity. Only the very finest doctors have the judgement to use it."

"In other words, let nature take its course," Carrie interpreted very drily, wondering if Dr. Burridge thought he had invented nature, and if God would one day tick him off for such arrogance.

"It's a sad truth that many hospital beds are filled with patients suffering iatrogenic diseases," he proclaimed, continuing his medical jargon. "A wise doctor knows when to leave well enough alone."

Carrie decided the wise doctor needed pinning down again. "What does iatrogenic mean?"

Dr. Burridge gave a delicate little cough. "Uh, a physician-induced condition."

"Doctors' guinea pigs," Carrie retorted with forthright indelicacy. "I thought as much."

"As I said before, it's often best to let nature take its course."

"So you're not advising me to do anything other than what I am doing."

A sly twinkle entered the doctor's eyes. "There's only one other thing you can do that will bring about a more rapid recovery."

"What's that?" Carrie asked sceptically.

"Fall in love, my dear. That's the greatest healer. Definitely the greatest healer. Fall in love. I can give you no greater advice."

Carrie regarded him with grave suspicion. Was he playing Dominic's hand for him, or had the doctor himself perceived too much from that first meeting in Dominic's office? "That, I'm afraid, is far too extreme," she said drily.

"Not at all," the doctor disagreed with a confident smile. "Love is extremely useful and beneficial."

Carrie didn't argue. The man obviously meant well. She could have told him that two beneficial weeks of falling in love was not useful at all when it was totally crushed by the overwhelming weight of an eight-year aftermath of emotional wear and tear. However, Carrie didn't voice any of these concerns. She gave Dr. Burridge the benefit of a confident and dazzling-with-health smile as she saw him out, so that he would never have any reason to come back.

With her conscience eased by the thought that the doctor's report would cover any legitimate concern Dominic had for her, Carrie continued her dogged efforts to find a new situation for herself and Danny.

She had finished writing another application two days later, and was feeling somewhat let down that all her efforts so far had been of little avail. She began idly flipping through the rest of the newspaper, even to the social pages, which she rarely read. A photograph caught her eye. She did not have to read the caption to know who it was. Alyson Hawthorn. Alyson Savage, Carrie corrected herself.

Her first impulse was to quickly turn the page and shut the woman out of her mind. To look at Alyson only reminded her of Dominic. And that hurt too much. She thrust the newspaper away from her and determinedly ignored it by going out to post the application.

But somehow, when she returned to the apartment, a dreadful fascination drew her to the photograph. Carrie told herself it was morbid curiosity about the kind of life that Dominic's wife led. However stupidly masochistic it was of her to want to know anything about it, she couldn't help herself. She had to look, to read, to prove she was doing the right thing by denying Dominic the relationship he wanted with her.

Alyson was not alone in the photograph. She was with a man who looked old enough to be her father. And probably was, Carrie thought, until she read the caption that accompanied the photograph. "Smiles from proud parents-to-be, socialite Alyson Hawthorn and brewery magnate Howard Slater, who confirm they will be married as soon as their separate divorces have been finalised."

Carrie's eyes read and reread the words, hardly daring to believe them. Alyson had reverted to her maiden name. And she was pregnant. But not by Dominic.

Her heart ricocheted around her chest as the meaning of the caption finally sank into her mind and gave birth to a wild leap of hope and joy.

Dominic's marriage to Alyson was over!

He was free!

As good as free!

There was no impediment to pursuing a relationship with him, a lifelong relationship! And Dominic wasn't being immoral or amoral in asking her to stay with him. There *was* a possible future for them!

Dear heaven! She had come so close to making the worst mistake in her life. If she hadn't followed the compulsion to read about Alyson, she would have left Sydney without ever knowing that she had every right to a chance of happiness with Dominic. As it was, she had kept him waiting for an answer for almost three weeks.

Carrie leapt to her feet and raced to the telephone, agitated at the thought that he might have given up because of her long silence. Her fingers trembled as she dialled the number Mrs. Coombe had written down for her. Her mind was a jumble of chaotic thoughts: fear, hope, need and deep desperate love all clamouring for expression.

The dragon's authoritative voice scythed through the chaos, wanting to know who was calling her. Carrie tried to calm herself, to speak rationally, to think how best to bridge the gap that she had created in her ignorance of Dominic's true marital status.

"It's Carrie Miller, Mrs. Coombe," she announced.

"Oh, my dear!" Authority cracked into instant anxiety. "What's wrong? What can I do?"

"Everything's fine, Mrs. Coombe," Carrie quickly assured her. "I was wondering if I might speak to Mr. Savage at some time. I know he's a very busy man, and there's no hurry, but I'd be grateful if you could let me know when it's convenient."

Silence.

"I don't want to interrupt anything," Carrie gushed on. "If you'd let me know when to call back...."

The dragon breathed some fire. "Priorities are priorities. Any call from you has top priority. And I know an *urgent* call when I hear one. Just hold on a second, my dear. I'll put you through immediately."

Carrie barely had time to recover from learning she was top priority in Dominic's busy world when his voice came on the line, sending a delicious rush of warmth right down to her toes.

"Carrie? What's wrong?"

"Dominic, I shouldn't intrude. There's nothing really wrong." She couldn't seem to get her thoughts in any order at all.

There was a strained alarm in his voice as Dominic tentatively filled in for her emotional confusion. "You're not disturbed by Dr. Burridge coming around, are you, Carrie? He didn't find anything wrong?"

"No. I'm a lot better. Didn't he tell you?" She rushed the words out.

There was a clearing of his throat. "Yes. You hadn't called, and I was worried."

"I'm sorry for leaving it so long, Dominic, but I..." She took a deep breath and plunged straight to the point of the call. "I've made up my mind. I would like to see you again... if you still wish to."

There was a moment of electric silence, then, "Carrie..." It was a bare, ragged whisper, like a half-strangled release of long-held control. "That would be wonderful," he added with definite fervour.

A wild dizziness whirled through Carrie's head. But it was not from any sick weakness. It was relief and joy and the turbulent release of all her long-repressed emotions. "I owe you so much. I thought...if you're free tonight, I could cook you dinner. It's the least I can do for—"

"I'm free. What time?"

A relaxed warmth pervaded his voice. Carrie had the immediate and strong sensation that if Dominic had not been free when she rang, he was now. He was good at cancelling appointments. For her. When she needed him. The fatuous smile on her face spilled into her voice.

"Whatever time suits you."

"Is six too early? I could leave the office as soon as I tidy things up and come straight over."

Suddenly words bubbled over each other. "Well, Danny and I usually have dinner at six-thirty, but—" She was going to add that six was fine. She didn't get the chance.

"Then six-thirty it is. I'll be there."

"Danny would like that. He loves the school, Dominic."

"Carrie, I don't want to put you to any trouble. I could take the three of us out to dinner."

"No. I want to cook for you, Dominic. Something special. It'll be my pleasure."

"And mine." There was a deep sigh. "I'll look forward to it, Carrie."

"So will I," she echoed with heartfelt feeling, then hung up as she felt tears pricking her eyes.

Maybe it was still madness to want him so much, she thought shakily. A mass of uncertainties started crowding in on her, tearing destructively at her newborn joy. Maybe Dominic wanted her out of some rebound effect from losing Alyson. His pride had to be hurt over his wife getting pregnant by another man.

Perhaps that was why he had frozen when she had called Danny her baby that first day...why he had wanted to take her home with him...why he had been thinking of his wife when Carrie had mentioned the gossip his actions would stir. There could hardly be anything more satisfying than parading a former lover around his home while Alyson was playing live-in lover to some magnate who was trying to recapture his youth. Tit for tat.

Dominic's desire for her had to be partly motivated by a need to retaliate, to wound his wife's pride by repeating a conquest that had niggled Alyson in the past.

Perhaps by pretending that it had always been Carrie he had really wanted, it made everything more acceptable to him. And she was right here, on hand, still obviously vulnerable to his attractions. It was so much easier for him to use her than to seek anyone new.

He might not have anything permanent in mind at all. Only another fling until he recovered from the wounds inflicted by Alyson.

With a fierce flash of resolution, Carrie quelled all the fears. It was stupidly self-defeating to be thinking along such negative lines. Dominic had to feel something for her. All she had to do was look at how much he had done for her and Danny. She couldn't believe it was only out of kindheartedness for underdogs, as Alyson had claimed. It had to be more than that. It might not be the kind of love she wanted, but it was something for her to build on.

She was no longer the inexperienced nineteen-year-old he had first met. She could hold her own in any sophisticated society now. She could show him to-night what a good hostess she was capable of being for him, if that was the kind of thing that was important to him. Which, given his position in the world, had to be. But over and above that, she would love him more than any other woman would. She had so much to give him if he really wanted her for always. At least she could try to make him want her for always . . . as she wanted him.

There was a chance that everything could work out.

Even the slimmest chance was better than nothing!

It meant so much, not only for her, but for Danny, as well.

Please, God, let it work out right, she prayed with almost feverish passion. Let him love me for what I am. Don't let me be deceived again. This means far too much. For everyone!

CHAPTER TEN

DOMINIC ARRIVED TEN minutes earlier than the agreed time of six-thirty. Carrie had just finished dressing in her favourite gold and beige sundress and was still in her bathroom brushing her hair when the buzzer went. It was Danny who admitted him to the apartment while Carrie tried to steady her fingers enough to apply some lipstick.

She didn't know whether it was apprehension or excitement that made her feel so nervous, but the moment she walked into the living room and saw Dominic again, the wild acceleration of her pulse left her in no doubt that she was in danger of losing her head as well as her heart.

Although he was early, he had obviously taken the time to change out of his business clothes. He wore superbly tailored grey trousers and a silk sports shirt patterned in navy and grey and white. Somehow his virile masculinity was even more pronounced in casual attire, and his whole image was less formidable and far too attractively approachable. Carrie's more intimate memories of him were instantly reawakened.

"Look what Mr. Savage has brought you, Mum!" Danny cried excitedly.

But she didn't need to look at the obvious courtship symbols—the sheaf of red roses, the box of imported chocolates, the bottle of Veuve Clicquot champagne. One look at Dominic was enough. His eyes told her what was on his mind as they clung to hers with compelling intensity, searching, wanting, stirring the response she could not hide from him any longer. He smiled, a slow smile of intense satisfaction.

"You look beautiful, Carrie," he said softly.

And somehow the years fell away, and it was just like that first smile he had given her at Jupiters Casino. She felt totally ravished by it.

"You do, Mum," Danny agreed with a cheeky grin. "You're not even skinny any more."

She gave a self-conscious laugh, aware that her skin had flushed with pleasure. She forced her legs forward, telling herself to appear graceful in every way. "You shouldn't have brought these gifts, Dominic. You make it so hard for me to return some of your generosity when you keep being more generous," she chided him with what she hoped was a charming smile.

"Just to be with you is more than enough return for me, Carrie," he said, his vivid blue eyes glowing with a warmth that heated her blood further.

Maybe it hadn't been a fantasy at all, she thought wildly. Maybe it had been as real as she had believed it was at the time—before Alyson and the others had turned it into something ugly—as real as it felt now. But she was so vulnerable to the desire. She *wished* to believe he truly cared for her, but she was not the only one who could be hurt by it this time. Carrie sternly warned herself to be cautious, to hold back until there was no shadow of doubt about Dominic's sincerity. She had to shield Danny from the kind of pain she had once suffered.

"I'll take these out to the kitchen and find a vase for them," she said as she took the roses.

"I'll come with you and open the champagne," Dominic quickly offered.

"Can I open the box of chocolates so that I can be of help, too?" Danny piped up.

"After dinner," Carrie replied, struggling to keep some command of her voice.

The next two hours proved a long struggle to keep command of anything. The many years of training provided an automatic control that stopped her from spoiling any part of the dinner she had prepared, but she didn't really taste a thing. Only Dominic's compliments on her cooking assured her that her efforts were successful. And very much appreciated.

Danny's presence helped to lend an air of normality to the evening. He chattered away to Dominic, claiming at least half of his attention. Carrie was intensely gratified by Dominic's interest in her son. There was not the slightest hint of condescension in his conversation. Indeed, it seemed to Carrie that he listened avidly to Danny's account of their life in Fiji as though he couldn't hear enough about it.

Occasionally what Danny told him evoked amusement, but quite often he flashed a look of pain at Carrie, as though the way they had lived caused him some inner distress. Of course, it had not been a life of material luxury—not the kind he was used to—but Carrie was quite proud of the way they had managed, and although Dominic didn't voice any criticism, she inwardly bridled against any adverse appraisal he might make of it.

On the whole, however, he was charming, and she couldn't take offence at anything for long. Eventually, of course, Danny's bedtime had to be announced. He then wanted to show off his new bedroom to Dominic. Carrie was quite happy to let them go off together while she stacked the dishwasher and made coffee.

It was a mistake that she very quickly regretted.

She had told Danny to get ready for bed and hadn't even considered the possibility that he might think of singing. The distinctive sound of his much-prized ukulele should have warned her, but she imagined Danny telling Dominic that it had been presented to him as a farewell gift by the Fijian staff on the island resort where they had last lived. However, her complacency was instantly dashed the moment she heard his clear child soprano voice lift into the traditional Fijian farewell song. *"Isa lei, na noqu rarawa..."*

A chill ran down her spine. She dropped everything and raced down the hallway to his bedroom. *"Danny!"* she almost shouted in her need to stop him.

His voice faltered as he took in her disapproving frown. "Dom asked me to sing it for him," he excused himself, bewildered by her vehemence.

"Dom?" It was Carrie's turn to look bewildered. Her gaze moved swiftly from the boy sitting cross-legged on his bed to the man who was sitting in the orange office chair swivelled around to face Danny.

"I told Danny he could call me that," Dominic explained, the blue eyes gently challenging her over his right to do so. Quite clearly his relationship with Danny was being fastened to a degree of intimacy that Carrie hadn't expected. Not this soon!

She tore her gaze from his, more worried about the other challenge he might make. "Danny, I told you it was your bedtime," she said reprovingly.

"Aw, Mum! Only a few minutes longer!" he wailed in protest. "Dom wanted me to sing *'Isa Lei.'* I was just telling him that I sang it for the boys in my class, and the teacher took me to the choirmaster during recess, and I had to sing it for him, too. He said he was going to put me in the school choir straight away."

"You didn't tell me that," Carrie said in some exasperation.

"It only happened today. I forgot about it until just now. I can't remember everything. I only just remembered the choirmaster said he hadn't heard a voice as good as mine since Dom was at school."

Carrie's heart stopped dead. She couldn't bring herself to look at Dominic.

"One chorus wouldn't hurt, would it?" Dominic put in mildly.

Carrie took a deep breath to calm her inner agitation. This scene was going way too fast for her, taking them right out into the middle of unknown depths. She had no idea where it might stop. Yet her fears and apprehensions could be unfounded. Dominic's mild tone of voice suggested nothing more than an interest to hear Danny sing. She had to make a decision, and to appear too adamant might arouse suspicions she had already laid to rest. She made up her mind.

"One chorus," she said sternly.

"And a verse," said Danny, and before she could contradict him, he was plucking out the tune on his ukulele.

It was the happiest of songs, and the saddest. So often through the long years it had filled her heart with ungovernable emotion and brought tears to her eyes. Somehow the words were inextricably linked to her brief relationship with Dominic, and even now she automatically translated what Danny was singing in Fijian.

> Isa, Isa, you are my only treasure
> Must you leave me, so lonely and forsaken
> As the roses will miss the sun at dawning
> Every moment my heart for you is yearning
>
> Isa lei, the purple shadows fall
> Sad the morrow will dawn upon my sorrow
> Oh! Forget not, when you are far away
> Precious moments beside Nanuya Bay.

Danny was obviously drawn by nostalgia to sing the chorus one more time. Carrie couldn't stop him now. The damage was done. And to compound matters, Dominic joined in, singing *"Isa Lei"* in harmony, humming the words he didn't know.

Carrie looked on in horror. Her worst fears were being realised in front of her eyes. Dominic was not only suffering the hurt of losing his wife, pregnant by another man, but he was looking with more and more yearning towards Danny. He really believed he had found his son, and Carrie could not see any way of laying that thought to rest now.

And where did that leave her? She didn't want Dominic to want and love her because of Danny. However selfish it was, she wanted Dominic to love her for herself.

The last haunting note wafted wistfully into the air. Carrie's eyes darted from one to the other, trying to assess what each was feeling. Although Danny had never voiced it, she knew he wanted a father figure— that was only natural—and she certainly didn't mind that person being Dominic. If their relationship was going to be permanent.

"That was beautiful, Danny," Dominic remarked quietly.

"Gee! I wish we could do that more often," came Danny's heartfelt desire. "Mum's great, but she can't sing a note."

"I can so," Carrie put in desperately.

"Not like Dom, Mum."

It was a fact she couldn't refute.

"I've got a guitar at home," Dominic slid in smoothly. "If you like, I could bring it next time I come, and we could all have a sing-along together."

"That would be super, Dom!" Danny enthused. "I'd love to learn guitar," he added without any subtlety whatsoever.

Dominic laughed. His eyes danced up at Carrie. "Well, if your mother says it's OK, I could teach you some. But she's the boss, Danny."

Relief poured through Carrie. Everything *was* all right. Dominic wasn't assuming anything he shouldn't.

"It's OK, isn't it, Mum?" Danny appealed eagerly.

"As long as you don't impose on Dominic, Danny. You mustn't ask for more than is offered," she gently chided.

Danny shot a worried look at Dominic. "I didn't mean you had to."

"It's OK, Danny. I'd like to," came the firm assurance.

Boy and man smiled happily at each other, their blue eyes mirroring an inner understanding that obviously gave them both the same kind of satisfaction.

"Bed," Carrie choked out huskily, moving forward to take the ukulele from Danny and lay it on the desk.

He was well content to snuggle down, cheerfully bidding them both good night. As he returned Carrie's kiss, he whispered, "Ask Dom around tomorrow night, Mum."

"We'll see," she murmured non-committally. "Now be a good boy and go to sleep."

Dominic went ahead to the living room as Carrie turned out Danny's light and closed his bedroom door. She stood in the hallway for several moments, gathering her composure, telling herself it would not be wise to let things move too fast where she and Dominic were concerned. That was what she had done before. It behove her to tread more carefully this time.

She decided to get the coffee first. Then, when she went into the living room, she would have something to do, and she wouldn't feel so tense, so aware of the intimacy that Dominic seemed intent on building between them. It was best to keep this a friendly social occasion, as far as possible. Only time could prove just how sincere Dominic was about wanting what he said he wanted.

When Carrie came in, bearing a tray that contained a plate of the special petits fours she had made, as well as the coffee things, Dominic was standing by the long windows, apparently viewing the city and harbour lights. He turned the moment he heard her step and stepped forward quickly to take the tray from her.

"No. It's all right, thanks," Carrie rushed out with a somewhat nervous smile. "Please ... sit down and relax, Dominic."

He subsided onto one of the smaller sofas that flanked a long chesterfield. "I do like this suite you chose, Carrie," he remarked appreciatively. "Very comfortable."

"This is all Gina Winslow's work, Dominic," she hastily corrected him. "I didn't choose anything, really. Gina did ask me my preferences in style and colour, and somehow we always seem to agree on what would look best, but I honestly haven't pushed my ideas. I wouldn't do that."

A whimsical little smile flitted over his mouth. "Well, I must use Miss Winslow on more projects in future. She obviously has a fine touch."

"And amazingly efficient," Carrie added, delighted that Dominic was pleased with the new interior decoration and wanting to give Gina all the credit she deserved. "She's done all this so quickly. If it wasn't for the dining room suite being delayed two months, you'd have this apartment back in operation next week, Dominic, and I'd be off and out of your hair."

For some reason, that idea didn't meet with his approval at all. He frowned. "There's no hurry on it. In fact..." He hesitated, frowning even more heavily.

"You mustn't worry about me," Carrie put in quickly. "I'm quite well enough to get a job now."

He looked startled. "You mustn't even think of getting a job yet, Carrie," he protested vehemently. "You look well, but you're better off to take your time. It's just not worth the risk."

He leaned forward, his eyes stabbing at hers in urgent appeal. "And you're certainly not to consider moving from here. At least, not until... well, not until all the decorating's finished, anyway. And there'll

probably be more hold-ups on that than Miss Winslow
has anticipated. Only when it's all finished will it be
time to consider a move somewhere else. I'm not
about to put you out in the street. Surely you know I'd
consider your needs ahead of anything else, Carrie.''

It certainly seemed that way, but as much as it
pleased Carrie to believe him, she was still wary of
letting herself depend on him for too much. ''I can
support myself and Danny, Dominic,'' she said quietly. A flood of painful embarrassment scorched her
cheeks as she forced herself to add, ''Not to the stan-
dard you're accustomed to, but—''

''Don't, Carrie!'' he broke in, his face twisting with
anguish. ''You've had it so hard all these years. I want
to make it a little easier for you now. Please…it's bad
enough, knowing what you've been through with no
one to help.''

''I had lots of help,'' she insisted, pride leaping to
the fore once again. ''The Fijians are the loveliest
people on earth, particularly where children are concerned. Danny never wanted for loving minders
whenever I needed them. And love and being loved is
what living is all about. Danny never went short on
that commodity. He's always been a happy child.''

''And you? Were you happy all these years, Carrie?''

She dropped her gaze from his intense probe and set
about pouring the coffee. ''Some times have been
happy. Some not,'' she stated evenly. ''Life isn't exactly carefree when one has responsibilities.''

''I would like to make your life carefree, Carrie,''
Dominic said softly.

She finished pouring the coffee, although how she
managed not to spill any was a minor miracle. Then

slowly she lifted her gaze, gently mocking the determined purpose she found burning in his. "That's not possible, Dominic. Because I'm not carefree. I do care. About a lot of things." She offered him a wry little smile. "But thank you for being so kind to me. And to Danny."

His mouth twisted in irony as he bent forward to stir sugar into the cup she had pushed towards him. "Danny's a fine boy, Carrie. You've done a marvellous job of raising him. I'd be very proud of him . . . if he were my son."

Her heart contracted. The temptation to confess the whole truth quivered on her tongue for several moments before she swallowed it back. One pleasant evening together was no test for what had to be a lifelong commitment.

"I *am* very proud of him," she said stiffly.

Dominic seemed to stir his coffee forever before finally putting down the spoon and lifting his cup. His face looked tight. His eyes searched hers carefully before he spoke again.

"I'm looking forward to spending more time with him. You really don't mind about my suggesting the guitar?"

"Of course not. I used to love—" She was going to say when you played and sang to me, but she pulled herself up at the revealing phrase and self-consciously substituted other words. "Do you still enjoy playing?"

His grimace was self-mocking. "I'm afraid I let it slide years ago. Somewhere along the line I lost my joy in music."

Carrie frowned. "Then why make such an arrangement with Danny?"

The blue eyes caught hers in compelling need. "I want to try again, Carrie," he said softly. "I want to try a lot of things again. Things that I once cared about...very deeply. But without the right kind of people to share them...they became meaningless."

Alyson could make anything meaningless, Carrie thought bitterly. She didn't understand, would never understand, why Dominic hadn't seen that for himself before making a marriage commitment with such a mean and despicable woman. But that was over now. Nothing could be gained by dwelling on the past. If she could give Dominic the future he wanted...

She smiled. "I'm afraid Danny expects you to be super, Dominic. You'd better start practising again if you want to live up to his expectations."

He relaxed into a happy grin. "I'm sure I can manage enough chords to satisfy a seven-year-old. But I will practise. I don't intend to let my...singing partner down."

Carrie wasn't sure if she had imagined that slight pause in his speech or not. For one mind-stopping moment she had thought he was going to say "my son," but he had continued so smoothly that she decided it was her own supersensitivity on the point that had raised the spectre.

"You'll have to tell me when you're ready for a concert," she invited. "Danny would have you come again tomorrow night, but I guess that would be pushing it."

"Not at all," Dominic denied quickly. "If tomorrow night wouldn't be pushing it for you, I'm only too happy to oblige. Just say what suits you, Carrie. I don't want to impose on your hospitality."

"I enjoy cooking for an appreciative guest," she assured him. "But promise me you won't bring any more gifts."

"I'll try to restrain myself." His rueful smile suggested a double meaning that the sudden simmer in his eyes reinforced.

Carrie picked up her cup to cover the wild surge of desire that rushed through her body. Neither of them seemed to have anything to say while they drank their coffee. The silence lengthened, sharpening the physical awareness that Carrie had tried so hard to keep at bay. Her mind strove frantically to find another line of conversation. Something safe!

Dominic did not help.

His cup clattered on its saucer.

He stood up, tension screaming from every line of his body. "I think I'd better go, Carrie," he said stiffly.

Disappointment stabbed through her. She set down her cup in such a hurry it tipped over. She leapt up from the lounge, her body a mass of shrieking nerve ends, her mind a whirl of uncertainties. Her eyes sought his, desperately needing to know his feelings.

"I've enjoyed the evening, the company and the dinner very much," he said, as though forcing the words through a grimly held barrier of restraint. Then his face cracked into a rueful grimace. "I don't want to strain my welcome, Carrie."

"You couldn't, Dominic." The words spilled out artlessly, her need for him too pressing for any dissembling.

He made an awkward helpless gesture. She saw the struggle on his face. "Carrie... this means too much to risk putting any foot wrong. Alone with you I find I can't trust myself to behave as I know I must."

"How must you behave?"

It was a crazy thing to ask—playing with fire—yet she couldn't stop herself from asking it. The desire he had been trying to suppress flared into his eyes. His chest expanded as he dragged in a deep breath. The battle for control went on.

"It's been a long wait, Carrie," he rasped. "I can wait a bit longer...until I've proved whatever it is I have to prove to you. So that you can trust me. If I go now then tonight's been all right, hasn't it?"

The note of desperation in his voice scoured Carrie's soul. "Yes." It was an explosion of her own pent-up feelings. "Yes," she repeated, but her eyes mirrored the uncontrollable need that was churning inside her, the need that so desperately wanted to be answered, the need that had been waiting so long, so very long....

"Carrie..." He stepped towards her, his hands lifting, reaching out, curling into fists, dropping. Anguish twisted across his face. He shook his head. "I must go. Thank you for...for letting me come."

"Dominic..."

It was a cry, straight from her heart, without any plan or thought, totally heedless of any consequence. She never knew afterwards if she stepped towards him at that critical moment. He had started to turn away from her. Her cry arrested the action. Their eyes locked, a raw aching desire leaping between them, compelling beyond any common sense or control, and the distance that separated them was abruptly and violently closed, the impact of their bodies so mind-shattering that all coherent thought ceased.

There was only feeling... Dominic's strong arms around her, crushing the softness of her body to the taut muscles of his... The heat of his mouth sweeping over her hair in a passionate flurry of kisses... The wild drumbeat of her heart, pounding its need to break through the heaving walls of their chests to reach his... Hands moving in feverish possessiveness... Heated flesh seeking heated flesh... Lips meeting, devouring, their mouths feeding the desire that yearned for more and more expression, that could never be satisfied with anything less than the total coming together that their bodies wanted.

"If this is wrong...I don't know what's right," Dominic groaned, his lips still sipping at hers. "Tell me, Carrie. Tell me you want this as much as I do."

"Yes..." There was no other response she could make. It was drawn from her soul, drawn from the dark well of loneliness that had ached to have this man, right or wrong....

And Dominic didn't wait for any other answer. He swept her off her feet and headed for her bedroom, driven by a need that couldn't bear to face up to questioning anything.

CHAPTER ELEVEN

PERHAPS IT WAS Dominic's breathing that woke Carrie from her light sleep. Her head was cradled on his shoulder, his arm curled around her, holding her firmly against his body. Even in sleep it did not seem that Dominic wanted to let go of her. It was a beautiful place to be, next to him, intimately coiled together. To Carrie, it was like coming home. Instinctively she felt it was the place she rightfully occupied, and always had.

They had made love so many times, her skin was highly sensitised to the slightest touch. The brushing of his legs against her own as he rolled onto his side was enough to arouse a leap of awareness, and she opened her eyes, instinctively wanting the wonderful intimacy they had shared to go on.

The morning light filtering through the curtains shocked her into another awareness. Her eyes darted to the bedside clock. Just past five. Danny didn't usually wake until about six-thirty. Carrie relaxed again, a sweet contentment curving her lips as she turned to the man who lay beside her.

Dominic...

His name was an exultant song inside her as her eyes roamed over the firm musculature of his shoulders and slid down the strong breadth of his chest to where the bed sheet lay loosely over his hips. He had always had a magnificent body, in Carrie's opinion, and just the sight of it excited her now. She gently lifted the sheet lower. She loved the firm swell of his bottom. It was perfect. And his powerfully muscled legs. She shivered with remembered pleasure as her gaze ran over his thighs, the sprinkle of dark hairs that had rubbed so deliciously against the satin smoothness of her skin.

She couldn't resist touching him. All last night it had been like opening a treasure trove that had been buried for years, all the contents known and loved, yet all the more precious and thrilling for having seemed lost but now found once more. Totally enthralling magic, and the reality of it—the sweet intense reality—had to be affirmed again and again. Even now, to feel the warmth of his skin, the slight contraction of his muscles as her fingertips slid over the erogenous zone just below his hip, the delicious fit of her hand around the firm curve of his buttock...her stomach twisted with the glorious pleasure of knowing he was hers to touch.

She leaned forward to kiss the vulnerable curve of his neck, and the tips of her breasts brushed his chest. Her nipples tingled into aroused excitement. With sheer sensual wantonness she rubbed them over his skin as her lips trailed to his shoulder and her hand glided forward, over his stomach.

With my body, I thee worship....

The words of the old marriage service slid through Carrie's mind, and she sighed in happiness at the thought of being married to Dominic. Having him like this, being with him, for always. He did love her. She was sure of it now. And she would make him see that she could be whatever he wanted in a wife. Not just in bed, but by his side in every capacity.

She suddenly found he was fully aroused. In the same moment of this discovery, Dominic's arm tightened around her, cuddling her closer, instantly drawing her gaze to his face. His blue eyes were wide open and glowing with pleasure. He smiled at her startled look.

"You can wake me like that any time, Carrie," he said, his voice furred with seductive sensuality.

She laughed a little self-consciously, happy that he was happy and that he could still desire her despite the excesses of the night, but at the same time realising that she was now bared to the light of day and her body could not bear the same scrutiny as his. There were faint stretch marks on her breasts and her stomach from her pregnancy, and she didn't want Dominic to see them.

"Is it time for me to go?" he asked, a trace of anxiety in his voice.

"Soon."

"How soon?"

"Danny rarely wakes before six."

He heaved a sigh of relief, checked his watch, then grinned at her. "That gives us plenty of time." He hitched himself up on the pillow and lifted a hand to stroke her hair away from her cheek and tuck it behind her ear. "I won't leave you until I absolutely have to," he stated, his eyes so warm and loving that heat tingled under her skin.

He bent his head and kissed her with tantalising lightness. Carrie lost all concern about her body and wound her arms around his neck, inviting him to take whatever he wanted of her. He kissed her again and again, teasingly sensual, slowly exciting them both towards the passionate hunger that simmered in both of them and needed so little fuelling to flare into compelling need.

His hand trailed down to her breasts and his palm revolved gently over the erect nipples, exciting them into a tight hardness. Carrie sucked in a quick breath as arrows of pleasure shot through her body. Her eyes clung to his, unable to hide the wanting, and the simmering desire in his was sharpened by a glitter of exultation.

"I love the feel of your breasts, Carrie," he murmured, slowly cupping the fullness in his hand. "So soft and womanly."

He shaped them to his mouth and hands, his tongue playing erotic dances around her nipples. Carrie felt herself drowning in the sweet pleasure of it. Slowly he increased the pressure, drawing on the sensitive flesh in a rhythm that sent fierce darts of sensation pulsing through her. She cried out as he built a tormenting need with his mouth. Her hands dragged through his hair and raked down to his shoulders. Her spine arched convulsively. He slid a hand between her thighs to soothe the aching desire for fulfilment.

"Dominic...please..." she moaned, as her body spun out of control.

He moved, carrying her with him as he rolled onto his back. "Take me, Carrie," he commanded, his eyes blazing with a fierce need, his hands supporting her quivering body, positioning her towards him. Slowly, tremulously, she absorbed his flesh within her own, and the heady excitement of seeing the expression on his face change, his eyes dilating, darkening, watching her with ever-deepening intensity, lent an exquisite awareness to the sensations spreading through her.

His hands glided lovingly over the soft curves of her body. "You are so exquisite, Carrie. The touch of you, the sight of you, the scent of you, the taste of you. To feel myself immersed in you like this...that's the greatest wonder of all."

All the love she had ever felt for him flowed through her like a tidal wave, and she could not, did not want to, deny him the words he had asked her to say weeks ago.

"I love you, Dominic."

"I know," he replied softly. There was a flash of fierce resolution in his eyes. "We will never be parted again. No matter what!"

A crest of exultant happiness bubbled into a delicious urge to tease him. "We can't stay locked together like this forever!"

A wicked delight sparkled back at her. "It seems like a great idea to me."

"Mmm..." she purred, trying an undulating movement with her hips.

Dominic sucked in a quick breath. His whole body went rigid for a moment. Then he grabbed her waist, pinning her to him as he swung her down on the pillows and took control, driving Carrie to a plateau of wildly pulsing sensation, faster, deeper, exciting a swirling tension that sent a tingling heat to her feet, her hands, her body, her brain, and just as she felt the spilling heat of his climax, her whole body spasmed in response, seeming to melt with a gushing joy around him.

He hugged her close for a long time afterwards, rubbing his cheek over her hair, stroking her back in long, sensual caresses. Finally he tilted her face up to his and kissed her with a sweet fervour that curled its loving reassurance around her heart.

"It's time, Carrie," he murmured. "I guess I should be leaving now."

"Yes." She sighed in reluctant resignation. "Thank you, Dominic."

He gave her a rueful little smile. "It hurts, but I wouldn't do anything that would distress you. And there is the promise of tonight."

"Yes." She smiled back, her eyes rewarding his caring with a deep glow of appreciation. "Don't forget to bring your guitar."

He laughed and dropped a kiss on her nose. "You are the music of my life," he said, then gently disentangled himself to get out of bed. "And I'll remind you of that tonight. With guitar and without it," he tossed at her as he headed for the bathroom.

Carrie sat up and hugged her knees, feeling so happy she could burst from it. Her eyes roved around the lovely bedroom that Gina had decorated for her, newly delighted by everything she saw, the elegant curtains in the lemon and apricot and pale green floral, with their apricot sashes and piping; the armchairs in the same fabric with the apricot silk cushions leaning against the armrests; the pale green lamps with the fluted apricot lamp shades; the magnificent secretary, which had to be a terribly expensive antique; the matching side tables; the chevalier mirror—Carrie loved everything.

And now she could stay here.

Dominic wanted her to stay here.

At least until . . . She remembered Dominic's pause before he added about the decorating being finished. He had meant until their relationship was settled.

Carrie was certain of that now. After all, he had wanted to take her to his home at first, and she suspected that was what he really wanted. But he was being careful not to rush things, to make sure it was right with her. And she was glad of that. She wasn't prepared to move into Dominic's home unless he was prepared to marry her.

He hadn't yet talked about marriage, only about not being parted again. Carrie sternly told herself to be patient about that. She had to show him that she could make him a suitable wife. At the present moment he could very well be shy of marriage anyway, after the disaster with Alyson. Besides, his divorce wasn't through yet. At least time was on her side in this new situation.

The question she really needed to have answered was the one that had tortured her over the years, and even more so lately. What had Dominic seen in Alyson Hawthorn that had made him choose to marry her?

It didn't really make sense that money and property had influenced his choice of wife. Surely Dominic's family had been wealthy and prestigious enough not to require a merger with another well-established family.

Carrie conceded that a similar background and social standing did make for an easier understanding between two people, but to her mind, Dominic's character and personality had been so different to Alyson's. On the other hand, it was probably true enough that opposites attract. Yet Dominic hadn't actually shown any great attraction towards Alyson.

It seemed to Carrie that there had to be something Alyson had—some particular quality that Dominic had seen as of special value to him in a marriage.

Something that had typified Alyson as wife material, over and above an emotional love he felt for anyone else.

And if that was the case, Carrie needed to find out what it was so that she could cultivate it. It was not just idle curiosity. She had a real need to know. Now that she had another chance with Dominic, she did not want him to find any shortcomings in her, or in their togetherness.

He came out of the ensuite bathroom, freshly washed and shaven, and he looked so splendid that Carrie's train of thought was completely lost.

He gave her a rueful grin. "Keep looking at me like that, Carrie, and all my good intentions will fly out the window. You're far too tempting, my love."

She laughed and pulled the sheet up over her breasts and tucked it under her arms.

"I'm not sure that's any better," he complained.

"I think you should get dressed and stop flaunting yourself at me," Carrie retorted in kind.

He laughed, enjoying the relaxed atmosphere between them, then set about picking his clothes up from the floor.

Carrie took great pleasure in watching him dress. Somehow it lent an extra intimacy to all that had gone before. It would be like this every morning if they were married, she thought. Or did Dominic only want them to be lovers?

That uncertainty lingered in her mind, prompting the question about Alyson. Carrie hesitated. Perhaps she should wait. She had the feeling that she might be opening a Pandora's box of troubles that was better left shut. If Dominic had been deeply hurt by his

marriage, it would be foolish of her to remind him of
it.

Yet if he loved her... And after last night, could he
possibly care about Alyson any more? The need to
know pressed the decision. And she had already
waited so patiently for so long, trying not to hurt anyone, that for once her own need came first.

"Dominic..."

He looked up from tucking his shirt into his trousers and smiled, the blue eyes bright with anticipation
of whatever she might say to him.

Carrie took a deep breath. "There's a question I'd
like to ask you. If you don't want to answer it, it
doesn't matter," she added hastily, apprehensive
about spoiling the mood between them.

"Ask away," he invited blithely.

"Well... would you mind telling me..."

She wasn't aware that her green eyes were filling
with vulnerable appeal, but she felt tension streaking
along all her nerves. Dominic looked at her quizzi-
cally as she hesitated again. Carrie ended up blurting
the question out in a rush.

"What did you find so attractive about Alyson
Hawthorn, Dominic?"

His hands stilled. His whole body seemed to be
poised in utter stillness. His face was frozen in an expression of shock. Carrie's mind screamed at her that
she had made an awful mistake. The past was the past.
It was stupid, stupid, stupid to drag it up when the
future beckoned so brightly.

The shock on his face slowly faded into dawning
comprehension, a comprehension that seemed to ap-
pal him. "Carrie..." His voice was a harsh rasp. His

throat moved in a convulsive swallow. "What made you think I found Alyson Hawthorn attractive?"

Her heart felt as though it was tumbling over itself. Bewilderment was followed by a painful storm of confusion. "Well, there had to be some reason..." The look on Dominic's face made it clear that whatever he had felt for Alyson was long gone. "I shouldn't have asked. I'm sorry. It doesn't matter."

"It does matter!" He advanced towards her, the blue eyes probing with an intensity that carried a blazing need to draw answers from her. He sat on the bed beside her and took hold of her shoulders, forcing her to look up at him. "Carrie, I know this is important. You have to tell me."

Her confusion grew worse. This was all the wrong way around. It was *he* who had to tell *her*. She shook her head. She should have waited.

"Please, Carrie... tell me one reason you thought I found Alyson attractive."

The urgency in his voice only served to heighten the unreality of what was going on. Carrie couldn't understand him. Never would. She tried to get the circling chaos into a straight line. "I could never understand what you saw in her," she said dully, wishing he would just answer her or let the subject drop.

"And if I said I saw nothing at all?"

Her eyes filled with pained accusation. Why was he trying to deceive her now? What point was there in it? Why couldn't he just give her the truth? That part of their lives was over. He didn't have to cover up and turn it into something different. All she had wanted was to understand. Surely it wasn't asking much for him to tell her.

"Then why did you marry her, Dominic?" she demanded, forcing him out of all evasion.

She felt the gasp of air hit his lungs. Horror and disbelief were stamped on his face. "Marry her!" The words came from his lips in violent rejection. "Marry that sly manipulative bitch? Carrie, I wouldn't have touched Alyson Hawthorn with a bar of soap, let alone..."

His head jerked in anguished denial. His hands lifted from her arms in a gesture of helpless appeal. He rose from the bed and paced around in extreme agitation.

Carrie watched him in a daze of spiralling shock. "You didn't marry her?" She forced the words from the mess that was her mind.

"No!"

The explosive negative completely shattered any equilibrium she had left. She stared at him, trying to steady herself, trying to take in the implications of this revelation. He must have changed his mind about marrying Alyson. And if he wasn't married to her, he was not getting a divorce from her.

"You married someone else," Carrie said, and the words seemed to come from a great distance. Her ears had a strange ringing in them.

"Carrie..."

It sounded like a protest. She saw his struggle to bring himself under control. The strain showed clearly on his face, but the observation only registered at the dimmest edge of her mind. He came to the bed and sat down, taking her hands this time, his fingers rubbing roughly over them as if seeking to reach under her skin. His eyes held an agonised plea.

"Yes, I did marry someone else," he acknowledged. "I'm sorry if that hurts you. Her name was Sandra Radcliffe. She wasn't there that summer. As far as I know, you never met her."

His face was tinged with hopelessness. Somehow he knew how important this was to her, but with their differing attitudes towards love and commitment, it was also clearly impossible for him to know why. Even to Carrie, the implications were only starting to sink in.

"It doesn't matter," she said defensively. "I shouldn't have asked." But she knew it did matter and couldn't keep the despair from her voice.

The words rushed from him, trying to bridge the gap of years that had been so suddenly shattered like fine crystal, the shards stabbing out in all directions. "Please understand, Carrie...."

She could hear the note of pleading in his voice and she did want to understand. She desperately wanted to. So she gave him all the attention she could muster.

"I'd spent years trying to find you, and I'd finally given up hope. Life was so empty...lonely...and then I met Sandra. I didn't love her as I love you. Never did. But I was thirty by then. And I did want children."

He didn't realise that the timing of his marriage—or the reason for it—didn't matter at all. The inexorable truth was that Dominic wasn't free. He had a wife. And Carrie had been a party to committing adultery all night. She hadn't known that. There was no wilful intent behind what had happened. She wasn't really guilty of taking another woman's husband. But it had happened.

She dully remembered that Dominic had meant to leave without touching her. He had even admitted it was wrong... although it felt right.

But it wasn't right!

It could never be right.

He was married to another woman.

"As it turned out, Sandra couldn't have children," Dominic continued sadly. "But she needed me, Carrie...."

"Of course," she whispered. Her mouth had gone completely dry. "I understand, Dominic."

She understood perfectly. Any woman married to Dominic would need him. For the rest of her life. And she certainly understood his desire now for Danny to be his son. But she couldn't bear to hear him talk about his wife. Not when the memory of their illicit intimacy was pulsing so painfully through her heart.

"I think you'd better go now. It's getting late," she said flatly.

He frowned. "About Alyson, Carrie..."

"I had a wrong idea about Alyson. That's all," she cut in quickly. Strange how her mind could work on a level that sounded quite sane and sensible while her whole bright new world was crumbling into ruins around her. "And now I know it was wrong. I don't want to go on about it. I'd rather you dropped the whole subject, Dominic. I feel enough of a fool as it is."

Conflict chased across his face, the need to pursue his own interests battling against her plea for forbearance. Frustration and disappointment finally gave way to reluctant resignation. "You just want to go on from here. Is that it, Carrie?" he asked softly.

"Yes," she said on a rush of sheer relief. She would have said anything to stop him involving her in a discussion about his marriage. Just the thought of that other woman who couldn't have his children waiting at home for him ...

"I didn't mean to upset you." His eyes searched hers anxiously, obviously wanting to put everything right between them before he left. "Believe me, I'm content just to have you again, Carrie. Any way I can."

Her whole body ached for the contentment she had just lost. "Yes," she agreed. It was the easiest word to say. Her conscience accused her of having said it far too much lately, where Dominic was concerned.

"Then I'll see you tonight," he said, and leaned forward to kiss her goodbye.

She knew she shouldn't respond to it, but a terrible surge of despair gripped her heart, and before she knew what she was doing, she had flung her arms around his neck and was kissing him back as though her very life depended on it.

When Dominic finally lifted his mouth from hers, he shook his head wryly and drew in a deep breath. "Tonight," he said, as though he needed to repeat the promise of what was to come before he could force himself to go. He stroked her cheek in a last tender salute. "Tell Danny I'll bring my guitar."

Carrie nodded, too choked up to speak.

Dominic smiled and left, shutting her bedroom door very quietly behind him, careful not to make any noise that might wake Danny before he could depart.

Carrie sat staring at the closed door for a long time, her heart fighting fiercely against her conscience. She could let that door open again and keep Dominic in her life . . . be his kept woman on the side. And maybe he would divorce his wife eventually and marry her.

And maybe he wouldn't . . . if he could have her any way he wanted. His wife needed him.

Besides, how could she be a party to hurting a woman who was innocent of any wrongdoing? Who had married Dominic in good faith and had every right to have that good faith returned. While Carrie had no rights at all . . . except Dominic's love for her, and her love for him.

There was a rap on the door and Danny's voice piping behind it. "Mum, are you awake?"

"Just a minute!"

She scrambled from the bed, scooped up her clothes that had been so heedlessly discarded last night, threw them into a cupboard and quickly dragged a housecoat over her nakedness.

What about Danny's rights? she cried inwardly, as she opened the door to her son. But she knew that that was no argument. It had never been an argument. She would not use her child to force anything from Dominic. Especially not now.

Danny's vivid blue eyes sparkled up at her. "Did you ask him, Mum?"

She frowned, struggling to drag her mind off its inner torment. "What, Danny?"

"Dom. To come tonight. With his guitar."

The eagerness in his face twisted Carrie's heart. Was it right to keep a boy from his father? Wasn't a part-time father better than no father at all? Dominic could be so good for him.

"He has other commitments, Danny," she temporised.

"Oh!" His face fell in disappointment.

And how many other disappointments would we have, when Dominic had to be with his wife? What excuse had Dominic given for his absence last night? What excuse would he think of for tonight? When would he start making excuses to her and Danny? How long would he be a part-time father to Danny?

Carrie shook her head. She couldn't live with that situation. It was just as well she had held her tongue last night. Better for Dominic not to know that Danny was his son. Better for Danny not to know that Dominic was his father. Maybe they could just be friends . . . given time.

Carrie savagely mocked that thought.

It was no answer to her dilemma.

But she had to find an answer.

Before tonight.

CHAPTER TWELVE

JUST FOR ONCE, luck was on her side.

The answer was delivered in the mail.

It came in the form of a reply to one of Carrie's job applications. A positive reply. She was offered the position of top cook in a motel restaurant at Mudgee. Accommodation was provided. A telephone number was given. Would she call and confirm arrangements? The management needed her quickly and desperately. They wanted her to take up the job as soon as possible.

It meant she could once more be completely independent. She had somewhere to go, somewhere to live, and she would be earning an income that would support her and Danny. She was in a hopelessly compromising position here in the APIC company apartment, with Danny attending a school for which Dominic had paid the fees—albeit without her knowledge or permission. With this job, she could pay him back all that was owed. In money terms, anyway.

As much as it broke her heart to leave Dominic again, especially after last night, if he was really prepared to make a life with her and Danny, the choice was open to him. Even though it was a terrible choice to make, and someone was bound to be hurt.

He could get out of his marriage, or he could stay with it.

If he decided on the latter, then she and Danny were better off on their own. Part-time love without total commitment was not something she could ever be really content with.

She called the Mudgee motel and accepted the position. The manager told her what train she could catch from Sydney. She said she would be on tomorrow's train. She did not intend to walk out on Dominic without a word this time. She fiercely wished she hadn't all those years ago. Dominic had changed his mind about marrying Alyson Hawthorn. He said he had loved her—always had—and only married someone else because he had given up hope of ever finding her again.

If that was the case, if he asked his wife for his freedom, Carrie would wait for him. And she really meant *wait*. There would be no more lovemaking until Dominic was free. Otherwise...well, she had to tell him she could not accept any other kind of future with him. It wasn't right. And never could be right.

She was in the midst of packing when the buzzer announced a visitor. Carrie immediately assumed it must be Gina and went to admit her. She was startled when the dragon announced herself. What was Mrs. Coombe doing here in the middle of a working day? Carrie had put a stop to the shopping visits weeks ago. Nevertheless, she could hardly refuse her entry. The woman had been kind in her own authoritative fashion.

Carrie waited in the lobby, hoping to head off any further interference from Dominic's secretary. Mrs. Coombe stepped out of the elevator carrying a guitar case. She bestowed a benevolent smile on Carrie.

"Hello, my dear. My goodness, you have had an amazing effect on Mr. Savage!" The grey eyes actually twinkled. "Bringing a guitar to his office and singing! I've never seen him so happy! He had to go off for a conference at Peppers, up in the Hunter Valley, and he said to drop the guitar off with you to save him coming back to the office. But he won't be late, dear. The helicopter will be waiting to whiz him back to Sydney."

Carrie was so taken aback, as well as being highly embarrassed by this uncharacteristic burst of confidences from the dragon, that she didn't have wits enough to stop the formidable lady from charging into the living room and leaning the guitar case against one of the sofas.

"Oh, this is nice!" The steely grey eyes swept around, not missing any detail of Gina's decorative genius. Carrie got another smile, a veritable beam of approval. "So comfy and pleasant. I do admire your taste, dear."

Carrie heaved an impatient sigh. "It's Miss Winslow's work, Mrs. Coombe. I had nothing to do with it."

The dragon made a click of annoyance with her tongue. "Of course! Well, I must say she's done a marvellous job. Would you mind if I had a little peek in some of the other rooms?"

Since Mrs. Coombe was the top executive secretary at APIC and probably had the responsibility of arranging accommodation for clients, Carrie felt she had no option but to accede to the request.

"Of course I don't mind." The buzzer rang again and Carrie seized on the excuse not to accompany her.

"Please excuse me, Mrs. Coombe. You go right ahead and look all you want."

It was Gina, and Carrie was only too pleased to admit her. Apart from being spared the dragon's undiluted company, she wanted to say goodbye to her friend and tell her how pleased Dominic had been with her work. It was always a pleasure to have one's talents and hard work praised, and Gina certainly deserved every accolade going. She was a super person, apart from anything else.

However, the moment she stepped out of the elevator, Gina wrinkled her pert nose in good-humoured frustration. "Bad news, I'm afraid. You know I told you the dining room suite would be two months away. Well, there's been a further delay on materials, Carrie, and they won't guarantee a time for delivery. We're just going to have to wait and see."

"It doesn't matter to me, Gina," Carrie assured her, "although I am sorry you're being held up on the job. Oddly enough, Dominic—Mr. Savage—said only yesterday that you'd probably run into more delays."

"Is that a fact?" Gina said with a crooked little smile.

"Yes. And he thought you'd done a brilliant job so far. He even said he'd be considering employing you for other projects."

The crooked smile turned into a grin of dazzling proportions. "I sure would like that, Carrie. This job has been an absolute dream!"

"Are you rushing, Gina, or have you got time for a cup of coffee?" Carrie pressed anxiously.

"Coffee would go down very well," came the feeling reply. "I've been dashing around all morning."

They moved towards the kitchen, only to be halted by the sight of the dragon, charging down the hallway with the light of battle in her eyes, her bosom heaving as though she was stoking the engine room for the fire to be breathed.

"What is the meaning of all this packing?" she demanded to know.

Carrie grimaced. It was none of Mrs. Coombe's business, but that was obviously no consideration in her mind. She had the bit by the teeth and was in no mood to be fobbed off. Carrie decided there was little point in evading the issue. Dominic had already left the office for his conference and would be coming here straight afterwards. What did it matter if the dragon was told before he was? It didn't change anything.

"I'm packing because I'll be leaving here in the morning, Mrs. Coombe," she stated evenly.

"Leaving!" The Dragon and Gina chorussed in unison, each with the same note of appalled horror.

Carrie frowned at both of them, bewildered by their vehement reaction. "You know that my being here was only a temporary arrangement. I've got myself a job somewhere else, with live-in accommodation."

Carrie didn't want to tell them where. She had images of Dominic following her because he couldn't have what he wanted. If she had to cut free of him, better to do it cleanly, as she had in the past.

"You *can't* take a job somewhere else!" the dragon puffed in righteous indignation.

Carrie was beginning to feel a bit angry herself. This really was no one's business but her own. "I have the right to do anything I want, Mrs. Coombe," she stated sharply.

That took some of the steam out of the dragon, but she eyed Carrie with stern censure. "You really are the most ungrateful creature I've ever met!"

"Me? Ungrateful?" Carrie could hardly believe her ears. "To whom? How have I ever been ungrateful?"

Mrs. Coombe drew herself up in formidable authority. The grey eyes glittered intense disapproval. "When Mr. Savage went to the expense of buying this apartment for you, and having it decorated entirely to your taste—"

"Mrs. Coombe, you are totally and terribly wrong!" Carrie broke in, appalled that Dominic's secretary should have leapt to such conclusions. "In your position you should know better. This apartment is not for me. It's owned by APIC and it's used for the company executives and their associates and clients."

There! Take that, Carrie thought belligerently. They were Dominic's exact words.

The dragon snorted smoke. "APIC has nothing to do with this. The company has never bothered with any such thing."

"Truly!" Carrie argued vehemently. "You just don't know."

"I? Not know?" Eyebrows shot up in haughty scorn. "My dear girl, I have been in the confidence of Mr. Savage, and his father before him, for over twenty years. There is nothing I don't know!"

"Well, you're wrong about this!" Carrie returned stubbornly, refusing to submit to sergeant-major bully tactics.

"I most certainly am not! There was an extreme penalty clause in the contract Mr. Savage had to sign for it. If settlement of the contract was delayed and not effected within six weeks of exchange, he had to pay many thousands of dollars a week in punitive damages. All to have this apartment immediately available so he could move you into it that very day! Even the agents found it stunning and inexplicable. It was one of the worst deals Mr. Savage has ever made in his life. Simply because it had to be done so quickly. *For you!*" she finished triumphantly.

Carrie stared at her in stunned disbelief. "You've got to be joking," she murmured weakly.

It earned a disdainful snort. "I've never made a joke in my life! Not for any reason! Never!" The sergeant-major swung her unshakable authority onto Gina. "Tell Miss Miller your instructions from Mr. Savage!" she commanded.

"Mrs. Coombe..." Gina fidgeted. Her eyes swung warily from one antagonist to the other. "I can't do that," she began uncertainly. "I gave my word to Mr. Savage."

"Please do as you're told. In this matter, I speak for Mr. Savage himself," Mrs. Coombe said in her best no-nonsense voice. "I chose you in the first place. I'm now ordering you, on Mr. Savage's behalf. So do as I tell you or the consequences—believe me—will be that you will never work for APIC again," the sergeant-major threatened.

Gina turned troubled eyes to Carrie, but Mrs. Coombe's threat was sufficient. Her mind had been made up for her in no uncertain terms. "It's true...all of it. My brief, from Mr. Savage, was to ascertain what you liked and do my best to please you with all the furnishings. He wanted you to be happy here, to have all the things you would love. Cost was to be no object. Anything at all you fancied. I was to get it for you one way or another. But I had to be careful not to let you realise that it was all being done especially for you. And I had to do it quickly so you'd be completely comfortable as soon as possible. Except for one important piece of furnishing that I had to hold back on."

"The dining room suite," Carrie murmured numbly.

"Yes. Mr Savage called me this morning and told me to make the delay a lot longer." Gina heaved a rueful sigh. "I'm sorry that it was kind of deceiving you, Carrie, but I couldn't see any harm in it. And you have been happy with what I've done. I've really enjoyed working with you. Giving you the pleasure Mr. Savage wanted you to have. And just being with you. Please believe that."

"Yes," Carrie whispered, too dazed to question what anyone said any more. She sat down on the nearest sofa and tried to make sense of all that Dominic had done for her. *Cost no object...* From the time he had left her that first afternoon, before he had even seen Danny, or suspected that her son might be his. He had done all this, set it all up, spent thousands and thousands of dollars, more...just for *her!*

"Why?" she murmured. It was so insanely extravagant. Her eyes lifted to the dragon, blindly seeking answers. "How could he do it?" Particularly when she had fought against any further involvement with him, Carrie thought, trying to absolve herself of any blame. For Dominic to just go ahead and...

"When Mr. Savage sets out to do something, he does it!" the dragon informed her categorically. "As to why, surely that's as obvious as the nose on my face." She sniffed for good measure, showing her nose in all its majesty. "Even if you don't love *him,* at least you could show some small smidgen of gratitude."

"Mrs. Coombe..." All the anguish of mind and heart that had wracked Carrie since early this morning poured into her voice. "What about his wife?"

"What about his wife?" came the wrathful retort. "That ended nearly two years ago. At the same time as his father died. Do you realise how crippling it is to have the two people closest to you die at almost the same time?"

It was a rhetorical question. She didn't expect a reply to it. Nor did she get one. Carrie simply stared at her, rendered totally speechless as revelations gushed from the dragon's mouth like an endless stream of fire, scorching away any possible objections Carrie might have to Dominic's interest in her.

"There's been more than a decent mourning period for Sandra. Surely to heaven you can't begrudge him some happiness now. After all he's been through, what with his father, then Sandra... and you looking so thin and ill that he was afraid you might have cancer, too.... And the grief that caused him... And then you refusing to go to hospital. Or see doctors. Taking the same wilful self-destructive attitude Sandra did..."

"His wife... Sandra... she died?" It was the one important fact to come out of Mrs. Coombe's torrent of indignation. Other things she could think of later, but a dreadful pressure was lifting off Carrie's brain, and her heart was already leaping with a surge of wild strength.

The dragon frowned her displeasure at Carrie. "Of course she's dead. Don't you know the first thing about Mr. Savage? He is the most honourable man I know. In business and out of it. Are you so ignorant

not to even realise that Mr. Savage would never interest himself in another woman if he had a wife? And
there's few men I can say that for!''

"I thought…'' Carrie dragged in a deep breath and
expelled it in a long shuddering sigh of sweet relief.
"I've made the most terrible mistake.''

"You certainly have!'' A finger shot out and
wagged sternly at Carrie. "That man deserves some
consideration. From you. A great deal of consideration. If there's one thing I can't stand it's base ingrat-
itude. And it's about time you gave him something
back instead of pursuing your own selfish desires. Instead of going on with this harebrained idea of getting a job and leaving, you could begin by saying
thank you, and then—''

"Oh, I will, Mrs. Coombe. I will!'' Carrie cried,
and startled the old lady into spluttering silence by
springing up from the sofa and hugging her and kissing her on the cheek. She wasn't a dragon after all. A
good watchdog, maybe, but not a dragon. And Carrie could have hugged her for a lot longer, but she
wasn't sure Mrs. Coombe's dignity would stand for
that. As it was she was ruffled into helpless bewilderment.

"You will what?'' she asked.

"Give Mr. Savage a lot of consideration. And show
him some gratitude,'' Carrie burbled.

"Well…so you should.''

"And I'm terribly grateful to you for explaining it
all to me,'' Carrie said with deep sincerity.

Mrs. Coombe recovered her usual composure. "Not
at all. What has to be done, has to be done. And I'm
the person to do it.'' She eyed Carrie sternly. "Just
don't let Mr. Savage know what I've told you. That

was at my discretion. Of which I have a lot. But Mr. Savage might not appreciate it straight away. Men can sometimes be very difficult in matters of pride.''

''And, uh, Carrie...'' Gina chimed in. ''If you don't mind, I'd rather him not know that I spilled the beans, too. I mean...well, I'd really like to get into more of Mr. Savage's projects...with Mrs. Coombe's help.''

In a flood of emotion, Carrie gave her a hug, too. ''Don't worry about a thing. You have my promise. And thanks for making a beautiful home for me, Gina.''

She laughed and hugged her back. ''You've been the easiest client I've ever had, Carrie. A dream job. And let me tell you, if I had a guy like Dominic Savage wanting to make me happy, I'd grab him fast and never let him go.''

''It's not quite as easy as that,'' Carrie said ruefully. ''There are things between us....''

Like confessing the truth about Danny. And explaining why she had not told him before. She couldn't just go on from here, even if Dominic was content to do so. The past had to be cleared away. And that could not be done in front of her son.

She swung back to Mrs. Coombe, her eyes filling with anxious appeal. ''May I ask you one more favour?''

''I'll do what's necessary, at my discretion. But if I can help in this situation, I will.'' Mrs. Coombe's stern demeanour was softening.

''It's Danny. I want to be alone with Mr. Savage for a while. If it could be arranged...''

''I'll pick Danny up from school and take him to a late afternoon screening of a film. Then we'll have hamburgers and chips. My boys always loved doing

that. Don't you worry about him. We'll enjoy ourselves immensely. I'll bring him home at seven. Is that
time enough?''

"If it's not too much trouble," Carrie breathed in
grateful relief. "You are a real treasure, Mrs. Coombe.
Thank you so much."

"Not at all." She brushed Carrie's words off, but
her face actually glowed with pleasure. "Mr. Savage
has a very nice voice. He should sing more often."

She cleared her throat and addressed Gina in her
sergeant-major voice. "Miss Winslow, we'd better be
going. You have a lot to do. You have to speed up the
dining room suite now that we all understand one another. And change anything Miss Miller would like
changed. But that part can wait until tomorrow. Miss
Miller won't have time to discuss such things today."

The grey eyes fixed their command onto Carrie
again. "You have a lot to do. Those job arrangements have to be immediately cancelled, and everything unpacked again and put away, and, uh, getting
yourself ready for Mr. Savage's visit."

"You're right, Mrs. Coombe," Gina agreed, but
there was a wicked twinkle in the eyes she turned to
Carrie. "Lots of considerations."

A lot more than Gina could ever imagine, Carrie
thought, a nervous flutter starting up in her stomach.
But it had to work out right in the end. It just had to.
Dominic loved her. More than she had ever dreamed.
And she loved him.

And there was Danny... their son. Dominic had to
be told. However unpleasant the consequences might
be from the explanations she had to give, there was no
way to avoid telling the whole truth now. She owed it

to Dominic. And much much more. If he could find it in his heart to forgive her, to understand . . .

It was a risk she had to take anyway. There was no way around it, and Carrie didn't want a way around it. Only the truth would serve their future happiness now.

CHAPTER THIRTEEN

FORTUNATELY THE MANAGER of the Mudgee Motel had another applicant for the position Carrie had to refuse. Carrie hated letting anyone down, but Dominic had her first consideration and always would from now on.

Unpacking did not take long.

Carrie wasn't sure when Dominic would arrive. Most probably he would think she expected him at six-thirty, like last night, but she willed him to come earlier. She needed far more than half an hour alone with him.

Since Danny would not be having dinner with them, and she remembered that Dominic liked Italian food, she prepared a special lasagne, which could be popped into the oven anytime. She couldn't make up her mind what to wear, finally deciding it didn't matter. Dominic loved her anyway. She prayed that he would still love her, despite what she had to tell him.

Alyson had more than lied to her. Mrs. Coombe had insisted that Dominic was an honourable man, and an honourable man wouldn't have made love to her if he was engaged to marry someone else. She hoped Dominic could forgive her lack of faith in his love, that he would understand what she had done and why. If only she had waited for him that day. She had been such a fool not to have given him a hearing before she left, to have let her mind be poisoned by that lying bitch of a woman instead of listening to her heart.

All the wasted years.

The pain.

Alyson had cheated all of them.... Dominic, herself and Danny. Carrie asked herself why? Maybe Alyson just couldn't bear anyone else to be happy, to be in love, and she had been jealous because of what Dominic and she had shared. What had she said—"gooey green eyes"? But in the end, Alyson had only succeeded in her cruel manipulation because Carrie had not believed enough! She hadn't believed that Alyson could be so evil, and she hadn't believed that Dominic could have such friends if he didn't share their attitudes, and she hadn't believed he truly loved her... as she loved him.

Carrie was still churning between guilt and hope and fear and despair and desperate love when Dominic turned up. It was just past five-thirty as he stepped out of the lift, and all Carrie's turbulent emotions crystallised into one pure beam of overwhelming love. He had come... He was here for her, the man she had wanted to have with her for so long. She threw herself into his arms and hugged him so tightly that Dominic was startled.

"Carrie? What's wrong?" he asked anxiously, his hands automatically moving to soothe any distress.

"I just love you so much, Dominic," she breathed huskily, revelling in the scent of him, the feel of him, the caring he had always shown her. Always.

He gently tilted her head and smiled at her, the blue eyes shining with a deep blaze of happiness. "I'm so glad you can say that, Carrie. Right up until last night I was afraid I was going to lose you again. It sure is a good feeling to know that everything's all right."

But it wasn't. Not yet. And he saw the inner disquiet flit over her face. "Something is wrong, isn't it?" He frowned, his eyes suddenly darting to the living room. "Where's Danny?"

She eased back a little from his embrace and screwed her courage to the sticking point. "He's gone to a film with Mrs. Coombe, Dominic. I asked her to mind him. I want to talk to you alone."

He tensed and looked even more concerned. "Carrie, if you're worried about anything, we can work it out."

"I hope so, Dominic," she said fervently. "Come in and sit down," she pressed, linking her arm around his and drawing him into the living room. "Would you like a drink?" she asked, nerves playing havoc with her resolution.

"Not right now, thanks, Carrie. I'd rather hear what you want to say first."

He was right. No point in prolonging the agony. She saw him settled on one of the sofas, but found her inner agitation too great to sit down herself. She wandered over to the windows before forcing herself to turn and face him.

"I haven't been fair to you, Dominic," she blurted out in a rush of shame.

His expression changed from concern to a wary watchfulness. "In what way, Carrie?" he asked softly, careful to withhold judgement.

She felt a tide of heat sweep up her neck and burn into her cheeks, and it took every ounce of her willpower to hold his gaze, despite the guilt that was making knots of her stomach. "I didn't believe you loved me," she answered bluntly.

He nodded slowly, still with that wary reservation in his eyes. "But you do now," he said.

"Yes. And I'm sorry it took so long to—"

"That doesn't matter to me, Carrie. Only having you matters," he asserted quietly.

She shook her head, her cheeks flaming even more painfully. "You don't understand, Dominic. This morning..." She took a deep breath. "This morning, when you said what you did about Alyson Hawthorn... all these years I've believed something very different."

"I realised that, Carrie," he said soothingly.

"No. You can't know. I—I made a mistake. A terrible mistake."

He rose from the sofa and gently slid his hands around her shoulders, giving them a light reassuring squeeze. His eyes were soft with compassion. "Carrie, I said I'd never criticise you and I never will," he promised her tenderly. "I know you would only have done what you believed was right at the time."

She couldn't stop the tears that blurred her eyes. She didn't deserve his understanding or his wonderful generosity, but she was intensely grateful for them.

"It was Alyson who came between us, wasn't it?" he asked gently.

"Yes." She choked the word out, working hard to swallow the growing lump in her throat. "But it wasn't only her. All the women said it was true. Every one of them. On the beach that afternoon. Although I already knew that I didn't fit in with... with your social set. Somehow I was outside them. Apart. Even so, I waited to hear it from you. For you to explain why you did what you did with me... to me. I couldn't believe it... didn't want to believe it."

"Carrie, what did they say?"

"Alyson Hawthorn was wearing an engagement ring. She said that you'd given it to her and that you were going to be married. And that I was just a little fling on the side. They said everyone—you and your friends—had that kind of casual sex...and it didn't mean anything."

"And that's why you accused me of playing musical beds."

She nodded, her eyes begging his forgiveness.

"Carrie, I swear I was never like that," he insisted earnestly. "And I never had anything to do with Alyson. She frequently gave me the come-on, but I never once took her up on it. Or showed any interest in her. Maybe that wounded her ego, or maybe she thought she'd stand a better chance with me if she could get you off the scene."

"I guess I played right into her hands," Carrie agreed sadly. "I believe you now, Dominic. But it was very convincing with the others backing her up. And when you finished surfing, you didn't come looking for me. You talked to her. Stayed with her. Sat with her and the others. And I thought then that I wasn't what you wanted. I couldn't ever be like you...like them."

"That was my fault," he murmured with a deep sigh. "I should have acted sooner." His eyes pleaded for her understanding. "I knew what was going on, the way they were treating you. That afternoon, when I came out of the water, I'd decided what to do. I wanted to take you away from them, but foolishly, in my pride, I thought that was running away. A defeat. I took Alyson by the shoulders—I wanted to throttle her—and I gave her an ultimatum. Leave you alone, or get out."

"I thought you hadn't noticed...or preferred to ignore it. That you were going back to Alyson."

The pained look that crossed his face was full of savage regret. "I noticed. But Alyson was all sweetness and light. She said you were still out shopping. Not back yet. I decided to stay with them, make my peace, so that they would be nicer to you. Underneath it all, I realised I would never have anything more to do with them after that holiday was over."

"But they were so superior."

"Oh, Carrie, it was you who was so superior. They resented and were jealous of you."

"But why?"

"Because you had what they didn't. You had a soul, Carrie. A beautiful receptive soul that knew how to love. And an innocent heart that didn't know how to put anyone down or hurt or destroy. The ring Alyson showed you was probably the engagement ring that she kept when a disillusioned friend of mine decided he didn't want to marry her. Alyson was all take and no give. She didn't care about anyone but herself. And as I lay on the sand with them that afternoon, listening to their smart remarks and sophisticated cynicism, I felt more and more ashamed to be in their company. I just wanted to be with you."

Carrie's heart ached with misery as she realised how dreadfully she had misinterpreted Dominic's actions that day. "I can only say... you looked relaxed, content to be with them."

"I did leave them, Carrie," he said, his eyes urgently seeking to impress that truth on her. "I went back to the apartment to wait for you. I waited and waited, and then began to worry that you'd somehow been involved in an accident. I rang the police but there'd been no accident reported. Then I went into the bedroom and realised there was nothing of yours lying around...."

He dragged in a deep breath. "At first I couldn't believe it. You couldn't have just walked out on me without a word. I ransacked the bedroom, trying to find something, anything of yours...but there was nothing left, nothing. And I didn't have your home address. All I could remember was the suburb where you lived in Sydney. I went to the hotel where you'd stayed before you came with me, but there was no booking there in your name."

"My mother made the booking for me," Carrie remembered, her chest growing tighter and tighter at this evidence of his caring.

"There was no Miller listed." The frustration in his voice carried even more conviction. "None at all!"

"My mother's name was Wainwright. She married again after my father died."

Dominic groaned. "Carrie, there are one thousand, five hundred and twenty-seven Millers in the Sydney telephone book. Or there were, when I got around to ringing every one of them, trying to find you. But the first thing I did was fly down to Sydney, because a number of buses had already left Surfers'. I knew you'd come on a bus and I thought you'd leave on one. I met every incoming bus for weeks, even after your vacation time had ended and I knew you had to be back at work. I was sure you would step off one of them, that the next passenger had to be you. But it never was."

The pain in his voice was too real to doubt, the details of all he'd done so vivid they shamed Carrie even further. The train of circumstances that had worked against both of them meeting again was one of those cruel and merciless ironies of fate that no one could have foreseen.

"I got off the bus at Taree," Carrie explained, the ravages of her painful regret making her voice husky. "I didn't want to go straight home. I knew Mum would ask about you, because I'd rung to say I was staying on. And I wasn't ready to talk. It was all too raw, too...shaming. And then, about a week later, a group of women I'd met offered me a lift back to Sydney in their car."

"Oh, Carrie, Carrie..." He wrapped her in his arms and hugged her tightly to him. "You had nothing to be ashamed of...nothing... And I tried so hard to find you... Everything I could think of. I used to drive around the western suburbs on weekends, hoping I might spot you somewhere. I asked after you at countless restaurants. I cursed myself a thousand times for not asking more about your life instead of talking endlessly about mine."

"I wanted to hear about yours, Dominic. Mine was so narrow and ordinary. You opened a new world to me."

"An empty world...without you, Carrie."

And he kissed her like a starving man, as though time was still an enemy, and he must take what he could to fill the emptiness lest a future of plenty was only a mirage that might disappear at any moment. Carrie responded with equal passion, wanting to reassure him that she was his to have and always would be from this moment on.

"I'm sorry, Dominic," she said softly. "Sorry for all the pain I've put us both through. Because I did love you. I never stopped loving you. If only I had stayed long enough to—"

"Don't blame yourself, Carrie," he cut in with a fervour that swept away any guilt on her part. "I was so blind not to see how the situation could affect you.

What I was used to...was not for you. Nor for me, either. Although it took your leaving to open my eyes to that. Too late," he murmured regretfully.

"We have the rest of our lives," she reminded him hopefully.

His face relaxed into happy relief. "Yes, thank God! And I never thought I'd ever thank God for someone being sick, but I have, Carrie. For the sickness that brought you back to me...even though it struck horror in me at the time."

She reached up and stroked his cheek in apologetic appeal. "I'm sorry about your wife, Dominic. I didn't know about Sandra and how she died until Mrs. Coombe told me today."

He frowned.

"When she brought your guitar, I asked her," Carrie explained quickly. "I didn't know whether you were still married or not and..."

"Oh, Carrie!" Anguish twisted across his face. "Forgive me, darling. It never even occurred to me that you didn't know. Even this morning when you asked about Alyson..."

"There was a photograph of her in the newspaper, and a caption saying she was getting a divorce and marrying some other man. I thought you were free, Dominic. And that's when I called you...."

He shut his eyes tight. His jaw clenched. "My God! Do you mean to say that all my future happiness was bound up in the fluke chance of your seeing a photograph of Alyson in a newspaper?"

"Just for once, God was on our side," Carrie whispered, hoping Dominic would forgive her worst mistake as easily as he had forgiven the rest. "There's something more I've got to tell you, Dominic."

He slowly opened his eyes, looking at her with fierce resolution. "Nothing will ever separate us again, Carrie. Nothing that you or I or anyone can say will make any difference to that. I want you to marry me. Promise me now that you will. I couldn't bear to have anything more come between us. I don't care what it is you have on your mind. Say you'll marry me."

His intense forcefulness on the point swept the last of Carrie's fears away. Love and happiness billowed from her heart and radiated in her whole face. "I will. Whenever you say. I want very much to be your wife, Dominic, and share our lives together. And there's something else we share, too."

"What's that?"

"Our son."

She searched his eyes anxiously, but there was not the slightest shadow on the joy that spilled into them. And the smile that had started when she had accepted his proposal of marriage widened to a huge grin.

"So Danny *is* mine," he said with an expression of glorious satisfaction. "I felt so sure of it."

"You had it right that day we took him to your school," Carrie rushed out. "I don't know what went wrong with the precautions we took, but there was no other man, Dominic. I was afraid of what you might do if I admitted Danny was yours. I thought you were married to Alyson and—"

He threw back his head and laughed, then picked Carrie up and twirled her around as though she were a child. Although when he gathered her in his arms he quickly reminded her that she was very much a woman.

"So he *was* premature," he said exultantly. "And when you came to me asking for help to get *your* baby back from the welfare people, it was really *my* son you were asking me to help.''

''Yes, I'm sorry, Dominic.''

His eyes laughed away any concern. ''Carrie Miller, you have a hide!''

''If there had been any other way, I would have done it. I knew I was taking a high-risk step, but I was desperate, Dominic. Truly desperate.''

''You'll never be that way again, Carrie,'' he assured her. He suddenly chuckled. ''As to it being a high-risk step for you, let me tell you, I've been taking a few high-risk steps myself in my desperation to keep you in my life since that day you walked back into it. I guess luck had to fall my way sooner or later. And it did!''

She couldn't tell him she knew about the apartment and the decorating. She had given her word to Mrs. Coombe and Gina. But she loved him all the more for every step he had taken to ensure she would end up where she belonged. With him.

''You do like Danny, don't you?'' she asked anxiously.

''I love him.''

There was nothing halfhearted about that response. ''He's got your eyes,'' Carrie said ruefully.

''And my voice,'' Dominic added proudly, then laughed in sheer pleasure. ''I was dying for you to admit it last night. When you didn't, I thought it meant I had to prove a lot more to you.''

''I almost died, too. When Danny started singing. I just thought it was better to wait . . . to see.''

''He likes me, Carrie.''

She laughed. ''Of course he does! How could he not? His first question this morning was about you. Whether you were coming tonight.''

"He's a great kid."

"Mmm...very like his father."

"When do we tell him?"

"Tonight, if you like. But it might be better to get him used to the idea of you first," she added worriedly. Danny was bound to ask some touchy questions that would take some delicate answering. Even so, she did not want to deny Dominic anything now.

"You're right. We'll approach it slowly," he agreed, immediately appreciating that some finesse was required. Then he sighed with huge satisfaction. "Tonight is the best night of my life. You...and Danny as well. When do you expect him home, Carrie?"

"Seven o'clock."

"Then we've got some time to fill, and there's still a lot I want to know about you. Why you left home and went to Fiji, what happened to your mother and the rest of your family...so much that I don't know."

They sat on the chesterfield, Carrie half-sprawled across Dominic's lap so that he could stroke her hair and kiss her when he wanted to.

She told him that she barely remembered her real father, who had died when she was six years old. They had lived in Perth then. When her mother had remarried, they had moved right across Australia to Sydney to start a new life, and she had lost all contact with her father's family. Her mother had been an English immigrant so she had no family of her own in Australia. When her second marriage ended in divorce, she was settled here and had no reason to return to Perth. She had supported Carrie through her pregnancy and minded Danny while Carrie finished her apprenticeship as a chef. Soon after that she had suffered a stroke. It had killed her.

"That must have been a dreadful shock to you... your mother going so suddenly," Dominic murmured sympathetically.

"She left an awful hole in our lives... mine and Danny's," Carrie acknowledged sadly. "I felt then that I couldn't stay in Sydney. It was too hard, having no one but Danny and knowing you were living so close, just across the city. The temptation to contact you was worse than ever. I thought the only way I could get on with my own life, without you haunting me all the time, was to get right away."

"So you went to Fiji," he said, a rueful irony in his eyes. "I didn't think of looking for you there, Carrie. Although I've actually been there on vacation twice in the last eight years."

"I was trying to forget you, Dominic." She sighed and stroked his cheek, her eyes reflecting his rueful irony. "But I never did. And when I came back, it wasn't only for Danny's education. Underneath it all, I wanted to be near you again."

The green eyes filled with poignant memories as she studied the face she loved so dearly. "In the song Danny sang for you, 'Isa Lei,' there's a line—'Every moment my heart for you is yearning'—and that was how I always felt, Dominic."

"So did I," he murmured, and kissed her with all the sweetness of knowing that the long yearning had finally come to an end.

They were supremely content just to hold one another and be together, enjoying the wonderful freedom of total trust and love, knowing they could say anything or do anything and it wouldn't be misconstrued or rejected. Time flew by and they were so immersed in each other that the buzzer announcing Mrs. Coombe's arrival with Danny startled them. But their response was quick and full of joyful anticipation. Dominic stood in the lobby with Carrie, his arm around her in an extremely possessive fashion as they waited to greet their son and his minder.

The lift doors opened.

"Dom!" Danny shrieked in surprised pleasure.

"If it's okay with you, Danny, I think we could make that Dad," Dominic declared. "Your mother has just consented to marry me." He lifted brilliant blue eyes to his secretary. "You may be the first to congratulate us, Mrs. Coombe."

"My hearty congratulations, Mr. Savage!" she enthused, stepping forward to shake Dominic's hand. Then she clasped Carrie's, her grey eyes glinting with approval.

"Does this mean you're going to be my father for always?" Danny asked, almost jumping out of his skin with excitement.

"Absolutely," Dominic confirmed. "You're stuck with me for life, Danny."

"That's great! I always wanted a dad. You've done real good, Mum."

Carrie had to laugh. "Thank you, Danny." Dominic had handled the matter beautifully, just as he handled everything beautifully. Later on, after their relationship was cemented, would be time enough to reveal that Dominic was Danny's real father. Let the trust between them build. . . .

"Very good, indeed!" Mrs. Coombe agreed, beaming approval at all of them. "I must be going now. A happy night to all of you."

"Thank you, Mrs. Coombe," they chorused in joyful unison.

She stepped into the lift, and to Carrie's eyes she seemed to emanate an aura of bright benevolence. Not a dragon, Carrie thought. Nor a sergeant-major. Nor even a good watchdog. A fairy godmother, that was what she was, underneath all the iron-plated armour.

Then the doors closed on her.

But she left behind the magic.

"Well," said Dominic. "I brought my guitar, Danny. How about a song?"

"Yes, sir!" Danny yelled and dived past them into the living room as he spied the guitar case.

Dominic's arm tightened around Carrie's shoulders as they followed their son. "Shall we try the Hallelujah Chorus?" he mused softly to her.

"Can you play it on guitar?"

"No. But it's singing in my heart."

"In mine, too."

"How would you like a honeymoon in Fiji?"

"Nanuya Bay?"

"Absolutely."

"That would be the loveliest place in the world."

"That's where your friends are. We'll go there often, Carrie."

They smiled at each other, knowing that nothing on earth would ever separate them again. Their togetherness was complete.

GUILTY PASSION
Jacqueline Baird

CHAPTER ONE

REBECCA cast a look around the lecture theatre, before taking her seat in the front row, beside her boss. It was almost full. 'You were right, Rupert, it does seem to be popular,' she conceded, smiling at the man sitting next to her.

'Aren't I always?' he grinned. 'Shh. Here he comes.'

She returned his grin. Rebecca had come to the anthropological lecture only because Rupert had insisted. Rupert and his wife Mary had been students together with Benedict Maxwell, tonight's speaker.

'Good evening, ladies and gentlemen, I am flattered by your presence here tonight and I trust my experiences and discoveries of the past several years will live up to your expectations. If I become too boring you have my permission to walk out.'

Boring! The sound of his voice alone was mesmerising. Rebecca's head shot up, her startled glance colliding with dark, golden-flecked eyes that held her gaze for an instant before flicking to her companion. The man possessed a sexual magnetism that ignited a totally unexpected feminine response deep inside her. The breath caught in her throat, her heart missed a beat; nothing like this had ever happened to her before. Her large violet eyes widened to their fullest extent, her lips parted in an astonished moue. She knew him. It was insane—she had never met the man before—but deep down in some secret part of her she recognised him. Everything about him seemed so familiar...

5

Common sense told her she was being ridiculous but never in her life had she reacted so physically to a man. A slow heat suffused her body, she shook her small head in an instinctive gesture of denial, but it was futile as she felt herself being drawn under the spell of the man's vibrant personality.

He held centre stage with an ease and command few men possessed. He was tall, probably about six feet, superbly built with wide shoulders and a broad chest, tapering to a neat waist and long muscular legs; not an ounce of flab marred his large frame—the physique beneath the tweed jacket and expensive trousers was that of a man in peak condition.

Rebecca listened, entranced, to his tale of adventure and hardship. Six years ago he had set off on an expedition through the Amazon jungle; twelve months later he was reported dead by his guide and porters. They had seen him swept down the river and over a waterfall; no man could have survived the accident. But miraculously he had returned to civilisation a year ago, after having spent four years living and studying a hitherto unknown tribe of Indians. His book on his exploits was to be published the following week, and Rebecca had no doubt it would capture the imagination of a much larger public than the usual anthropological studies.

If he wrote half as well as he told a story, there could be no doubt about it, she thought, captivated, and hanging on to his every word. He painted pictures with his voice, his expressive features, a mere twist of his sensuous lips highlighting a point he wanted to make.

Little was known of him, but now he had appeared on the academic scene and shaken it to the core. Some of the more conservative anthropologists had a hard time hiding their jealousy. But Benedict Maxwell, ignoring the criticism, was embarking on a round of public lectures to keep the plight of the South American Indians

and the devastation of the rain forests alive in the eyes
of the world, and hopefully the world leaders would be
forced to find a solution to the ever-increasing problem.

Rebecca was a hundred per cent in favour of his ideals,
but, even if she had not been, just watching him would
have convinced her.

His hair was black and rather long, a few wayward
curls curving over the collar of his jacket. Taking his
features one by one, he was not strictly handsome. His
broad forehead, and black, rather bushy eyebrows, gave
his face a rather sinister slant, along with a rather large
crooked nose, and a hard square jaw. The overall impression was one of power and determination. But his
eyes were truly beautiful...

Rebecca had never known two hours pass so quickly,
and she was on her feet and applauding loudly when he
finally concluded his lecture. For a second his golden-
brown eyes rested on her and fancifully she was reminded of some large jungle hunting cat, but then a
frown marred his rugged face and the moment was gone.

She turned excitedly to Rupert. 'He was brilliant, absolutely brilliant.'

Rupert laughed. He was a big rumpled-looking man
with a shaggy mane of grey hair that reinforced the impression. When her father was ill Rupert had employed
her as his research assistant. Then, when her Dad had
died some months ago and she had sold the family home,
she had become Rupert and Mary's lodger.

He reached out and slung a casual arm around her
slender shoulders. 'You too.' He shook his large head.
'I don't know... first Mary went into raptures when she
heard Ben was coming, and now it looks as if you're
smitten as well.'

Rebecca laughed, and, tossing her head in a vain attempt to disperse the giddy feeling Benedict Maxwell had
aroused in her, she teased, 'Shame on you, Rupert, you

know Mary has eyes for no one but you, and of course tiny Jonathan.'

'Yes.' A satisfied smile creased Rupert's face, and Rebecca knew why. His wife had given birth to a baby boy a week ago, their first child after ten years of marriage. Mother and child had returned home only yesterday. 'Look, would you mind going to the party at the Chancellor's rooms and making my excuses? I'll call in later. First, I want to check on Mary.'

'Of course, Rupert. Give them my love,' she smiled.

Still smiling, Rebecca walked across the quadrangle and made her way to the administration block. She stopped outside the Chancellor's door then turned quickly and headed for the ladies' toilet. The nervous flutter in her stomach she put down to indigestion, but in her heart she knew she was only lying to herself—the thought of meeting Benedict Maxwell face to face filled her with a trembling excitement she had never experienced before. Pull yourself together, my girl, she told herself, and, placing her handbag on the washbasin, she studied her reflection in the mirror above.

Was that flushed, sparkling-eyed girl really her? She was behaving like a fool. Determinedly she splashed cool water on her face and dabbed it dry, and, opening her bag, she carefully repaired her make-up—what little there was of it. A touch more mascara on her long, thick lashes, a fresh covering of pink gloss to her full lips, and with a sigh she viewed the result.

It was hopeless. She was educated, intelligent and good at her job as a researcher for Professor Rupert Bart, a senior lecturer in law—she was a match for any man. Unfortunately, at five feet tall, with large pansy eyes, and long black hair that, although pinned up in a chignon, had a nasty tendency to curl, plus a shape that was a little too curvaceous, she looked like a seventeen-year-old Lolita! She winced at the thought, an ugly memory shadowing her eyes.

She sighed; even the severely cut straight blue silk shift could not disguise the fullness of her breasts, the feminine curve of her hips. The great man would never notice her. Even if he did, he would never take her seriously on sight. No man ever had...

Rebecca stood in one corner of the lavishly furnished room and listened to the conversations going on around her with half an ear, intensely aware of the man who held court in the middle of the room, surrounded by some of the best brains in Oxford. She had given Rupert's apologies to the Chancellor, and could not help noticing that the man's secretary, Fiona Grieves, a tall redhead, had latched on to the guest of honour and was clinging to his arm like a limpet.

Chancellor Foster had casually introduced Rebecca to Benedict Maxwell, and as she had stood tongue-tied he had murmured a polite response, and with a purely social smile that had not reached his eyes—in fact he had looked almost disapproving—he had continued his conversation with Fiona. Rebecca, hurt at his offhand manner, quietly slipped into the background, but from her relative seclusion she feasted her eyes on the man of her dreams.

'Rebecca, it is not like you to be hiding in a corner—come and let me introduce you to Benedict.'

She jumped at the sound of Rupert's voice and, placing her glass on the window-sill beside her, she reluctantly walked the few paces to where he was standing with Benedict, Fiona and the Chancellor. She felt a complete fool. She opened her mouth to say they had already been introduced, but Rupert cut in.

Flinging his arm around her shoulder and drawing her into the little circle, he said, 'This is Rebecca, my personal assistant. You remember old Bruiser, Ben? Well, this is his daughter, and just as clever as the old man was.'

'Bruiser? Rupert!' she admonished lightly, while wishing the ground would open and swallow her up. Why Benedict Maxwell affected her so strangely, she had no idea, and she wasn't sure she liked the feeling.

Rupert laughed. 'Sorry, pet, it was our nickname for him. Blacket-Green equals Bruiser!'

She managed to smile, until Benedict Maxwell turned and, freeing his arm from Fiona, fixed his brilliant leonine eyes on Rebecca.

'The late Professor Blacket-Green's daughter?' Surprise and some other emotion she did not recognise coloured his voice as he questioned her.

'You knew my father?' she asked quietly.

'I attended a few of his lectures. He died recently, I believe.' His hooded lids half closed, masking his dark eyes as he added, 'My condolences. I know what it feels like to lose someone you love.'

She recognised the sympathy in his deep, melodious tone, and her earlier apprehension vanished; she was completely captivated, and it showed as she smiled up at his ruggedly attractive face.

'Thank you.'

His dark gaze slid over her from head to toe, and there was no mistaking the masculine interest in his scrutiny. She did not question why he had barely noticed her when they were first introduced, but basked in his obvious male appreciation.

The rest of the evening passed in a dream for Rebecca. Benedict insisted on getting her a glass of champagne, and keeping her by his side, a hand placed casually on her slender shoulders. The conversation was lively and informative, and eventually light-hearted as Rupert insisted on showing everyone a photograph of his new son.

'Where is Mary tonight?' Benedict queried.

Whereupon Rupert regaled Benedict with all the technical details of the birth with obvious pride, ending on a joking note, 'But Mary reckons the boy is too young to be deprived of his food source just yet. So my personal, live-in assistant here, who got a double first last year—quite some achievement for such a tich——' he patted Rebecca on the head, much to her fury '—was detailed to look after me, to keep my spirits up. Along with this.' And, lifting a half-full glass of whisky to his lips, he drained it.

'You live with Rupert?' The censorious tone of Benedict's voice was obvious.

'No... Well, yes.' She stumbled over her words in her haste to explain. Did all women feel like this, she wondered, when they met the man of their dreams? She was desperate that this man should have a good opinion of her. 'I mean, I'm lodging with Mary and Rupert. I sold my father's house, and I intend to buy a small apartment, when I decide where I want to live, but in the meantime Mary asked me to stay and help with the baby and everything...' She was babbling, and her voice tailed off as her violet eyes were trapped and held by brilliant gold.

He smiled down into her bemused face. 'I understand, Rebecca.'

She was sure he did; she felt a sensuous longing to reach out and trace the full line of his lips, to feel them against her own. 'Thank you,' she murmured, not really sure what she was thanking him for, or where her erotic fantasies were coming from.

Benedict lifted his hand and gently tilted her chin with one finger. 'It's rather crowded here, and I would very much like to get to know you better, Miss Blacket-Green,' he drawled softly and before she knew what was happening she found herself backed into the corner of the large bay window.

'So, Rebecca, tell me—what does a young girl who hardly looks old enough to have left school intend doing with a first from Oxford? Surely not work as a researcher for old Rupert all your life?' One dark eyebrow rose enquiringly.

To Rebecca's astonishment she found herself telling him all her hopes for the future. 'I had intended to go to Nottingham for a year and get my postgraduate Certificate of Education, and then into teaching. But with Father ill I stayed at home and looked after him until his death six months ago.'

She did not regret it. Instead it had allowed her to accept the fact of his death that much more easily.

'So what are you going to do now?' Benedict asked quietly.

'Well, in September I'm going to complete my education, albeit a year late. Eventually I hope to teach high school history and French.'

'Teaching... not very ambitious for a girl with your——' he drawled the word '—qualificatons.' His lingering glance added a sensuous message—he was not just referring to her academic achievements—while the hand on her shoulder slid around the back of her neck.

She trembled at the warmth of his touch, and went pink with embarrassment, and a flash of anger. It was one of her pet hates when people derided the teaching profession, and somehow she had expected better of Benedict.

'Your attitude surprises me, Mr Maxwell, considering your education.' She knew from Rupert that Benedict had a first in maths as well as a B.A. and a D.Phil. 'I hate the kind of attitude, which seems to be prevalent in our country, that people only go into teaching for lack of any real ambition.' She tilted her head at his urging, and was stung by the gentle amusement infusing the darkness of his rugged features. 'I'm sorry if my

opinions amuse you. But you are not the first person to
suggest I should take up a more lucrative career. The
City, or business. Do you know I was even approached
by Chase Manhattan of New York?' She came to an
abrupt halt, as Benedict laughed out loud.

'Well, well, you are quite a surprise, Rebecca; you look
so cool and controlled when really you're quite a little
firecracker.'

She flushed bright red; his hand still curved her slender
neck and suddenly she lost all her anger, as the caress
of his strong fingers sent shivers of awareness tingling
down her spine. 'I'm sorry, I'm afraid I talk too much.
With all you've seen and done, my aspirations must seem
very boring,' she managed, wondering why her voice
sound so husky.

'Not at all, Rebecca, and I apologise if my earlier
comment offended you. It wasn't meant to. I think
teaching is a very laudable profession, and, as for finding
you boring, you couldn't be more wrong. Everything
about you intrigues me.'

She looked at him uncertainly; he sounded sincere.
The golden-brown eyes darkened, an unmistakable
message in their depths as they lingered on her flushed,
upturned face then very deliberately dropped lower to
where her full breasts thrust taut against the soft silk of
her dress. Her blush deepened and she was more flustered than she had ever been in her life. She raised her
hand to her throat in an unconscious attempt to conceal
the pulse that beat heavily under her skin.

'You will make a wonderful teacher, though I think
you may have problems with the young men.'

'Because I'm small?' she answered resignedly. He had
disappointed her. Rupert was always teasing her with
that fact.

'No, your size is perfect, but you look so young, all
the male students are bound to fall in love with you.'

'I'm twenty-two,' she bristled.

Benedict slowly trailed long fingers back around to her shoulder, and gently squeezed. 'I didn't mean to offend you, Rebecca, but at thirty-four everyone in their twenties appears young to me.' He pulled her tight against his side. 'But not too young... Am I forgiven?' he murmured throatily.

She could not disguise the tremor of awareness that the contact with his hard body aroused in her. Her breast brushed lightly against the fine wool of his jacket and the tightening of her nipples made her catch her breath. Her glance lifted to his face, her eyes wide and wondering, she lifted her hand and placed it on his chest; she could feel the slow, steady thump of his heart beneath her fingertips, but she was unaware of the total intimacy of her gesture, and in that moment she would have forgiven the man murder.

'Yes, oh, yes,' she murmured. One part of her mind was answering his question while another, more primitive part was accepting the vibrant masculine demand in his darkening gaze.

Benedict captured the small hand that lay on his chest, turned it palm-up and, raising it to his lips, planted a soft kiss in the middle of her palm. 'I think we understand each other, you and I...'

She was captivated, completely enthralled, her violet eyes darkened to deep purple, her lips parted seductively. She felt as though she was drowning in the dark golden depths of his eyes.

'Now is not the time or the place, Rebecca. Dinner tomorrow night. I'll call for you at seven.'

She loved the sound of her name rolling huskily off his tongue. 'Yes,' she whispered, her breathing erratic, as he lowered his dark head and planted another kiss on her softly parted lips.

'Duty calls, I have to circulate.'

Rebecca's circulation had gone berserk at the touch of his lips on hers, the blood flowing through her veins like wildfire.

'Goodnight for now, little one, but don't forget me.' He smiled down into her delicate flushed face. 'Until tomorrow.' His hand dropped from her shoulder, he tapped her chin with one long finger. 'And don't worry, Rebecca, I like my ladies chin-high.' He grinned and winked as he walked away.

How long she stood with a silly grin on her face, she had no idea. It was only when she looked around her that she realised what a spectacle they must have made. She could see the knowing smiles on quite a few female faces, but she didn't care. She had met Benedict for the first time tonight, but already she was in love with him. She knew it with absolute certainty.

'Well, my pet, old Ben has certainly knocked you for six, if your soppy expression is anything to go by.' Rupert's voice brought her back to reality with a jolt.

'Is it so obvious?' she asked quietly, tearing her gaze away from where Benedict stood, once again surrounded by people, to focus on her boss.

'I'm afraid so, little one. But a word of warning. Benedict is not the sort of man you should cut your milk-teeth on.'

'I'm not a baby, I do know about sex.' She grinned at Rupert. 'Benedict is taking me to dinner tomorrow night.' Just saying the words out loud thrilled her to the core.

'Ah-ah. Before you do anything foolish, girl, I suggest you have a chat with Mary. She knows Ben better than me. They were good friends as students. He is a very complex man, and, to be brutally frank, I think a bit out of your league.'

'Thanks, friend,' she responded drily. 'You're a great confidence-booster.' She watched as Rupert ran a huge hand through his untidy mass of grey hair, and almost felt sorry for him, he looked so perplexed.

'Oh, hell, Becky, you know what I mean. Just be careful—and now let's get out of here.' He watched her scan the room for the man they had been discussing and when she found him, even Rupert could see that the look that passed between Rebecca and Benedict would have lit coals.

She responded to Benedict's rueful shrug of broad shoulders, and a softly mouthed, 'Tomorrow,' with a brilliant smile and a very determined nod of her lovely head.

Rebecca, with one last lingering glance at Benedict, allowed Rupert to lead her out of the overcrowded room, and down to the quadrangle. Arm in arm, they strolled through the streets of Oxford. Rebecca thought the town had never looked more beautiful. Early June, and the students had almost finished their exams. The old place vibrated with young voices filled with exultation and relief.

The mellowed stone of the great colleges gleamed faintly silver in the fading light, and Rebecca's heart sang with unaccustomed joy. She walked on air for the ten minutes it took to reach the large brown stone terrace that was her temporary home.

Sitting across the table from Mary in the kitchen, her small hands curved around a cup of cocoa, she tried to remain cool in the face of Mary's demand to know what Maxwell's lecture had been like.

'OK, Rebecca,' Mary exclaimed. The older woman drained her cocoa-cup, and replaced it on the table, before fixing Rebecca with gimlet blue eyes. 'Why don't you forget the high ideals to save the world and tell me what really happened?'

Rebecca sat up straight in the chair, a wry smile curving her full lips; was she really so transparent? Even Mary, who was ordinarily completely engrossed in her new role as mother, noticed her emotional upheaval.

'Benedict Maxwell has happened,' she said bluntly—prevarication was not her style.

'Ah! So it's Ben who has turned you from a beautiful woman into a radiant one. I should have guessed. He always did have a disastrous effect on the female of the species, even as a student.'

'I wish I had known him then,' Rebecca mused; the thought of Benedict as a child and young man, all the years he had lived before she had met him, filled her with mixed emotions. Was it jealousy? No, surely not. Just greed; she had an avid desire to know every little thing about the man who had so instantly captured her heart.

'Tell me about him, Mary.' She looked at her companion, and flinched as a horrible thought struck her. Had Mary been one of his women? She was a very pretty lady, tall with brown hair and laughing blue eyes, and the personality to match. Benedict might have been her lover...

'No, he wasn't my boyfriend,' Mary chuckled, accurately reading Rebecca's thoughts. 'But we all went around in the same group. As for telling you about him, I don't know what to say. Apart from exchanging Christmas cards for a few years I've never seen him in the flesh since we left college. He must have changed quite a lot, in the intervening years, from the shy young man I knew.'

'Shy?' Rebecca exclaimed; somehow that was not a trait she would ever have associated with Benedict.

'Yes. Well, perhaps shy is not the right word. Reserved maybe.' A reminiscent smile curved Mary's wide mouth. 'Most of the time, that is, but I remember one occasion, the end of our second-year exams. We were all at a party, and I reckon it was the first and only time Ben got drunk.

He and I talked all night. I know his father died when
he was ten, and within months his mother had married
again, Ben was shunted off to boarding school and by
the time he was twelve he had a baby brother.'

Rebecca's heart ached for the young boy losing his
father and stuck away in a boarding school. Her own
mother had died when she was nine, and she could appreciate the loneliness Benedict must have suffered.

Mary continued, 'He was a very complex young man.
I know he explained his mother's quick remarriage by
saying she was a timid woman who needed the support
of a man. I got the impression he felt a shade guilty
because he was too young to give her what she needed.'
Mary sighed. 'The naïve intensity of youth! The woman
probably wanted a man in her bed... Anyway, apart
from that one evening, Benedict never discussed his personal life again. There's not much else I can tell you,
except I liked him.'

'You've told me quite a lot already. I know you
probably think I've flipped my lid, but just hearing you
talk about him fills me with pleasure.' Rebecca grinned,
her eyes sparkling with mischief. 'I'm seeing him tomorrow night and will carry out my own investigation—
I can hardly wait.'

'I can see it's only his brilliant mind you are interested
in, nothing so crass as his gorgeous body,' Mary teased,
and they both burst out laughing.

When their laughter stopped, Mary reached across the
table and took Rebecca's hand in hers. 'Don't get me
wrong, I know you're a very capable lady, but when it
comes to affairs of the heart you don't have much experience. Benedict is a lot older than you, and I don't
want to see you get hurt. Be very sure it's not just a case
of hero worship, before you do anything stupid.'

Rebecca squeezed Mary's fingers, and, with naïve
honesty, responded, 'I have never felt like this about a

man before. I just know deep down he's the one for me, and if I get hurt, so be it.'

Later, much later, she was to realise the bitter truth of her words.

CHAPTER TWO

REBECCA looked at the jumble of clothes covering her bed, and sighed. Benedict would be here in half an hour, and here she was, still standing virtually naked except for tiny white lace briefs, trying to decide what to wear.

It was her own fault, she thought, a snort of self-disgust escaping her. If she had not spent the best part of the Saturday afternoon washing her hair, doing her nails and wallowing in the bath for hours, reliving in her mind her meeting with Benedict, and fantasising about the evening ahead, she might have had the sense to go out and buy something to wear. Now, she was all made-up—well, made-up for her. A moisturiser was all she needed and a slight touch of mascara on her long lashes, but she was stuck with the rather sparse wardrobe she had acquired as a student, and added to only briefly in the past year.

Finally, she opted for the last garment in her wardrobe. Still in its plastic cover was the rose-coloured silk suit she had bought only days earlier, in anticipation of baby Jonathan's christening. What the hell? she told herself. I can buy something else. And carefully removed it.

The pencil-slim skirt hugged her hips and ended just on her knee. The matching camisole with shoe-string straps prevented her wearing a bra, but one quick glance and modesty had her grabbing the fitted silk short-sleeved jacket and slipping it on. Double-breasted, it fastened with two buttons neatly at her trim waist. She surveyed the whole ensemble, pleased with the result. As long as she kept the jacket on she'd be fine. Quickly she applied the new matching soft pink lip-gloss to her full lips.

She pivoted in front of the cheval-glass, and wished, for the hundredth time, that she were taller, before slipping her feet into moderate-heeled navy sandals. It wouldn't be so bad if she could wear four-inch heels, but the one time she had tried she sprained her ankle.

Still, Benedict had said he liked his ladies chin-high, she consoled herself. She viewed her hair with some misgivings. She had swept it up at each side and held it with two gilt combs, allowing the long black tresses to fall in shining waves down her back. She should have pinned it all up; a more sophisticated image might have helped her look older. She reached for the comb...

The ringing of the doorbell set her heart pounding. Too late now... And, grabbing her lipstick, she shoved it in a small navy clutch-bag, and dashed out of the room.

Careful, she told herself and forced her feet to slow down. She heard the sound of Mary's voice and laughter and the deeper, more earthy tone of Benedict, as they renewed their acquaintance.

She was halfway down the stairs when she caught sight of Benedict; her breath caught in her throat and she almost fell down the last few steps.

He moved quickly across the hall and caught her arm. 'Steady, Rebecca.'

She had the sinking feeling she would never be steady in this man's company in a million years, and for the first time since meeting him the force of her feelings for him scared her.

Tonight he was dressed in an immaculate silver-grey suit, his silk shirt a soft blue. A grey and blue striped tie drew her attention to his strong, tanned throat. Slowly she raised her head, as his eyes roamed hotly over her body and face. 'Hello, Benedict,' was all she could manage, unable to tear her eyes from his.

'You look absolutely beautiful, Rebecca. You must always wear your hair loose for me.' And, raising his other hand, he slid his fingers through the thickness of her hair, pulling a few strands over her shoulder, his long fingers tracing the length down over the soft swell of her breast in an erotic gesture that sent shock waves of pleasure arcing through her body...

'I can see I'm *de trop* here. Have a good time, children.' Mary's voice broke the spell that bound them. 'And don't keep her out all night,' she added to Benedict.

'We will, Mary, and don't worry; unlike her other men friends, I will bring her back safely.'

What other men friends? Rebecca thought, not sure how to take the obvious cynicism in his tone. But, when Benedict encircled her slender waist with one arm to escort her from the house to the waiting car, his touch knocked every sensible thought from her head. She slid into the passenger-seat, and, fighting down the nervous tension that engulfed her, she sank back against the soft leather upholstery. In a way his car surprised her, when she came to her senses enough to notice it was a top-of-the-range Mercedes. Academics in England were not particularly well paid.

'Alone at last.' Benedict grinned as he slid in behind the driving-wheel and started the car. 'I thought my days of courting in a car were long over, but I have a horrible suspicion that, as long as you live with Rupert and Mary, that will be my fate.' He cast her a sidelong glance, his golden-brown eyes sparkling merrily. 'Unless I can persuade you to move in with me,' he teased.

'I might if I knew where you lived,' Rebecca said lightly; she knew he was only flirting but she could not help her pulse racing at the thought of sharing a home, a bed, with this gorgeous man by her side.

'I have a hut in the Amazonian rain forest or a place in London. Which would you prefer?'

She chuckled. 'Guess.'

Benedict's light-hearted banter set the tone for the rest of the evening. They drove out of Oxford to a small roadside inn that looked like something from a picture-postcard—thatch-roofed and old oak beams.

Over a quite simple meal of steak and salad followed by cheese and biscuits Rebecca finally relaxed. The bottle of fine Bordeaux wine helped. It was amazing how much they had in common, she thought wonderingly, as the conversation moved from theatre, to music, to politics, and, at Rebecca's insistence, to Benedict's time in the jungle. He made her laugh with his anecdotes but she knew it had not been easy for him. He had been badly injured when the Indians found him, and it had taken over a year before he had recovered his health and then another three before making his seemingly miraculous return to civilisation.

'I am an honorary member of the tribe, and have my own hut; perhaps I can tempt you to share it with me?' he grinned.

'Surely the chief gave you his daughter? Isn't that what usually happens?' she prompted teasingly.

'The offer was made. Unfortunately all the unmarried girls were barely thirteen and somehow I couldn't bring myself to have sex with a child. I adopted a celibate lifestyle.' His gaze darkened perceptibly and she gasped at the expression in his eyes. 'But, since meeting you, that's about to change. You don't strike me as the sort of woman to deny herself the pleasures of the flesh,' he decided sensuously.

'Coffee, sir.' The waiter broke the tension that arced between them.

Rebecca did not know whether to be flattered or insulted by his comment, and to hide her disquiet she blurted the first thing that came into her head. 'The poor

man probably thinks you're some kind of paedophile,'
she gibed. 'Or mad, Benedict.'

His gaze was fixed on her beautiful face, and slowly
he reached across the table and took her small hand in
his much larger one, his thumb gently stroking the palm
of her hand. 'I am mad—mad about you. I love to hear
you say my name in that breathless tone.' He lifted her
hand and pressed a kiss on the pulse that beat rapidly
in her wrist. She shivered and would have pulled her
hand free, suddenly embarrassed—there were other
people around. 'No, Rebecca, don't back off now; your
honesty was one of the first things I noticed about you.'
He tightened his grip. 'You know what's happening between us, don't you?' he demanded hardly.

Rebecca swallowed the lump that formed in her throat,
almost choked by her own emotions. It was not just her,
her heart sang. He felt it too, this familiarity, this secret
knowledge of each other. She tried to tell herself it was
too quick—love at first sight was a myth—but still she
murmured softly, 'Yes, oh, yes.' Her violet eyes, wide
and full of longing, searched his rugged features, and
the desire she saw in his told her all she needed to know.

'If you keep looking at me like that, Rebecca, I'm
going to drag you out of here by that magnificent hair
and I doubt if we'll make it past the car park.'

She flushed bright red and hastily looked down at the
table. 'I'm sorry, it's... I don't know.' And, bravely
raising her head, she said, 'I've never felt this way
before.' She was incapable of dissembling.

'I want to believe that, Rebecca. God, how I want to
believe that.' For a second she imagined she saw shock
in his eyes but she must have been mistaken, as he slowly
shook his dark head. 'But an intelligent, beautiful
woman like you must have had many admirers. Is there
anyone now I should know about?'

'No, Benedict, not now, not ever, only you.'

Abruptly he dropped her hand and sat back in his chair, his eyes narrowing speculatively. 'I find that hard to believe but I'll take your word for it.' He paused. 'For the moment.'

Rebecca did not understand what he meant, but before she could ask he had beckoned the waiter. 'Let's get out of here; suddenly the place seems too crowded.' Passing a bundle of notes to the waiter, he stood up, and held out a hand to Rebecca.

Back once more in the car, Benedict turned towards her, sliding one long arm around her slender shoulders, then he lowered his dark head and she knew he was going to kiss her. 'I want you,' he murmured against her lips, before covering her mouth with his own.

She trembled in his arms, the heat of his taut body engulfing her, the pressure of his mouth on hers almost painful in its intensity, as he kissed her hard and long. The force of his passion at first surprised then swamped her. She responded with all the fervour of a young heart awakening to love. When his hand slid inside her jacket and then eased down her camisole, she tensed, wary at the intimacy, but as his hand cupped her breast, his thumb teasing the hardening peak, an intoxication she had never dreamed of flooded through her slender body.

'Benedict,' she whimpered as his head dropped lower and his mouth covered the madly beating pulse in her throat, while his hand continued to caress her burgeoning breast.

She was aflame with a need, a hunger, she could not control, did not want to. The blood pulsed through her veins like wildfire. She raised her arms around his shoulders, her small hand burrowed into the silky strands of his black hair, holding him to her. She felt no shame; surely this was what she was born for...

Benedict groaned and slowly raised his head; carefully he eased her away from him and, with hands that shook, he straightened her clothing. 'God, Rebecca, I almost took you in the car park after all. You have a devastating effect on me, little one.'

'I'm glad,' she whispered fiercely, still aching for his caress, his kisses. 'I think I'm falling in love with you, and it would be terrible if it was all one-sided.' She tried to laugh, knowing she had told him more than she should.

Benedict cupped her small face between his palms. His golden-brown eyes burned into hers. 'It's no joke, Rebecca. I feel the same as you do, but here is not the place to show you.' He pressed a swift kiss on her swollen lips, before he let her go and turned to face the front. 'I'd better get you home before Rupert sends out a search party. But make no mistake, Rebecca, this is just the beginning for you and me. I promise.'

They drove back to Oxford in a companionable silence. Benedict accepted her invitation for coffee, but to her chagrin Rupert joined them. Still, she consoled herself, Benedict had said it was just the beginning and she believed him. Later, when he left, she walked to his car with him. Surely he would ask to see her again; he must . . . she thought furiously, and she had no idea how expressive her small face was as she murmured, 'Goodnight, Benedict,' knowing she could delay him no longer.

'If you keep looking at me like that, Rebecca, I will be tempted to bundle you in the car, and take you back to London with me,' he teased.

'I wish you would,' she joked, half seriously.

He pulled her into his arms, and, bending his head, kissed her long and hard. 'I'm lecturing on Monday at UCL, but I will be in touch.'

By the following Wednesday Rebecca's sense of euphoria was fading fast. She had hardly been out of the house, but Benedict had not called. Finally, at Mary's urging, she agreed to go to the local historical society's monthly meeting. She sat through the talk and film show, only half aware of what was going on, but worse, when she returned home, Mary met her with a wry smile. Benedict had called.

'Oh, no. I knew I should have stayed in.'

'Rubbish, girl. He said to tell you he'd called and...'

'And what?' Rebecca demanded, unable to stand the suspense.

'I've invited him to stay the weekend. He will be arriving Saturday, but he'll call tomorrow night to confirm when.'

Rebecca flung herself on Mary. 'You darling.'

On Thursday night Rebecca waited by the phone. When it finally rang she was filled with an unaccountable nervousness.

'The Bart residence,' she answered, hoping, after a few false alarms, that this call would be Benedict.

'Rebecca. I'm honoured, I've finally caught you in. What happened? Have you worn out the young beaux of Oxford?' he drawled mockingly.

'Benedict,' she said, hurt he could imagine she would dream of going out with anyone else. For a horrifying moment the thought crossed her mind; perhaps Benedict had heard about her brief twenty-four hours of notoriety years ago. No, he couldn't possibly—he had not even been in the country at the time. Anyway, she could explain the unfortunate episode. Benedict would understand, but not yet. She wanted nothing to mar her newfound love. Hastily she began explaining the reason for her absence the night before, while telling herself she was worrying unnecessarily.

'It's all right, Rebecca, I believe you, but to get down to business. I'll be with you at about three on Saturday afternoon. OK?'

'Oh, yes!' she breathed happily, and dismissed the odd feeling that he did not believe her as so much nonsense.

* * *

June gave way to July and Rebecca would have given way to Benedict if he had asked her... But he hadn't.

She stood looking out of the window of the living-room, waiting for him to arrive. She spoke to him frequently on the telephone and for the past three weekends he had returned to Oxford and stayed with her, and Mary, Rupert and baby Jonathan... Perhaps that was the problem.

A secret smile curved her full lips, but not any more... This weekend she had the house to herself. Rupert had taken the family to his parents in Devon to show off the new grandson.

Rebecca could barely control her excitement. She loved Benedict and she was almost sure he loved her. They'd shared intimate dinners, gone to concerts, spent one glorious Sunday sailing up the river, and the passionate kisses they exchanged each time he arrived and departed left her weak at the knees and longing for more.

She smoothed her damp palms over her slim hips. They would be alone, completely alone, for two whole days... Her heartbeat raced at the thought, then leapt as she saw his car draw up at the door. She ran through the hall, opened the door, and flung herself into his arms.

'Now, that is what I call a welcome!' Benedict growled, before lowering his dark head and kissing her firmly on the mouth.

He ended the kiss far too soon for Rebecca, and as he eased her away from him his eyes narrowed in knowing amusement. 'What have I done to deserve this passionate welcome, little one?'

She searched his rugged face with hungry eyes, drinking in the sight of him. 'Nothing,' she murmured in response, 'but I've missed you.'

'I know the feeling,' he said quietly. 'But how about letting me get in the door? Rupert, man of letters that he is, will not appreciate a couple making love on his doorstep,' he drawled mockingly.

'He won't know.' She couldn't wait to tell him. 'We have the house to ourselves; they've gone to his parents for the weekend.' She grinned broadly and, grabbing Benedict's arm, led him into the hall. She closed the door behind her and turned towards him. 'Now I've caught you,' she teased, and, standing on tiptoe, flung her arms around his neck.

'Is that what you want?' His large tanned hands spanned her narrow waist, and lifted her so her face was on a level with his. 'To catch me? Or is this more to your liking?' And, swinging her high over his broad shoulders in a fireman's lift, he strode through the open door into the living-room.

She screamed, 'Benedict, put me down!' With her head hanging down his back and his strong arms wrapped firmly round her thighs, she was powerless to break free. 'You'll drop me.'

'I wouldn't dream of it, my darling girl,' he declared with a chuckle, then she was falling in a helpless bundle on to the large shabby leather sofa.

She lay on her back, her legs splayed apart, her hair a tumbled mass of black silk falling around her face and over her shoulders. She had no idea how seductive she looked: her brief white shorts barely covered her hips, the knitted T-shirt she was wearing had ridden up and left a teasing glimpse of naked midriff. Laughing, she stared up at Benedict. 'I think you've spent too long with the natives, my man.' She chuckled, 'You Tarzan, me Jane,' her wide pansy eyes, lit with laughter, clashing with his.

His golden gaze glittered over the vivid flush in her cheeks, the unconsciously wanton posture of her lovely body. A hint of derision flashed in the darkening depths, as Benedict bent over her and with one hand stroked the

hair from her face. 'Are you trying to pretend a tiny
beauty like you has never been picked up by a man
before?'

The smile left her face. She had the oddest impression
he was not referring to being bodily lifted, but something else entirely. 'My father used to,' she responded
quietly.

He was towering over her, his strong legs encased in
form-fitting black jeans that revealed the musculature
of his thighs, and more. Her blush deepened, and she
hastily raised her eyes to his broad chest, the thick curling
body hair visible where he had left the top three buttons
of his checked shirt unfastened.

Rebecca swallowed hard, her pulse racing, suddenly
aware of their complete privacy. She stirred uneasily on
the sofa, and began to rise.

'No. Stay where you are,' Benedict commanded, and,
placing a hand on the top of her thigh, he nudged her
slightly as he lowered himself down beside her. 'What
did you say earlier about our having the house to ourselves?' he husked throatily, and, placing one hand on
the back of the sofa, with the other he gently traced the
line of her mouth.

Her lips parted of their own volition and lazily she
reached slender arms up around his neck. God, how she
loved him! she thought, mesmerised by the dark gleam
in his wonderful eyes. The tantalising male scent of him
filled her nostrils, and she wanted nothing more in this
life than to lose herself in the warmth, the strength of
his virile male body.

With the pad of one long finger he gently rubbed the
inside of her bottom lip, his piercing gaze holding her
captive. 'I want you, Rebecca, and I think you want
me.'

'Oh, Benedict. I do, I do.' She had no thought of
denying him.

'Do you love me, Rebecca? Really love me?'

A stray beam of sunlight slanted across his darkly tanned face, touching his black hair with gold, like a halo around his proud head, and for a moment masking the expression in his eyes. He looked like a Greek god to Rebecca; how could she help but love him?

'I love you, Benedict, I feel as though I always have, and I know I always will,' she told him.

His head swooped down and his mouth found hers. She whimpered as his teeth nibbled her lips, teasing, then suddenly, as she arched against him, her fingers burrowing in the thick dark hair that curled the nape of his neck, he groaned, his strong arms wrapping her tightly to his hard frame, as he deepened the kiss, his tongue probing the hot, dark secrets of her mouth with a greedy passion.

Abruptly he broke the kiss, and straightened up; with one hand on the soft curve of her breast he held her down on the sofa. Rebecca smiled up at him dazedly, her eyes like twin stars in the perfect oval of her flushed face. The smile faded, as she surprised an arrested expression on his rugged face.

'You, my dear, are dynamite—a real firecracker—and if I don't get away from here soon I'm liable to do something we may both regret.'

'I won't regret anything, Benedict, I promise.' And she raised a small hand, and did what she had been aching to do for weeks: trailed her fingers down his strong throat, and inside his open shirt, stroking over a hard male nipple buried in soft, silky hair.

'Now, I wonder how many men you've said that to?' He grasped her wrist and pulled her hand free.

'None. Only you.' Was he jealous, she wondered, or was it something else? She wished he would not talk like that, as though he doubted her. She shivered . . . Someone walked over her grave . . .

'Sit up, make yourself decent, if that's possible.'

'I don't think I liked that crack,' she muttered, sitting up and decorously tugging her T-shirt down.

Benedict did not respond; instead he put his hand in his back pocket, and drew out a small jeweller's box. His eyes were half closed and his thick, curling lashes almost brushed his cheek as he studied the box in his hand. 'This is something that belongs to you, Rebecca. I think you should have it before we go any further.'

Rebecca's heart slammed against her chest, her hand trembled, as she reached out. She lifted moisture-filled eyes to Benedict's face but he avoided her look. This wonderful man, who had braved all sorts of hardship in the Amazon, was shy. His vulnerability touched her, and a great rush of love almost caused her pain.

He placed the small red box in her outstretched hand, and slowly she opened the lid. It was exquisite—a deep violet-red stone surrounded with tiny diamonds.

'It's beautiful, Benedict, and I'm the luckiest girl in the whole world. Put it on for me.' And, holding out her left hand, she trembled as he slid the small ring on her finger.

'You like it?' he asked, still avoiding her eyes.

'I love it, the same way I love you, Benedict.'

'That figures,' he laughed, but somehow the sound was harsh.

Poor man, he really is nervous, she thought and, pushing her way on to his knee, she curled up in his lap. She could sense the tension in him, and, wrapping one arm around his neck, she extended her other arm, her fingers splayed, the better to admire her engagement ring. 'I love rubies.' She sighed her contentment.

'It's a garnet,' he corrected her flatly.

'Whatever,' she whispered; at last confident of his love, she planted a soft kiss on the strong brown column of his throat. 'I'll treasure it all our married life,' she mouthed against his satin-smooth skin.

Benedict murmured, 'I'm sure you will.' But she never heard the sarcasm in his voice as, tilting her chin with one long finger, he kissed her lightly on the lips. 'I'm sorry, Rebecca, but I can't stop. I only called down today to give you the ring. I have to go straight back to London; I'm appearing on a television chat show this evening.'

His news dimmed the happiness in her eyes. 'But what about us? Our engagement day and you're going to leave me. At the very least we should have a drink to celebrate.' She couldn't hide her disappointment.

'No, sorry, I'm driving.' Benedict lifted her off his lap, plonked her back on the sofa, and stood up.

'But we have tons to discuss, like a date for the wedding.' Just saying the words made Rebecca smile. So maybe they couldn't be together straight away, but they had all the time in the world, she realised. They would be man and wife. She was so happy; all her wildest dreams had come true.

'I will only be in England until the end of August, then I have to be in New York. Perhaps...' He hesitated.

With a radiant face she jumped up, not letting him finish the sentence. 'It only takes a couple of weeks to arrange a wedding and then I could come to America with you.'

Some expression in his eyes made her heart miss a beat.

'That's not a bad idea, but there are quite a few other considerations. I'll think about it and we can discuss it next week. There's no hurry, and I'm sure you're a great little organiser; whatever we decide, I have no doubt you will manage,' he drawled mockingly.

Rebecca smiled at his teasing, never registering the mockery. 'Whatever you say,' she sighed happily. She looked at the ring sparkling on her finger and all it represented: a glowing future with the man she loved. Nothing could dent her euphoria.

Rebecca wiped her sweaty palms on her thighs; she had acted on impulse, rushing up to London on a Thursday, hoping to see Benedict. She could not wait till Saturday; she needed reassurance. Sometimes she had to pinch herself to make sure her new-found happiness was true, but this morning she had awakened with a premonition of doom that nothing could dispel.

As the taxi trundled through the London streets she perched on the edge of the seat, her hands tightly clasped to stop them trembling. She was nervous, her stomach full of butterflies. It was stupid, she knew, but she couldn't help herself. She looked at the small diamond ring on the third finger of her left hand, and took a deep, calming breath.

She had come to London shopping—at least that was her excuse. Since their engagement, three weeks ago, she had seen Benedict every weekend, and he regularly telephoned, but somehow they never seemed to get round to discussing a wedding date.

'Here we are, miss.' The taxi driver's voice startled her, and, sitting up straight, she fumbled in her purse for the money he requested.

Handing over a few notes, she said, 'Thank you, and keep the change,' before gathering her parcels and sliding out of the car.

She looked up at the smart white house, the heavy black iron railings and the impressive columns of the portico. In a terrace of similar houses overlooking Regent's Park, 'Nash' if she wasn't mistaken, it was much grander than the apartment she had expected.

What if he wasn't in? she panicked. He had written down his London address the last time they were together, so surely he could not object to her calling?

She held her parcels in front of her like a shield, and, lifting her hand, she pressed the gleaming brass bell. He was her fiancé, for God's sake! What was she worrying about...?

The door swung open and she looked up into the face of a complete stranger. An old man in a dark suit.

'Yes, madam. May I help you?'

'I—I was looking for Benedict Maxwell's apartment,' she stammered, checking once again the slip of paper in her hand.

'Who is it, James?'

It was the right house. 'Your fiancée,' Rebecca sang back, relieved at the sound of Benedict's voice.

'What the hell...?' Benedict appeared. 'It's all right, James, I'll deal with this; you can go on up now, I won't need you any more this evening.'

Rebecca stifled a nervous giggle. A butler called James—she couldn't believe it. Then, raising her eyes, she stared at her fiancé, and hardly recognised him. Just looking at him made her mouth go dry, and set her heart pounding. He was dressed in an immaculate black dinner suit, the jacket a perfect fit, taut across his wide shoulders, a snowy white silk dress shirt contrasting sharply with the polished mahogany colour of his ruggedly attractive face—a testament to his long years in a much warmer climate.

'You'd better come in, Rebecca.'

'Benedict, I thought you lived in an apartment,' she said stupidly as, with a hand at her elbow, he ushered her into a wide marble-floored hall, a beautiful curved staircase the centre-piece.

'In a way I do. The third floor is an apartment for James the butler and his wife—she's my housekeeper.' He stared at her lovely, perplexed face, and noticed her agitation. Almost curtly he said, 'Perhaps you could enlighten me. Why are you here?'

One glance from his dark eyes and Rebecca was putty in his hands. She found herself aching to be held in his arms, to feel his lips on hers, to know the touch of his strong hands on every part of her. The sheer intensity of her passion for him frightened her. She did not know this woman she had become and, worse, she was no longer so sure she knew Benedict.

'Well, I thought I would surprise you; I had some shopping to do.' She held up her parcels and quickly he took them from her hands, and placed them on a convenient table.

'You certainly surprised me, darling, but very pleasantly.' And, dropping a swift kiss on her brow, he placed one arm around her shoulders, and led her through wide double doors into a beautiful room.

'I hope you don't mind, but I thought, as I was in London, I'd take a chance on finding you at home. I know you're coming on Saturday, but I wanted to talk...' She was babbling, and couldn't stop.

'Rebecca, slow down, and sit down,' Benedict commanded sternly. 'Let me get you a drink, and relax. You don't have to explain; as my fiancée you have every right to call on me any time.'

She gulped and sat down on the large velvet sofa Benedict indicated. 'I just wanted to...' But she was talking to his back as he turned to a magnificent polished wood bureau, almost ceiling high, the glass panels tiny diamonds edged in brass instead of the more common lead.

She sank back against the high back of the settee and looked around with interest and amazement. Two long sashed windows let in the early evening sunlight, heavy dark green velvet drapes were caught back with ornate brass holders. Thick oriental carpets covered the magnificently polished strip-wood floor... A globe of the world stood on a small occasional table along with a pile of *National Geographic* magazines—the only sign of disorder in an extremely elegant room.

The walls were covered in pictures, one or two obviously good oil paintings, a few watercolours, and, to her surprise, a large selection of cartoons. A couple of the late Mark Boxer's caricatures caught her eye. She had read of the artist's untimely death from a brain tumour and it had struck a chord in her mind. She recognised the drawings from an article printed in one of the Sunday papers when they were going on auction at Christie's.

'You look rather pensive; thinking of another man, are you?' Benedict's voice cut in on her wayward thoughts. He was at her side, a crystal glass with a good measure of brandy in it held out towards her. 'Or perhaps an old lover?'

'Good heavens, no,' she responded instantly, taking the glass. 'Quite the reverse. I missed you,' she told him honestly. Surely he must be aware of how utterly enslaved she was? Her thinking mind questioned for a second if it was wise to be so dependent on another person for one's happiness, but she quickly dismissed the thought.

She looked up into his dark eyes and her stomach clenched in fear. He looked so intense, as though he could reach down into her mind and read her every thought. Suddenly his mention of a former lover made her wonder again if he had heard about the old scandal. She should have mentioned it, she knew, but somehow the time had never seemed right.

'So,' he said softly, 'you couldn't wait to see me. I'm flattered, darling, and I apologise if I was less than polite when you arrived, but I'll make up for it by taking you out to dinner, hmm?'

He was standing in front of her, his broad shoulders blocking out the light. Impressive didn't begin to describe him, and she wished he had been casually dressed; somehow he seemed less approachable in formal clothes. Strong and powerful, he exuded a raw male virility like no other man she had ever met. He sparked an instant reaction inside her that she was helpless to control, didn't want to...

'I've been tramping around London for hours; I'm not really dressed for going out.' She looked down at her now rather crumpled, pretty print summer dress, and back to his formal attire, and then it hit her. 'I'm sorry. I should have rung. You are obviously on your way out.' Why else would he be dressed in an evening suit? she thought uneasily, and drained her brandy in one gulp, nervously replacing the glass on a small side-table.

Benedict took a step back and half turned so that his expression was hidden from her, and she wondered why she should suddenly feel a chill. She glanced at the window; had the summer sun gone down? No, but it was after six in the evening, the warmth had gone. That must be it...

'No, you're quite wrong. I've only just returned home. You know how it is—the media are mad keen on environmental issues, and suddenly I have become flavour of the month. I've been recording a show for the BBC— hence the clothes. If you will give me a minute, I'll change.' He turned and smiled down at her. 'OK?'

Relief flooded through her and her confidence soared. 'I'll come with you,' she teased. 'I wouldn't mind having a look around your home, I'm already stunned by the grandeur of the place. I had no idea anthropology paid so well.'

She did not notice the cynicism in his smile as he held out his hand and she trustingly put hers in it. He dragged her to her feet. 'It doesn't. This was my father's house, and now mine, and I will be delighted to show you around. You could stay the night.' Golden-brown eyes.

clashed with violet, and for a long, tense moment the air crackled with electric tension.

It was what Rebecca wanted but...

'Your silence is its own answer.' One dark brow arched sardonically. 'You prefer to wait for the band of gold, hmm?'

'No,' she quickly denied. How could she explain her sudden virginal fear? Couldn't he see all she wanted was to be held in his arms and kissed senseless?

For weeks she had been aching with frustration for this man. She would quite happily have gone to bed with him the very first night they met. Instead, apart from a few passionate kisses as he had left her at weekends, they had hardly been alone together.

Benedict rubbed her engagement ring casually with his thumb, his sensuous mouth curved in a knowing smile. His eyes dropped to the soft swell of her breast, the hardening nipples visible beneath the light cotton dress. 'I think I can guess what's on your mind,' he mocked. 'You really are a very precocious young lady, Rebecca, and I might just oblige. I'm only human, and celibacy doesn't suit me either...'

'Oh, Benedict,' she murmured, swaying towards him. 'I came today because I needed to see you, to have your arms around me, to know that what I'm feeling is real and not some dream that will vanish...' She tilted her head, her soft, full lips brushing his, and closed her eyes.

'I thought it was to talk,' he laughed huskily, and her eyes flew open in surprise.

'Yes, that as well,' she admitted ruefully. A stray beam of sunlight glanced across the room, catching Benedict's head, casting strange shadows over the planes and valleys of his strong face. For a second she had the impression of a cynical, ruthless arrogance about him. Far removed from the easygoing, slightly reclusive man she had fallen in love with.

'You're beautiful, Rebecca, and, with your passionate nature, the man isn't born who could refuse you, not want you for his wife.' He said the words almost angrily before bending his dark head, his mouth opening over hers, his tongue pressing against her teeth. Willingly she parted her lips for him, her own tongue tentatively stroking his.

She whimpered as his arm tightened around her back, his mouth suddenly hard and bruising as the kiss deepened into a deep, searching thrust for more. She arched shamelessly against him as his hand stroked down to cup her breast. Benedict groaned deep in his throat, his mouth leaving hers to trail teasingly down the graceful curve of her neck. She slid her small hands inside his jacket, one hand stroking up his broad back, the other roaming lovingly over his muscular chest. She felt the tension in him and rejoiced that she was able to arouse him as instantly as he aroused her.

His hard thighs moved restlessly against her as the hand at her back tangled in her long hair and wrapped it around his wrist. The quick, sharp tug broke through Rebecca's sensual daze.

'Benedict,' she murmured, half protesting, as he held her slightly away from him. The warmth of his breath against her throat, the heavy beat of his heart beneath her small hand, intoxicated her. Surely he felt the same, she thought dizzily. Why was he stopping?

She stared up into his flushed, handsome face. His dark eyes, burning black, fixed on her full, love-swollen lips. 'I will not take you like some love-starved teenager on the living-room floor.'

Daringly she responded, 'So take me upstairs. I'm tired of behaving myself, Benedict. I love you and want you, and we are engaged,' she pleaded shamelessly. Her body ached for him, every hair every pore was sensitised to his touch, the warmth, the heat of him. She did not think she could stand any more frustration.

'Do you? I wonder,' he drawled, glancing at her flushed face before swinging her up in his strong arms.

Rebecca frowned, wondering at the evident cynicism in his voice; surely he wasn't unsure of her? 'Yes, and I will always love you,' she told him simply, and, curling her arms around his wide shoulders, she nuzzled his ear, as he briskly walked out of the room and up the stairs.

'Can I be sure of that?' he murmured softly, as with one shoulder he nudged open the door of what was obviously his bedroom.

Rebecca took no notice of her surroundings. Her whole world was Benedict, and she gazed at him with wide, wondrous eyes as he laid her down on the huge bed.

She watched in fascination as he shrugged off his jacket, his hands going to the buttons of his shirt.

'How many men have drowned in your pansy eyes, I wonder? You're incredibly beautiful—there must have been other men in your life. Other loves.' The statement was really a question, and his dark gaze roamed intently over her slim, seductive body, coming to rest, with a strange intensity, on her small face.

Rebecca smiled softly, as realisation struck. He had asked her before about other men; it was obvious he was jealous, he needed reassurance, and, dear heaven, she knew the feeling. Just the thought of any other woman in Benedict's arms made her feel sick...

'No other men, Benedict, darling, no other love, not ever,' she murmured, her hands reaching out to him, as though by touching him she could convince him of the truth of her words.

His gaze lingered a moment on the garnet glittering on her finger. 'You sound so positive, so honest,' he murmured as he finally removed his shirt. 'But surely

you must have had a boyfriend? After all, you are
twenty-two; a teenage romance, perhaps?' Something
flashed in his eyes, but she didn't notice.

Her hungry gaze was roaming over his naked, hair-
roughened chest; his skin gleamed like brown satin in
the soft evening light. She watched, mesmerised, as his
long fingers dealt expertly with the buckle of his belt,
and she gasped as he stepped out of his trousers, the
tiny black briefs he wore barely covering his blatant
masculinity.

He caught her staring and, lowering himself down on
the bed beside her, he arched one brow enquiringly, a
teasing smile playing around his sensuous mouth. 'Don't
be afraid to confess, darling, I want to know everything
about you; the moment I saw you I knew fate had declared we should be together. Nothing you say will make
me change my mind, I promise.'

Confess what? she thought, bemused. Oh, yes, boy-
friends... His words were all the reassurance she needed;
he had fallen in love with her on sight, his feelings were
the same as hers, and there should be no secrets between
lovers, so dazedly she began to explain, 'There was one
young man.' The scandal had upset her father, but she
knew Benedict would understand. His hand stroked
gently over her knee.

'When?'

'I was seventeen.' His hand slid higher beneath her
skirt, and she trembled; all thought of detailed explanations vanished like smoke on the wind, as his seeking
fingers stroked the flesh of her inner thigh.

'And?' Benedict rasped as his other hand dealt deftly
with the buttons down the front of her dress.

'Nothing,' she groaned. 'He died.'

CHAPTER THREE

HOURS or perhaps only seconds later, they were both naked. Rebecca did not know how or when, because time had ceased to exist. The only reality was Benedict. It had always slightly frightened her, the passion this man aroused in her, but now, in the circle of his embrace, she forgot her fears.

She put her mouth to the hollow of his throat and tasted the tanned flesh, intrigued to realise that his pulse leapt, and the muscular body tensed at her caress; his muffled curse surprised her, but did not deter her. The taste of him, salty and all male, fascinated her, her hand spread out across the soft hair of his chest and traced the narrowing line down his flat stomach. She was lost in a world of the senses, enthralled by the perfection of his male beauty. She felt his stomach muscles clench as her fingers explored lower, learning him by touch.

Rebecca hesitated as he muttered something and groaned, and in a movement that took her by surprise he rolled her over and under him. His mouth trailed a line of fire down her throat to her breast, and a shocked gasp escaped her. Then his large body blocked the evening light, and for a second she feared the huge, dark shadow blotting out the world; then his hand cupped her breast and his mouth closed over one rosy nipple, tasting and suckling the hard tip.

Her body arched in a spasm of delight, every nerve quivering and tightening to an aching tension. She felt the heat of his body and with trembling hands she reached out and stroked the shape of him from chest to thigh.

'I want you, I can't help it.' Benedict's guttural moan vibrated across her heart as his mouth teased each breast in turn.

She whimpered tiny little erotic cries of keen encouragement. She was swamped by the force of her own latent sensuality which she had never known she possessed. His strong hands caressed her burning flesh, finding the secret, hidden temple of her womanhood, stroking the hot, moist, sensitive flesh.

Nothing in her life so far had prepared her for such a tumult of erotic sensations. Her body welcomed and gloried at his touch and feverishly she sought to return the ecstasy. Her slender fingers slid across his thigh, cupping the maleness of him in a bold caress. She felt his muscles lock rigid in an attempt to restrain his response, then his hand tore hers from his body, pinning it above her head in one violent motion.

'God forgive me, Gor——'

A swift stab of pain and she cried out, her slender body clenching for an instant in rejection as he made her his with one powerful thrust.

'No, no, I don't believe...' Benedict grated.

But Rebecca, the pain subsiding, was drowning in a hot molten flood of desire. She clung to his broad shoulders, her fingernails digging into his flesh, while her body sheathed the strength and force of his masculinity, knowing and welcoming its master.

Benedict stilled, every muscle in his large frame locked in an intolerable tension; she looked up into his tight, darkly flushed face and begged, 'Don't stop. Please...'

Her words unleashed a wild, savage passion that should have terrified her; instead she met him thrust for thrust. She was swept along in a maelstrom of emotion, and she clung to him, her slender legs wrapped around his waist, as he took her higher and higher; she could sense the awaiting pinnacle, and cried out as the tension almost tore her apart.

She sobbed his name, the world exploding around her as he took her with him into the swirling vortex. He touched her womb, his harsh, guttural groan swallowed by her mouth, as the liquid of life flowed between them. She knew he had captured the very essence of her being and absorbed her into him. They were one...

Rebecca had read about sex, but nothing in the world had prepared her for the reality. It wasn't possible, she thought, her body trembling in the aftermath of release, that any other two people in the universe could experience what had passed between herself and Benedict. His head lay on her shoulder, great, shuddering breaths racking his huge frame. She reached a hand to stroke the hair from his damp brow to tell him her thoughts.

He raised his head and caught her wrist, holding it with a grip of steel. His breathing slowly returning to normal, he said with barely contained rage, 'You were a virgin. Damn you to hell, Rebecca!' And, rolling off her, he swung his feet to the floor, presenting her with his back.

Her new-found euphoria dwindled beneath his hostile words. What had happened? Why did he resent the fact she had been a virgin? It didn't make sense. Pulling herself up into a sitting position, she tentatively reached out a hand to his stiff back. 'What's wrong?' she asked softly, fearfully.

At the touch of her fingers, he jumped up and swung around to face her; totally unconscious of his own nudity, he stared down at her with dark, hostile eyes. 'I guessed you were evil, but my God, to think Gordon, the poor sod, went to his grave never knowing what it was like to have a woman. What did you do, string him along

with a few kisses until he was out of his mind with
wanting you?'

Rebecca shivered, not with cold, but with the slow,
icy chill that crawled up her spine and encircled her heart.
'I don't understand,' she whispered; her violet eyes lifted
to his and fell beneath the blazing anger she saw registered there.

'That's right, hang your head in shame, you bitch!'

His scathing words cut her like a whip, but bravely
she raised her head. She still wasn't sure what had happened, but the mention of Gordon filled her with fore-
boding. She could explain that episode in her life;
Benedict would understand, she told herself. He loved
her and she had done nothing wrong.

'What was it the papers called you? A pint-sized
Lolita. A pocket Venus.' His gaze ran the length of her
naked body, blatant with contempt. Rebecca held her
head high, and with trembling hands she brushed the
tumbled mass of her black hair over her shoulders. She
was too shocked to speak. She said nothing. Earlier she
had been going to explain her one unfortunate relationship, but Benedict's persuasive, sophisticated lovemaking had washed the thought from her head. Now it
was too late...

His dark eyes followed the movements of her hands
then settled insolently on her bare breasts before slowly
rising to her pale face. 'I have to agree with them. On
the outside you are everything a man could want—intelligent, beautiful, perfectly formed and passionate—
but inside, where it counts, you have none of the female
virtues, no warmth, no compassion.'

She looked at him, the man she loved, the man she
had given everything to only moments earlier, and did
not recognise him. Her eyes roamed over his large, still
sweat-wet body; she had traced those muscles with her
fingers, kissed those lips. She shook her head to dispel

the image. This towering naked man, bristling with hostility, was a stranger. How could he turn on her so?

'Nothing to say, Rebecca, no defence?'

'I didn't think I would need to defend myself to my fiancé,' she said bleakly. 'I thought you of all people, Benedict, wouldn't believe the gutter Press, and anyway it all happened years ago. I was barely eighteen.' She wondered how he had found out. Not that it mattered. It was enough that he had, and immediately thought the worst of her. She had expected better from the man she loved.

Benedict laughed, a harsh, guttural sound. 'The Press do exaggerate occasionally, but my own mother showed me Gordon's diary—his last entry before he died.'

'Your mother?' she murmured. What in God's name had his mother got to do with it? She was totally confused.

'Yes, Rebecca. Gordon Brown was my half-brother and you destroyed him,' he said with pitiless certainty.

Rebecca moaned, a soft, low sound; suddenly Benedict's actions made a horrible kind of sense.

'Now I think you're beginning to understand...Rebecca.' He drawled her name. 'Derived from the Hebrew. Charmer. Ensnarer. Tell me, my love, my fiancée, how does it feel to be the one ensnared for a change?' he demanded malevolently.

How does it feel? The question echoed in her head. As though she were breaking into a million pieces, she thought. But she would not give Benedict the satisfaction of knowing how close he had come to destroying her. Slowly she turned and slid her trembling legs over the opposite edge of the bed from him, she grabbed the edge of the sheet and wrapped it around her numb body, and, with a terrific effort of will, she rose to her feet. Only then did she turn to face him, the wide, rumpled bed between them.

'The coroner's verdict was accidental death,' she said softly. Why was he blaming her? She had been completely innocent of any involvement.

'Yes, but we both know why—to save embarrassment to a good Catholic family. Mother never showed the court the diary, her young son's outpouring of a hopeless love. You were leaving him the following day, and would never wear his ring.'

Benedict walked around the bed and snatched her left hand in his, his thumb rubbing her engagement ring. He watched her, a strange, feral glitter in his golden-brown eyes. She looked down at their joined hands.

'Gordon bought the ring for you years ago, but you wouldn't take it from him. Ironic, isn't it? You almost snatched my hand off when I gave it to you,' he drawled cynically. 'But then you love me; I should be flattered.' With his free hand he tilted her chin, forcing her to look at him. 'Isn't that so, Rebecca?'

She flushed with humiliation at the taunting words. 'No.' She breathed the lie. She loved Benedict, not this vengeful stranger. How could she love this man when his hatred of her was blatant in his every glance?

The taut muscles of his hard body flexed at her denial, and his hands dropped from her, as though her touch were somehow contaminating. She could feel the anger emanating from him and, pulling the sheet closer round her small frame, she tucked it sarong-style beneath her armpits, and stepped back only to find her feet hopelessly tangled in the trailing silk and herself tumbling forward.

Benedict's strong hands caught her and held her steady against the hard warmth of his naked body.

'Actions speak louder than words, darling, and what your lips deny, your body aches for,' he said with harsh triumph, his insolent gaze dropping to her full breasts, the hard nipples clearly outlined against the soft silk of the sheet.

Scarlet-faced, she tried to push him away. 'No.'

'Not fifteen minutes ago you were begging me to love you. Now I think you might appreciate and begin to feel some of the anguish my brother felt when you refused his love,' Benedict said gloatingly, and, lifting her up as though she weighed no more than a feather, he dropped her back down on the bed.

'Stay there and think about it while I shower and dress. Then we'll talk.' The last sounded like a threat.

Rebecca had to get away...to think... She jumped up and in a frantic scramble around the floor found her panties and bra, then she quickly struggled into her clothes. It had all gone so horribly wrong; her premonition of doom that had sent her running to London had proved to be true. She was hurting too much to think clearly, but she knew she had made a complete and utter fool of herself.

Benedict was right when he said she had almost snatched his hand off to wear his ring; she cringed at the memory. The happenings of the last few weeks ran through her mind like an express train, and in a flash of blinding clarity she saw it all. Benedict did not love her, never had, even the act of love they had shared was false. She remembered his, 'God forgive me,' or had it been 'Gordon'? He had never wanted to make love to her, she had thrown herself at him.

With fingers that shook she fastened the last button on her print dress, then carefully removed the ring from the third finger of her left hand. With it went all her hopes and dreams of love and marriage.

She raised her head as Benedict sauntered back into the room. He looked magnificent; his dark hair, wet from the shower, was swept back smoothly from his broad forehead. He had slipped on a blue cotton velour jogging suit, and the pants clung lovingly to his muscular thighs, subtly outlining his virile masculinity.

Rebecca flushed, her stomach clenching in pain for what she had lost. But self-pity had always been an emotion she despised. So she choked down her emotions and proudly raised her eyes to his. She held out her hand, the ring nestling in her palm.

'You can have this back. I understand perfectly, Benedict.' He had wanted revenge and he had used her to get it.

'Good God, no, you keep that little bauble; it was meant for you. If I ever give a woman a ring it would be worth a hell of a lot more than that.'

Rebecca glanced at his arrogant, taunting face. Dear heaven, what a fool she had been. How had she never noticed the cruel twist to his mouth, the ruthless element in his nature? She hadn't because she had been blinded by love...

She could not look at him, it hurt too much. Slowly she let her gaze roam around the room. The lavish drapes, the inches-thick cream carpet, and, lastly, the enormous bed. It was like the rest of the house, elegant and very expensive. She did not fit here, never would. Her fingers closed over the ring in her hand; Gordon had never told her about the ring, but then he wouldn't have, not when he'd found out. He would have wanted to spare her the pain of losing him. Her lips curled in a soft smile. He had been that sort of boy. Always caring for others.

'Rebecca.' Benedict touched her shoulder. She stiffened.

'Don't touch me.' She raised moisture-glazed eyes to his. 'You're wrong about one thing, Benedict. Gordon bought this ring with love in his heart; any ring you gave a woman would be worth nothing in comparison. You don't have a heart.'

She had the consolation of seeing his face darken with barely controlled anger. 'You dare say that to me? I read Gordon's last entry in his diary, and I quote.'

In a voice laced with cynicism he continued.

Becky, I love her. Sweet Becky. But I know now she will never wear my ring. She burns like the brightest star in the heavens, a brilliant future awaits her. While for me life is over.

'The poor fool was besotted by you, and you killed him as surely as if you had stuck a knife in him. Don't talk to me about heart,' he sneered. 'You don't know the meaning of the word. But by God, I am going to teach you.'

Rebecca brushed the back of her hand across her eyes, whipping away the tears, deeply touched by the quotation. But what did he mean, he was going to teach her?

'I don't think so,' she said quietly. She wanted nothing more to do with the man. She stepped around him, heading for the door, and escape. She felt as though she were living through a nightmare and if she did not get away soon she might break down completely. She was teetering on the edge.

Think practically, she told herself, opening the door. If she hurried she could catch the last train to Oxford.

'Where are you going?' The staccato question halted her in mid-stride. 'I haven't finished with you yet.'

Slowly she turned and looked back at Benedict. 'Yes. Yes, you have.' In a couple of strides he was beside her; reaching out, he caught a handful of her long hair. 'Let go of me,' she said tightly, 'I have a train to catch.'

His sensuous mouth curved in a knowing smile. 'But you wanted to stay the night, Rebecca,' he mocked. 'You want me, you know you do.'

She wrenched away from him, and when he made to follow her she turned on him, her violet eyes blazing with anger. 'I've heard of mad scientists but you beat the lot,' she said scathingly. 'I wouldn't want you if you were the last man on earth.'

To her astonishment he laughed. 'That might be awkward, as we are engaged to be married.'

She glanced up at him; his golden-brown eyes shone with mockery and something else she did not recognise. Then the full extent of her stupidity hit her. Engaged? What a joke! 'You never intended to marry me, did you?'

His dark eyes narrowed on her pale face. 'I never actually asked you, so what do you think?' he responded mockingly.

Rebecca, shamed, could not answer. She knew, and, swinging on her heel, she walked along the hall and downstairs. Mechanically she picked up the parcels from the hall table, and left the ring. Benedict's hand on her arm stopped her at the front door.

'Wait. You can't wander around London at night. I'll drive you to the station,' he said curtly.

She sat in the far corner of the seat, as far away from Benedict as she could get. She felt like ranting and raving, screaming her anguish to the world, but instead she clenched her hands in her lap, her knuckles white with the strain. She would not give the swine the satisfaction of knowing how he had hurt her.

'I'll drive you back to Oxford,' Benedict said, breaking the icy silence.

'No, thank you. I have my rail ticket.'

'So what? It will be quicker by car.' He shot her a sidelong glance, a grim smile twisting his lips. 'I don't mind the drive.'

The conceit of the man, the arrogance, amazed her. 'Well, I do,' she fired back. 'The quicker I get away from your hateful presence, the better I will like it,' she said through clenched teeth.

His strong hands tightened on the driving-wheel, as he spun the car in a quick arc and headed for the station. 'I take it by that comment you're breaking our engagement?' he enquired, flashing her a brief, oddly intense glance.

With bitter cynicism she answered him, using his own earlier words, 'What do you think?'

He brought the big car to a halt in the station forecourt. Rebecca reached for the door-handle.

'Rebecca, wait.' Turning in the seat, he caught her by the shoulders, his dark eyes searching her small face. 'I never intended...' He hesitated. She had never seen him uncertain before, and, for all her desire to escape, she did wait.

'I didn't mean it to end like this, and well...If there are any repercussions...I'll help you.'

A hysterical laugh escaped her. Repercussions? Who was he kidding? She would be suffering from this night for the rest of her life. 'Thanks, but no, thanks.'

'I insist Rebecca; if you are pregnant I want to know.'

What little colour she had left vanished. How could she have been so dumb? Dredging up every last ounce of will-power she possessed, she stared straight into his dark eyes and lied her head off. 'Really, Benedict, I know I might have given you the impression to the contrary, but I'm not a complete idiot. You said yourself once that I was a great organiser. I started taking the Pill weeks ago. You have nothing to worry about.' Not waiting for his response, she opened the door and slid out of the car.

Benedict made no attempt to stop her. She walked quickly away, stiff-backed with her head held high, and she never looked back. Please God, she prayed, give me

strength. Let me get on this train and home before I fall
apart.

She sat huddled against the window of the train, staring
out into the darkness, the lights of the city flashing and
dazzling her eyes. She was in a state of shock, totally
numb, but she knew that somewhere in the dark shadows
of her mind lurked an agony not to be borne. Her
thoughts slid back in time, a sad, reminiscent smile
quirking her full lips. Gordon Brown, poor gentle, caring
Gordon, he would have been horrified to know how
Benedict had used his ring...

It had been the summer before she started university.
Her father had taken a holiday home for six weeks at
Sidmouth in Devon. The small seaside town was re-
nowned for holding the best folk festival in England every
summer, and her father had been a devotee of folk music.

It had been the middle of July, the first week of their
holiday, when Rebecca had met Gordon Brown. She had
been walking along the water's edge, enjoying the sun
and sea, when she was almost hit by the boom of a sailing
dinghy swinging around in the wind; she had ducked
just in time but fallen on her backside on the hard pebble
beach.

A young man, a tall, golden-haired Adonis, had
dashed out of the water and helped her to her feet, and
that had been the start of their friendship. He had told
her he was a first-year student at Essex University, and
he had kidded her about her being a brain-box when she
had shyly informed him she was going up to Oxford in
September.

Over the following weeks they had spent almost every
day together. He had taught her to crew the dinghy for
him, they had walked for miles around the headlands,
lunched in excellent little restaurants in the small but
beautiful villages of Seaton and Beer, and generally

enjoyed themselves. Gordon's pride and joy was a little red Mini car and in it they had travelled over Dartmoor, and all the surrounding countryside.

She rarely, if ever, saw him in the evenings; those were devoted to his mother. He had asked her once or twice to join them, but she refused. Her own evenings were reserved for her father.

Looking back, she realised he had not said much about his family—only that his mother was French but had spent most of her life in England, as his father had been English. Gordon was holidaying with her mainly because both his father and his older half-brother had died the previous year and his mother was completely devastated and needed his loving care. Gordon confessed he missed his father, but he had never been very close to his brother, so it had not affected him as much as his mother.

It had been the last week of August and almost the end of the holiday when the tragedy happened. With hindsight Rebecca recognised all the signs had been there, but she was too young to realise it at the time. On the Monday, she had not seen Gordon—he had had business in London—but on the Tuesday they went sailing and he had caught his head a nasty crack on the boom.

Laughing, she had told him he should be more careful or get a bigger dinghy, if he wanted to keep his head, but he had not laughed. Instead he had said quite soberly, 'A crack on the head won't make any difference to me now, Becky; the damage is done.'

Rebecca had wondered what he meant, but hadn't bothered querying his statement. It had been a beautiful day, a day out of time; they had tied the boat up at a little cove and picnicked on the beach. After they had eaten they lay side by side on the blanket, and for the first time, Rebecca had some inkling of the depths of

Gordon's feelings for her. Oh, they had exchanged kisses
once or twice, but that was all.

This day was different. He leaned over her, his boyish
face oddly serious, his golden-brown eyes dulled with a
haunting sadness.

'Becky, I want you to know the past few weeks have
been the most perfect of my life, and if circumstances
had been different——'

'Gordon, why so serious?' she cut in, not sure what
to say to him. 'I've promised to spend tomorrow with
Dad. We're going fossicking at Lyme Regis, but we will
still have another day before I leave. And after that we
can write to each other; I'll persuade my father to come
back next year.'

Gordon smiled a truly beautiful smile then very gently
kissed her lips. 'Yes, Becky, you do that.' And somehow
in that moment he had seemed much older than his years.

A sigh escaped her. She could understand his entry in
the diary that last day. He had known he was terminally
ill and had obviously decided he could not give her the
ring, with the commitment it implied. He was too caring
to burden her with his problem.

She rested her head against the back of the seat, closing
her eyes. The regular, rhythmic beat of the train was
oddly soothing. It had all been so long ago, and she had
thought the episode was forgotten, until tonight and
Benedict.

She had never seen Gordon again. The following day
she had spent with her dad, and, on returning to their
apartment on the seafront at Sidmouth late in the
afternoon, she had been accosted by a complete stranger.
Before she knew what was happening a flash bulb had
gone off in her face, and a horrible little man was flinging
questions at her.

'Gordon Brown was your boyfriend. Had you fought
with him? Was that why he was on his own today? Do

you think he drove over the cliff deliberately? Was his death suicide?'

Rebecca had been stunned and completely numb; the staccato questions rained down on her like machine-gun bullets. She had no idea what she replied, and was grateful for her father's support as he hustled her into the apartment.

It had been a twenty-four-hour sensation at the time, created by one of the most disreputable newspapers. A photo of Rebecca, her long hair tumbling about her face in disarray, and dressed in scanty shorts and sun-top, had appeared on the front page. WAS IT ACCIDENT OR SUICIDE? the headline screamed, and they had dubbed her a 'pint-sized Lolita'.

The irony of it still made her smart. When the inquest was held a week later, the verdict was accidental death. The same newspaper printed the result in three sentences on page twenty-one. Her father had attended the inquest and told her about it afterwards.

Poor Gordon, Becky thought sadly, he had never stood a chance. The coroner's report had explained everything. Gordon had attended the medical centre at the university in May, complaining of headaches. Tests had been carried out and a massive brain tumour diagnosed. The Monday before his death he had visited a specialist in London, only to be told it was inoperable. He had known he was going to die. The pathologist's report had confirmed that Gordon had suffered a massive brain haemorrhage and in all likelihood was dead before his car went over the cliff.

An elderly couple who had been talking to him only minutes before confirmed he had complained the sun was giving him a headache and he was going home. They had watched him get into the little Mini, and it was obvious he was about to reverse away from the edge of the headland, as his arm was along the back of the pass-

enger-seat, and he was looking behind him. But for some
inexplicable reason he missed the gear and the car slid
forward and over the cliff.

'My dear, are you all right?'

Rebecca's eyes flew open, and hastily she brushed a
tear from her cheek as her startled gaze settled on the
lady seated opposite her on the train.

'Yes, yes, thank you,' she murmured, jolted back to
the present by the old lady's intervention.

'Are you sure? You look very pale.'

'Yes, I'm sure,' she responded, trying to smile. She
wished she were home in the safety of her own bedroom,
but she had to hang on for a while longer...

CHAPTER FOUR

QUIETLY Rebecca let herself into the house and tiptoed up the stairs. It was well past midnight but, with a baby in the house, one never knew at what hour of the night Mary or Rupert would be up, and the last thing she wanted was to bump into either of them.

She closed the bedroom door behind her and slumped against it, her handbag and parcels dropped unheeded at her feet. With hands that shook she unbuttoned her dress and let it fall to the floor, then, walking like an old woman, she crossed the room and collapsed on the small bed.

Like a small, wounded animal, she crawled under the coverlet, burrowing down in the bed to hide. She pulled the pillow down with her and, gripping it tightly, she buried her head in the soft down and finally let the tears fall.

She cried and cried, great, gulping sobs that shook her small body from head to toe, the sound muffled by the soft pillow. How long she cried, she had no idea, until at last, her throat raw, her eyes dry, her slender frame ceased shuddering; but the pain, the hurt, it went on and on...

Slowly she turned on her back and, pushing the pillow under her aching head, she gazed with dull, sightless eyes at the ceiling.

Benedict Maxwell, the man she had loved, had hoped to marry, was responsible for her agony of mind and body, and the worst part was knowing he had acted with a brutal, cold-blooded deliberation to achieve just this result.

The first time she set eyes on him, Rebecca had thought she had met her soulmate. What a fool she had been! Of course Benedict had seemed familiar. Why wouldn't he? His golden eyes were exactly the same as his younger half-brother's had been. If she had not been so smitten, so damned gullible, her analytical mind might have recognised the likeness earlier. Instead she had dreamt of love and happy-ever-after.

Rebecca groaned; thinking clearly for the first time in hours, she cringed at her own stupidity. It was all so obvious. Benedict had barely noticed her when they were first introduced. It was only when Rupert gave her full name that Benedict had turned the potent force of his masculine charm upon her.

The next day Mary had tried to warn her, and Rebecca, in her conceit, had told her, 'Deep down I know he's the one for me, and if I get hurt, so be it.' How prophetic those words had been. The same night, on her first dinner date with Benedict, he had asked her about any other admirers, and she had eagerly avowed he was the one and only man for her. At the time she had wondered why he had said he would believe her 'for the moment'. Bitterly she realised he had been stringing her along to cause her the maximum pain, and she, dear heaven, had helped him. So many comments she had dismissed as irrelevant now made horrible sense.

Rebecca moved restlessly; she longed for the oblivion of sleep, anything to stop the memories, but it was not to be. Her mind spun on oiled wheels, recalling every word every gesture of her time with Benedict. Her body burnt with aching frustration, never to know the touch of his hands, the warmth of his lips, the ecstasy of his possession. How could she survive without him?

If only he had not made love to her, she thought bitterly. The agony of having known the wonder of being
his completely, only to discover he cared nothing for her,
had forced himself to take what she had so blatantly
offered, tore at the very heart of her womanhood, destroyed her pride.

The grey light of dawn was lighting the sky, when she
finally faced the most crushing, humiliating fact of all:
she was partly to blame for the situation she now had
to endure. Benedict was wrong about her relationship
with his brother, wrong about her. But one comment he
had made was perfectly true, and she could not deny it.
He had never actually asked her to marry him. He had
given her the ring, and she had immediately jumped to
the conclusion that he was proposing marriage. She had
even felt touched because he had avoided her eyes, and
she had assumed he was nervous.

Her shame and humiliation were complete. No wonder
he'd been in no hurry to fix the wedding day. He had
never intended to marry her. He'd wanted revenge for
his brother and she, fool that she was, had given him
the rope to hang her by.

A baby's cry broke the morning silence. Rebecca stiffened where she lay. Young Jonathan was making his
wants known. She glanced at her watch. Dead on time.
Six-thirty every morning, the little one awoke, demanding his feed.

She could hear Mary moving around in the room
across the hall, and knew she could not delay the inevitably painful discussion much longer.

Half an hour later, she swung her legs over the side
of the bed and stood up. She lifted her slender arms over
her head and stretched. Rebecca winced and dropped
her hands, her muscles aching in places they never had
before. Determinedly she convinced herself it was the
result of her sleepless night and had absolutely nothing

whatsoever to do with Benedict's passionate lovemaking. No, she corrected, there had been no love on
his part.

Pulling on her old towelling robe, she gathered up bra,
panties, a pair of jeans and a sweater, and headed along
the hall for the bathroom. Safely behind the locked door,
she stripped and stepped into the shower-stall. Turning
on the tap, she turned her face up to the warm spray,
letting the water wash over her. Picking up a bar of toilet
soap, she lathered her slender body from top to toe. Her
long hair trailed in black tails down her back, as over
and over again she repeated the process in a feverish
attempt to wash every touch, every lingering scent of
Benedict from her flesh.

A knock on the bathroom door brought an end to her
frantic washing. A wry smile curved her full lips. That
would be Rupert. It was a lovely old house Mary and
Rupert had intended modernising but, as Rupert had
been offered a post at Harvard in the USA, starting in
the autumn, they had postponed any renovations; hence
one bathroom was shared by all.

Benedict must have really felt he was slumming it,
staying here, she thought bitterly, memories of his elegant
home fresh in her mind. Obviously he had been prepared to put up with any inconvenience in order to carry
out his scheme to hurt her.

Bile rose in her throat, and for an instant she thought
she was going to be sick as she recognised just how de-
viously Benedict had behaved. Fighting down her nausea,
she quickly rubbed herself dry with a large fluffy towel.
A slow-burning, bitter anger took root in her mind as
she hastily donned her clothes. He had used her friends,
the ring, anything and anyone, in order to break her
heart.

Rebecca stood in front of the washbasin and neatly
wrapped a towel round her soaking hair, turban style.

She stared at her pale, hollow-eyed reflection and made
a silent vow. Neither Benedict Maxwell nor anyone else
would ever know just how well he had succeeded. It
would be hard, but for her own pride, her self-respect,
not by a look or a word would she ever betray how much
he had hurt her.

She thought of her late father. He had fought a killing
illness with spirit and determination; surely she could do
as well with an unfortuante love-affair? The hardest thing
to accept was, she was as guilty as Benedict in a way.
She had not behaved very intelligently and now she was
paying the price.

She opened the door. 'It's all yours, Rupert,' she told
him, and ran downstairs.

She straightened her shoulders and hesitated for a
second outside the kitchen door. It was about to begin.
She walked into the homely room. Mary was seated by
the kitchen table, on a low nursing chair, feeding
Jonathan. She raised her head and smiled, but at the
sight of Rebecca the smile quickly turned to a frown.

'Really, Becky, you should have stayed in bed. You
look haggard as hell. What time did you get back last
night?'

'Thanks Mary, and good morning to you too,' Rebecca
muttered as she walked across the room and, leaning
against the pine work-top, switched on the kettle.
'Coffee?' she prompted, her back to Mary.

'It's ready in the percolator.'

'Oh, thanks.' The percolator sat in the middle of the
kitchen table, two cups beside it. Carefully she poured
out a cup of coffee, willing her hand not to shake, then,
with apparent nonchalance, she pulled out one of the
ladder-backed chairs and sat down facing Mary. 'How
is hungry Horace this morning, my favourite godson?'
she asked with a smile for the tiny bundle lying in his
mother's arms, determinedly gulping down his bottle of

formula. Mary had given up breast-feeding the week before.

'A hell of a lot better than you.' Mary's blue eyes searched Rebecca's face. 'You look as though you haven't slept a wink. Nothing wrong, is there?'

She could think of no easy way to say it. 'The engagement is off.'

Mary jerked upright and young Jonathan yelled as his bottle fell out of his mouth. 'Off? What do you mean, off?'

'I'm sorry, Mary, I know I've caused you a lot of trouble, Benedict staying here and everything, but the engagement was a mistake.' She did not want to explain the true reason, but she owed Mary some explanation. 'I met him yesterday in London, and we had a long talk and agreed we were incompatible.'

'Just like that? But Rebecca——'

'No, Mary, I really don't want to discuss it,' She cut her off bluntly, and, draining her cup of coffee, she stood up. 'If you don't mind I'd like to use the phone in the study. I know I said I would help you with the baby, but would you mind terribly if I went away for a while? I thought I might go and stay with Josh and Joanne if they'll have me.'

'Of course I don't mind, Becky; you look as if you could use a holiday. But don't you think you're being a little hasty? Take it from me, I know—one fight doesn't mean you have to break up. I bet Benedict will be here any minute, full of apologies.'

'It's no good, Mary, my mind is made up. Just take my word for it.'

Maybe it was something in Rebecca's tone but Mary stared at her, her smooth brow drawn in a deep frown. 'I think you really mean that.' She hesitated, her sharp eyes surveying the young girl standing so stiffly before her. 'If you didn't fight...it must have... Wait a minute. You were late last night.'

Rebecca could almost see the older woman's brain ticking over, but she could do nothing to enlighten her. Then, to her stunned amazement, Mary blushed.

'I know, Rebecca. You were a virgin, and last night you and Benedict...'

Now it was Rebecca's turn to blush.

'Oh, you poor girl,' Mary went on. 'You made love and bells didn't ring. That's it, isn't it? But it's no reason to break up. The first time is quite often less than perfect for any woman. Not everyone clicks in the sexual stakes immediately; with some couples it takes time. Don't be put off, Benedict will soon teach——'

'Mary, you don't understand.' Rebecca couldn't listen to any more. 'I don't want Benedict. Is that plain enough?' she said sharply, and was immediately contrite. 'Sorry, Mary, but trust me—I know what I'm doing. And if you'll excuse me, right now I have a call to make.' Head up, she walked stiffly out of the kitchen and across the hall to the study.

It hardly seemed possible that one's life could change so drastically in twenty-four hours, Rebecca thought wearily. She sat down at the leather-topped desk, and, resting her elbows on the desk, she propped her head in her hands and gazed vacantly into space.

With hindsight it was glaringly obvious that Benedict had no intention of committing himself to her. He had never introduced her to a single friend of his, and there must be plenty. Carefully making sure only to visit her at her home, only mixing with her acquaintances...so only Rebecca was humiliated...

Wearily she straightened and picked up the telephone. Joanne and Josh, pals from college and now husband and wife and living in Northumbria. They had been so pleased for her when she had last called, and told them she was engaged. How would they react when she told them it was off? And could they put up with a visitor for a few weeks? she thought wryly.

Rebecca need not have worried; once she had spoken to Joanne it was all arranged. With a relieved sigh she carefully replaced the receiver. Now all she had to do was pack her bags and drive off...

A light knock on the door heralded the arrival of a very worried-looking Mary, carrying a tray with coffee and biscuits on it. 'I thought you might need something, love,' she said, placing the tray on the desk.

Need... What she needed was a time machine to whisk her back a couple of months, but failing that a strong coffee would have to suffice. 'Thanks,' she murmured, taking the cup from her friend's outstretched hand.

'Are you sure you know what you're doing, Rebecca?'

'Yes, very sure. I can't explain now, but perhaps some day. I only know Benedict Maxwell is not the man I thought he was, not the man I thought I loved. You and Rupert were both right—you told me at the very beginning to be careful. I should have listened...'

The phone rang, a jarring sound beside the soft voices. 'I'll get that.' Mary jumped to answer it. 'You've had enough.'

More than enough. How long she could hang on to her sanity, she did not know. She tensed.

'Yes, I'm sorry, Ben, but Rebecca has been using the phone.'

Rebecca carefully bent forward and placed her coffee-cup on the floor, the action easing the swift stab of pain she felt in her stomach as she realised it was Benedict calling. Taking a deep, calming breath, she straightened up.

'Becky——' Mary held the phone out '—it's Benedict. He wants to talk to you.'

The swine, the arrogant, heartless swine. How dared he ring her now? Hadn't he hurt her enough? she thought furiously. She had just spent the most humiliating few hours of her life, and all because of him. She jumped to her feet, violet eyes blazing. 'Well, tell Mr Benedict Maxwell I do not wish to speak to him, see him or hear his name mentioned ever again.'

'I guess you heard that, Ben.'

Rebecca didn't know what Benedict replied and didn't want to. But she hesitated on her way to the door at Mary's cry of outrage.

'Ben, I have a young baby in the house; he is asleep at the moment and I want him to stay that way. You can't keep ringing all day and night.'

Rebecca marched over to the desk and snatched the phone from Mary's hand. 'Yes, Mr Maxwell?''

'Really, Rebecca, surely you know me well enough—especially after last night—to call me Benedict.'

His mocking response was just what she needed to hold on to her anger. 'On the contrary, Mr Maxwell, last night showed me I didn't know you at all,' she declared icily, as the door closed on Mary's exit.

'Lying naked in my arms, making those erotic little whimpering noises, you quite happily called my name. I seem to remember you begging me to get to know you completely,' Benedict drawled throatily, the amusement evident in his tone.

Stamping down on the sensual images his words evoked, she replied, 'Was there something you particularly wanted, or do you just like making obscene phone calls? If that is the case I suggest you choose a number at random and stop bothering me.'

'Do I bother you, Rebecca?'

'Not any more. And by the way I have told Mary the engagement is off, but perhaps you would like to stick a notice in *The Times*,' she said sarcastically. She wouldn't put it past the devil to make her humiliation as public as possible.

'That was what I wanted to talk about,' Benedict volunteered, the amusement vanished from his voice. 'I had hoped to catch you before... Well, anyway, what I mean Rebecca, is there is no reason to break our engagement. I thought about it al—last night, and I realised maybe I overreacted a bit.'

She gasped her astonishment. What the hell was he playing at now? He actually sounded contrite.

'I realised I can't blame you alone for Gordon's death.'

For a moment Rebecca's heart soared—he had discovered the truth—but as he continued she turned from white to pink to red with fury.

'After all, you were very young. Young girls do flirt. You probably didn't realise how much a man feels in certain situations. You were still a virgin, a very beautiful, romantic young girl. You probably didn't realise what a tease——'

'Stop right there.' Rebecca snapped. He actually had the colossal nerve, the arrogance, to try to make excuses for her...

'I have heard quite enough. We are finished. *Kaputt Finito*. And as for you...I suggest you take yourself back to the Amazon and your half-baked theories of my character with you, and stuff them where the monkey stuffed his nuts. In future you would do better to stick to the study of primitive tribes—you're obviously on the same wavelength.'

His laughter had her clenching her fists with anger.

'Crude, Rebecca, crude... Though it doesn't surprise me—you always were a little firecracker, and now I know you give the same explosive response in bed. I can't help thinking, Gordon aside, you and I could have a very fruitful adult relationship.'

Benedict was certainly showing his true colours now, she thought sadly, all her rage evaporating like air out of a burst balloon. The conceit of the man—he would kindly overlook the fact that he thought she was responsible for his brother's death for a bit of good old-fashioned lust. He hadn't a decent principle in his whole body, and she had been a complete and utter fool to think otherwise.

'Why have you called, Benedict? To gloat,' she answered her own question.

Perhaps the blunt finality in her tone got through to Benedict, or maybe he had lost interest in goading her, because his reply was voiced with a cool formality. 'No, Rebecca. When you were sitting on the train last night, I thought you looked rather upset. I only called to assure myself you got home safely.'

'Thank you for your concern, but it was quite unnecessary,' she drawled sarcastically. 'Goodbye.' And, slamming down the receiver, she gripped the edge of the desk with her small hands, her head bowed as she fought to retain her self-control. Her legs were trembling, barely able to support her.

Eventually regaining some semblance of control, she went looking for Mary, and found her in the kitchen. 'It's arranged. I'm going to Corbridge for a while.'

'Yes, love, It will do you good to get away. But you know we're here if you need us.'

'Thanks.' Rebecca's violet eyes glazed with tears. Thank God she had friends like Mary and Rupert. 'I don't know what I would do without you and Rupert.'

'Hey, come on, Becky. What are friends for? Only don't forget to come back for the last Sunday of August—Jonathan's christening.'

'As if I would,' she smiled through her tears.

* * *

Rebecca slid into the driving-seat of the Ford Sierra, and, with her suitcase stowed in the back, and explicit instructions on how to get to Corbridge, she waved goodbye to Mary and started the engine. Some seven hours later, with her head aching, she saw the welcoming sign of the village on the roadside.

She drove into the little market square. At one end was an old stone church, and the other three sides were a mixture of houses and shops and, luckily, a parking space.

Josh and Joanne lived in a teetering three-storeyed house overlooking the square, and just as Rebecca raised her hand to press the bell the door was flung open and, in a flurry of embraces, she was dragged enthusiastically into the house. It had been over a year since their last meeting at a party in Oxford to celebrate the end of their university years.

Josh had been lucky enough to get a job with Northumbria County Council as an archaeologist and Joanne worked for a legal firm in the adjoining market town of Hexham. Their small stone cottage backed on to the river Tyne and the garden, steeply terraced, ran down to the softly flowing water. The house rang with laughter and love, and anticipation of a happy event.

At first Rebecca almost resented the happiness her friends shared. Each morning she pulled herself out of bed, usually after a sleepless night or worse. When she slept her dreams were full of Benedict, and the touch of his hands, the warmth of his lips were so real; and then she would wake, her body flushed and wanting, and know it was all a dream. Sadly that was all her relationship with Benedict had ever been.

But gradually the peace and beauty of her surroundings began to soothe her bruised heart. She drove all over the county, parking her car at various spots along the route of Hadrian's Wall and walking for hours. She visited Housesteads, the Roman fort, and from there walked miles along the top of the wall.

There was something remarkably levelling about standing on a wall that was thousands of years old and thinking of the men, beginning with the Roman legions, who had spent centuries guarding this wild landscape. Finally she could see her actions of the last few months in perspective. So she had an unfortunate love-affair. So what? In the space and timeless beauty of the Northumbrian landscape, she began to realise that life was too short to dwell on past mistakes. Man's span on earth was all too brief in the greater scheme of things, and she would only be compounding her foolish behaviour if she allowed a few weeks with Benedict Maxwell to overshadow her whole life.

By the time Rebecca was once more on the road back to Oxford she had regained some peace of mind and some of her confidence. The bitterness she felt towards Benedict would probably always be with her. But she was lucky. She had good friends and an interesting career to look forward to, and in time perhaps she would find the perfect partner...

The red painted door was so familiar. Rebecca raised her hand to knock, but before she got the chance the door was flung open, and she was clasped in a warm embrace.

'Rebecca! It's good to see you,' Mary cried, and, holding her arm, led her into the living-room. 'But I have some rather bad news.'

'Jonathan? He is all right?'

'Yes, he's fine, getting fatter by the minute.' Mary turned worried eyes on her young friend. 'But that dumb ox of a husband of mine has done something so stupid, I could throttle him.'

'Rupert?' Rebecca queried, sinking gracefully on to the shabby sofa. She knew the man was a bit absent-minded but she could not see him doing anything to hurt his family deliberately. 'What has he done?'

'Benedict Maxwell rang yesterday.'

Rebecca swallowed hard, fighting down her instant reaction to the sound of his name, and, with a lightness she did not feel, she said offhandedly, 'So?'

'He rang to confirm that he was still standing as a godfather to Jonathan and he'll be down tomorrow for the christening. Rupert, fool that he is, said, "Yes, fine," and has only seen fit to tell me half an hour ago. I'm sorry, love. I've tried to get in touch with Benedict, but so far no joy.'

'Is that all?' Rebecca laughed lightly, wanting to save her friend's obvious embarrassment. But her insides churned sickeningly. She had not thought she would have to face Benedict again, and certainly not tomorrow. The gall of the man was fantastic. Mary had asked them both to be godparents, but that was when she had thought they were engaged. The least he could have done, given the circumstnces, was bow out gracefully. He was just doing this to torment her.

'Rebecca, I know you said it was a mutual decision for the two of you to part, but, my dear, I have known you for four years, and I know you're hurting. If there is any way I can stop Benedict coming, I will.'

'Don't bother, Mary, I'll be all right, honestly.' But she could not hide the tremor in her voice. Coming back to this house had awakened memories she had tried so hard to forget.

Mary walked over and sat down next to her on the sofa. Rebecca made no protest as Mary gathered her hands in hers. 'Sometimes it's better to talk, love.'

Whether it was the touch of human warmth, the softness of Mary's voice or just weeks of bottling up the truth, Rebecca did not know. But for the next fifteen minutes she found herself confiding everything that had happened between herself and Benedict and the story of Gordon.

'You poor child,' Mary crooned, sliding an arm around her shoulders.

For a moment Rebecca allowed herself to wallow in the comfort of the other woman's sympathy, then, with a deep sigh, she straightened. 'I'm OK now, Mary. My holiday has helped me put things in perspective, and you've nothing to worry about tomorrow. I'll be fine at the christening.'

'I don't give a fig about that... Well, I do. But I can't believe Ben could be so thoroughly rotten, though I suppose in a way I'm not surprised. True, I knew him as a boy at college, but he was very reserved then and somehow, meeting him fourteen years later, I sensed a hardness about him; but, after what had happened to him, I thought, What can one expect from someone who has spent years cut off from civilisation? But to deliberately set out to hurt you... Words fail me.'

'My sentiments exactly, Mary. And now, if you don't mind, I think I'll go to bed. We have a busy day ahead of us tomorrow.'

It was another beautiful summer day; the sun beat down from an azure sky. Rebecca had spent all morning helping in the kitchen, running back and forward to the back garden, where the buffet was to be held, setting up trestle-tables, anything she could find to keep herself busy. She didn't want to think about her forthcoming meeting with Benedict.

Finally Mary hustled her off upstairs to get ready for church. 'One hour exactly. Get ready!'

Rebecca watched from the bedroom window as the cars pulled up in the street outside. She said a silent prayer of thanks. Rupert and Mary's parents had arrived first, so at least now when Benedict turned up she would not be left on her own to entertain him, while Mary got the baby ready for the short journey to the church.

She smoothed the slim pink silk skirt over her slender hips—too slender... The last and only time she had worn the outfit was for her first dinner date with Benedict. Well, it was stupid to be sentimental about clothes, she told herself firmly, and defiantly buttoned the jacket.

Only she had lost a bit of weight in the past few weeks and where once the small, fitted short-sleeved jacket had fastened snugly around her waist there was now room to spare, and the skirt no longer clung to her hips. Still, it wasn't too noticeable. Worriedly she chewed her bottom lip; if her suspicion was correct loss of weight would very soon not be a problem. With one last glance in the dressing-table mirror, she patted her neatly curled chignon and left the room.

With furtive glances at her wristwatch she carried the tray of drinks around the living-room, Rupert's booming voice, full of happiness, almost concealing the sound of the doorbell. Fortunately his mother-in-law jumped up and answered it. It could only be Benedict. Tom and Rose Wiltshire, the other godparents, had already arrived.

Rebecca felt the hairs on the back of her neck stand on end, her heart missed a beat, and she berated herself for being so stupid. Taking a deep breath and slowly exhaling, she turned around and not by a flicker of an eyelid did she betray her nervous tension as she coolly walked across the room and offered the latest arrival a drink.

'Whisky or sherry, Mr Maxwell?' she proferred, avoiding his eyes. 'Help yourself.'

'Hello, Rebecca.' Her violet eyes followed the progress of his large, tanned hand as he reached out, his long fingers curving around the chubby thickness of a crystal glass. 'A whisky will do fine—and Benedict, please.'

She could not tear her gaze away from the light smattering of black hairs at his wrist, the edge of his immaculate white silk shirt peeking beneath the grey silk sleeve of his jacket. She followed his hand as he raised the glass to his mouth, and quite unconsciously the tip of her tongue flicked out and licked her dry lips, as for a moment she remembered the touch of his sensuous mouth on her own.

'Surely after the intimacy we have shared you can't insist on calling me Mr Maxwell.'

His words stabbed her like a knife. She raised her eyes to his, and for a moment it was as though they were the only two people in the room. His golden gaze was strangely intent, no trace of the triumph she had expected evident there.

'You wore that outfit on our first date. You looked beautiful then, and you look even more beautiful now.'

He had the nerve to remind her. He was actually flirting with her. She wanted to smack his handsome face, she was so mad, but instead she replied calmly, 'Did I? I don't remember.'

'You do. But I suppose your denial was to be expected.' His dark head inclined towards her. 'Are you all right, Rebecca?'

Was she all right? Good God, if only he knew! It had been a month since their last meeting, and she had spent the last two weeks worrying. She was almost sure she was pregnant. She was clinging to the forlorn hope that emotional upheaval had disturbed her monthly cycle, but the nausea she had suffered that very morning led her to suspect the worst. But there was no way on earth she would tell this man ...

'I'm fine, thank you,' she bit out. 'Excuse me, I have to attend to the guests.' She could not get away quick enough.

'Rebecca, wait.'

'Ah, Becky, you darling, give me a drink quick and let's get this show on the road before baby Jonathan here decides to have another screaming fit.'

Rebecca expelled a sigh of relief at Mary's timely intervention, and in the general exodus for the cars to the church she managed to avoid Benedict.

Standing by the font of the old church with Benedict beside her, his sleeve brushing her shoulder, she could not help but be aware of him. She cast him a sidelong glance. He looked devilishly attractive, his dark hair, slightly longer, now curved the collar of his perfectly tailored jacket. He moved slightly and his muscular thigh rested against her; she jerked away as though she had been electrocuted, and barely managed to respond to the minister. Luckily no one seemed to have noticed her confusion.

Except Benedict. He turned towards her, his dark eyes lit with amusement. 'We're in a church, Rebecca, you're perfectly safe ... For now.'

The whispered words ignited her anger but there was nothing she could do about it; nevertheless it took all her self-control to prevent herself giving him a hefty kick in the shin. The conceited swine.

Back at the house Rebecca tried to avoid Benedict, but everywhere she moved he seemed to appear at her elbow. She fixed a smile on her face and talked vivaciously to everyone but him.

'I'll get you alone in the end, Rebecca,' he drawled softly, close to her ear.

Over my dead body, she thought, bitterly moving away, and breathing a sigh of relief as Fiona Grieves arrived with the Chancellor and his wife. Fiona made a bee-line for Benedict, linking her arm with his, and gazing adoringly at him.

Rebecca told herself she didn't care, the other woman was welcome to him, but her gaze kept straying to where he stood. A powerful, dynamic man, he drew people to him by the sheer force of his presence. He looked up and their eyes met. Benedict winked...

Amazement was quickly followed by disgust with herself and she lowered her gaze. She took a deep breath; it was almost over, and she had survived. But she could not relax, her nerves were tied in knots.

Perhaps indoors, away from the crowd, might give her some measure of relief, she thought as she strode into the living-room. The christening presents were laid out neatly on a table and idly she read the accompanying cards, smiling at 'Go for the set' beside a silver napkin-ring.

'If I were in your shoes I wouldn't be smiling.'

Fiona! How had she managed to tear herself away from Benedict? Rebecca thought cattily, when out of the corner of her eye, through the open door, she saw Mary ushering the man into the study across the hall.

'Oh, I don't know; I think the party is going rather well,' she replied, politely ignoring the other woman's innuendo.

'Come off it, Rebecca. You had the greatest catch of the decade and let him slip away.'

'An anthropologist can hardly be called the greatest catch of the decade. A multi-millionaire, maybe,' she opined mockingly, wishing Fiona would shut up.

'You don't know. I honestly believe you don't know.' The red-haired head was thrown back and she laughed.

The high, false sound grated on Rebecca's taut nerves and no way was she going to ask the question Fiona was evidently waiting for.

'My dear, Benedict Maxwell is a millionaire and more. Surely you have heard of M and M, the Anglo-French electronics firm?' Fiona waited and when Rebecca still stared blankly at her she continued, 'Montaine and Maxwell. The whole story was on the Jeff Kates show on television a couple of weeks ago. He interviewed Benedict and made him furious by suggesting he wasn't a genuine anthropologist and his discovery of the tribe and everything was all pure luck.'

'That's ridiculous.' Why Rebecca was defending Benedict's academic achievements, she had no idea.

'You know what they say. Money comes to money, fame to fame and all that. Apparently Benedict was on a two-year sabbatical from the family firm. When he was presumed dead, his uncle, Gerard Montaine, ran the company virtually on his own. But now Benedict is back and chairman of the board.'

Rebecca stared open-mouthed at Fiona. M and M was Benedict's. She had heard of it—anyone who ever read the business pages had. They had done a vast amount of the electronics work on the Channel Tunnel. Of course. Gordon had told her his mother was French. Benedict's mother... Good God! She had been an even bigger idiot than she knew.

'Rebecca, I want a word with you.' Steely fingers grabbed her arm and she found herself looking up into the darkly flushed face of Benedict. 'Alone,' he snarled, anger in every inch of him.

Something or someone had evidently rubbed the great man the wrong way; the air crackled with tension. But Rebecca had no intention of allowing herself to be used as the scapegoat. He had done that to her once already, never again...

'Benedict, darling, I thought you were never coming back,' Fiona's high-pitched whine intruded.

'Get lost, Fiona, I want to talk to my ex-fiancée.'

Rebecca almost felt sorry for the other girl; her beautifully made-up face turned scarlet and, with a haughty toss of her head, she walked out of the room.

'That was rather brutal, but true to form,' Rebecca observed coolly. Benedict's hand on her arm tightened. 'Let go of me,' she snapped.

'After we have had our little talk you can go to hell, but first I want an explanation.'

One quick glance at his dark face and she allowed him to lead her across the hall and into the study. She would never forgive herself if he caused a scene at the christening. She would not allow this man to spoil one of the happiest days of Mary's life.

Benedict was controlling his temper by a thread. It was evident in every line of his body, the tight, hard mouth, and the glitter of rage in his golden eyes. What had upset him, she could not imagine, but a shiver of fear snaked down her spine as the study door was slammed shut behind her.

'Now, Rebecca, just what the hell have you been telling Mary? I have never been so insulted in my life. Not five minutes ago I was raked over the coals for my despicable behaviour, by a woman I have known for years. Mary was sorry—if she could have contacted me, I would have not been needed as a godfather to her son. And it's all your doing.'

Rebecca groaned, she should have guessed. Mary was staunchly loyal, and very outspoken. The glimpse earlier of Mary and Benedict, entering this room, suddenly made sense.

'Why such outrage, Benedict? Surely it was no more than you expected?' She forced herself to stay calm,

though inside she was sick with misery. It had never occurred to her that Mary would tackle Benedict...

'I didn't expect to be virtually accused of rape,' he
snarled, and, his hands closing on her slender shoulders,
he hauled her tight against his huge, taut body. His dark
head swooped, and before she could react his mouth
savaged hers in a brutal kiss, his fingers tangling in the
mass of her black hair, with one tug dismantling the
smooth chignon.

Rebecca flinched, her hair cascading around her
shoulders. Then inexplicably the kiss gentled and he
murmured husky words against her mouth. To her shame
she sighed a soft sound of surrender. He straightened
up, and held her at arm's length, his glittering gaze intent
upon the pink, swollen curve of her mouth, the tell-tale
flush on her lovely face.

'If Mary could see you now she would know you for
the liar you are. Seduced you for revenge—what a joke!
You couldn't keep your hands off me,' he said scathingly.

It was worse than Rebecca had thought. Not only had
Mary confronted him about the break-up, but she had
obviously added her own suspicions about Rebecca's reaction to his lovemaking.

'I...I didn't lie to Mary. She is my friend, and—and
I told her the truth.' She stuttered over the words. Just
when she thought she had begun to get her life in order,
it was starting all over again. Benedict...was she never
to be free of him...?

'Your version—Gordon isn't around to deny it.'

She thrust the pain away at the mention of his half-
brother, and, very composed because she was keeping a
tight rein on her fast-rising temper, she said, 'Gordon
would have agreed with me. He was a wonderful, caring
young man. Something you would know nothing about.'

'By God, woman, you're truly remarkable! I look in
those wide, innocent violet eyes, and even I could be

fooled for a second. But I know just how destructive you can be. Poor Mary is as deceived by you as Gordon was. I've known the woman since we were teenagers, and in four short years you twine yourself around her affections so much so, you tell her what a big, bad ogre I am, and years of friendship are destroyed.' She stumbled backwards as Benedict thrust her away from him. 'You disgust me!' he snorted contemptuously.

Rebecca looked at him slowly through her thick lashes. He was standing motionless, arrogant contempt in every line of his hard body.

'What, no come-back, Rebecca?' He drawled her name as if it were an insult.

It was the last straw for Rebecca, and, straightening, she proudly raised her head, while with one hand she brushed her tangled mass of night-black hair from her face. 'You're pathetic, Benedict. My father once told me everyone is responsible for his or her own actions, but you—you're a coward and a cheat.'

'I've never hit a woman, but you could well be the first,' Benedict growled, taking a step towards her.

'It wouldn't surprise me. Nothing you do could surprise me any more. I've finally got your number, Mr Maxwell. You needed a scapegoat to assuage your own guilt... Mary, the friend who has only had a couple of cards off you in donkey's years, told me you were never there for your mother. Poor Gordon, as you like to call him, was a hundred times better a son. Where were you when your family needed you? Swanning around in Brazil.'

Rebecca saw the colour leave his face, his lips tightened to a thin line edged in white as he struggled to control his fury, but nothing could stop her. She wanted to hurt him as he had hurt her.

'Gordon told me he was spending the holiday with his mother because she needed him... He was that kind of young man. Unselfish. But then, how would you know, Benedict? You barely knew the boy.'

Benedict flinched, and she knew she had hit a nerve, but she didn't care. Nothing could stop her now.

'He told me his mother was distraught at losing her husband, and at your presumed death. He missed his father but, as he had rarely seen you, it didn't bother him as much. So if you want to lay blame anywhere, try laying it on yourself, you selfish bastard. And, before you call me a liar again, I suggest you read the autopsy report on Gordon. For a man who is supposed to be a scientist, your research is sadly lacking.'

She stalked across to the door and Benedict made no move to stop her. She turned, with her hand on the door-knob, and as a parting shot she added spitefully, 'Maybe that television chappy was right, Mr Multi-Millionaire. Your success in the Amazon *was* luck...' Rebecca flounced out of the study without a backward glance, she was so furious.

If she had stayed she would have seen Benedict Maxwell collapse in a chair and bury his head in his hands...

CHAPTER FIVE

'*MERCI.*' Rebecca picked up the cup of coffee the waiter had placed on the table, took a sip, and sank a few inches lower in the chair. A soft sigh of contentment escaped her. No one made coffee like the French. For the first time in three days she was alone and at peace.

The marina at Royan sparkled in the June sun, the sailing boats lying low in the water, their tall masts creaking and jingling in the strong breeze, the sound blending melodiously with the chattering voices of the locals enjoying the Sunday holiday.

Her attention was caught by a young boy crying as his ice-cream plopped on the pavement, and she was achingly reminded of her own son Daniel. It was the first time she had left him with Joanne and Josh, and she missed him dreadfully. But as a single parent she had to look after her career.

Her gaze strayed to a large yacht navigating the entrance to the harbour. A gleaming white cruiser, it was too big for the narrow berth of the marina, and tracked the harbour wall to dock at the open wharf. A tall, dark-headed man appeared on deck. He jumped lightly to the shore, his tanned body gleaming in the afternoon sun. Rebecca could not see his face, but there was something oddly familiar about him, the lithe way he moved, but before she could pursue the thought the peaceful setting was shattered by the strident cry of a young girl running towards the café.

'Mrs Blacket-Green ... Mrs Blacket-Green!'

Rebecca groaned, and looked up as the girl stopped in front of her. 'What's wrong, Dolores?' She eyed the well-developed sixteen-year-old, and frowned at the apology for a bikini she was wearing. 'And didn't I tell all you girls not to leave the beach without some clothes on?'

'Yes, miss. But please, miss, you have to come quick. Dodger persuaded Mr Humphrey to go out on a hobby cat and now they're in real trouble.'

Rebecca jumped to her feet. Extracting a few francs from the pocket of her trousers, she dropped them on the table, and set off at a run down the hill towards the beach. The large, dark man standing on the wharf was forgotten. She never noticed him turn to watch them, or the arrested expression on his rugged face.

The school trip to France had started off badly. On Friday, when they left England, Miss Smythe, her co-driver, had jammed her hand in the door of the minibus, and, as her other colleague, Mr Humphrey, didn't drive, Rebecca was left with the task, along with much of the responsibility for looking after a group of sixteen-year-old schoolchildren.

Oh, God! What damn fool thing had Humphrey done now? Rebecca asked herself, as she reached the beach. Miss Smythe was at the villa, preparing the evening meal, but Rebecca had felt sure Humphrey could manage on his own for a few minutes. Looking across the water, obviously she had been wrong. Travelling fast towards the entrance of the Gironde estuary and the Atlantic beyond was a hobby cat, the wind full in a large white sail and two figures getting smaller by the second clinging to the canvas deck.

'Dolores, get the rest of the pupils, and meet me at the shoreline,' she ordered, dashing across the sand. Then, to Rebecca's immense relief, she realised that the antics of the two on the cat had been spotted. Three life-

guards shot past her, and as she watched they jumped
into a motorised dinghy, and in minutes reached the sail-
boat and fastened a line to it.

Rebecca sighed with relief as the boat was towed to
the shore. With her fast-beating heart returning to
normal, she walked to the water's edge, gathering up her
charges as she went. There were nine—five boys and four
girls, with the iniquitous Dodger, Mr Humphrey, Miss
Smythe and herself making up the party of thirteen!
Some omen...

She watched, a worried frown creasing her face, as
the men stepped ashore, while the rest of her pupils
cheered. Once she had assured herself no harm had come
to the would-be sailors, her relief gave way to anger.

'Right, you lot. Sit down! Not you, Mr Humphrey—
perhaps you could go and get the sports gear while I talk
to the children.' She eyed him with exasperation. A tall,
ginger-haired, bespectacled young man, in the four years
Rebecca had taught at the large comprehensive school
in one of the poorer areas of London, Mr Humphrey
had definitely proved himself the most unlikely man to
control the street-smart kids.

'Silence!' she shouted, viewing the motley collection
with jaundiced eyes until she found the culprit. 'Right,
Dodger, perhaps you would care to explain your
behaviour.'

'I fancied a sail, miss. We are on holiday.'

Three days and already she was a nervous wreck. 'Let
me tell you. All of you. Unless you smarten your ideas
up, I will drive the bus back home tomorrow.' She was
totally unaware of the startling picture she presented. A
tiny, beautifully shaped woman, with short black curly
hair, dressed in cut-offs, a skimpy black Lycra boob-
tube, and a pair of battered Reeboks on her dainty
feet...haranguing a group of teenagers all bigger than
her.

'This trip started with an accident and but for the life-guard today would have ended in catastrophe. How you dared pretend you could sail, Dodger——' her eyes fixed on the youth responsible for the trouble '—when I know the nearest you have been to sailing is a rowing boat on the Serpentine in Hyde Park, is completely beyond me. An——'

Loud masculine laughter stopped her and, unsuspecting, she looked around. The catastrophe had happened after all. Benedict Maxwell. She recognised him immediately, her heart slamming against her ribcage in shock. Five years since their last meeting, and he had laughed then, she recalled, all the old bitterness returning, but with it a sense of pride. He could not hurt her now.

'Rebecca, Rebecca,' he spluttered between gales of laughter, 'you achieved your ambition, I see.' His golden eyes lit with amsuement, flashed around the group. 'Where do you teach? At a school for delinquents?'

He was standing a few feet away, naked except for brief khaki shorts, his wide shoulders shaking with mirth. Pointedly she turned her back on the laughing man, not deigning to answer him, and carried on in a firm voice, 'I want you, Dodger and Thompkins, to pick two teams and set up a game of football. Hopefully that will keep you out of trouble for an hour or two.'

'Hey, miss, the bloke is still there. Why don't you speak to him?' Dolores piped up. 'He's not bad for an old guy.'

Rebecca didn't want to speak to Benedict, she didn't even want to acknowledge his existence, but her lips twitched. 'Old guy.' He would love that...

'This old guy is perfectly capable of speaking for himself. Why don't you children jump to it and do as your teacher said? Football. Now.'

Rebecca had not realised Benedict was so close. A large hand curved over her shoulder, and she flinched at the impact on her smooth flesh. With a quick shrug she stepped away. 'I am perfectly able to look after my pupils. I don't need your assistance.'

'Forgive me, Rebecca.' Amusement still quirked his sensuous lips, but his dark gaze was intent and oddly serious on her flushed face. For a second she had the impression he was asking more than his words implied. But she was quickly disabused of the notion when he added mockingly, 'but you look as if you need all the help you can get.'

'You're the last man on earth I would ask if I did,' she spat. What perverse twist of fate had brought this man to this beach in the south-west of France, on the very day she had arrived? Rebecca asked herself bitterly. She had hoped never to see Benedict again, and after five years thought she had succeeded.

'That's better, Rebecca. It's good to see you're the same little firecracker I knew.' His lips parted over gleaming white teeth in a wolfish smile. 'And loved,' he added silkily.

Liar. He had never loved her, and she had no intention of bandying words with the man. A scream was a welcome diversion and she turned her attention to the ball game. 'You were offside, Dolores,' she cried, ending what looked like becoming an argument, before calling to her colleague, 'Mr Humphrey, I'll take over. I think you've had enough sun for one day.' The action might stop her legs trembling...

'Not so fast, Rebecca.' A big hand closed around her upper arm.

She glanced up at Benedict. He was standing much too close; she could feel the heat, the power coming from his muscled body, his glittering gaze commanding her attention.

'I want to talk to you, I want to explain. I want you to give me a chance,' he declared hardily.

Five years rolled back, and for a second she was once again the besotted fool. She shivered. She had been wrong earlier. This man could hurt her again. If he ever discovered her secret...

'Still the same Benedict: "I want".' A muscle tensed along his square jaw was the only visible sign of his rising temper. 'Well, you will just have to want. It will be a new experience for you, I'm sure,' she said with cold cynicism. 'And get your hand off me.'

'You win for now,' he said quietly, setting her free, as Mr Humphrey walked towards them. 'I can see this isn't the right time, Rebecca. Will you have dinner with me tonight?'

'No. I will not,' she said bluntly, and she caught the predatory flash in his tiger eyes an instant before Mr Humphrey joined them. Saved, she thought, deliberately turning her attention on Humphrey.

'Thanks, Rebecca. I am starting to burn.' The young man grimaced. 'See you later.' And with a wave he loped off down the beach.

In her peripheral vision she picked up what looked like the start of another argument. She wanted to ignore Benedict but her innate good manners forced her to turn back to him. 'Goodbye, Mr Ma——'

'Not so fast.' He stepped closer, his size, the well-muscled contours of his big, near-naked body disturbingly intimidating. 'Why, Rebecca?' One dark brow raised in enquiry. 'What are you afraid of?'

If only he knew... A thread of caution warned her to be careful. Her violet eyes wide, and she hoped innocent, lifted to his. 'Snakes, maybe,' she said musingly, 'but certainly not you.' She watched him stiffen, his face tight as the meaning of her words sank in. 'You will have to excuse me. My pupils need me.'

And, swinging around, she ran across the makeshift pitch. She felt his eyes burning into her back, but forced herself to ignore his brooding presence on the sidelines. She concentrated all her attention on the game.

She heaved a deep sigh of relief when, out of the corner of her eye, she saw Benedict turn and walk back up to the road. Thank God! He had gone...

Midnight and the house was finally quiet. It had been a long day. They had spent two days in Paris, left early that morning and driven down to Royan, arriving at lunchtime, and Rebecca was exhausted. The house they were staying in was a lovely old building on the roadside, overlooking the beach. It belonged to Miss Smythe; she had bought it for a song a few years ago for her retirement. She intended eventually to turn it into a holiday centre for students with limited funds. It had three large reception-rooms, four bedrooms on the first floor plus bathroom, and another four attic rooms and bathroom. The boys had opted for the attics and the girls had the first floor.

Wearily Rebecca made her way upstairs and into her room, switching off the lights as she went. She shrugged off her clothes and climbed into bed, too tired to think. But an hour later she was still awake. She tried to tell herself it was the heat, but she knew she was lying. Benedict Maxwell was the sole cause of her insomnia.

Her mind went back to their last meeting five years ago. After storming out of the study she had spent ten minutes tidying herself up and pride alone had forced her to return to the christening party.

Benedict had been politely making his goodbyes, his anger at Rebecca held firmly in check. When he'd spotted her coming downstairs, he had strolled up to her and declared loudly, 'It was wonderful seeing you again,

darling, and I'm sure we will always be good friends.'
Then he'd had the audacity to kiss her.

She had been jumping with anger, too furious to
speak, and his laughter echoed in her head long after he
had left. The next day she had moved to Nottingham,
renting one room while she completed her teacher-
training course.

The days were bearable with lectures to occupy her
mind, but at night, alone, she cried and cried. Often the
dawn found her awake and hurting.

She visited Oxord once more for Rupert and Mary's
farewell party in October, and on her return to
Nottingham the full folly of her actions was brought
home to her. She finally visited the doctor and her pregnancy was confirmed.

She exchanged her bedsit for a two-roomed apartment,
and, spending Christmas with Joanne and Josh, she had
confided in them. They had been a tower of strength for
her. Daniel was born in the Easter break and Joanne
had stayed with Rebecca for over a month.

It had all worked out very well. Rebecca took her final
exams and passed with flying colours. She applied for
a teaching post in a London school, and was immediately accepted, then spent the rest of the summer with
her new baby, and house-hunting.

Rebecca flung her legs over the bed and walked across
to the window. Her eyes roamed over the wide beach to
the sea beyond, the waves gently lapping the shore like
a lover's caress, a full moon gilding the scene in silver
glow. She was filled with doubt, and it was Benedict
Maxwell's fault... Had she done the right thing? yes,
of course, she told herself, her eyes lifting to the star-
studded night sky, as if by some miracle the heavens
would confirm the correctness of her decision.

She shivered. A chance meeting and, if she wasn't
careful, her cosy life could be badly disrupted.

*　　*　　*

'I brought a friend, is that OK?'

Rebecca jumped, dropping the sausage she had been trying to fork off the barbecue. 'Damn!' she swore under her breath and slowly turned to face the couple strolling across the garden. Dolores, with Benedict Maxwell in tow, was grinning all over her young face, the rest of the group behind them.

'We met your friend and invited him to lunch.'

'I hope you don't mind?' Benedict came towards her, his golden gaze roaming over her scantily clad body with sensual appreciation.

Rebecca shivered inwardly, and wished she had dressed with more care—brief shorts and a bikini-top were no defence against Benedict's studied appraisal. But even more worrying to her peace of mind was, what was he doing here? Miss Smythe had taken the children to explore the town. How Dolores had ended up with Benedict, she couldn't imagine.

Her eyes skated over his large frame. He was wearing a black sleeveless sweatshirt that outlined the musculature of his chest, beige chinos hugged his hips, a pair of Gucci loafers on his feet—the overall impression all virile male.

'Yesterday I was mad you had cut your hair; I remember it spread on my pillow,' he said softly. 'But now I like it,' Then he ran one large hand through her short black curly hair.

She flinched beneath his casual caress, and the memory his words invoked, and hit out at him scathingly, 'I should have thought even you would have more sense than to chat up young teenagers.'

'Don't be stupid, Rebecca. You must know the only reason I spoke to Dolores was to find you.'

She believed him. The trouble was, she had not wanted him to find her again. He was a dangerous man, and she had far too much to lose... She turned wary, hostile

eyes to his, about to tell him to get lost, when Miss
Smythe cut in, 'Isn't it lucky we met your old friend Mr
Maxwell? Fancy your father being one of his lecturers
at university! What a small world it is. I was telling him
about my little accident——' she held her bandaged hand
before her '—and guess what?'

The flash of triumph in Benedict's eyes was enough
to tell Rebecca that she was not going to like the answer.

'His yacht is here in the harbour for a few days, while
some minor repairs are carried out. So he has kindly
offered to help with the driving for a couple of days.
Also the children are going for a trip on his boat on
Thursday. Isn't that great?'

Stifling a groan—it was worse than she thought—
Rebecca said firmly, 'Really, I don't think we can impose
on Mr Maxwell like that.'

'Nonsense, Rebecca, it's my privilege,' Benedict
drawled mockingly. 'What are friends for?'

She shot him a fulminating look; it was obvious he
had spent the last hour winning the confidence of her
two collegues and the children. She could just imagine
their faces if she told them the truth. He had seduced
her and given her a child...Daniel. The thought of her
son cooled her anger; she had to be careful. One slip
and Benedict might find out more than she wanted him
to know. Screaming her hatred of him was a non-starter.
Much better to play him at his own game. Pretend to
be friends, and in a few days' time she need never see
him again.

'Well, if you're sure it won't be too much trouble?'
she queried lightly, amazed at her own acting ability.
'Your help with the driving would be much appreciated.'
The kids would drive him mad in half a day and it would
serve the swine right, she thought gleefully.

'It will be my pleasure, Rebecca.'

Little did he know... She had no doubt his experience was zilch. He was in for a rude awakening. Confidently she turned to the large trestle-table with long benches running either side and began setting out the food.

Rebecca was not quite so confident when she realised the only place left to sit was at the end of the bench next to Benedict, and when his hard thigh brushed her naked leg she quickly edged away.

'Nervous, Rebecca? There's no need. Have a drink,' he drawled softly, and, picking up the large bottle of cheap wine, he leant over her and filled the beaker beside her on the table. 'It should be champagne to celebrate our reunion.'

His throatily voiced comment was a teasing breath across her cheek, his golden eyes glittered wickedly down at her, and in that instant she knew she was not immune to his charm and never would be.

'Hardly a reunion,' she said carefully.

A lazy smile curved his hard mouth. 'Oh, but yes, Rebecca, and I'm hoping for a lot more,' he drawled, his gaze dropping from her lovely face to her full breasts, arousing an unwanted shiver of awareness inside her. 'I'm looking forward to tomorrow and accompanying you to Cognac. Wednesday is a nature trail, I believe, and Thursday we go sailing.'

'There's no need,' she snapped, forgetting her early conviction to beat him at his own game.

'Oh, but I think you do need me, Rebecca.'

She flushed and looked away. She didn't need him, she didn't need any man, she told herself sternly.

'To help with the children, of course. Dolores tells me you're here until Friday, so perhaps we could have that dinner after all,' he said blandly.

Stupid, stupid, stupid, Rebecca castigated herself. Of course Benedict had not meant she needed him personally. 'Dolores has a big mouth,' she muttered.

'Now, now, Rebecca; is that any way to talk about your pupils?' he admonished with a chuckle.

She ignored him and savagely speared the sausage on her plate, wishing it was Benedict's face. As for Dolores... She would have to have words with that girl. God knew what else she might tell him. It was a short step from gossiping about Rebecca's school duties to her personal life, and she could not allow that to happen. Lifting the plastic beaker to her lips, she took a long swallow of wine in an attempt to steady her nerves. Then, replacing it on the picnic table, she munched on a sausage. When she finally had enough control to raise her head, and tune into the conversation, to her horror she saw that Benedict was arranging with Miss Smythe and Mr Humphrey for him to take her out to dinner on Wednesday evening.

'No, really,' she cut in. 'I couldn't leave you two on your own with the children.'

'Rubbish, Rebecca, you'll be doing most of the work the next couple of days, of course you must have a night out with your old friend. I won't hear otherwise,' Miss Smythe insisted.

Rebecca's violet eyes flashed fire at the man beside her. His smug, self-satisfied grin, and the triumph in his eyes, made her clench her teeth to prevent herself cursing out loud. Benedict Maxwell was an expert at manipulating circumstances and people to suit himself. If he was determined to spend the next couple of days with their party, and to get Rebecca alone, he must have some ulterior motive for it. With a terrific effort of will she retained her self-control. It would be more to her advantage to expend her energies on trying to find out exactly what he was up to...

She tilted her head to one side, and for the first time since meeting him again she really studied him. He was thinner, the lines bracketing his mouth much deeper, the once-black hair now streaked with grey. He looked a lot older than she remembered; still, he was almost forty. But it wasn't the signs of age that made him look different—the hard character of the man was etched into his rugged features. Or perhaps it was because she no longer saw him through a rosy haze of love; her vision had cleared, and she saw him for what he was: a dangerous man...

'So will I do?' Benedict asked drily. 'You're looking at me as though you've never seen me before.'

An embarrassing tide of colour swept up her throat and she could have kicked herself for being caught staring. Instead, picking her words with care, she replied, 'Five years is a long time, I don't know you; but from what I remember of you——' she deftly brought the subject back to the present '—I find it difficult to believe you would willingly spend time with a group of schoolchildren. I would have thought the Riviera was more your style.'

'How would you know my style, Rebecca? After you broke off our engagement you refused to even acknowledge my existence,' he said with bitter cynicism.

She broke off their engagement? 'Hardly surprising,' she snorted inelegantly. Who was he trying to kid? Had the man lost his memory?

'I know I was wrong, but I wrote and explained, apologised. I hoped you would reply, but I understood and accepted it when you didn't. But surely after five years you can forgive me?' he demanded, frustration evident in his voice.

He had lost her. Benedict had never written to her in his life.

'I want to be your friend, Rebecca—lay the ghost of the past once and for all. Yesterday, when I saw you at the harbour, I couldn't believe my luck. My one thought was at last I had a chance to put things right between us. A letter is never really satisfactory.' His deep voice was compelling but Rebecca could not believe what she was hearing.

Thankfully Miss Smythe interrupted the low conversation with, 'Well, if you all help to clean up, the rest of the afternoon can be spent on the beach.'

Benedict looked around as though he had forgotten there were other people present, and swore under his breath. He glanced back at Rebecca.

'We will talk, and that's a promise.' The threat in his tone was unmistakable and, not waiting for her reply, he got to his feet. With all the charm at his disposal he regretfully took his leave—business to attend to. With one last penetrating look at Rebecca, he added, 'Miss Smythe tells me we leave at nine in the morning. I'll see you then.'

'Yes, fine, goodbye,' she gritted, galled to have to agree, but she had no option.

For the rest of the afternoon Rebecca kept a sketchy eye on her pupils, while going over and over in her mind everything that had happened since yesterday afternoon and the reappearance of Benedict Maxwell in her life.

Could she have handled the situation any differently? she asked herself a hundred times over. The answer was always no. With his easy charm he had completely captivated Miss Smythe, and she was the senior teacher. Rebecca was obliged to go along with what her colleague suggested. Cutting Benedict dead, or allowing her bitterness to show, would serve no purpose. He would probably see it as a challenge and be even more persistent or, worse, suspicious. An inquisitive Benedict was the last thing she needed. Yes. She had done the right thing. The next few days would be hard, but then back to London and safety.

Later, after dinner, she made a quick telephone call to Josh and Joanne in Corbridge and spent a happy five minutes talking to Daniel. He was having a great time with young Amy to play with, and did not appear to miss her in the least. Afterwards she wandered outside, unable to settle. Benedict's reappearance had disturbed her more than she wanted to admit. Daniel was the image of him; she had not quite realised how very alike they were until today, and the thought was oddly disturbing...

Sitting in the front passenger-seat of the minibus, she cast a sidelong glance at the driver. Benedict looked positively brimming with health and vitality, his rugged features somehow more relaxed. She couldn't see the expression in his eyes as he was wearing dark glasses, but, by the upward curve of his lips, he was a man content with the world.

Rebecca was loath to admit it, but it was a relief to have someone else drive. She had not relished the thought of doing it all herself.

'Why the frown, Rebecca?' The softly voiced question caught her unawares. 'Is it such a hardship to be in my company?

Her full lips curved up in a smile. 'No, nothing like that; in fact I was just thinking how lucky we are to have you along. I like driving, but it's good to have a break,' she replied truthfully.

'I'm sorry Miss Smythe hurt her hand, but her loss is my gain, so I'm not complaining.' He turned his attention back to the road, adding wryly, 'Except about the dilapidated state of this vehicle. It amazes me you managed to drive it from England.'

'It's perfectly all right, only a bit old; it needs gentling along, that's all,' she defended.

He shot her a cheeky grin. 'Like me.'

She turned and looked out of the window, warmed
by his achingly familiar grin but determined not to respond. It would be all too easy to fall for his practised
charm, and that was the road to hell, she knew, to her
cost. She was a mature adult, she told herself, and had
more sense than to make the same mistake twice.

As they drew nearer to their destination Benedict explained the history behind the making of cognac. All
along the roadside were the vineyards and invitations to
sample the wines that were eventually blended to make
cognac. Brandy made anywhere else in the world was
not allowed to call itself cognac.

When they finally pulled up in the centre of town, the
children who had been half-hearted about the trip were
now raring to go. Benedict had fired their imagination,
Rebecca realised, something she would not have thought
him capable of.

'Why the strange look, Rebecca?' he queried, taking
her hand and helping her down from the bus.

'I never had you down as someone who would get
along with children,' she reluctantly explained.

Not letting go of her hand, he said, 'I love children;
I hope to have my own some day.' A teasing grin spread
across his handsome face as he removed his glasses and
bent his head down to hers, adding, 'How would you
like the job, Rebecca?'

She gasped and pulled her hand from his, a bright tide
of red sweeping her delicate features. 'No, thank you,'
she muttered, avoiding his eyes, and hastily she began
shepherding the boys and girls into some kind of order.

'Embarrassed—a woman of your experience? I wonder
why?' His questioning gaze narrowed on her flushed
face, and quickly she turned, before he saw more than
she wanted him to.

'Kids, follow me,' she instructed, not bothering to answer him.

Rebecca breathed a sigh of relief, as Benedict walked past her, ruthlessly suppressing an unexpected feeling of guilt. She had almost given herself away; she would have to be more careful in future.

The distillery was fascinating, a huge building down by the riverside. They toured the Cognac and Cooperage Museum, which included some pieces dating back to the Middle Ages. Then they boarded a passenger ferry to cross the river to the ageing warehouses, where millions of litres of brandy aged in casks, each row containing the harvest for a single year, going back over a century.

'Goodness, Benedict, the smell in here will be enough to make my lot tipsy!' Rebecca exclaimed as the young guide told them all to sit on chairs at one end of the dark warehouse for a film show.

'Not to worry, sweetheart; as long as I stay sober you'll be fine,' he murmured, sitting down beside her.

When they all finally emerged into the bright afternoon sunlight, Rebecca felt slightly disorientated, but with Benedict's arm flung casually across her shoulder she quickly recovered, and felt dizzy for a completely different reason.

In the visitors' hall the full range of cognacs were on sale, and as Benedict spoke to the guide Rebecca bought a bottle of V.S.O.P. fine champagne cognac. It would be a nice present for Josh and Joanne, she thought, and the least she could do, considering the favour they were doing her.

'Careful. Acquire a taste for the stuff and you lose control,' a deep voice drawled provocatively.

'It's for a friend,' she said quickly.

'A male friend?'

'Yes,' she muttered, wishing Benedict would not tower over her in quite such a domineering fashion.

'Lucky man,' he said curtly, then smiled. 'But perhaps not so lucky. He isn't here and I am.' And, bending down, he brushed her forehead in a brief kiss, before placing his arm possessively around her shoulder and tucking her into his side. 'Have you got all you need? We're holding up the queue.'

Flustered by the sensual warmth of his touch and the unexpected kiss, Rebecca grasped her package tightly with both hands. Was it only she who felt the tension between them? she wondered frantically.

'Yes, thank you,' she said in a tight voice. Her decision of yesterday to play along with the man, as the easiest solution, was beginning to lose its appeal. The effort to hold him at a distance was exhausting and playing havoc with her nerves.

Rebecca stepped into the antique bath full of hot, scented water and slid down until the soft bubbles reached her small chin. Ah, luxury! she sighed. With six females sharing one bathroom she fully appreciated the sacrifice her pupils had made in insisting she could have the bathroom for an hour. But she was not so appreciative of the way she had been forced into dining with Benedict.

For the last two days he seemed to have filled her every waking hour. From their leaving the cognac factory on Tuesday until this evening the time had flown, and she had to admit it had been quite fun.

A reminiscent smile curved her full lips. Today they had driven along the Route Verte to Saint-Fort-sur-Gironde, lunched at the only hotel—Le Lion d'Or—and afterwards they had driven on a few miles to the Moulin de Sap, a large wooded area with a narrow stream meandering through it. In the heart of the wood a timber hut had served as a bar, with a few pedal-boats for hire to explore the waterway.

The children had hired pedalos for an hour and Benedict had insisted she accompany him on one. A chuckle escaped her; she could still see the hurt look of frustration on his face when after half an hour he had tried to turn the boat around in the ten-foot-wide stream.

First they had run aground at the front then at the rear, and in the process one pedal broke. Thompkins and Dodger had come up behind them, hooted at Benedict's struggles then commented cheekily, 'Maybe it's not such a good idea to go on his yacht tomorrow, if his expertise with a pedalo is anything to go by.' Laughing, they turned and left.

When Benedict finally managed to point the boat in the right direction he pushed the one pedal hard, rocking the craft. A jangling sound echoed in the silence as all his loose change fell out of the pockets of his shorts and into the water.

Rebecca had tried for two days to retain some formality between herself and Benedict, but she was fighting a losing battle and at the look of chagrin on his face she had burst out laughing.

His furious eyes met hers, then his lips twitched, he chuckled, and finally his laughter joined hers.

Still smiling, she stepped out of the bath and rubbed her small body dry with a huge beach-towel, then, wrapping it firmly round under her armpits, she headed back to her room.

She sat down at the battered dressing-table and studied her flushed, lightly tanned face in the mirror. She had mixed emotions about the evening ahead. She could not deny the tingling feeling of excited anticipation at the thought of dinner with Benedict. But her common sense told her she was being a fool to risk it.

Later, Rebecca shifted uneasily in the soft leather seat of the white Mercedes, her fingers tugging nervously at the hem of the jade silk dress in a futile attempt to cover her knees. The dress was a mistake. A Bruce Oldfield original, the bodice a wisp of silk that draped in a deep V back and front, fastening at the side with one button, a matching belt circled the waist, the skirt a straight wrap-over with two small soft pleats in the front. It had been an impulse buy in the January sales. She must have been mad!

It was the most daringly cut thing she had ever worn, and tonight, when Benedict first caught sight of her, his expression said it all. His face had revealed a variety of emotions, going from the friendly smile he had adopted over the past few days, to shock, then a slight frown, and culminating in what she could only describe as blatant lust.

They had travelled for about ten minutes and Rebecca could feel the tension building in the silence. Her thoughts skidded guiltily between the past and present. They were travelling fast, the road winding between sweet-scented pine forests.

'I don't want to go too far,' she blurted, breaking the silence.

'In that dress? You could have fooled me.' Benedict shot her a sidelong glance, his smile one of wicked amusement.

She flushed. 'I mean I don't want to travel too far. I don't feel right, leaving my colleagues to deal with the children while I gad around,' she explained, ignoring his provocative statement.

'Don't worry, Rebecca. As for going too far, we're almost there.'

The tyres screeched as Benedict swung the car around a corner and into a side-road, and Rebecca was flung across the seat, so she ended up against him. She straightened abruptly, putting some space between them. Her bare arm burned where it had come into contact with his. She told herself it was the ninety-degree temperature of the area, nothing more, but the excuse was wearing thin after two days of frequent such contacts, even to her ears...

'Mechers is a nice little village and the restaurant rather unusual. I think you'll like it, Rebecca, so relax and enjoy, hmm?'

He was right. At first she was puzzled as he drove the car up a hill, through the village, to the top of a cliff overlooking the sea, and parked.

'Where is the restaurant?' she asked dubiously.

'Soon all will be revealed. Trust me.' And, sliding out of the car, he walked round the front and opened the passenger-door, helping her out, with one strong hand cradling her elbow.

The evening air was heavy with the fragrance of flowers mingling with the salty tang of the sea. To her amazement Benedict led her to a small gate, through, and down steps cut into the cliff-face where a large natural shelf formed a wide veranda, with a man-made wall to prevent anyone plunging the hundred and fifty feet down into the sea. The restaurant was a group of caves, carved out of the rock.

'This is fantastic!' she exclaimed. The view of only sea and sky was unreal. 'It's like the secret grotto in a fairy-tale.' She turned shining eyes up to Benedict. 'It's beautiful. Thank you for bringing me here.'

He was not looking at the view, his gaze fixed intently on her lovely face. 'You're beautiful,' he said, his voice husky and vibrant with desire.

For a moment she simply stared at him, aware of a need, a sense of longing, she had not felt in years. He looked overwhelmingly male, dangerously so. Perfectly tailored beige trousers hugged his lean hips, and a complementary short-sleeved silk shirt lay open at his throat, revealing the beginnings of black body hair. 'So are you.' Horrified, she froze to the spot. She had spoken aloud.

Benedict searched her face for a few seconds, and then he smiled slowly. 'We were lovers once, and now I would like to think we're friends. It's not a crime to admit we still find each other attractive.' His eyes slid down to her cleavage where the soft curve of her full breasts was clearly visible, then back to her small face. His golden eyes darkened appreciably. 'I'm giving you fair warning, Rebecca; I want you...'

Rebecca gave a small gasp of alarm and stepped back quickly. She was burning, she could feel the heat through the soles of her sandals to the top of her head. How much longer could she blame the climate?

'Can we eat outside? I like the idea of dining hanging over a cliff...' She was babbling, but his declaration had completely unnerved her.

Benedict's hand grasped her wrist and gently he urged her to sit down at a table overlooking the estuary. 'Yes, we can eat outside.' And, sitting down opposite her, he relinquished her wrist and casually picked up the menu. 'Will you allow me to order for you?' he asked with a faint curve of his hard mouth.

How did he do that? One minute he looked all predatory male, and moments later he was smiling gently. Rebecca moistened her dry lips. 'Yes,' she murmured with a tentative answering smile of her own. Perhaps she had heard him wrong before...

Benedict ordered champagne, and after the first glass Rebecca began to relax; by the second, she was suddenly filled with a sense of adventure. She had been acting responsible and concerned for years, but tonight she felt like a different person, and it was only for the one night. What could go wrong?

Over a delicious meal of asparagus in a creamy sauce followed by a marvellous platter of fresh seafood, the

conversation flowed easily. Benedict laughed at some of
her stories about teaching and she responded as he regaled her with his account of his first voyage on his yacht.

The sweet arrived, a fantasy of ice-cream and
meringue, and as Rebecca licked her lips after the last
mouthful Benedict asked lightly, 'Do you still see Mary
and Rupert?'

'Rupert took a post at Harvard. I try to keep in touch,
but Mary isn't a letter-writer; I've had a card a couple
of times——' She broke off, remembering the ac-
cuastion she had once hurled at him.

'Yes, I know. I was in America when they arrived; we
had lunch. Mary is a very loyal friend—I had a devil of
a job persuading her to give me your new address. Why
didn't you answer my letter, Rebecca? Had I really hurt
you so badly?'

Warning bells rang in her head. 'I'd like a coffee,' she
said, attempting to change the subject.

One dark brow arched sardonically, as he met her
glance, then he turned to the waiter. 'Coffee for two,
and two cognacs,' he instructed, before turning his dark
gaze back to Rebecca's wary face. He reached across the
table and covered her hand with his... She wanted to
snatch her hand back, but thought better of it when she
registered his expression.

He was watching her, his intelligent eyes filled with
curiosity and a hint of exasperation. 'Why do you shy
away whenever I attempt to mention the past, Rebecca?
It's almost as though you feel guilty about it. Yet everything that happened between us was all my fault. We
need to talk about it. I want to explain. That last day
in the study, you were partially right——'

'Please, Benedict, don't spoil a pleasant evening,' she
cut in. 'I can't see the point in raking over dead ashes.'
She had enough guilty feelings of her own, and they were

growing larger by the day, the more time she spent with
this man...

'Are they dead?' he demanded tightly.

She swallowed hard and forced herself to ignore the
soft rub of his thumb against her palm, clamping down
on the erotic sensations his lightest touch aroused. He
was much too perceptive; she should have remembered
he was an extremely successful businessman with a razor-
sharp brain, who for a hobby studied the evolution of
the human race. A shiver of apprehension shuddered
down her spine. He would be a formidable adversary to
anyone who crossed him.

'I was very young, when I first met you. Now I am a
very busy teacher who loves her career. I never look back,
but to the future.' She made herself squeeze his hand,
as she smiled deep into his eyes. 'It was great meeting
you here in France; your help has been fantastic. Let's
just forget the past.'

Would he buy it? she wondered, astounded at her
acting ability. Or was it acting...?

Benedict eyed their entwined hands for a few seconds,
then looked up at her with a strange expression.
'Yes...but please just answer one question. Why did
you not answer my letter?'

Letter—he kept going on about some letter, and she
had no idea what he was talking about. 'Perhaps because I never received any letter from you,' she said flatly,
dragging her hands free.

'But you must have done. Mary gave me your address
in Nottingham, and I wrote to you in November, explaining I knew you were innocent of any involvement
in Gordon's death, and apologising.'

'Did you?' she commented, not believing him for a
moment.

'You don't believe me!'

'It doesn't matter.' The coffee and cognac arrived, and she breathed a sigh of relief, but it was short-lived—as she reached for the cup Benedict once again trapped her hand in his. His other hand tilted her chin so she was compelled to face him.

His golden eyes held her captive. 'Rebecca, after we parted I went to France and I did what I should have done in the beginning; I asked my uncle exactly what had happened when Gordon died. He showed me the autopsy report, and he had no doubt at all it was accidental death. He had attended the inquest personally. When I questioned him about my mother's view—that Gordon had committed suicide because his girlfriend had dumped him, and the ''accidental'' verdict had been a kindness to a Catholic family—Gerard quickly disabused me of the notion. Seemingly Mother had been unstable for some time, since the death of her second husband, and my presumed death. When Gordon died she had gone to pieces completely. She had found his diary among his personal effects and jumped at the chance to blame someone for his death. You...'

'Please, Benedict...' Rebecca shook her head.

His hand fell from her chin to the table. 'Please hear me out, Rebecca. When I first met you I had only heard my mother's version of events, and you were right. I did feel guilty. I hadn't been there for her when she lost her husband, and you were correct when you said I wasn't as close to Gordon as I should have been. I did use you as a scapegoat in a way, and I have never forgiven myself for it. I had some crazy notion I could make up for not being there when Gordon needed me. I don't know.'

His hand tightened on hers. 'I met you, and you were so lovely, so full of life...and Gordon was dead.' He shook his head as if to clear his mind, a look of helpless frustration in his dark eyes. 'I want you to know I deeply regret my behaviour. I told you all this in the letter, and

I hoped you could see your way to forgiving me. But
you never replied, and I accepted it.'

His eyes told of his deep regret, the sadness in their
depths too real for her to doubt him.

'I never, ever got the letter, Benedict,' she said quietly.
She believed him, and, looking back, she could see how
it might have happened. 'I had a bedsit when I first
moved to Nottingham, but after a couple of months I
moved into a one-bedroom apartment; perhaps your
letter went to the first address, I don't know...' She tailed
off as the full import of his confession struck her. If she
had heard from him then, would she have done things
differently? Would she have told him about Daniel? His
explanation had opened up a Pandora's box of might-
have-beens, and suddenly she was tormented by doubts.

'Do you believe me now, Rebecca?'

'Yes, yes,' she murmured, but it was all too late, she
thought sadly, unable to look at him. The shock of
knowing he had tried to get in touch with her and had
some excuse for his behaviour was almost more than she
could take in, but it did not alter the fact that he had
never loved her...

Benedict threw back his head, taking a deep breath
of the night air. 'God, Rebecca, I feel as though a huge
weight has been lifted from my shoulders.'

She looked up into his handsome, smiling face. The
relief on his rugged features was obvious; the trouble
was, that same weight had descended on *her* shoulders.
How could she tell him he had a son? Did she want to?

She grasped the brandy glass in front of her and raised
it to her lips. Slowly she sipped the fiery spirit, trying
to compose her shattered nerves. The revelations of the
evening took some getting used to. The towering presence
of Benedict opposite was a comfort, but also a threat,
and she needed time to decide what to do...

Benedict, as if sensing her uncertainty, put himself out to be pleasant.

He told her more about this part of France, as the evening sky darkened and the first stars appeared. There was no one else eating on the terrace, and, with darkness surrounding them and the soft sound of the water lapping against the base of the cliff, Rebecca had the weird feeling that they were the only two people in the world.

Eventually Benedict stood up and drew her to her feet. She shivered slightly in the cool night air, and it seemed perfectly natural for him to put his arm around her and hold her close to the warmth of his masculine body. Still holding her, he paid the bill and led her back to the car. For some reason the journey back seemed shorter, Rebecca thought, as he stopped the car on the road outside the villa.

'It's a beautiful night; shall we stroll along the beach?' he asked quietly.

Maybe it was the drink, but she didn't care and, with a soft smile, she agreed to his request.

Like two children, they dashed across the road hand in hand and down on to the sand. Rebecca kicked off her sandals and Benedict picked them up, carrying them in one hand while his other arm encircled her slender shoulders.

Where the road turned away from the beach the pine woods stretched down to the sand. The scent of pine and the heady feeling of Benedict's hand gently caressing her bare shoulder conspired to break down the protective barriers Rebecca had errected around her emotions over the years. In a dream she wandered along, the sand still warm against her bare feet. Surely she was entitled to one night free of responsibility, one night of magic...?

'Rebecca?' Benedict chuckled softly, and turned her, wrapping her close against him. 'I've been talking for the last few minutes,' he said into her hair. 'Where were you?'

'Here.' She smiled guilelessly up into his rugged face and, lifting her hand, with one finger she gently outlined his mouth. 'What were you saying?' she murmured.

He caught her hand, and placed it deliberately on his shoulder. 'I was saying thank you for this second chance, and promising not to rush you into anything you don't want; it's enough to know you've forgiven me.' He took a deep, rasping breath. 'But now I don't know if I can keep that promise,' he ended huskily.

She wasn't aware she was giving him a second chance or even wanted to, Rebecca thought muzzily, but, as his hand drifted down over her full breast, his other hand tightened convulsively round her waist, hauling her hard against him. His dark head lowered and his lips found hers. This was where her play-acting of the past few days had led her. This was what she had been afraid of, she thought with a flash of insight, before the warmth of his kiss deepened and she was incapable of controlling her own response.

Her arms went around him and he held her tightly against him. She knew she was playing with fire, but his masculine arousal was very evident and unbelievably exciting as he moved his hard thighs erotically against her. Rebecca moaned softly, knowing she should put a stop to this intimacy, but her senses were swimming with pleasure, and a restlessness began to uncoil deep within her.

'God, you feel so good. You don't know what you do to me, Rebecca. I've wanted you like this for years.'

His rough, deep voice was thick with passion and she barely registered when he lowered them both to the sand. She wrapped her slender arms around his neck, her mouth seeking his; she was floating in a whirlpool of desire, and she writhed against him as his hand slid inside the bodice of her dress, his long fingers stroking her hardening breasts. His tongue darted between her lips, exploring her mouth with an urgent passion as his body rocked over hers.

Benedict pulled back and stared down at her; his hands deftly unfastened the belt at her waist and the one button that held the dress in place. 'This damn gown has driven me crazy all night,' he groaned, turning back the silk. 'You're exquisite, Rebecca—tiny, but so voluptuous, absolutely perfect.'

She gazed up at him; the moonlight cast planes and shadows over his dark features but there was no mistaking the burning passion in his golden eyes. She smiled a smile as old as Eve, reached up and unbuttoned his shirt. Then he caught her hands and spread them either side of her lush, near-naked body, her lace briefs her only protection from his hungry gaze.

Slowly he bent his head and with incredible gentleness suckled the hard nub of her creamy breast, first one and then the other, till she thought she would cry out with the ecstasy of it. Allowing one of her hands to go free, he stroked long fingers gently down her flat stomach, easing beneath her briefs to the warm dampness between her thighs.

Her back arched involuntarily. 'Please...' she moaned, her hand gliding down his broad chest to his trim waist, her fingers tugging at his belt.

'Rebecca, my love, tonight I want to love you as I should have done the first time. Slowly, slowly.'

The mention of the first time was like a douche of cold water. Her body clenched in instant rejection, and she grasped his wrist and writhed for a totally different reason, trying to get away.

'Rebecca, no. What is it?' Benedict groaned.

Fighting down the urge to haul him down to her, she cried, 'I'm not protected,' and sprang to her feet.

Fumbling with her dress, she pulled it haphazardly
around her. He caught her ankle.

'It's all right, I have something,' he said urgently.

Her breathing was erratic and the ache of frustration
was eating at her control. But she saw red at his words.
'Yes, you would!' she cried, and, kicking free, she picked
up her sandals and stormed off down the beach, fastening
her dress around her trembling body. The swine would
be prepared! Shame he hadn't thought of it last time.
No, she didn't mean that, she loved her son... But
Benedict was rich and powerful, he wanted her now, tonight—she did not doubt that for a minute. But what
of tomorrow, and the rest of her life?

No! There was no future for her with Benedict.
Perhaps, years ago, they might have made a go of it.
But not now. She had responsibilities. It was too late.
Wasn't it? She shivered, the night air cold against her
hot flesh.

'Rebecca.' Benedict caught her arm. 'Why? We are
free, consenting adults!' he exclaimed.

'You might be, but I'm not,' she said sadly.

'The man you bought the cognac for,' he growled.

Suddenly she saw a way out. 'Yes, that's right.'

'I'm sorry, I shouldn't have come on so strong.'

His apology took all the fight out of her. She looked
up at him; he was breathing deeply, fighting to control
some emotion she could only guess at. 'No, you
shouldn't,' she agreed. But he carried on as though she
had never spoken.

'I had no right, but I give you fair warning, Rebecca.'
And, wrapping her in his arms, he held her still and close
to his heart, her head resting on his chest. 'I fully intend
to give your boyfriend a run for his money. Your loyalty
does you credit, but I want you and I think you want
me...'

'I...' She wanted to deny him.

'Shh, Rebecca.' His strong arms enfolded her, soothing, caring. 'Tomorrow we'll spend the day together, and I'm going to visit you in London.'

She sighed. 'Only the children and Mr Humphrey are coming with you on the yacht.' His grip tightened and hastily she explained, 'Miss Smythe and I are spending the day cleaning the villa and packing, ready for an early start on Friday.'

'You work far too hard, little one, but you're right. It's probably better that way. I'll bring the children back so tired, they won't object to staying in the last night, and you'll be free to have dinner with me.'

That was not what she'd meant, but the idea had appeal. This new caring Benedict was someone she could easily grow very fond of. As for visiting her in London, she didn't know... It would present an awful lot of problems. But there was no harm in dreaming for another day. Was there?

'Yes, OK, dinner tomorrow night.'

'Thank you, Rebecca.' Benedict tilted her chin, and kissed her softly swollen lips, before gently tucking her into the curve of his arm, and together, in a peaceful silence, they walked the last few hundred yards back to the villa.

Curled up in her bed, Rebecca told herself she was a mature, sensible woman, and Benedict appeared to be a reasonable man. Perhaps if she told him about Daniel tomorrow night... perhaps they could be friends. She didn't for one minute admit to herself any further interest. She didn't dare...

CHAPTER SIX

SUNDAY evening, school tomorrow, and Rebecca ached all over. With a weary sigh she sank down into the armchair, and closed her eyes. She had been driving solidly for three days, and was absolutely exhausted. Friday across France and back to London. Saturday from London to Corbridge in the north, to collect Daniel, and today back to London.

Thank God it was all over; the past week had been one of the most traumatic in her life, but her secret was still safe. Daniel was fast asleep in the next room, and she could finally relax.

The trouble was, her conscience would not let her. For years she had carried in her mind a picture of Benedict as a totally despicable man, who had wreaked havoc on her young heart for revenge. But in the past week she had seen a different side to him. There was no way he could have faked his obvious delight in the children's company. But most unsettling of all was the letter he had written and she had never received.

She did not question for a moment the truth of his story. She could see all too easily how it had happened. When she had returned to check the mail, Mary had not written until the New Year in response to Rebecca's Christmas card bearing her new address.

Rebecca was forced to question her firmly held conviction that Daniel was better off not knowing his father, and she could not quite dispel the nagging sense of guilt these doubts aroused in her. Wearily she rubbed her aching eyes with her fingers before running her hands through her black curly locks.

What the hell! It was all academic now. She would never see Benedict again. Luckily for her, he had cancelled their Thursday night date; she had been on the brink of revealing all, and making a disastrous mistake. Dolores had told her, when they had returned from the day's sailing, that a Miss Grieves had met the boat and Benedict had gone off with her.

Obviously he had been stuck in Royan for a few days, and by sheer coincidence it had allowed him to apologise for a less than noble part of his life. Having obtained her forgiveness, he was able to carry on with his life with a clear conscience. She ignored the painful stab of regret for what might have been. It was too late. Five years too late ...

Rebecca looked around her comfortable living-room; the french windows leading to the small garden caught the late evening sunlight. She had bought the ground-floor apartment when Daniel was four months old. The price had been astronomical—not much less than her father's house had sold for—but it had proved worth it. Daniel loved playing in the garden. She had chosen London because, as an unmarried mother, it was easier to get a teaching job in the capital where they were desperate for teachers, and would not enquire so closely into her personal life. Even so, she had stuck a cowardly 'Mrs' in front of her name, though she had never worn a ring.

With the maturity of years she recognised that, at twenty-two, for all her brilliance as a scholar, she had been very unworldly. Her father had always protected her and instilled in her his values. When other girls left home for university, Rebecca had remained with her father, and even after his death she had jumped at the chance of moving in with his colleagues Rupert and

Mary. She had never actually had to stand on her own,
until she was pregnant, so it was hardly surprising that
she balked at actually declaring herself an unmarried
mother. Now she realised it had been a bad mistake. She
had been lucky so far, but eventually Daniel was going
to want some answers about his father, and she knew
she could not lie to her son...

Slowly getting to her feet, she pushed the unsettling
thought aside. It was something she would have to face
in the future, but right now she was exhausted. She retrieved the two suitcases from the hall and carried them
straight into the bedroom. The bed, with its pretty rose-
sprigged duvet that matched the curtains and cushions,
looked very inviting. She tightened the sash of her short
towelling robe—she had shared a bath with Daniel—then
resignedly set about unpacking the cases. Gathering a
bundle of dirty washing in her arms, she headed for the
kitchen.

She switched on the kettle, then loaded the washing
machine, added soap and slammed the door shut.
Spooning instant coffee into a mug, she poured the now
boiling water on to it, added a spoonful of sugar—she
needed the energy, she excused herself—and added a
dollop of cream. Re-entering the living-room, she collapsed once again into the armchair and took a long
swallow of the hot, soothing liquid.

A loud knock on the door broke the blessed silence.
Rebecca, draining her coffee, rose to her feet, a wry smile
on her soft lips. Mrs Thompson from the first floor, no
doubt—a widow who adored Daniel and quite happily
looked after him when the occasion arose. Unfortunately,
however, she was a terrible gossip, and Rebecca was not
in the mood tonight.

She opened the door and her mouth fell open in shock.
Conservatively dressed in a dark navy suit, Benedict

stood on the doorstep, his expression grim and somehow menacing.

'Hello, Rebecca, aren't you going to invite me in, old friend?' he drawled mockingly, and before she could speak he had pushed past her and strode into the living-room.

'Wait a minute.' She finally found her voice, and hurried after him. 'What do you mean by barging into my home?'

'Where is he, Rebecca?'

Every vestige of colour drained from Rebecca's face, and she clenched her hands in the pockets of her robe to disguise their trembling. Benedict stood, his powerful presence somehow filling her small room.

'To whom are you referring?' She raised defiant eyes to his face, hoping to bluff it out.

She was prepared for his anger, but the icy fury in his golden-brown eyes froze her to the spot, and his words shocked her by their savagery.

'My son, you bitch,' he ground out between clenched teeth. 'I could strangle you with my bare hands for what you've done.'

In that moment Rebecca could well believe him, and she took an involuntary step back. She had always been afraid this nightmare moment would come some day, but now it had arrived she was struck dumb; not one excuse or explanation came readily to mind.

'Nothing to say, Rebecca, no excuses?' A muscle tensed along his square jaw as he fought to restrain his anger. 'He's mine, Rebecca, isn't he?' he demanded in a deep, savage growl. 'Daniel Blacket-Green, born...'

As he reeled off Daniel's date of birth Rebecca knew beyond doubt that there was no way she could bluff her way out of the situation. How he had found out, she couldn't imagine. 'Who told you?' She heard her voice, shaky with fear, and wondered if it belonged to someone else.

'It sure as hell wasn't you,' he snarled. 'You even labelled him a bastard—no father's name on the register. How could you do that to my child?'

Rebecca dropped her head, flooded with guilt. 'I—I never thought...' She stopped. How could she tell him about the pain, the fury she had felt towards his father when Daniel was born, and her fear that Benedict would claim him, without revealing how much his past treatment of her had hurt? At the time she had walked away from him with her head held high. How could she now expose her true feelings? He would immediately realise just how much she had loved him, something she had vowed never to reveal. She crossed her arms over her waist in a helpless gesture of self-protection. Standing before him like this, the intensity of his anger was like a physical force enveloping her.

'Never thought?' He gripped her shoulders, and gave her a shake that forced her head up to meet his. 'Liar, you thought all right, too damn well.' His eyes burnt black with fury. 'You must have known you were pregnant when I wrote apologising and begging to see you. Didn't you?'

'I never got your letter,' she denied shakily.

He sucked in his breath. 'I've only your word for that.' His fingers bit into her shoulders, and for a second she feared he was going to do her some violence. A long shudder rippled through Rebecca's body, he felt it, and it was as if in some way it helped him regain his control.

A harsh laugh escaped him. 'You're right to be afraid, Rebecca. I treated you badly, but, by God, you got your revenge, denying me four years of my son's life!'

'Daniel is my child,' she finally managed through trembling lips. But it was as though she had never spoken.

'They say revenge is sweet; I trust, for your sake, the past four years were sweet, because you're going to spend the next forty or more paying for them,' Benedict declared with a mocking cynicism that made her blood run cold.

She stared at him in horror. 'What do you mean?'

His eyes held hers unfalteringly. 'I want my son,' he answered softly, 'and—' he deliberately dropped his gaze to where the loose lapels of her robe exposed the soft curve of her breast '—taking you won't be too much of a hardship,' he concluded silkily.

'You're mad. You can't be serious?' she cried.

For a second Benedict's eyes gleamed again with anger. 'Mad? Yes, I was when I discovered I had a son I knew nothing about, but, luckily for you, in the past forty-eight hours I've come to terms with the fact.' He smiled, a brief twist of his hard mouth, totally humourless. 'You and I will be married by special licence in three days, and, to answer your question, I've never been more serious in my life.'

How she would have responded, Rebecca was never to know, because at that moment a small voice interrupted.

'Mummy, can I have a drink of water?'

Benedict's hands fell from her shoulders and he turned towards the boy. If Rebecca had not been in such a panic to get Daniel away from Benedict, she might have noticed the look of vulnerability, the moisture in the man's dark golden eyes.

'Yes, of course, darling.' She dashed across the room to where her son stood in the doorway, dressed in a sleepsuit with a huge picture of Bugs Bunny on the front, and, rubbing the sleep from his eyes with a small fist, he looked utterly adorable—and the image of his father. 'Come to the kitchen with Mummy.' She grabbed his hand, but with the curiosity of the young Daniel refused to move; his sleep-hazed eyes had settled on the strange man.

'Who are you Mr Man?' he asked easily.

Benedict walked over and knelt down beside him. 'I am your daddy, Daniel,' he said softly.

Rebecca gasped in horror. How could he blurt it out like that? Then she choked at the excited expression on Daniel's face.

'You mean, you're my daddy, my very own daddy?'

'Yes, I am your daddy and you are my son,' Benedict assured him solemnly, and gently he reached out and smoothed the black curls from the small sleepy face. 'How about letting me get you that drink of water and tucking you up in bed?'

'Yes, please.' And then, needing his mother's approval and reassurance, he turned large golden-brown eyes up to Rebecca. 'Is he really my daddy? Not like Josh, but a proper daddy, just for me?'

He said it with such longing, tears glazed her eyes. She had not realised how desperately he wanted a father of his own. At two years old, staying with their friends for the summer holiday, he had asked about his daddy and Josh had laughingly told him he would be his daddy—Daniel could share him with his daughter Amy. Oddly enough Daniel had never mentioned it again, and Rebecca had been too much of a coward to bring the subject up.

'Answer him, Rebecca,' Benedict demanded bluntly, rising to his feet to face her, but still holding Daniel's hand firmly.

Her eyes fell beneath the blazing contempt in his. 'Yes, this man is your daddy,' she said softly.

Daniel threw his short arms around the only part of Benedict he could reach—his muscular thigh—and, turning a blissfully happy face up, he said, 'I'll show you where the kitchen is, Daddy.'

Rebecca felt a swift stab of pain like a knife-thrust in her stomach, as two pairs of identical golden-brown eyes smiled at each other. Jealousy at their instant rapport turned her stomach. Daniel had been hers alone, since he was born. Now Benedict had appeared and it hurt to see how instantly Daniel accepted him.

'Daddy, Daddy, I've got a daddy,' his little high-pitched voice sang ecstatically as he skipped across the room, tugging Benedict along with him by a fistful of trouser leg, to the kitchen.

Rebecca collapsed into the nearest chair, and buried her head in her hands. Benedict had appeared and turned her cosy little world upside-down. She couldn't believe it, didn't want to... But the sound of laughter coming from the kitchen was all too real.

Slowly she raised her head, and, taking deep, even breaths, she forced herself out of the panic-stricken shock that had engulfed her for the past half-hour. She was over-reacting, she told herself determinedly. She was a strong, mature woman, who had suffered a good few knocks in her twenty-seven years, and always bounced back. From Gordon, her father's death, to the affair with Benedict, and finding herself a one-parent family.

So what if Benedict did want Daniel? There was no way he could take him away from her; she was his mother... She was worrying unnecessarily. Of course Benedict had a right to be furious on discovering he had a son he knew nothing about. But surely once he had calmed down he would see reason, Rebecca consoled herself. Only a couple of days ago he had stood her up for Miss Grieves; no doubt that same Fiona Grieves who had chased Benedict at Oxford had caught him. His ranting about marriage must be just so much guff. No. She had nothing to fear. She would give Benedict access rights to Daniel maybe once a month, and an occasional holiday...

Her confidence slightly restored, she looked up as
Benedict strolled back into the room, carrying Daniel
on his shoulders. 'It's time you were in bed, young man,'
she said lightly.

'It's all right, Mummy, Daddy's taking me, and he's
going to stay here, and I'll see him in the morning.'

'You...' The 'can't' froze in her throat at the stormy
warning in Benedict's dark eyes.

'I'll talk to you later, Rebecca; now show me the way
to the bedroom.'

Rebecca stood at one side of Daniel's bed, while
Benedict sat on it, reading him a story. That had always
been her job, she thought resentfully. Benedict looked
up at her; the cold mockery in his eyes told her he knew
exactly how she was feeling, and she could not control
the shameful tide of red that washed over her face.

'He's asleep; come along. You and I have some arrangements to make.'

She flinched as his large hand on the small of her back
guided her out of the room. If he noticed he made no
comment, but Rebecca could feel the warmth of his hand
like a burning brand through the soft cotton of her robe.
Suddenly she was intensely aware of her state of un-
dress. She turned quickly. 'If you'll excuse me, I'll get
dressed.'

'Don't bother, you look perfect the way you are.'

She glanced up at him. He loomed over her, huge and
darkly threatening, and suddenly she felt small and very
vulnerable. Cautiously she stepped back, turned and
walked into the living-room.

She dropped tiredly on to the sofa, but kept a wary
eye on Benedict. He removed his jacket, flung it on the
armchair, unfastened his tie and sat down beside her,
his trousers tautening along his muscular thighs as he
stretched his long legs out in front of him with negligent
ease.

'Make yourself comfortable, why don't you?' she prompted sarcastically, unwillingly aware of his hard masculine body only inches away from her.

'Thank you, I will.' And before her astonished eyes he removed his tie, flinging it to join the jacket on the chair opposite, then casually unbuttoned his white silk shirt almost to his waist.

'What do you think you're doing?' she snapped.

His narrowed eyes met hers. 'Exactly what I want to do. And from this moment on that is precisely how our relationship is going to continue. I do as I want! You do as you're told! Do I make myself clear?' he demanded icily, his tone of voice totally at odds with his casual appearance.

She bit back the angry retort that sprang to her lips. Arguing with him would not help the situation; she needed to keep a cool head, it was her son she was fighting for. Slowly counting to ten under her breath, she managed to put her thoughts into some kind of order. Carefully folding her hands in her lap, she began, 'Benedict, I realise we have to talk—obviously it has been a shock for you meeting Daniel for the first time, and I can understand your desire to keep in touch with him.' She studied her folded hands rather than look at him. 'But we are both mature adults, and I'm sure, with a little compromise on both sides, a suitable arrangement can be reached.'

'What would you call a suitable arrangement for a man who has not seen his son in four years?' he queried silkily.

'I'd be quite happy to let you see him once a month and, say, one holiday a year.' She turned her head slightly, watching to see how he accepted her suggestion. His mouth tightened into a hard line. 'Well, perhaps once a fortnight,' she blundered on.

'Try once a day, and you'll be almost there, Rebecca,' he prompted, a steely note creeping into his voice. 'I don't intend to put up with anything but your full capitulation. We will be married, as I told you before, in three days' time.'

Rebecca's fragile control of her temper snapped. 'Don't be ridiculous; there's no way I'll marry you, and you can't make me. Daniel is my son...'

'Our son.' Benedict's hard gaze fixed intently on her furious face, he gave up all pretence of ease, and, with a speed that shook her to the core, one strong arm gathered her to his broad chest, and his other hand curved round her throat, tilting her face to his.

'You would deny me even now—when the evidence of your own eyes must tell you Daniel and I should be together!' His eyes were dark golden chips of fury. 'What kind of woman are you? God, I could still strangle you for what you have done, but first—first, I'd kiss you senseless, and make love to you till you begged for mercy!'

His hand tightened at her throat and for a second Rebecca truly feared for her life—she had never seen such inimical anger. So much for her mature adult compromise, she thought irrelevantly as his head swooped down and he found her mouth before she could avoid him.

She struggled, trembling under the savage ferocity of the kiss, aware of the barely controlled fury in his large body. The hot, violent onslaught went on and on, crushing her lips until they felt numb. When he finally released her, she croaked angrily through swollen lips, 'You hurt me!''

His hand trailed from her throat, sliding under the edge of her robe. 'Maybe, but it did me a hell of a lot of good,' he rasped, the anger glittering in his eyes darkening to a much more dangerous emotion.

She tried to jerk away, quivering from head to toe, but his strong arm was like a ring of steel around her, lifting her so she was lying across his lap. 'Oh, no, Rebecca, I haven't finished with you yet,' he muttered, his free hand sliding to cup her full breast, the pad of his thumb stroking the dusky tip.

She was helpless in his hold; her head fell back and she stared into his flushed, taut face, her violet eyes wide with alarm and a rising sexual awareness. She could not move, hypnotised by the intention in his dark, watchful gaze, and the swift heat flooding through her at his continued sensual caress.

Once more he bent his head but this time his mouth was gentle, probing with a skilful, tempting expertise which ignited a flame deep inside her. She opened her mouth, welcoming his thrusting tongue as she kissed him back. She felt his hands wandering from her arm to her thigh, from breast to breast, and his mouth swallowed her low groan of pleasure.

Her own hands, now at liberty, stroked his naked chest, feeling the satin-covered muscle and hair with tactile delight.

He buried his head in the side of her throat, his mouth burning a trail of fire lower. Somehow she was lying on the couch, her robe wide open and Benedict poised over her; as her small hands moved around the back of his head, she could feel the tension of the muscles in the nape of his neck. She curled her fingers into his dark hair, unconsciously urging his head lower.

His strong hands caressed her almost-naked body lovingly, gently. 'Benedict,' she moaned; she could not deny the craving of her body any more. She wanted him with an urgency, a deep-rooted need she had not felt in years.

'Yes, Rebecca, yes,' he murmured, then he caught one taut nipple gently between his teeth. She cried out as he bit lightly, while his hands stroked down over her flat stomach. He raised his head. 'Our son nestled here,' he said throatily, and his large hand spread across her flat stomach, then slid lower to the soft black curls at the apex of her thighs.

'You want me, Rebecca.' He took her hand and laid it against his hard masculine length. 'Tell me, Rebecca, say it.' His mouth touched her creamy breast again. 'Say it . . .' he demanded unsteadily.

She was trembling all over, every nerve-end on fire, her heart pounding until she thought it would burst. 'I want you, Benedict,' she groaned. Her fingers touched the zip of his trousers, she needed to have him naked . . . now . . . She was beyond reason; his hands and mouth were driving her crazy.

His hand caught hers, and for a moment he lay still over her; a little cry of pain escaped her as he crushed her fingers. She felt his body shiver. Why had he stopped her? Then abruptly he sat up.

She smiled up at him, her love-swollen lips pouting for more, only to find him watching her, his teeth clenched in a cruel smile and his dark eyes glittering with pure masculine triumph. Slowly his gaze slid insolently over her naked body,

'You want me, but not tonight, sweetheart,' he drawled. 'You have to marry me first . . .'

She stared up at him. The light beading of sweat on his brow was real, he was as affected as she. So why? At first her brain, her body, could not accept what had happened, then she realised he was waiting, his intent gaze probing her wide violet eyes, anticipating her re-action. She went hot then cold. What had she done? One touch and she had caved in completely, and Benedict was openly gloating at the fact while brutally rejecting her. Scarlet with humiliation and frustration, she fumbled to pull her robe around her trembling body, shamefully aware of the triumph in his watchful eyes.

'Try and control yourself for three more days,' he taunted.

Rebecca moved her shapely legs to the floor and sat up, with her head bent. She busied herself tying the belt of her robe firmly around her tiny waist. She could not face him; the frustration, the pain was eating her inside, and she wouldn't give him the satisfaction of seeing her distress. Breathing carefully, she forced her screaming body under control.

'No, I will not marry you,' she said quietly, and bravely she turned, making her eyes stay steady on his arrogant face. He hated her; she had seen it in his face, felt it in his anger. She would have to be crazy to even consider the idea.

'You're a fool Rebecca. Does your boyfriend realise how easily you turn on for another man, I wonder?' he drawled cynically, adding 'And to think on Wednesday evening I apologised for rushing you. But now I have proved to my own satisfaction that you're more than ready. You want me... I'm quite prepared to take you along with Daniel. But if you insist, I'll just take Daniel.'

So that was why he had rejected her—to humiliate her, to prove a point... and perhaps to get revenge for her own rejection of him, she thought bitterly. Vengeance was his style, as she knew better than most.

'I won't allow it,' she asserted, and she was not just talking about Daniel; on an unconscius level she was telling herself she would never again allow this man to sexually manipulate her.

'I would have preferred not to go to the courts, but...' He shrugged his broad shoulders. 'I have the power, the money, if that's what you want.'

'No, you can't do that,' she cried, but the implacable look on his handsome face told her he could and would. Worse, she had a terrible feeling he might win. How could she, a single parent who placed her child in a day

nursery while she went to work, possibly compete with
what Benedict had to offer?

'It's your decision, Rebecca.' He smiled coldly.

The swine knew she had no choice. She dared not risk
losing her son; he was her life. And, with that realisation uppermost in her mind, reluctantly she responded
in a strained voice, 'All right. I will marry you.' She
caught the flash of triumph in his eyes and impotent
anger hardened her tone. 'But first I think I'm entitled
to know how you found out about Daniel.'

'Quite by accident. The first day in Royan I heard a
girl shouting *Mrs* Blacket-Green all over the harbour. I
recognised you immediately, and realised I must have
misheard. I thought no more about it until Thursday on
the yacht, when Dolores, probably imagining she was
helping the course of true romance, told me what a wonderful person *Mrs* Blacket-Green was. My suspicion was
aroused. Yours isn't a common name, and the likelihood of your marrying a man with the same name must
be about a billion to one.'

'Dolores, the mouth,' Rebecca groaned. She should
have guessed. Why, oh, why had she ever allowed the
children to go on the yacht without her?

'Yes, she's a very talkative young girl. With a little
careful prompting I discovered you were either a widow
or divorced and you had a young child.

'It struck me as odd. You and I had spent the best
part of four days together and yet you never once mentioned you had a child. Thursday evening I called an
agency in London and had you investigated. You can
imagine my amazement when late Friday I was given the
full details of your deceit. I came straight to London,
and waited all weekend for you to arrive.'

She stared at the grim lines of his face. For a second
she thought she saw pain in the depths of his dark eyes,

but a moment later she almost laughed out loud at her foolishness.

His eyes narrowed icily on her small, composed face, and she shivered at the contempt she read in them.

'Make no mistake, Rebecca, you will never deceive me again. On Wednesday you become my wife. You have until then to arrange your affairs.' He stood buttoning his shirt, picked up his jacket and tie and, turning back to where she sat frozen on the sofa, he added, 'I use the word "affair" advisedly. The man Josh—get rid of him... No one is going to act as a father to my son.'

'But Josh——'

He cut in before she could explain. 'I don't want the sordid details, just get rid of him—and any other men you are involved with... Understood?'

What did he think she was—some sex-mad lunatic? An imp of conscience whispered inside her head that he had some justification, the way she had reacted in his arms moments earlier. She stomped on her wayward thoughts. His opinion was not important; let him think what he liked—she didn't owe him any explanation. He was forcing her to marry him, demanding his son. He had it all... Unconsciously her eyes followed his movements as he slipped on his jacket and fastened his tie. He was powerful, dynamic, all male, and as her eyes reached his face she realised he was furious.

'Answer me, damn you!'

She had to search her memory for what he had said.

'Yes, I understand completely.' She rose, her dark head held high, and moved towards the door. She opened it and stood to one side. 'I would like you to leave now.' Her emotions, her life were in turmoil and she could stand no more.

For a moment Benedict stood, his face flushed with barely contained rage that she could find no reason for.

Then, like a shutter falling, his dark eyes narrowed expressionlessly on her pale face.

'Perhaps I should call home—a change of clothes would be useful,' he said smoothly. 'Give me your key and I'll let myself in.'

'In where?' she muttered.

'I promised Daniel I would be here in the morning. I intend to keep my promise, but don't worry—I'll sleep on the sofa.'

'But...'

'The key.' Benedict smiled coldly. 'You look haggard. Have an early night and tomorrow we'll spend the day together.'

Like a robot, she crossed the room, picked her bag off the table, withdrew the spare key she always carried, and without speaking held it out. She did not feel she could bear to speak another word to the man, or she would break down completely.

He gave her a long, hard stare, then, swinging on his heel, he left. She heard him move down the hall, the front door open and close surprisingly quietly.

Rebecca heard the thump of her heart in the silence, her legs began to tremble, and she stumbled to the chair and sank down on it, shaking in every limb. Shock, delayed reaction, she thought vaguely. Then the pain that had been lurking on the fringe of her consciousness for hours hit her.

Forcing herself to her feet, she walked stiffly to the dresser and the bottle of whisky left over from Christmas. She had never liked the stuff but now she filled a glass and downed it in a few gulps, the instant warmth that flooded her frozen body bringing some relief, but the chaos in her head could not be stilled. She refilled the glass...

Benedict had stormed back into her life and completely rearranged it. Her own inherent honesty forced her to admit he had some right. She had always suffered from a nagging sense of guilt over her decision to deprive him of his child. Deep down she had realised that Benedict would have insisted on marriage if she had told him she was pregnant, but she had been so hurt at the time and, yes, passionately angry; her pride would not have allowed her to marry a man she knew cared nothing for her.

Now, she had no choice. If she wanted to keep her son she had to marry his father. It was that simple. Pride was no longer a factor, and what hurt most of all—made her thinking mind scream, no!—was the way he had deliberately set out to show her her own weakness. With cold calculation he had aroused her sexually, then callously rejected her.

She shivered. She had known from their first encounter all those years ago that Benedict had a vast capacity for revenge, so his behaviour tonight was not surprising—he was running true to form. Yet only hours ago, on the evidence of a few days in France, she had seriously considered she might have misjujdged him!

A mirthless laugh echoed in the silence of the room. A few kind words and a smile, and she was as big a fool as ever. No, that wasn't quite true, she told herself; he might be able to make her respond sexually, but never again would she mistake lust for love... Mechanically she walked into the kitchen, removed the washing, and flung it into the drier; the normal mundane chores were still necessary, even if she was falling apart inside. From the hall cupboard she withdrew a couple of blankets and sheets, throwing them on the sofa in the living-room. The swine could make up his own bed.

Finally she made her way to bed. She would marry Benedict for Daniel's sake. She would play the part of his wife to the full, but with the certain knowledge that she could never love him. She had too much self-respect to fall in love with a man who had such a vengeful side to his nature. She would never allow him to hurt her again, she told herself.

She ignored the tiny voice of conscience whispering that only a few days ago she had believed his explanation and apology for his behaviour in the past, and forgiven him. She slipped off her robe and crawled into bed, not expecting to sleep, but the exhaustion and emotional turmoil of the last week took their toll, and she slept. Some time later she half opened her eyes at an unfamiliar noise. It's only Benedict, she thought drowsily, and sunk back into sleep, unaware that her subconscious mind had found comfort in his presence.

CHAPTER SEVEN

'MUMMY!' A small body catapulted itself on to her stomach. Rebecca groaned, half awake. 'It wasn't a dream, Mummy, my daddy is here and he helped me dress.' She closed her eyes. God, what had she done?

'Are you awake, Mummy?' A finger poked at her eye.

'Yes, darling,' she muttered, and, turning her head, glanced at the travelling-clock on the bedside table. Seven-thirty. Oh, hell, she'd overslept!

'Coffee and toast OK?' a deep voice drawled smoothly.

'Daddy's made breakfast,' Daniel said proudly, scrambling off the bed, and dashing to his father.

Stunned, Rebecca stared at Benedict. He had obviously showered and shaved—his dark hair was damp and brushed severely back from his broad forehead. Dressed in tan pleated trousers and a crisp cotton shirt, he was all clean-cut, virile male. She squashed her wayward thoughts and tensed as he stood towering over her, a bland smile on his handsome face and a loaded tray in his hands.

'Put that down, and leave—I have to dress,' she said curtly, carefully pulling the sheet up under her chin. Naked beneath the covers, she felt at a hopeless disadvantge.

'Good morning to you too, Rebecca; I never knew you were a grump in the morning,' he drawled mockingly, but did as she suggested, and, with Daniel's hand in his, he added, 'Come on, son, Mummy wants to be alone—women can be funny that way,' and left the room. She felt like throwing something at him, the joint laughter of the two males in her life infuriating her. But worse was to follow.

After hastily washing and dressing in a slim grey skirt and prim white blouse, her uniform for work, she drank the near-cold coffee, ate the toast, and, straightening her shoulders, walked into the living-room. They were sitting on the sofa, talking, but when she moved forward two pairs of identical golden-brown eyes turned on her.

She swallowed on the sudden lump in her throat, and said stiffly, 'Thank you for your help, Benedict, but we must hurry. I have to drop Daniel at his nursery for eight-thirty and get to school.'

The ensuing argument was not pleasant. Benedict insisted they were going to spend the day together.

'I have to work, I can't just walk out on my teaching commitment and, anyway, I like my job.'

'When we're married you won't need to work,' he declared flatly. 'What difference will a couple of days make?'

'A couple of days? I have to give a term's notice!' she cried in exasperation. The time was ticking by, she was going to be late in any case, but suddenly, to her surprise, he capitulated.

'OK, I'll drive you to school, but Daniel stays with me.' And, turning to the little boy, he added, 'How about it, son? You can tell me what you want to take to your new home and help me get everything ready for the removal firm.'

'Are we going to live with you, Daddy? All the time?' Daniel exclaimed with delight.

'Of course; now I've found you I'll never let you go,' Benedict declared in a voice deep with emotion.

Rebecca looked on in impotent fury; the man was leaving her no escape.

'Mummy too?' Daniel queried, rushing to catch Rebecca's hand, suddenly not quite so sure of the massive changes taking place in his young life.

'Certainly, Mummy as well.' Benedict smiled as he moved to place an arm around Rebecca's shoulder, and she froze as he lowered his dark head and quite deliberately kissed her full on the lips. 'Your mummy and I are to be married, we're going to be one happy family.' His golden eyes burnt down into hers, daring her to deny him. 'Aren't we, Rebecca?'

She looked down at Daniel, and the excited anticipation in his little face squeezed her heart. 'Yes, Daniel, it's true.'

At lunchtime, standing in the headmaster's study, with Benedict and Daniel by his side, she had to clench her teeth to prevent herself screaming at the manipulating swine.

The headmaster congratulated her on her forthcoming marriage, and happily waived her notice. The fact that Benedict had presented the school with a new minibus and a large donation to the school fund was obviously worth a lot more than her services.

'You have cost me my job. How dare you do that?' she demanded of Benedict as she angrily slid into the passenger-seat of a gleaming metallic-blue Jaguar. His money could buy him anything, including her...

'It was for your own good. Daniel has spent almost his whole life in nursery school. He deserves some time with his mother,' he said bitingly.

He used the one argument she could not honestly disagree with, and she was immediately on the defensive. 'I spend as much time with him as I can, but I have to earn a living, and I enjoy teaching.'

Benedict shot her a sidelong glance, as he manoeuvred the car through the busy London traffic. 'I'm not suggesting for a moment you've neglected him,' he said quietly. 'In fact you're to be complimented—he's a wonderful little boy and obviously well brought up. But there's no longer any need for you to work. Later, when Daniel is older, I don't mind if you want to work. You're an intelligent woman, I can understand your desire to continue with your career—I'm not a complete chauvinist.'

His attitude surprised her, and the unexpected compliment brought an unwanted flush of warmth to her pale cheeks.

'Daddy is taking us out for lunch, Mummy, to a proper restaurant, and then I'm going to get a toy,' Daniel's voice piped up from the back seat. 'A be-bea...a late birthday present.'

Rebecca looked over her shoulder, thankful for the interruption. Warming towards Benedict was the last thing she needed! 'Whose idea was that?'

'It's all right, Mummy, you're going to get all new clothes as well. Daddy said, when he looked in your bedroom, you haven't enough to fill a suitcase.'

'Exactly what have you been doing this morning?' she demanded acidly, slanting Benedict a frowning glance. Seconds ago she had worried about softening towards him. She must have rocks in her head...

'Relax, Rebecca. As my wife you have a position to uphold, and I couldn't help noticing, when I checked your apartment, you have very little in the way of personal possessions.'

'How dare you?' she spat, absolutely furious at the thought of him mooching through her things.

'Are you fighting with Daddy?'

Rebecca bit her lip in frustration. 'No, darling, we're only talking.'

After that she remained silent, as the full enormity of what she was doing sank into her emotionally exhausted mind.

Meekly she allowed Benedict to lead her into Harrods. In the restaurant she forced the unwanted food down her throat, and tried to smile. She hadn't the heart to spoil Daniel's day. He was so happy. He clung to Benedict's every word. Finally, when the meal was over, she got reluctantly to her feet. Daniel was champing at the bit to reach the toy department.

'Benedict, what a surprise—shopping with the family! How droll.' Fiona Grieves entered the restaurant, loaded down with parcels, just as they were about to leave.

'Something like that,' Benedict responded with a smile for the elegant woman. 'What about you? Is this what we pay you for—shopping?' he teased easily.

'Well, I just had to get something for the wedding,' she simpered.

Fiona was coming to the wedding. Rebecca clenched her teeth to prevent a caustic comment escaping.

'You remember Fiona, Rebecca?' Benedict prompted, an arrogant, mocking smile curving his hard mouth, and she felt like slapping him.

'Of course, but I didn't realise she worked for you, dear,' she responded with saccharine sweetness, her eyes going from one to the other. They made a perfect pair, she thought cynically. The elegant redhead, and Benedict, with a casual suede blouson jacket draped across his broad shoulders, tall and dark, the sophisticated wordly male.

'Didn't I tell you Fiona is an invaluable member of our management team? Has been for some years.'

Why did Rebecca get the feeling that he rejoiced in imparting that snippet of news? Suddenly she felt tiny, completely insignificant in her prim grey suit, and hopelessly out of her depth. She looked around for Daniel;

it was because of him she was putting up with this, she thought sadly. But where was he? 'Daniel!' she exclaimed worriedly.

Benedict, immediately concerned, said, 'Wait here, he can't have gone far,' and walked off.

'Well, Rebecca, I suppose I should congratulate you. You've finally landed him, but I wouldn't get too used to being Mrs Maxwell. Benedict wants his son. Once the boy is old enough to do without his mother, you'll be yesterday's news.'

Sadly Rebecca recognised that Fiona wasn't even being spiteful—her blue eyes were smiling.

'Make the most of it while you can, and aim for a big pay-off. I'd do the same in your shoes,' the woman added.

Before she could comment, Benedict returned with Daniel in tow. Rebecca bent down and hugged Daniel, and only when a strong hand gently squeezed her shoulder did she straighten, raising large violet eyes to Benedict, a lingering trace of worry in their depths.

'Don't worry, sweetheart, he's safe, and I'm just beginning to realise how hard it must have been for you, looking after him on your own.' A soft smile curved his hard mouth, and his golden gaze, wry and strangely tender, held hers. For an instant an invisible bond seemed to hold them captive. Then Fiona shattered the moment as she loudly proclaimed her congratulations once again and left.

As far as Rebecca was concerned the day went from bad to worse. In the toy department Benedict got his eye on a toy car, a perfect replica of a Jaguar that actually had a battery-powered engine. Within seconds Daniel was in the driving-seat and the assistant was extolling the virtues of the car. Rebecca was horrifed to hear Benedict say they would take it. It cost not a few hundred but thousands of pounds.

'You can't possibly buy that,' she remonstrated with him as he stood at the cash desk. Daniel was still sitting happily in the car, and the assistant had moved out of earshot to deal with the credit card. 'It's obscene, spending so much money. In any case it's more your idea than Daniel's. You're stupid about cars. A Mercedes in France, a Jaguar here... What are you trying to do, start a collection? I will not have my son spoilt; he appreciates the value of money even if you don't.'

'Our son, Rebecca,' he corrected icily. 'For four years you deprived me of all knowledge of the boy. One expensive present is nothing compared to all the birthdays I've missed.'

The return of a beaming assistant silenced her for the moment, but as they left the department she could not contain her anger. 'It's a ridiculous present. Have you thought for one minute where he's going to use it? I presume you do still have the same house in London? Somehow I can't quite see Daniel riding around a marble-floored hall.'

'Next week we're going to look for a place in the country, so you have nothing to worry about...'

Just like that! She was going to live in the country. 'I've already put Daniel's name down for the local infants' school near my apartment.'

'So cancel it. You would like to live in the country, Daniel?' He addressed the question to a grinning little boy. 'Have a dog and maybe a pony?'

'I'd love it, Daddy, and I could drive my car!'

'Bribery and corruption,' Rebecca muttered softly, but the look of joy on Daniel's face silenced her.

In the designer-gown department Rebecca gave up... Benedict brought all his considerable charm to bear on a simpering assistant and Rebecca found herself parading back and forth in front of him and Daniel. Whenever she tried to argue, Benedict was not above using

blackmail—a pointed aside to Daniel on the lines of,
'You like Mummy in that, Daniel?' Or, 'That colour is
one of my favourites, what do you think?' And naturally Daniel agreed with his Daddy—the man could do
no wrong in his eyes. Rebecca was amazed at the camaraderie that had developed so quickly between father and
son, and not a little miffed . . .

The final straw was when they both laughed hil-
ariously at an over-long skirt she tried on. Then Daniel
turned to his father and asked, with a worried frown on
his young face, 'Do you think I will grow as big as you,
Daddy?'

He might as well have added, Or end up a shrimp like
his mum, Rebecca thought miserably. She listened to
Benedict reassure the young boy, her hard won self-
confidence draining away drop by drop.

Later they returned to her apartment, but only long
enough to collect Daniel's few treasured possessions; a
teddy and a small assortment of toys, plus his favourite
duvet with Superman on it. A couple of suitcases easily
held Rebecca's few belongings.

Benedict had flatly refused to allow them to spend
another night in the apartment, curtly telling her he had
no intention of sleeping on a sofa, nor did he intend
letting her out of his sight before the wedding.

Her goodbye to Mrs Thompson, her neighbour, was
not as painful as it might have been, as Benedict once
again turned on the charm, and by the time she left the
building Mrs Thompson was convinced that Rebecca was
the luckiest woman alive.

Rebecca walked down the aisle of St Mary's church on
the arm of Mr James, the butler, a small, ethereal young
woman in an exquisite cream silk gown. The bodice,
richly embroidered with pearls, was boned and followed
the contours of her breast, the waistline dipped, ending

in a flattering V over her flat stomach; the skirt, gently flared, fell to her knees. A stole of richly embroidered silk skimmed her shoulders, creating an air of modesty. Satin high-heeled shoes the same colour encased her tiny feet, and a small cluster of fresh rose-buds entwined in her black curls complemented the small posy she carried in trembling hands.

It was supposed to be unlucky for the bridegroom to see the bride's outfit, wasn't it? A grim smile twisted her lips. Benedict had chosen hers—that was some omen for the years ahead, she thought bleakly.

Hazily she was aware of the guests seated either side of the long aisle. By some miracle Benedict had arranged, in a few days, a church service, attended by his uncle Gerard Montaine and his wife, their daughter, her husband, a niece and two nephews. Gerard's son Jean-Paul was acting as best man, and there were a few friends, including Fiona Grieves.

Rebecca had not wanted to invite anyone, but Benedict, with typical ruthlessness, had overruled her. So Dolores, her bridesmaid, in a complementary blue dress, was waiting at the altar, with Daniel, in a velvet suit, white shirt and bow-tie, by her side.

She caught sight of Mrs Thompson and her lips twitched in the semblance of a smile. The old woman was in the front row, wearing the most enormous hat.

Rebecca stood at Benedict's side, barely listening to the priest, until he reached the part of the service where she had to respond. She couldn't do it! It was sacrilege. She turned her head and for the first time since entering the church she looked at Benedict. She opened her mouth to say no, but before she could speak his hand gripped her wrist. His leonine eyes burned down into hers, and somehow the moment of panic was gone.

Her small hand trembled as he slipped the plain gold band on her finger, and when she realised she had to

return the gesture and slip an identical band on his finger
her whole body trembled.

Later, at the reception in a smart French restaurant
in Mayfair, Rebecca was still trying to understand what
had happened. Maybe he had the power to hypnotise
people, she thought wryly. God knew, he was powerful
enough in every other way!

She had eaten none of the exquisitely prepared food,
and now the noise and laughter going on around her was
making her head ache. Benedict's constant attention was
adding to her confusion. He was all smiles and gentle
touches, and not one sarcastic remark had escaped him.
She glanced up as he rose to his feet to speak. His speech
was short and witty and very flattering to her. She studied
his strong face for any sign of hypocrisy, but could find
none. What was he up to?

For the past three days the atmosphere between them
had been one of chilly politeness, only Daniel's presence
preventing any outward show of hostility. On Monday
evening, when they had arrived at his house, Daniel could
not contain his excitement and had run around exploring like a whirlwind. By the time Rebecca had finally
calmed him down enough to sleep in his new bedroom,
but with his own duvet, she had been utterly drained.
She had joined Benedict for dinner, and he had sat in a
brooding silence for the duration of the meal. She had
said a curt goodnight and gratefully retired to one of
the guest-rooms.

Yesterday they had all gone to the Tower of London—
Daniel's choice—and she had had to watch the growing
rapport between father and son with mingled feelings of
jealousy and resentment. Last night had been an ordeal
as Benedict's family had descended on the house for an
impromptu party.

'Had enough, darling? Your smile is slipping,' a deep voice drawled as a long arm circled her waist and drew her to her feet.

Her stomach kontted at his touch, and she parted her lips in a patently false grin, gazing simperingly up at him beneath thick eyelashes. 'Sorry, darling.'

Ignoring her sarcasm, Benedict said, 'Have I told you how unbelievably beautiful you look in that dress?' His dark head bent. 'But, even better, very soon the perfect little body inside it will be mine.'

His breath, warm against her skin, disturbed the soft tendrils of hair around her small ear, and she tensed in his hold; his hard, powerful body pressed against her, aroused feelings, a want inside her that her mind had to battle to control. She lowered her eyes, unable to withstand the stated intent in his darkening gaze. She smiled with relief when his aunt captured his attention and she was free.

'Really, miss, you look absolutely fab… No one would ever guess you were once a teacher.'

For once Rebecca was glad to hear the girlish chatter. 'Thank you, Dolores—I think,' she responded with a grin. 'I'm not sure that is a compliment.' If it weren't for Dolores she would not be in this mess, the thought flitted through her mind, but she could not really blame the young girl. It was obvious Dolores thought this wedding was a fairy-tale come true, and Rebecca hadn't the heart to disillusion her. Politely she moved around the room, hopefully making the right noises, until finally she found herself alone with Gerard Montaine.

'I was hoping to have a word with you, Rebecca,' he said in charmingly accented English.

She looked up at him in some surprise; they had met last night but hadn't really spoken much. 'That sounds ominous,' she teased.

'No, my dear. I wish you both all the happiness in the world, but I do feel I owe you an apology. Benedict has told me all about your previous relationship.'

Her eyes widened in shock, a dull tide of colour running up her face.

'No, please, don't be embarrassed. I just want you to know...'

And to Rebecca's amazement Gerard confirmed everything Benedict had said he had written to her.

'I blame myself for——'

'Really, this isn't necessary,' Rebecca cut in.

'Allow an old man this indulgence. I think it is for me, and perhaps for you.'

She had the oddest feeling that Gerard Montaine understood more about her hasty marriage than most.

'Unfortuantely, on the advice of my sister's doctor, we just ignored her imaginings, hoping they would go away. When Benedict returned, I told him Gordon's death was an accident, and I never realised until later that his mother had told him differently, and he had believed her. It was only after your engagement was broken that Benedict came to me and asked again about Gordon, and told me what had happened. Of course I swiftly put him right, but it was too late—the damage had been done.'

'Thank you,' Rebecca murmured. It was nice of Gerard to bother, but it could not change anything. Benedict hated her for not telling him about Daniel, and he now believed she had got his letter all those years ago and ignored it, simply to get her own back. Not that it mattered what he thought of her, she told herself; Benedict had never loved her... A loveless marriage then, or now, what difference did it make...?

As if her thoughts had reached out to him, he was at her side, his smiling eyes sliding from Rebecca to Gerard. 'Flirting with my bride? Shame on you, Uncle.' And they

all laughed; if Rebecca's laugh was a bit strained, nobody
seemed to notice.

Then it was time to go. Daniel appeared, pulling on
the hem of her skirt, his little face flushed, his bow-tie
askew. 'This is the bestest day of my life! Now I have a
mummy and a daddy all my own. Josh——'

'All right, son,' Benedict cut in. 'Remember what we
arranged this morning; no tears, a kiss for Mummy, and
be a good boy for your uncle.'

Rebecca looked from one to the other, and the happy,
smiling face of the little boy contrasted sharply with the
hard, dark mask Benedict turned on her. She shivered.
The easy, laughing bridegroom had reverted to type; obviously the act for his friends was over. She bent and
gave Daniel a cuddle and a big kiss, and it was only
when he began to squirm impatiently in her hold that
she reluctantly released him.

'You left him for a week with your lover—a few days
at the seaside with my uncle's family will hardly bother
him,' Benedict said in a hard undertone.

Searching his harshly set features, fleetingly a thought
crossed Rebecca's mind. Could he possibly be jealous of
Josh? Was that the reason for his sudden change in attitude? No. She dismissed the idea. He had just reverted
back to his usual sarcastic self.

'Daniel could come with us,' she protested yet again,
although she knew it was futile—they had had the same
argument countless times yesterday. She could not ignore
the suspicion that Fiona had been right. It had already
begun; Benedict was trying to wean her son away from
her.

His jawline hardened. 'No. For appearances' sake we'll
spend a couple of days alone.' He clasped her wrist and
for the next few minutes she suffered through the enthusiastic and some ribald farewells.

It was almost a relief to sink into the soft leather up-holstery of the hired Rolls, and Rebecca let her head fall back and closed her eyes. Thank God! The pretence was over.

But not quite; when the car stopped at the Regent's Park house Benedict, without a word, picked her out of the car, swooped her up in his arms and carried her over the threshold.

'Put me down,' she demanded, but she might as well have been talking to herself.

'Tradition dictates I carry you,' he jeered, and strode on up the wide staircase, subduing her struggles as effortlessly as if she had been a baby. He shouldered open the door to the master bedroom, and, once inside, kicked it closed.

Her heart thumped erratically, but Benedict—damn him!—hadn't lost a breath. Had he always been so huge, or was it fear that appeared to make him so much larger and more powerful? 'What are you playing at, Benedict? There's no one here to witness your act,' she prompted, the slight quiver in her voice revealing her apprehension.

His eyes bored relentlessly into hers as he slowly lowered her down the length of his hard body. 'You're my wife, the mother of my son. As you say, no more play-acting. Reality starts here and now. I'll wipe the memory of Josh and all the rest from your mind for all time, so you know once and for all who you belong to.'

The cold implacability of his words terrified her. Rebecca felt her feet touch the floor and she tried to wriggle out of his grasp, but his strong hands curved over her shoulders.

'Stop it,' he commanded, pulling her so close, she could smell the lingering traces of champagne on his breath. 'The dress has served its purpose, but now I think we can dispense with it.' His fingers pulled the long zip down the back of her dress.

'Get off!' she cried, grabbing at the front, but she was too late. Benedict's hands slipped the stole off her shoulders, his long fingers curled into the bodice of the dress and pulled it down to her hips, until it fell unimpeded in a pool of silk on the carpet. The speed of his attack dumbfounded her, leaving her almost naked beneath his gaze in the tiniest of lace briefs, a garter belt and stockings.

Folding her arms over her breast in protection, she frantically glanced around the room, searching for some escape. Her eyes stopped at the huge bed and the painful memory hit her like a fist in the stomach; she fought down the feeling of nausea. Nothing had changed in this room in five years, and the memory of the first time they had been here together froze her to the spot. Until that moment she had not really accepted the full consequences of the hasty marriage.

Slowly she turned her head. Benedict had removed his jacket, shirt and bow-tie, and one hand was unzipping his trousers, the other caught her shoulder. She raised her eyes to his harsh face, and she knew he had every intention of carrying out his threat.

Without thought she kicked out at him, her small foot connecting with his shin. His sharp intake of breath did not deter her, and, lowering her head, she went for his arm with small pearly teeth, but a hand in her short curls snapped her head back before she could connect.

'Still the same firecracker, Rebecca,' he drawled with mocking cynicism. 'Don't you know better than to waste all that fire on fighting me? You can't hope to win. Much better to save it for bed.'

'I can try,' she cried and, lifting her arm, struck out at his hard face. He caught her wrists and in a flash had spun her around, her back against his broad chest, her arms pinned to her sides.

'I think you need a little soothing, my sweet wife—a touch here.' His hand stroked down her throat slowly to cup her full breast, his fingers kneading softly. 'Now, isn't that better?' his husky voice taunted in her ear.

She tried to kick back at him, but instead he inserted one long leg between hers and she was in an even worse position. 'Let go of me, you brute.' Only by lying back against him could she keep her balance. She closed her eyes, hoping to blot out his presence. She wanted to scream at the unfairness of it. He was so much bigger, so much stronger, and she could feel the first tendrils of desire curling in her stomach. It was all very good telling herself it was only lust and meant nothing, she could handle it, but with her heartbeat racing she was no longer so confident.

'There, there, Rebecca; relax, let yourself go. It's been a long day,' his deep voice mocked her as his long fingers teased a deliberate feather-light path over the soft curves of her breast, circling the tightening peaks, before rolling them sensuously between his thumb and forefinger.

A low moan escaped her as every nerve-end in her body was aroused to a tingling, taut awareness, and still he continued tormenting her. One strong hand slid lower, pressing on her stomach, urging her closer, if that was possible. She felt the hard proof of his arousal at her back and her blood ran hot with wanting.

'Open your eyes, Rebecca. Know yourself, my little wanton,' he whispered, his mouth warm against her throat. 'Look in front of you.' His hand tracked lower, his long fingers stroking inside her tiny briefs.

Her eyes flew open at the intimacy of his caress, and she barely recognised the erotic picture before her. The mirrored door of the wardrobe reflected the two of them locked together. A hectic flush covered her whole body, the large man towering over and around her, broad, tanned shoulders glistening in the late afternoon sun, looked as though he would devour her whole.

'Please, please, stop,' she pleaded, but, even as she pleaded with him to stop, of its own volition her head tilted to allow his lips easier access to her slender throat.

'You want me, Rebecca. You know you do,' he rasped against her velvet-soft skin.

Her eyes flew wide as they met his. The passionate intent in his gaze, the wholly sensual curve of his firmly etched lips, invited her surrender, and to her shame she could not deny him. Need, want, too long denied, ran like molten lava through her veins. Had he always made her feel this way, this aching, all-consuming hunger? she wondered, arching back against him, trying to turn her head.

'Yes, yes—oh, yes,' she moaned as he finally turned her around, and his mouth captured hers in a greedy, insatiable kiss, a currrent of overwhelming emotion melting her bones.

He swung her up in his arms, his lips finding her breast as he carried her to the waiting bed. His weight came down on her, while his hands still explored every curve and plane, every tiny inch of her, dispensing with her remaining few clothes with an erotic expertise, slowly curling the stockings down her shapely legs, with scorching kisses trailing in their wake, and when he treated her garter belt and briefs in the same way, his mouth hot on her moist, intimate flesh, she cried out.

'Please...' She did not know if she was begging for him to continue or stop, her body arched like a bow-string, her slender arms curved around his shoulders, her fingers tracing the muscle and sinew of his broad back.

Benedict pulled away for a moment, shedding his pants, then she felt the glorious naked weight of him in

every pore of her body as he lowered himself over her,
sliding between her legs.

He took her with a sudden, passionate thrust, and for
a second her small body clenched in unexpected dis-
comfort. Benedict stilled inside her for a moment, allowing her body to accept him, the tension to build...
Then he moved, his deep, slow strokes filling her completely, and suddenly her fears vanished in a flash-flood
of passion. She clung to him, her nails digging into his
flesh, shuddering violently in a mind-bending ecstasy she
had only glimpsed before.

His powerful thrusts accelerated to a pounding rhythm
that she instinctively matched. Finally, when she thought
the tension would consume her, her burning, throbbing
body clamped to his, convulsed in an erotic dance of
life. Benedict jerked against her with a guttural, rasping
sound of completion, his large body thrusting violently
into the quivering silken softness of hers.

It was a long time before she stirred. Her mind seemed
incapable of registering the enormity of what had happened, while her body pulsed languorously beneath the
weight of Benedict's.

'Are you all right?' he rasped, and, easing himself up
on his elbows, he added, 'I'm too heavy for you.' His
eyes searched her flushed face, her swollen lips and lower
to her full breasts. 'You're so tiny and so beautiful, my
perfect, passionate little Venus.' His smile was one of
pure masculine triumph. Rebecca did not see the flash
of some other emotion, as she briefly closed her eyes in
embarrassment.

'Get off me,' she whispered, consumed with shame at
the ease with which he had seduced her. His broad
shoulders flexed, and a vivid image of the two of them
earlier, reflected in the mirror, flashed in her mind. The
calculating way he had made her aware of her own sensuality made her burn with resentment. 'I hate you,' she

muttered, turning her head away. Her brain registered the time on the bedside clock. God, it was barely an hour since they'd left the reception! Still daylight. She would never forgive him, never . . .

Benedict chuckled. 'Ah, Rebecca, you can hate me as much as you like, sweetheart,' he mocked as his lips sought the soft line of her neck, 'as long as this exquisite little body knows its master.' His hand stroked over her breast in a light caress, and to her horror she felt the stirring of renewed arousal.

Hands that had clung to his broad back only minutes earlier pushed at his damp chest. 'You're an animal,' she cried. 'You could have waited.'

'You can call me all the names under the sun but it doesn't alter the fact you wanted me.' He ran a taunting hand down over the naked curve of her waist and thigh. 'And still do.'

'No,' she choked as he quickly caught her failing hands and pinned them either side of her head. She shivered; his powerfully body was poised over her like some avenging angel, but the dark glitter in his golden eyes was pure devil.

'Yes, perhaps you're right, Rebecca, maybe I was a little hasty,' he drawled lazily.

'You were!' she exclaimed. She didn't trust his suddenly agreeing with her.

'Ah-ha . . .' His dark head lowered and once again his mouth sought hers. She was too weak to fight him, and she squeezed her eyes shut, as he murmured teasingly against her lips, 'This time I'll take you slow and easy, pure pleasure. Hmm?'

It was dark when Rebecca next opened her eyes. For a moment she was disorientated; her limbs felt heavy, her body aching, and when she moved her arm brushed hard, warm flesh. She stiffened, hardly daring to breathe,

as memory returned. The deep, steady sound of
Benedict's breathing told her he was asleep.

Moving cautiously, she eased out of the bed; with only
a pale moonlight to guide her, she silently crossed the
soft carpet to the bathroom. She closed and locked the
door behind her with a shuddering sigh of relief.

A quick look around the extravagantly furnished room
and she blushed at her own naked reflection in the mirror
on the wall. The marks of Benedict's lovemaking were
clear to see on her soft skin. Heat surged through her
as she recalled the long, slow assault on her senses.

The incredible intimacies he had subjected her to
should have horrified her, but to her shame she had responded with a wild abandon, and returned the favour.
She had explored his hard-muscled body with a tactile
delight, glorying in his muffled groans, fascinated by his
big masculine form.

She shook her head to dispel the erotic images and
walked into the shower-stall; turning on the gold-plated
tap, she stood under the cleansing spray. Methodically
she washed every centimetre of her flesh, in a vain attempt to wash away the memory of her husband's
possession . . .

Much as she would have liked to deny it, he had possessed her absolutely and, worse, deep down in the
innermost part of her being she knew she had wanted,
even welcomed his sensual mastery. She tried to excuse
herself. It was because she had been celibate for so long—
any man could probably have aroused her. But she knew
she was lying. It was only Benedict who had the power
to make her fall apart with just a kiss, a caress. She had
no defence against him, and sadly she realised she
probably never would.

Rebecca closed her eyes and allowed the warm water
to work its soothing effect on her tired body. She didn't
hear the shower door open, and almost jumped out of

her skin when a deep, masculine voice asked throatily, 'Mind if I join you?'

'No!' she exclaimed, stepping out of the shower and bang into Benedict. She pushed at his chest, putting some space between them, her pulse picking up speed as she tried to subdue her awareness of his large, hard body so close beside her.

'Pity, it can be fun,' he drawled sensuously.

She glanced up and flushed at the knowing gleam in his eyes. She looked down but the tiny black briefs he wore were barely decent. She gulped and stared straight ahead, but his broad chest, the darkly angling body hair, was no less intimmidating.

'No? Then here—allow me.' And, wrapping a large towel around her naked form, he began towelling her dry, his big hands strangely gentle.

'I can do that myself,' she said in a muffled voice, as he brought her body into close contact with his, holding her small, very wet head to his chest while he briskly rubbed her hair. The intimacy of the situation completely unnerved her.

'Why bother when you have a willing slave?' he drawled huskily, and, dropping the towel to the floor, he folded her in his strong arms, bringing her body into an even more intimate fit with his.

She squeezed her eyes tightly shut, trying to hold back the tears of self-pity. It was so unfair, she thought helplessly. If she was six feet tall, she would punch him in the nose, but fighting him was a futile exercise, as she had learned to her cost. She hated being so defenceless; she was a strong, mature woman, used to living her own life, and in a few short days it had all been taken from her.

Benedict tilted her chin with one finger, his eyes narrowed, dark and intent on her pale face. 'Are you all right?'

She felt his body stir against her and the evidence of his arousal seemed like the ultimate insult. A blind anger consumed her. 'No, I'm damn well not,' she said defiantly, her eyes misted with tears.

'You feel perfect to me.'

She spun away from his restraining arm. 'And you feel like a sex maniac to me,' she snapped back, her violet eyes no longer misty, but furious.

The masculine line of his mouth quirked with amusement. Reaching out a hand, he caught her arm, and, placing his finger over her lips, so that her eyes sparked even more angrily, he said, 'You can blame me for a lot of things, Rebecca, but the sexual chemistry between us is a mutual explosive force. You can't blame me for being a man.' His eyes assumed a mocking gleam. 'And I suggest you stop blaming yourself for being a woman.' His gaze angled down her naked body, taking in the soft, faint bruising of her flawless skin, the deeper pink areolae of her breasts, where not long ago he had suckled, then back to her furiously flushed face.

'Look at yourself. The signs of our mutually satisfying lovemaking are traced in your fair flesh, my little firecracker. So let's not pretend. If I'm a sex maniac, you were with me all the way.' He dropped her arm and, cupping her face in his hands, he pressed a swift, hard kiss to her swollen lips. 'So what does that make you?' he gibed, and with an arrogant smile he released her and, stepping past her, entered the shower cubicle.

The sound of his laughter was the last straw. 'Why, you egotistical bastard!' she exploded, but the sound of running water muffled her words. Spitting nails, Rebecca grabbed another towel and, wrapping it tightly around her chest, she slammed out of the bathroom. The fact that Benedict was right did not help her temper at all.

Returning to the guest-bedroom she had used for the past couple of days, she was even more infuriated to find all her clothes had been removed; she stormed back to the master bedroom, and flung open drawers. It was just as she had suspected. The housekeeper had transferred all her clothes.

Cursing under her breath, she found a bra and matching briefs; from the wardrobe she took the first thing she touched: a blue cotton blouse with a matching blue and cream patterned skirt—one of the outfits Benedict had bought. Hastily she dressed, her stormy eyes lighting on the clock. Ten. And suddenly her stomach growled. She was famished.

'Going somewhere?'

Rebecca stiffened at the blunt question. 'Downstairs to get something to eat,' she flung tersely. She glanced at Benedict. He was wearing only a brief towel, knotted low on his hips. Suddenly the room seemed far too intimate. She wanted to run, and bristled defensively, as he strode towards her.

Noting her reaction, his golden eyes narrowed in a brief frown. 'Relax, Rebecca.' He reached past her and drew a navy silk Paisley robe from the wardrobe. 'I've no intention of starving you.' And, dropping the towel to the floor, totally unconscious of his nudity, he stood in front of her and slipped on the robe.

'How reassuring,' she gibed, trying to ignore the potent appeal of his naked, sun-bronzed body.

'In any way,' he added provocatively, the sensual promise in his eyes unmistakable, and she darted out of the room like a scared rabbit.

The kitchen was immaculate stainless steel, all tiled, and with every known gadget. Rebecca looked around, and longed to be back in her own kitchen. It was never likely to happen—not for some years, if Benedict had his way.

Yesterday, she had reluctantly listed her home with an agent as available to rent. She was lucky, she supposed, Benedict had not insisted she sell it.

With a tired sigh, she crossed to the refrigerator, opened the door and peered inside. A wry smile curved her lips. Mrs James, the butler's wife and Benedict's housekeeper, had been very efficient. On the top shelf was a tray of cold cuts, and salad, plus a bottle of champagne.

She slammed the door on the champagne and meat; instead she took an egg from a basket on the counter and, turning on the gas cooker, she splashed some oil into the frying-pan. So what if fried food was fattening? The way she felt at the moment she couldn't give a damn! She popped two slices of bread in the toaster and had just cracked the egg into the hot fat, and taken a spatula from the rack beside the cooker, when Benedict walked into the room.

'Fried egg? Not a very romantic wedding supper,' he said with a smile. 'Still, if that's all you can cook, I suppose it will have to do.

'I'm not your slave,' she said angrily.

Her flash of temper seemed to amuse him. 'Temper, temper. Did your mother never tell you the way to a man's heart is through his stomach?'

She turned slightly. He was dangerously close, she could see the fine lines spreading from the corners of his eyes, and the amusement in their depths infuriated her. 'You're the only man I know who makes me angry, and, as for finding the way to your heart, if I did I would cut it to pieces,' she snapped.

Dark eyes met hers, deep and unfathomable, successfully masking his thoughts, but the hard line of his jaw clenched imperceptibly. 'I see you've drawn the battle-lines,' he said sardonically.

Mutinously she stared at him. He was wearing the Paisley robe, his legs were bare and the V between the robe's lapels revealed the soft black mat of hair on his chest. The sheer masculine strength of the man hit her like a physical blow.

Her hand holding the spatula trembled, and she was furious at her own weakness. The toast popped and thankfully she turned her attention to the food. She slid the spatula under the fried egg, trying to ignore Benedict's overpowering presence.

'Make mine over easy,' he murmured, his lips brushing her ear.

Whether it was the brush of his lips, his warm breath on her skin, or just the mockery in his tone that made her snap, she didn't know. But quite deliberately, instead of turning the egg over in the pan, she turned around and turned it over his head.

The look on his rugged face she would carry to her dying day. Incredulous did not begin to describe it. His dark brows drew together with puzzlement, as the yolk broke and trickled over his broad forehead, and down his nose.

Rebecca couldn't help it; her lips twitched, he looked so stunned and so funny. She could not resist gibing, 'An original Eggs Benedict!' and the laughter bubbled out, as she watched the hard white bounce off his shoulder and splatter on the floor.

CHAPTER EIGHT

'REBECCA!'

Benedict's roar stopped the laughter in her throat. Suddenly she was confronted by an absolutely furious primitive male animal. Nervously she looked around for a way of escape. She flinched as Benedict's hand reached past her and turned off the cooker; his other hand caught hers, and relieved her of the spatula, throwing it contemptuously over his shoulder. It landed with a clatter on the tiled floor.

'Now Ben—— Ah!' His name changed into a terrified squeal as he caught her shoulders, shoving her back against the refrigerator door.

'Eggs Benedict, you said, you little witch. Well, now you are bloody well going to eat it.' His head bent, his mouth crushing hers as his hard body slammed into her, sending a shock wave of fear mingled with a feverish pleasure jetting through her veins.

His hands were everywhere, moving from her breasts to hips, to thighs, in a savage exploration. He rubbed his face across her breasts, tearing her blouse open in the process. With his teeth he broke open her front-fastening bra. Rebecca swayed on her feet, her knees weakening as he pushed her skirt up around her waist and ripped her silk briefs away from her body.

Helplessly she clung to his wide shoulders, her body throbbing with a mercurial flash of aching desire, as he lifted her bodily off the ground, burying his face between her full breasts, his fingers digging into her rounded bottom as he lifted her higher. When his teeth bit the sensitive tip of her breast, her shapely legs, of their own volition, snaked around his lean waist. He entered her, driving repeatedly into the hot, wet centre of her womanhood. The sheer voracity of their coupling stunned her brain and finally she cried out, her slender body shaking in tumultuous release as Benedict thrust again, his large frame shuddering in a mutual climax.

She came back to reality when her feet touched the floor; she was aware of the icy coldness of the refrigerator door at her back while inside she was burning. Rebecca could not believe what had happened. They had come together in a blazing angry passion that had utterly consumed her mind. If anyone had told her yesterday that making love shoved up against a refrigerator door was erotic, she would have laughed her head off...

But now, raising her flushed face to look up at Benedict, she wasn't laughing. His dark golden eyes, full of remorse and something else she dared not put a name to, roamed over her delicate features. Lust no longer seemed the right word, she thought wonderingly.

'God, Rebecca, I'm sorry...' His deep chest heaved, and she rested her small hand on the dark, damp curls; she could feel the still rapid pounding of his heart beneath her finger tips.

'It's all right...' she breathed shakily.

'It isn't all right, damn it!' Benedict rasped. 'I swear I've never behaved this way with any other woman in my life.' He brushed a none-too-steady hand through the black hair falling over his brow in a gesture of bewilderment. 'You scramble my senses, enrage and infuriate me until I lose all self-control. You're so lovely and so tiny.' His dark eyes grazed over her slight but voluptuous body. With a snort of self-disgust, he began fastening her tattered blouse, his strong hands smoothing her rumpled skirt down over her slender hips. 'God,

what a wedding night! I'm sorry, Rebecca. I behaved . . . like an animal. I'm afraid . . . I hurt you.'

She smiled at him tenderly. 'No, no, you didn't hurt
me.' She wanted to smooth the worried frown from his
forehead, cuddle him as she would Daniel when he dis-
played that exact same expression—a mixture of sorrow
and guilt. Her violet eyes widened to their fullest extent.
His lovemaking could never hurt her... She loved him...
She could fool herself no longer. It wasn't lust or duty,
as her rational mind had tried to insist, but love, glorious love... She exulted in the discovery, her glowing
face turned to his, and then his voice pierced her
consciousness.

'Maybe not this time, but the way I feel about you,
one day it's bound to happen.' He spoke slowly, his
words husky and faintly slurred, as if he was speaking
his thoughts out loud without knowing it. 'I should never
have married you.' He brushed the back of his hand
across his eyes in a weary gesture.

Rebecca stared up at him, incapable of tearing her
gaze from his attractive but suddenly haggard features.
Her hand fell from his chest, her fingers curling into
fists at her side. Hysterical laughter bubbled in her throat
as the hopelessness of the situation struck her. She had
finally admitted to herself she loved Benedict, and
probably always had. While he had reached the totally
opposite conclusion; he hated her and should never have
married her.

'Benedict . . .' she said helplessly.

His face hardened into a familiar, impenetrable mask.
'You'll have to stay here for a while, but you don't need
to worry—I won't force myself on you again. I'll buy a
house in the country for you and Daniel. I'll stay in town,
and with your permission visit occasionally.'

She shivered, briefly closing her eyes against the pain.
He had it all cut and dried.

'You're cold, Rebecca, go to bed.' He turned to gesture around the kitchen. 'I'll clear the mess . . . we'll talk tomorrow.' His cold, clipped voice chilled her to the bone.

Slowly she walked out of the room, a wave of icy desolation sweeping through her; on trembling legs she mounted the stairs to the bedroom. Talk! What was there to say? She undressed and washed before she got into bed, but she couldn't sleep.

She was blinded by tears. They had been married for a few short, chaotic, frenzied hours, and in that time her emotions had run the gamut of just about every feeling known to the human race. Was it only three days ago that she had sought the sanctuary of her own bed in her apartment, upset at having to marry Benedict, but consoling herself with the knowledge there was no way she would ever love him? *Ergo*, there was no possibility of him hurting her again . . .

In her conceit she had considered herself far too realistic, too intelligent, to ever make the same mistake twice. There was no way she could love a man who had such a ruthless, vengeful side to his nature.

Yet now, lying in the bed on which they had made love only hours earlier, she could not deny she loved him . . .

Rebecca jolted awake, as a heavy arm crashed down on her. It felt like a lead weight cross her breasts. She turned her head on the pillow and in the gloom of the dawn light she made out the shape of Benedict beside her. He was lying on his stomach and his long arm was effectively pinning her to the bed.

Groggily she remembered coming to bed last night, tormented by the knowledge that she had fallen in love with her husband. She must have fallen asleep. She hadn't heard him join her.

She tensed, as he grunted something unintelligible. Was he waking up? No, but he was making it very difficult for her to breathe easily. Warily she tried to push his shoulder, and her hand stilled on his flesh. His skin was burning where she touched it; suddenly she was aware of the unnatural heat exuding from his large body. She heard him groan her name and instinctively stroked her hand caressingly over his shoulder. His skin was wet with perspiration...

Suddenly it struck her that this was no ordinary sleep; his breathing was heavy and laboured, interspersed with guttural words she could not decipher. Was he having a nightmare? Somehow she had always considered Benedict as some exalted, superhuman being, but now, as he unconsciously held her captive, she was struck by the realistion that Benedict suffered from the same frailties, was susceptible to the same dark fears, as the rest of the human race.

It was impossible for her to lift his arm, so carefully she wriggled up the bed until she was in a sitting position, then gently, with both hands, she managed to lift his arm from her legs, and slide out of bed. She switched on the bedside light, pulled on her robe and turned to stare down at him, her delicately arched eyebrows drawn together in a worried frown. This was no ordinary nightmare; something was wrong, badly wrong with him.

As she watched he flung himself over on to his back, the bedclothes twisting around low on his thighs. His muscular chest rose and fell erratically, his face was flushed and his dark hair, wet with sweat, was plastered to his brow.

'Oh, Benedict,' she whispered; sitting down on the side of the bed, she reached out and swept his hair back from his forehead. The heat was phenomenal, his temperature must be sky high, she thought fearfully.

She was reminded of Daniel when he had suffered from measles once, and her heart squeezed with love for him. He looked so helpless. Worriedly she chewed her bottom lip. It was all well and good staring at him with cow eyes, but what was she going to do?

She called his name, but his eyes remained firmly closed, his dark, curling lashes glued to his skin with moisture. Was it a summer flu? she wondered. But as the thought occurred he began to shiver, his muscular torso shaking as if in the grip of some virulent fever. Struggling with the tangled sheets, she managed to pull them up to his shoulders, her hand sliding over his sweat-slicked chest, when shockingly he raised his head, his eyes wide open, and his hand caught her wrist in a grip of steel.

'Rebecca, Rebecca, don't leave me, please. I...' His mouth worked but no sound came out.

'It's all right, Benedict, I'm here, but you're ill.' Who was his doctor? She had married him, slept with him, but in reality she knew so little about him. 'You need a doctor.' She saw his throat move as he swallowed hard.

'No, no doctor.' His dark eyes burned with a feverish light. 'Fever—cabinet in bathroom.' The words took all his strength, his eyes closed and his head fell back on the pillow.

She leant forward and gently replaced the covers around his now completely still form, panic clawing at her heart. Fever! What kind of fever? Ovbviously he had suffered from it before, but as far as she was concerned it could be anything. She sat by his side for a few minutes longer. Was he asleep or unconscious? She didn't know, but she couldn't sit here doing nothing.

Jumping to her feet, she shot into the bathroom, opened the large cabinet above the washbasin, and groaned, 'Oh, no.' There were half a dozen different bottles, and with trembling hands she painstakingly read

the labels. Four she could dismiss as proprietary brands
of pain-killers. But she was still left with two bottles.
She breathed a sigh of relief as she noted the doctor's
name on both.

Dashing downstairs, the bottles in her hand, she raced
into Benedict's study; a desk diary and a personal telephone directory lay on the large oak desk. In a matter
of seconds she was dialling the telephone nunmber of a
Dr Falkirk.

A gruff, sleepy voice answered her; briefly she explained the position, and was told to check—one of the
bottles should contain chloroquine.

She heaved a deep sigh of relief. 'Yes.'

'Good. No need to panic; we've been through this
countless times before. Mr Maxwell *will* forget to take
his tablets Mrs James.' Rebecca didn't bother to correct
him. 'Give him one three hundred milligram tablet with
a glass of water immediately. Keep him comfortble,
sponge him down, plenty of liquids, and I'll be there
directly after morning surgery.'

She wanted to scream at the man to come immediately, but common sense told her it would do no good.
Quickly she ran back upstairs, and filled a tumbler of
water in the bathroom, before entering the bedroom. She
choked back a sob. Benedict was lying as she had left
him, and the high colour in his cheeks, the perspiration
running down his brow, brought tears to her eyes.

'Oh, Benedict, please,' she murmured in anguish,
'wake up!' With the tablet in one hand and the glass of
water placed on the bedside table, she sat down by his
head and slid one arm beneath his massive shoulders.
How she got the strength to lift his heavy body, she didn't
know, but for a moment his eyes opened, and his glazed,
feverish glance skidded over her.

'Rebecca . . . you stayed,' he groaned.

'Shh, don't talk. Swallow this.' And, placing the tablet against his lips, she watched as he weakly opened his mouth. Supporting his head, she picked up the beaker of water. 'Drink, Benedict.'

She breathed a sigh of relief as his throat worked, swallowing the liquid in great gulps. His head fell back and down against her breast, a dead weight against her. But he was still awake, his sweat-drenched features contorting as, in a delirium, he rambled remorsefully and then raved angry, disjointed sentences that made very little sense to Rebecca.

'Gordon, I'm sorry... Betrayed you... Should have made sure... Sorry, sorry... Guilty, Rebecca.' He flung himself over on his side, out of her arms, his back towards her. 'Not the only reason...' He was breathing unevenly as he tossed about in feverish agitation. The way he cried her name brought a lump to her throat and confirmed her earlier fear. She was guilty in his eyes. Obviously he was sorry he had ever married her. What else could it be?

She leant over him; he might hate her tomorrow, but right now he needed her... and that was enough for her. Her tender heart ached to comfort him, when suddenly he flung hinmself over on to his back. Surprising her with his strength, he grasped her hands, holding them to his damp chest; she could feel his heart thundering erratically, and she battled to hold back the tears. It hurt her almost physically to see him this way.

His eyes, wide and surprisingly brilliant, bored into hers. 'Gordon... Rebecca. A guilty passion... I had no light. You understand... tell me you understand...'

Rebecca didn't, but she could not bear the lost, pleading look in his glittering eyes. 'I do understand, Benedict, and it's all right; please try to rest.' She blinked back the tears stinging her eyes.

Benedict, in a brief moment of normality, searched her lovely face. 'You're crying...for me, Rebecca?' A pitiful attempt at a smile twitched his full lips. 'You will stay.' And, as suddenly as he had awakened, his grasp on her wrists weakened and he fell back aginst the pillow, she hoped asleep and not unconscious.

Rebecca hurried to the bathroom and returned with a basin of water, sponge and towels. She had no idea how long she sat watching him, occasionally sponging his face, his chest; the bedclothes were damp. She would have to change them. But how? And all the time her troubled mind tried to make sense of his rambling.

What had he meant? 'A guilty passion' and 'not the only reason'. If she could decipher his ravings, she might understand him better. The ringing of the doorbell intruded on her troubled thoughts. The doctor! Carefully she stood up, and smoothed the bedclothes over Benedict's broad chest. He did not stir, he appeared to be deeply asleep. She flew downstairs and opened the front door.

'So Mr Maxwell has been naughty again.' The bluff Scots accent went well with the short, stout man who walked past Rebecca into the hall. He turned. 'You're not Mrs James.' His grey eyes, a hint of disapproval in their depths, searched her pale face.

'I am Mrs Maxwell, Benedict's wife.' It was the first time she had said the words out loud and it gave her a certain pride. 'Mrs James is on holiday,' she went on to explain, holding out her small hand in a conventional greeting.

Dr Falkirk positively beamed, his plump hand shaking hers so heartily, she could feel the vibration to her shoulder. 'Well, so the old devil finally got married. My congratulations. When was the wedding?'

Rebecca could feel the heat rising in her face. 'Yesterday,' she responded quietly. 'But please, don't you

think we should go up to Benedict?' To her astonishment the doctor started to laugh as he headed for the
stairs.

'Well, that could explain this attack—emotional upheaval is a prime cause of activating this particular
tropical disease, and very few things in life are more
traumatic for a man than getting married. Come on,
lass, let's have a look at him, and don't you worry. He'll
be as right as rain in a day or two.' Still chuckling, he
strode into the bedroom.

She stood by the bedside while the doctor took his
patient's pulse, lifted his eyelids and examined his eyes,
all without Benedict moving.

'Yes, just as I thought. He picked this up in Brazil,
you know. There are hundreds, no thousands, of tropical
diseases, a lot the medical profession don't even have a
name for. But we sorted this out the first year he was
back in England; nothing to worry about. Probably in
all the excitement leading to the wedding he has forgotten to take precautionary measures. You've given him
the dose of chloroquine? What time?' he asked briskly.

'Yes.' She looked at her wristwatch—ten-thirty in the
morning—and it was then she realised she was wearing
only a robe. Dear heaven, what must the doctor think
of her? She blushed scarlet, mumbling, 'I don't know.
About ten minutes after talking to you.'

'Hmm, we'll say six-thirty. Let him sleep for now, then
two more doses today, but tomorrow and the following
day he'll only need one; that will do the trick. One tablet
a week is all it takes to prevent this type of occurrence,
but he must have forgotten again.'

He hesitated, his grey eyes sliding over Rebecca from
head to toe, taking in her slight stature, and very red
face. 'If you are at all doubtful about looking after him,
I could bring in a nurse, or arrange for him to be taken
to a private nursing home. It wouldn't be the first time.'

'No. Oh, no!' she cried. 'I can manage, honestly I can.' Benedict needed her, and it was probably the only chance she would ever have to lavish all her love and care on him. No way was she going to allow some stranger to take her place.

'Excellent.' Dr Falkirk smiled. 'But if you're at all worried call me in the morning. Try to keep him in bed, or at least make him rest, and if you take my advice you'll persuade him to take you on a long honeymoon, away from work and nowhere near Brazil and his be-loved Indians. If he didn't keep going back there this would have cleared up long ago.'

'I'll see what I can do,' Rebecca said with a weak smile.

'A newly married man, he'll take no persuading; you're a very lovely young woman, and he'd be a fool to refuse.' He was still chuckling as she showed him out.

Returning to the study, she rang the hotel in Brighton where Daniel was staying with his new-found relations. With a few brief words she explained the situation to Gerard Montaine, and he seemed singularly unalarmed. After a short chat to Daniel, who was thoroughly en-joying himself with his new cousins, and was at that minute waiting to leave for a picnic on the beach, she replaced the receiver and hurried back upstairs.

Benedict seemed to be in a fretful kind of sleep. Rebecca watched him for a moment, and then quickly moved around the room, gathering clean underwear from a drawer, and a simple cool blue cotton summer dress from the wardrobe. Then she headed for the shower.

She did not dare linger, and within five minutes she was back at Benedict's bedside, where she remained through the long, hot hours of the fine summer day. At two o'clock she managed to get him to take his medicine and, with a great deal of effort and not a little embar-rassment, she bathed his naked, burning body and changed the sodden bedclothes.

Benedict swung between bouts of fever and sudden chills. His incoherent ramblings frequently interspersed with her name. She clung to his large hand, willing him to get better, while her own emotions fluctuated between happiness at her newfound love for him, and deep despair as to what the future might hold for her.

At one point she forced herself to go down to the kitchen, where she ate some of the cold cuts from the refrigerator without tasting anything, drank a cup of coffee and filled a jug with some orange juice for her patient, before returning to the sickroom.

The sun was setting in a glorious golden-red ball of fire, filling the room with a rose-pink haze, and Benedict was sitting up in bed, his hair ruffled, his golden eyes wild. 'Where have you been?' he demanded harshly, the evening light accentuating the planes and hollows of a face weakened by fever. 'I thought you'd left me.'

'Oh, Benedict,' she cried, rushing across to the bed; she placed the jug on the side-table, and unthinkingly grasped his hand. 'I wouldn't dream of leaving you alone. I just needed a drink.' She was sitting on the bed, cradling his large hand in hers without realising what she was giving away. 'How do you feel? I was so worried.' With her other hand she stroked the dark stubble on his unshaven jaw.

'Rebecca ... God! I thought ...'

For a second she was stunned by the naked vulnerability she read in his eyes, but before he could say any more she nervously interrupted. 'No, no talking, you must conserve your energy, and anyway it's time for your medicine. You must have a drink. Relax,' she said softly.

Benedict's lips twisted in a semblance of a mocking smile. 'My own Florence Nightingale.'

Hiding her face from him, she poured some juice into a glass. She loved him, but now he was coming to his senses she dared not let him see ... Composing her

features, she turned and held out the glass. 'Drink this.
And here's your tablet.' In her other hand she held out
the pill, but to her dismay Benedict had not the strength
to hold the glass; his large hand shook and instantly she
covered his hand with her own, guiding both juice and
pill to his dry, cracked lips.

His head fell back against the pillows. 'Thank...' He
sighed deeply, his eyes closed, and as she watched he
slipped once more into a troubled sleep.

Rebecca jerked her head up. She was propped uncomfortably on the side of the bed, the deep, even tone of
Benedict's breathing the only sound in the dark room.
Carefully she reached out and switched on the table lamp.
It was one o'clock in the morning and she was freezing.
She looked with loving, tender eyes at the man lying in
the bed. His fever appeared to have broken and his features were relaxed in what looked like a normal but deep
sleep. She shivered, her summer dress no protection
against the night air.

Benedict rolled over, muttering something in his sleep.
She eyed the narrow strip of empty bed longingly. Surely
if she was very careful she could wriggle under the bedclothes without disturbing him. Quickly she slipped off
her dress and shoes and cautiously slid under the covers.
With a weary sigh she closed her eyes. She'd rest, just
a little while, she told herself. Benedict seemed over the
worst, he was no longer burning up, and she was so
tired...

Rebecca was cosily curled up, her cheek resting against
the firm warmth of a very masculine chest. She was
floating in a dream between waking and sleep. A long
finger teasingly outlined her full lips. Benedict! She
sighed and drew the tantalising digit into the moist,
hungry heat of her mouth.

Benedict? Her eyes flew open, she pushed the hand
away and, fighting the tangle of sheets, she tried to pull
herself up to a sitting position.

There was a low chuckle from the man beside her, and
an arm with a surprising amount of strength for a man
who was ill kept her pinned to his side.

'Good afternoon, Rebecca.'

'Afternoon?' Some nurse she had turned out to be.

'One-thirty. Friday.' Benedict was leaning on one arm,
staring down at her, his dark eyes tired but clear, only
the gauntness of his features and the dark beard outlining his square jaw betraying the fever of the past thirty-
odd hours. 'I'm back to reality, thanks to you.'

'Your medicine!' she cried.

'It can wait, but you and I can't,' he stated hardily,
his hand tightening round her waist.

'But the doctor said...'

'I know what he said.'

'How could you? You were out cold when he was here
yesterday.' Her eyes, wide with puzzlement, stared up
into guarded dark ones. He wasn't making sense, perhaps
the fever still lingered...

'Was I?' he said in a dry voice. 'A man is at his most
vulnerable when ill. True, I was in the grip of a fever,
but at that point I was lucid enough to hear what was
being said. Maybe I refused to open my eyes because I
couldn't bear the thought of seeing you refuse to look
after me. I seem to remember asking you earlier to stay
with me...'

'You were rambling, you didn't know what you were
saying,' she excused him, stunned and not quite believing his admission of deceit.

'You're so generous, you shame me, Rebecca.' His eyes
darkened as if with pain.

'Benedict.' She placed her hand on his broad chest in
a gesture of comfort, and suddenly the feel of his warm

flesh beneath her fingers made her aware of the intimacy of their position. 'I'd better...'

'No, Rebecca, let me talk.' His hand moved to cup her chin so she was forced to look up into his dark, intense face. 'I woke up a couple of hours ago to find your slender arm around my waist. You were curled up against my back like a soft little kitten. For a moment I thought I had died and gone to heaven.'

She felt the colour creeping under her skin at the heated glow she saw in his eyes. Was it possible he cared about her? No, she answered her own question. 'Yes, well, you're still alive,' she replied, deliberately prosaic.

But Benedict ignored her and continued. 'Then reality struck. I have lain here for ages, watching you sleep, planning what I was going to say to you.'

'There's no need to explain...' The idea of him watching her sleep was oddly disturbing.

'Rebecca, I might never have the courage again.' His sensuous lips twisted in a wry smile 'Or perhaps be weak enough again, so please listen. I love you. I always have and I always will...'

CHAPTER NINE

IT WAS the last thing in the world Rebecca had expected. She was struck dumb, her mouth fell open, and her pulse-rate shot up like a rocket. In the lengthening silence she could sense the increasing tension in the air, but was incapable of response. She couldn't believe it... but oh, how she wanted to! And deep inside her she felt the first flicker of hope.

'Rebecca!' Benedict stared at her with a pleading hunger she had never seen before. 'I'm not asking you to love me. I don't deserve you, I know, but I...I thought...' For such a proud man, he was unusually hesitant. 'I know I said I would let you and Daniel go to the country together, but...well, maybe we could come to a more amicable arrangement... The other night I was a brute, but I swear it won't ever happen again... We could have a good marriage——' He stopped and, totally out of character, his gaunt face flushed with embarrassment, but a grim determination lit his golden-brown eyes. 'I thought, I hoped, because you have looked after me, changed me, bathed me—— I can't believe you would do that if you really hated me——'

'Benedict,' she interrupted cautiously, 'you're the one who hated *me*, for hiding Daniel from you. You said as much last night...'

'Are you mad?' he asked with an edge of anger. 'Whatever you thought you heard in my ramblings, it certainly wasn't that. I tried to tell you about Gordon. I seem to remember demanding you understand, and you said yes.'

'I was humouring you. You were delirious.'

'Hell's teeth, Rebecca, you are, without a doubt, the most infuriating, stubborn, obtuse woman I have ever met.'

This was the Benedict she knew and loved, she thought wonderingly, as he moved over her, supporting himself on his elbows each side of her body. She was intensely aware of his lower torso lying over her bare legs, her briefs the only barrier between herself and his naked body. 'I think you're still delirious,' she muttered quietly, but he heard her.

'Damn it, woman, I am not delirious! I'm trying to explain. Something I tried five years ago, and again last week in France, and again last night. But this time I am not letting you out of this bed until you *listen* and *understand*. Is that clear?' he snarled.

'Yes, Benedict,' she said meekly. God knew, there was so much confusion, so much hurt between them! It was way past time they tried to talk like civilised human beings, she thought, and there was Daniel to consider. For his sake alone she owed it to Benedict to hear him out.

'First I have to know, did you believe me last week when I explained about writing to you?'

'Yes, of course, and even if I hadn't, your uncle Gerard explained what had happened at the wedding reception. In fact he apologised; he seemed to think it was partly his fault you had believed what you did about Gordon's death.'

'Thank God for Gerard!' Benedict said bluntly. 'But I have a confession to make. I didn't tell you the whole truth in the letter.'

Warily she searched his sombre face, not sure she wanted to hear any more.

'I'd better start at the beginning, Rebecca. From the moment I saw you sitting in the front row of the lecture theatre...' he breathed deeply '...I was bowled over. A tiny, exquisitely proportioned girl with the face of an angel, huge pansy eyes sparkling with life, the most intelligent expressive features...everything about you fascinated me, and then I saw Rupert. I knew you weren't his wife, and immediately jumped to the wrong conclusion. Later, at the party, I couldn't look at you when you were introduced. I didn't dare, I was afraid of making a fool of myself. No woman had ever reached me so deeply before. Later I couldn't help myself when Rupert insisted on introducing you again. But when he said your full name I couldn't believe fate could play such a trick. The girl I had wanted on sight had belonged to my half-brother.'

Rebecca felt the flame of hope in her heart burn brighter as she listened to Benedict's deep voice. It was as if he was talking to himself.

'My mother had told me about Gordon's death—her version—and, as you know, foolishly I believed her, even though Gerard, without going into details, had already told me it was an accident. In any case Gordon had been dead four years, there was nothing I could do. But when I realised who you were I felt guilty as hell. I was lusting after my dead brother's lover. I was so mixed up; maybe you were the temptress my mother had said you were. I used Gordon as a defence, to fight my own feelings... I was obsessed by you. I wanted to possess you body and soul. I tried to stay away from you, but I couldn't. Suddenly it made sense that you had ensnared Gordon, because one look at you and *I* was completely enslaved.'

Rebecca looked up at him. The intensity of his words, the sincerity in his dark eyes, was very convincing; and hadn't it been the same for her? She had loved him on sight; was it so difficult to believe Benedict had done the same?

'I can't see you as anyone's slave,' she murmured softly, her gaze falling to his wide shoulders, the rhythmic movement of his broad chest only a hand span away. Unconsciously she reached out one finger, teasing a lock of softly curling body hair, a warmth building up inside her.

'I couldn't either at the time, though I seem to remember telling you on our wedding night I was your willing slave.' He caught her teasing finger and kissed it.

He had, but Rebecca had ignored his remark at the time, too full of her own anger and resentment. Dared she begin to believe he cared? She was still not convinced, and her doubt showed in the guarded look she gave him.

'I don't blame you for doubting me, Rebecca. But hear me out. I fought, God, how I fought against the emotions you aroused in me. I told myself the years in the jungle must have addled my brain. I didn't believe in love, never had and never would, but one glance from your sparkling eyes and my mind turned to mush. I lied to myself. As long as I could believe I was seeking vengeance for my brother, I had an excuse, and didn't have to admit that deep down I felt I was betraying him, lusting after his woman... The night I made love to you here in this bed——' his eyes darkened, and his head lowered, brushing a light kiss across her brow, as though he needed the contact '—it was the most wonderful and the most shattering experience of my life. To discover you were a virgin, had never belonged to Gordon, or any other man, left me so stunned, so confused, I didn't know what to think. I'll never forgive myself for the way I lashed out at you. The things I said about you and Gordon were just to cover my own guilty passion.'

'But you never intended the engagement or to marry me?' He might have lusted after her, but it still hurt, even now, to know he had not loved her.

'Yes, I did, Rebecca, I just hadn't admitted it to myself; but I spent the rest of that night awake and going over everything that had happened between us. I think I knew subconsciously even then that you weren't capable of what I had accused you of, and I knew without a doubt that I didn't want our relationship to end. Suddenly being engaged to you was vitally important to me, and marriage...yes, why not? I, who had never believed in the institution! In my conceit I thought all I had to do was telephone you in the morning and we would be back together. But I was too late, and too proud to beg.'

He had called, and he had suggested they carry on as before. Rebecca thought back. But only in a very casual way. Then she remembered something else that had always puzzled her. 'You said I looked upset on the train, but you never got out of the car at the station.'

'You didn't look back, Rebecca. If you had, you would have seen me running along the platform after you. I watched you sit in the window-seat with your head bent and tears in your lovely eyes, and cursed myself for fifty kinds of fool.'

She wanted to believe him—maybe if he had said something at the time, she would have done—but the years between had taught her caution if nothing else. 'You could have said something later at the christening,' she said quietly, a question in her voice.

'I intended to, but you were so cool, so composed. I was intimidated.'

'Now that I cannot believe.' She smiled up into his serious face. 'Five-foot-nothing scaring you...?'

'Rebecca, one frosty glance from your expressive eyes is enough to make me quake in my shoes. Haven't you realised that yet?'

She searched his handsome face with those same eyes and could see no trace of mockery; instead he looked grim.

'Then Mary made me so angry, suggesting I had seduced you. I was furious to think that you had discussed our lovemaking with her. I completely lost my temper with you.'

She remembered their fight in the study. He wasn't the only one who had lost his temper. She had made some very hurtful comments herself.

'I tried to tell you last night... No, the night before,' he corrected. 'You were right at the christening when you tore into me and told me I was trying to put my own feeling of guilt on to you, but it took me a long time to realise it.' For a moment there was silence as Benedict appeared to search for words, a distant look in his golden eyes.

'We were never a close family and I certainly felt no guilt when I took a two-year sabbatical from the family firm. My mother was quite content with my stepfather, who incidentally had been my father's right-hand man, and ran the business as well if not better than my dad had. Also young Gordon was earmarked for the business world, plus my uncle's son Jean-Paul; my presence wasn't essential. But with hindsight I can see, when I returned four years later and found out about the death of my stepfather and Gordon, I did feel guilty. I never seemed to be there when my mother needed me. Which is why I was inclined to believe her about Gordon's death. I felt as though I owed her my support, I'd been there so rarely for her.'

The pain in his eyes touched Rebecca's heart. She could understand his reasoning, even though she had been the

person hurt by it. 'I should never have accused you of
not caring for your family; you couldn't help being away
for so long.' She tried to console him. 'I had no right,
but I was so furious—hurt and furious,' she finally admitted, while her hand unconsciously stroked gently over
his chest, the heat of his body against hers. The content
of his words was inducing a melting warmth within her.
She let her other hand trace the hair arrowing down his
stomach, and she felt him flinch.

'Don't do that,' he rasped, his voice suddenly hoarse.
'I want to clear the air between us ... first.'

Flushing, she clasped her hands in front of her breasts.
She hadn't realised what she was doing, but his hard,
muscular thighs straddling her legs made her squirm
restlessly, and Benedict groaned.

'For God's sake, keep still! Or are you trying to
torment me?' His eyes clashed with hers, and for a
moment the naked longing she saw in the golden depths
stunned her.

'I was saying——' his mouth twisted '—I was trying
to tell you. You were correct, Rebecca, I did feel guilty,
hellishly guilty. From our first date, I knew in my heart
there was no way you could be in any way responsible
for Gordon's death. You were so honest, so open in your
feelings, but I ... I was so much older and terrified of
the way you made me feel. I'd never been in love before,
and in some crazy, mixed-up way I thought I had to
fight against it. But I wanted you ... God, how I want
you!'

He lapsed back into the present tense, much to
Rebecca's delight. She still couldn't quite believe his
earlier avowal of love, but gradually she was beginning
to accept that at the very least he cared something for
her.

'You have to understand, Rebecca, I felt as though I
was lusting after my brother's lover. Oh, I know Gordon

was dead, but he had loved you. Every time I held you,
kissed you, ached for you, it was with a passion riddled
with guilt.' He grimaced. 'I was so angry with myself,
and I took it out on you.'

'You had no need,' she said softly.

'I know that now, but at the time I felt as if I was
betraying Gordon. When I finally began to think
rationally, and realised there was no reason to feel guilty,
it was too late and I had lost you.'

Of course, in his delirium he had said she was right,
and mentioned a 'guilty passion'. Now she understood.
But could she believe him? Rebecca glanced up at him;
letting her hands slide up to his broad shoulders, she
searched his face. His handsome features were dark with
a two-day stubble which gave him a piratical air, but the
vulnerability in his shadowed eyes touched her heart.

'Can you ever forgive me, trust me again, as you did
when we first met, before I threw it all away?' he asked.

She stroked one hand around the back of his neck, a
warm tide of love sweeping through her, breaking down
all the barriers of hurt and pride she had built up over
the years. 'I can forgive you.' A glittering light flared in
his eyes. 'But can you forgive me?' she asked softly. 'I
quite deliberately deprived you of our son. When he was
born I was so furious that I was alone, so passionately
telling myself I hated you, I didn't even name you as his
father. I had no right to do that, not to Daniel and not
to you. I've spent the last four years feeling
guilty——'

'It doesn't matter, Rebecca,' he cut in, and planted
an affectionate kiss on her nose. 'When I found out
about Daniel, I was furious with you for keeping him
from me, but deep down inside I was delirious with joy.'

She sighed as his warm breath caressed her face. 'Because you had a son...'

'That, yes... but also because it meant at last I could make you marry me...'

'But if it hadn't been for Daniel, I would never have seen you again,' she said sombrely, knowing it was true.

Benedict moved, one arm locking around her waist; he rolled over on to his side, and held her imprisoned in the curve of his arm, with his free hand he stroked the tumbled curls from her brow. His dark eyes bored down into hers.

'How can you believe that, Rebecca? When I saw you again last week in France, I thought at long last the gods were smiling on me. I watched you on the beach with the children, and you were exactly as I had imagined you for years. I told myself that surely, after all this time, you would forgive me for my abominable behaviour, and give me a second chance.

'The two days we spent with the children gave me some hope, but you were wary. I didn't blame you for that, but you seemed willing to accept my friendship, and then when we went out to dinner and I realised you had never received my letter, but you still listened and appeared to believe me, I was euphoric. I was convinced I could win you back. I would have married you, Daniel or no Daniel, never doubt it,' he said fiercely, adding with a grim smile, 'have you forgotten the way I jumped on you like a sex-starved fool that night on the beach?

'No.' She would never forget; she had been seconds away from letting him take her, and she trembled at the memory. Her breasts rubbed against his chest and she could feel them swell against the soft lace of her bra. Benedict flung one heavy thigh over her slender legs, trapping her tightly against him, his own aroused state very obvious.

'I had it all planned. I was going to see you the next night, get your address, and visit you in London. I thought if I wined and dined you, courted you properly,

I could make you forget the Josh bloke you bought the cognac for.'

Rebecca felt him stiffen and could feel the tension in him, and noted the unasked question in his dark, intent gaze.

'Josh and Joanne are a married couple I've known since university. They live in Corbridge in the north of England and Daniel and I have spent most of the school holidays with them. They have a daughter, Amy, and when I had to take the school trip they looked after Daniel for me. That's why I bought the cognac.' She should have explained long ago, but her own stiff-necked pride had stopped her.

'Oh, God, is there no end to my idiocy?' Benedict groaned. 'At the reception, I was furious when Daniel mentioned Josh. I dashed you back here and virtually raped you, I was so mad with jealousy,' he said thickly. 'How can I expect you to forgive me? Once Dolores had dropped her bombshell about a child, I stampeded you into marriage simply because it was too good a chance to miss.'

'You implied I had received your letter and deliberately ignored it, to spite you. It hurt to think you had such a low opinion of me.' That still rankled.

His lips twisted in a wry, self-mocking smile. 'I was so furiously angry; I'd spent two days running back and forward to your apartment, and I was mad with jealousy. I had nightmare visions of you spending the weekend with Josh or some other lover, and by the time I finally found you at home I was ready to kill you for what you had put me through. But, once I'd met Daniel and we had put him to bed together, all I wanted to do was crawl into bed with his mother.'

'You could have done,' she said huskily. 'But you turned me down.' His rejection had hurt unbearably at the time.

'I was a fool. I wanted to prove to myself that the physical attraction between us was as strong for you as it was for me. I had the stupid idea that if I could leave you feeling frustrated you'd be all the more willing to marry me. Instead you went to bed and slept like a top, and I lay awake all night on that tiny hard sofa in a state of semi-permanent arousal.'

Rebecca chuckled. 'How do you know I slept like a top?'

'Because about four in the morning I gave up and decided to join you, only to see you sprawled across your narrow bed, deeply asleep.'

Meeting his eyes, Rebecca's lips parted in a slow, sensuous smile. 'You should have done,' she murmured throatily. Her slender arms curved around his neck. They still had a lot to sort out, a lot of adjustments to make, but she no longer doubted him, she realised, happiness bubbling inside her, and they had already wasted five years. They had a lifetime to talk...

At Rebecca's urging Benedict's dark head bent and his mouth burned along the soft line of her cheek as he whispered fiercely, 'I do love you, Rebecca; if you believe nothing else, you must believe that, and I swear if you'll give me another chance I'll spend the rest of my life trying to win your love.'

His lips moved against her skin and the vibration from his words seemed to echo right through to her heart's core. Her fingers tangled in the dark silk of his hair, holding him close. 'You won't have to try very hard.' She believed him, she had to, simply because she loved him.

Benedict jerked his head back, his piercing dark eyes intent upon her flushed face. 'You mean...?'

'Yes. I think I love you...' She breathed a deep, shaky breath; she had gone as far as she dared. Her tongue touched his lips, and she was trembling with the force of her emotions.

Benedict groaned and captured her mouth; the kiss was like nothing they had ever shared before. It promised tenderness and love, forgiveness and hope. He moved, rolling her over on top of him without taking his mouth from hers. His long fingers quickly dispensed with her bra, and his hands slid to her buttocks and the edge of her briefs.

She felt the shudder that rippled through his huge frame, and a responsive tremor shivered up her spine, then sanity prevailed. Lifting her head, she stared down at his darkly flushed face, the deepening passion reflected in his golden-brown eyes. 'You're supposed to be ill, Benedict, this can't be good for you.'

He slipped her briefs down, his hand lingering between her legs with devastating effect. She groaned, 'Be sensible . . .' and it was the last word she uttered for some considerable time.

Benedict touched his lips to the tender curve of her neck, and lower to her breast, and then nipped lightly with his teeth. One large hand moved up and down her back, over her bottom, sensuously kneading the rounded cheeks, while his other hand continued an intimate exploration between her thighs. She arched instinctively, fitting her soft feminine curves over the hard masculine frame.

'Rebecca, take me,' he rasped, his eyes holding hers. 'Show me you want me . . . this time.' His hands framed her face. 'Please.'

He was giving her control, and with a flash of insight she realised he needed her to show him she wanted him. Every other time they had made love on his insistence. A slow, sexy smile curved her full lips, as she sat up, her legs straddling him, taking his hard shaft deep inside her. She savoured the complete, full feeling, then slowly she moved, loving the control her position gave her. He was hers, and, throwing her head back, her small hands resting on his broad chest, she moved again, her muscles contracting around him, fierce, primitive pleasure flooding through her.

Suddenly she was no longer in control. His strong hands encircled her tiny waist, urging her on and down, his mouth closed over her breast and she cried out when he withdrew the contact. He growled husky, erotic words of encouragement, his big body bucking beneath her, stroking faster and faster as the tension built until finally exploding in a mutual, fiery rapture.

His huskily rasped, 'I love you,' brought a breathless smile to her lips, as she sank down on top of him. Exhausted, she sheltered in his powerful arms, feeling protected and at peace.

The ringing of the telephone brought a reluctant groan from Benedict, and, tucking her into his side, carefully pulling the sheet up and over them at the same time, he reached out a long arm to the bedside telephone. 'Yes? Benedict Maxwell speaking.'

Curled up against him, Rebecca listened to the one-sided conversation. It was his uncle, calling to enquire about his health.

'Let me speak to Daniel,' she murmured.

'Wait your turn, woman,' Benedict said, with a grin. She listened, a smile on her face as he talked to their son, the love and pride in his tone obvious. She let her hand roam down over his flat, hard stomach to his thighs, her fingers teasing him deliberately until, with a muffled groan, he muttered, 'You win, your turn,' and handed her the phone.

Her conversation was brief as Benedict returned her teasing, his large hands caressing with unmistakable intent. Assured Daniel was fine, she hastily handed the instrument back to Benedict, his uncle once more on the

line. Reluctantly reminding herself that Benedict had
been ill, she moved to the far side of the bed.

He shot her a puzzled glance then returned to his
conversation.

It was obviously business, but suddenly Rebecca stiffened at the mention of Fiona Grieves. She had forgotten all about the woman in the euphoria of her
husband's arms.

'Yes, fine. OK.' Benedict replaced the receiver and,
turning, reached for her. 'Now where were we?' he
growled throatily.

'Fiona Grieves,' she said flatly, holding him at arm's
length with one small hand.

'What about her?' he queried with a puzzled grin.

'How come she's working for you?'

'You're not jealous, are you, Rebecca, of me and
Fiona?' A grin of pure male satisfaction creased his
handsome face.

'No,' she muttered untruthfully, flushing scarlet.

He threw his head back and laughed out loud. 'You're
a terrible liar, Rebecca, your blush gives you away.'

'I'm getting up,' she said huffily.

Instantly serious, Benedict reached out and hauled her
back into his arms. 'Fiona means nothing to me. Three
years ago she came to me and asked if I could get her
a job out of the country. She was in a bit of a state;
after spending ten years as Chancellor Foster's mistress,
she had finally realised it was hopeless. He had no intention of ever leaving his wife for her.'

Rebecca's eyes widened in shock and disbelief. 'You
mean she was having an affair with him?' she exclaimed. But, looking back down the years, she realised
it could be true. The woman was always at Foster's side.

Benedict pressed a soft kiss to her head. 'Rebecca,
you must have been one of the few people in Oxford not
to know about it. Anyway, I felt sorry for her, and, my

suspicious darling...' he held her close, his hand rubbing gently up and down her back in comfort and reassurance '...that's all I have ever felt for her. I arranged with Uncle Gerard for Fiona to work in the Bordeaux office, and she does her work very well, by all accounts.'

'Oh,' Rebecca mumbled inanely.

'Haven't you realised yet how very much I love you? I won't allow anything or anyone to come between us ever again, Rebecca.'

As his arms tightened around her she wound hers firmly around his neck, love and happiness lighting her violet eyes, curling her full lips into a blazing smile of such beauty, Benedict caught his breath, before capturing her lips with his own.

Later they showered, a very long shower, and it was midnight before they made it downstairs to the kitchen for a makeshift meal of sandwiches, crisps and champagne, then returned to bed.

The sound in her ears had to be a drum, Rebecca thought in confusion, her eyes flying open. She sat up in bed, and a large hand reached in front of her, tucking the sheet around her naked breasts.

'For my eyes only.' A soft chuckle accompanied the whispered words. She flushed scarlet and shot a sidelong glance at Benedict; his muscular upper torso was propped against the headboard and he was laughing.

'Mummy, Daddy, look what Uncle gave me.' And a live torpedo shot across the room, a small drum on a rope around his neck, his little arms swirling the drumsticks like a demented dervish.

'I'm sorry about this. His uncle brought him back an hour ago, and I've tried to keep him amused, but he refuses to wait any longer to see you both.' Mrs James's apologetic voice battled against the unholy row, as Daniel stood at the bedside, banging away incessantly.

'Your uncle must really hate you, Benedict,' Rebecca murmured drily, casting a baleful eye from the drum to his handsome face.

'Who cares, when I have your love?' he said confidently. His sensual, reminiscent smile told her exactly what he was remembering, and she grinned.

Daniel stopped drumming. 'And mine, Daddy.'

Benedict leant forward and swung Daniel, drum and all, up in his arms, hugging him to his chest.

Rebecca swallowed hard at the moisture in her husband's eyes, her last doubt gone. He was going to be a wonderful father.

'Do Daddies and Mummies always lie in bed all morning?' Daniel asked, wriggling out of his father's hold and into the bed between the two adults, once more banging his drum.

'Obviously not with a son like you,' Benedict chuckled, wrapping his arms around both mother and son in an exuberant bear-hug.

Mrs James quietly withdrew; she'd cancel breakfast and make a brunch, she thought. She wiped the moisture from her eye with the edge of her apron. They didn't need her. They had it all...

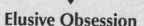

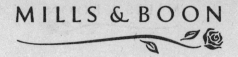

MILLS & BOON

Next Month's Romances

Each month you can choose from a wide variety of romance with Mills & Boon. Below are the new titles to look out for next month.

LAST STOP MARRIAGE — Emma Darcy
RELATIVE SINS — Anne Mather
HUSBAND MATERIAL — Emma Goldrick
A FAULKNER POSSESSION — Margaret Way
UNTAMED LOVER — Sharon Kendrick
A SIMPLE TEXAS WEDDING — Ruth Jean Dale
THE COLORADO COUNTESS — Stephanie Howard
A NIGHT TO REMEMBER — Anne Weale
TO TAME A PROUD HEART — Cathy Williams
SEDUCED BY THE ENEMY — Kathryn Ross
PERFECT CHANCE — Amanda Carpenter
CONFLICT OF HEARTS — Liz Fielding
A PAST TO DENY — Kate Proctor
NO OBJECTIONS — Kate Denton
HEADING FOR TROUBLE! — Linda Miles
WHITE MIDNIGHT — Kathleen O'Brien

Temptation

THREE GROOMS:
Case, Carter and Mike

TWO WORDS:
"We Don't!"

**ONE
MINI-SERIES:**

GROOMS ON THE RUN

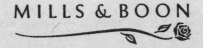

Starting in March 1996, Mills & Boon Temptation brings you this exciting new mini-series.

Each book (and there'll be one a month for three months) features a sexy hero who's ready to say "I do!" but ends up saying, "I don't!"

Look out for these special Temptations:

In March, I WON'T! by Gina Wilkins
In April, JILT TRIP by Heather MacAllister
In May, NOT THIS GUY! by Glenda Sanders

MILLS & BOON

MILLS & BOON

Just Married

Celebrate the joy, excitement and adjustment that
comes with being 'Just Married' in this wonderful
collection of four new short stories.

Written by four popular authors

Sandra Canfield

Muriel Jensen

Elise Title

Rebecca Winters

Just Married is guaranteed to melt your
hearts— just married or not!

Available: April 1996   Price: £4.99